THOMAS PULLED FIA HARD AGAINST HIM, AND HIS FINGERS ENCIRCLED HER NECK.

"Och, I think you mean to kiss me," she said. And she looked . . . excited.

Thomas was shocked. *She should be terrified, damn it!* "I will do more than kiss you," he said as he tightened his fingers. Her lush mouth curled into a smile. She closed her eyes and lifted her face to his.

He should have tried to scare her more, to frighten her into submission. He should have. But he didn't. He kissed her with every bit of passion that welled inside him.

Then, through a haze of raw desire, he became aware of a razor-sharp point pressed into his side.

Thomas opened his eyes.

Fia regarded him with a cool smile. In one hand, she held a knife that shone wickedly in the moonlight. In her other, she held his purse.

Thomas cursed. He'd played right into her hands! Gazing into Fia's fathomless eyes, Thomas found himself drowning. Drowning in the eyes of a wench who brought him the devil's own luck!

ONE LUCKY LORD

LORD

KIM BENNET

LOVE SPELL BOOKS   NEW YORK CITY

LOVE SPELL®

February 2000

Published by

Dorchester Publishing Co., Inc.
276 Fifth Avenue
New York, NY 10001

Cover Art by John Ennis, Ennisart.com

ISBN 0-505-52363-9

First, one great big hug to Rachelle Wadsworth, my best friend and critique partner extraordinaire. You are the best. And now, you have to dedicate your first book to me! Ha!

Special thanks to my critique partners—Millie Boyd, Elaine Houston, and Sherry Schlereth for helping me write the book of my heart. I couldn't have done it without you.

Also, thank you to the kind people at Duart Castle, www.holidaymull.org/members/duart.html, who patiently answered all 2,006 of my questions and made me feel as if I had come home.

Last, special thanks to Donald Maclean, President of Clan Maclean International Association, and Alasdair White, who minds the Clan's history forum, for collecting the historical information included in the Author's Notes.

For more information on Clan Maclean, check out their website at: www.maclean.org.

ONE LUCKY LORD

Chapter One

Duart Castle
Isle of Mull, Scotland
May 1567

It was one thing to fall. It was quite another to be shoved from the ledge of a second-story window.

With an ominous thud, Thomas Wentworth landed flat on his back, his head saved from the hard, rock-strewn ground by the fortunate placement of a thick patch of herbs. Light exploded before his eyes as the breath left his body in a whoosh and blessed blackness lulled him away from the pain.

"Och, Fia, you've gone and killed the man." A lilting voice crept silkily into his ears. Low and husky, it flowed through him, as rich as cream over fresh berries. " 'Tis an ill omen to kill the finest man you've ever chanced to see."

The luscious voice, evidently of a woman musing

aloud to herself, demanded his attention. Groaning with the effort, Thomas forced his eyes open and focused on the figure kneeling above him.

The moon made a nimbus around the thickest cloud of hair he had ever seen. As inky black as the darkness around them, it streamed in waves and curls, frothing in abandon across her shoulders. The end of one persistent curl brushed his ear, and he weakly swatted it.

"Bless Mother Mary, you're alive," she said, smoothing the hair from his forehead with a feather-soft touch.

"Aye, I live," he muttered, raising a hand to his throbbing head. He struggled to rise, yet before he could do more than lift his shoulders, the wench pushed him back to the ground.

"You can't get up 'til we know for sure you've no injuries," she said. Warm hands slid with agonizing lightness over his arms and legs.

He caught her wrists and pushed her away, the rough wool of her sleeves telling him that her position within the castle was menial at best. Despite her protests, he forced his aching body upright. "Leave me be," he growled unsteadily. "I can take care of myself."

"You're a Sassenach—an Englishman." A faint note of accusation hung in the air.

Thomas silently cursed his aching head that he had forgotten to disguise his voice with a Scottish accent.

She brushed a hand over his shirt. "And your clothing is much too fine for a man of simple means."

Thomas felt a flicker of annoyance. He had chosen his dark garments with the utmost care, knowing he needed to blend with the shadows should anything go awry.

Awry. The thought brought a twisted smile. In truth, little had gone right with this venture. Ever since he had crossed into Scottish waters, the famous Wentworth luck had been tested to the breaking point.

First, his ship had run into a gale off the rocky coast and had barely managed to hobble to safety. Once in port, Thomas had discovered that his horse had been sorely bruised by the rough crossing. It had taken three days to find a suitable replacement.

And now this. Shoved from a window and then accosted by a saucy wench. 'Twas yet another delay in his carefully laid plans. Thomas stifled his growing irritation. Delays caused risks, and risks were something he rarely took without exquisite preparation and consummate attention to detail. Hurried plans inevitably ended in failure.

Thomas Wentworth never hurried, and he never failed.

"What you were doing perched in the window, Sassenach?"

" 'Tis no concern of yours," he returned curtly.

"Och, I cannot agree. 'Twas me as opened the shutters and bumped you from the ledge. I have a certain responsibility for you now."

"You were the one who . . ." He ran a hand through his hair and grimaced as he touched a bruise. "Who are you? A housemaid?"

She chuckled, the sound low and melodious. "Oh, aye. You just ask questions, and I'll just answer them. I think not, Master Thieving Knave."

Her lilting voice tantalized him. Thomas leaned forward and sank his hand in the silken softness of her hair. Ignoring her gasped protest, he tilted her face until the moon slanted cold rays across the smoothness of her cheek. He briefly glimpsed a small, straight nose and the outline of a pair of very kissable lips before she pushed his hand away.

"Perhaps you don't remember," she admonished. " 'Tis a known fact that Englishmen have remarkably soft heads."

11

"No doubt you heard that from some heathen Scotsman wielding a claymore the size of a tree."

"A mite testy, are you? 'Tis no wonder, what with your head aching like a cracked rock. Not that I'm one to be giving advice, but if 'twas thieving you came to do, there are safer ways to be about it."

Could she have discerned his purpose? Thomas felt his inner pocket and heard the reassuring crackle of paper.

It could be called thieving, he supposed. He had never looked at it that way. His purpose was much larger, much grander than mere thievery. Thank God he had been climbing *out* of the window, his mission completed, when the chit knocked him to the ground.

His lip curled. "Are you a master thief to offer such advice?"

She shook her head, moonlight flowing across her hair like firelight on a rippling pond. "Not a master. 'Twas my first effort at reiving, and 'twas not near as exciting as I'd hoped."

"Exciting?" he echoed hollowly.

"Aye. 'Twas dull work 'til I knocked you from the ledge. Did you know you never so much as made a sound on the way down? 'Tis amazing, that. You fell like a great rock, with nary a cry 'til you landed in the garden. Then you went 'oof' like a—"

"For the love of St. Peter, cease your prattle!" Thomas hissed, casting an uneasy glance at the looming castle.

She laughed. "Don't fash yourself about being heard. There's no one home but the servants, and they're all ancient and as deaf as can be."

He wasn't going to ask, but some part of him wanted to feel her honey-smooth voice a moment more. "What were *you* doing in the great hall?"

"Trying to decide if I should climb out the window

like a proper thief or take the stairs. I took the stairs," she said with evident disappointment. "After watching you fall, I thought 'twas very possible I could have dropped my bag, and then all my efforts would have been for naught."

He felt a twinge of amusement at her casual attitude toward her less-than-honorable profession. "You're a saucy wench," he said with grudging admiration.

She chuckled, and the sound seemed to curl up in his lap and heat him in ways he'd never thought a mere sound could. "That's exactly what Duncan says."

For the space of a second, Thomas envied the unknown Duncan. "What's your name, little thief?"

"Fia." She rose and hefted a bag to her shoulder. It clanged and clanked like a sack of bells. "I just took a few candlesticks. I think they'll be easy to sell, don't you?"

He shook his head. She assumed he was some sort of king thief, up to his ears in helpful advice for a fellow brigand. He should have been insulted, but instead he found himself strangely hesitant to disappoint her. It was yet another sign that he should be on his way.

He took a deep breath and clambered gingerly to his feet, spacing them far apart to answer the swaying earth. He felt as though he were on the deck of the *Glorianna* in a full gale.

"Are you feeling well enough to be walking just yet?" Fia asked. "If you faint, you'll be caught for sure."

"I am not a thief. I was merely . . ." He halted and scowled. He couldn't tell her the truth, but he would be damned if he would allow her to think him such a varlet. " 'Twas for a wager."

She regarded him silently, then shrugged. "Well, you've not the voice of a commoner. 'Tis possible, I suppose. The rich can afford such nonsense." She raked a hand through her impossible hair, the gesture bringing more disarray than order. "Whatever your reason, I must be off. Duncan returns this morn."

"Duncan?"

"Aye, Duncan Maclean." She sighed at his blank expression. "The Earl of Duart. The laird. Didn't you know whose castle you were stealing into? 'Tis a paltry housebreaker you are, to be sure."

"You're mistaken," he said shortly. "Maclean is not to return for another week."

"He sent word he will be returning early to . . ." Fia hesitated, a note of uncertainty in her voice.

Thomas caught her arm. "Why is he returning so early?"

"Let me go," she protested.

He tightened his hold. "The name, sweet Fia, is Thomas. Now tell me what Maclean is planning." Without giving her time to consider, he turned her until the moonlight spilled across her face.

For a moment, he could only stare. Every glimpse of her had suggested that she was comely, but nothing had prepared him for the beauty he now faced. Her dark eyes sparkled with anger, surrounded by a thick tangle of lashes. Full and sensuous, her mouth begged to be tasted, while her flawless skin glowed warm and vibrant even under the cold caress of the moon.

"Why would I tell you anything?" She struggled to free herself, her bag clanging noisily.

Thomas smiled and pulled her hard against him. He pushed aside the wild abandon of her hair as his fingers encircled her neck.

"Think about it, my little thief." His mouth was but a whisper from hers, his thumbs resting suggestively at the delicate hollow of her throat.

"Och, I think you mean to kiss me." Her breath was ragged, her eyes fixed on his mouth. Her lips parted, and the edge of her tongue moved slowly across the fullness of the lower one. She looked . . . excited.

Thomas was shocked. *She should be terrified, damn it.*

"I will do more than kiss you," he said as he tightened his fingers. She winced, and he steeled himself against a sudden stab of pity. He hated to frighten her, but this was too important. There was so much more at stake than the cares of a Scottish wench.

To his surprise, her lush mouth curled into a sensual smile. "Kiss me," she murmured huskily. She closed her eyes and lifted her face to his.

He should have tried to scare her more, thought of a way to frighten her into submission. He should have. But he didn't. All he could think of was the promise of her lips and the delicate fragrance of heather that drifted from her hair.

He kissed her with every bit of passion that welled inside him.

Her bag of stolen goods dropped to the ground in a noisy jangle as she clutched at his loose shirt, pulling insistently. Her lips, soft and yielding, drank hungrily from his.

He brushed aside her entangling hair and tasted the sweetness of her neck. He traced the contours of her back and hips, stopping to pull her bodice from the waistband of her skirt. Her skin was deliciously warm and inviting. He pulled impatiently at the ties at her waist, his mouth ruthlessly possessing hers.

Through a haze of raw passion, he became aware of a razor-sharp point pressed into his side. Thomas opened his eyes.

Fia regarded him with a cool smile. "Let me go, Sassenach. 'Tis time you were on your way."

In one hand, she held a knife that shone wickedly in the moonlight. In her other, she held his purse.

15

Thomas silently cursed. No wonder she hadn't been frightened. He'd played right into her hands.

He released her, aware of the dull ache of unanswered desire. Cold, deadly fury raced through him. He thought about lunging for the knife, but he killed the idea as soon as it was born. The few servants might be hard of hearing, but he had little doubt a bloodcurdling scream would awaken every last one of them.

Thomas swore. "You common, thieving—"

" 'Tis your own fault, Thomas, laddie." Fia grinned and tucked the bag of coins into her bodice. "I had no notion to take aught from you 'til you tried to seduce me."

"Seduce *you?*" He laughed harshly. "One does not seduce a trollop. One pays, though I would never pay that much for time between your thighs."

Her hand tightened on the knife, her delicate eyebrows lowered. "Have a care, Sassenach. The laird will return at any moment. Leave whilst you can."

"I'm in no more of a hurry than you, comfit." Thomas took a step closer, careful to stay out of range of the knife.

Fia backed toward the beckoning shelter of the forest, her eyes fixed warily on his.

Thomas continued his slow advance, smiling with cold menace. "Tell me why his lordship returns in such haste, and I'll allow you to leave in peace."

"As though you had the choice of it," she mocked, though her gaze drifted toward the castle. The first fingers of dawn crept stealthily into the sky.

"Come," he urged, taking another step. "A little information for the gold you've stolen. 'Tis a fair exchange."

Fia regarded him soberly. To his immense surprise, she nodded. " 'Tis only fair. Maclean is returning to marry."

"Marry? Who?" His voice rang harshly through the predawn stillness.

She smiled, and he knew her answer before she even spoke.

"Me, Sassenach," her lilting voice taunted. "He comes to marry me."

And then she was gone.

Chapter Two

Fia peered through the brush and wondered what could possibly be keeping the Sassenach. She knew he would follow. He had been too angry not to.

She noted the brightening horizon. If she were back at the castle now, she would be rising to the familiarity of her own comfortable chamber with its red velvet hangings and thick carpets. She would be snug, warm, and safe, not hiding in the damp, cold woods from an irritated Englishman.

She almost laughed out loud. She couldn't imagine a more fortuitous beginning for her adventure.

And what an adventure it was. At this very moment, tucked into a leather pouch and tied to the back of her horse, were the plays she had painstakingly written over the past six years of her so far very uneventful life.

Fia patted her sack of silver and felt a bubble of excitement. She had carefully planned every step of the journey. Soon she would be in London and, with any luck, a playwright before Duncan caught up with her.

She frowned at the thought of her cousin. The sad truth was that Duncan *had* decided to marry her.

"Aye," she muttered with distaste, "he's decided to marry you off to the first qualified man as stumbles through the castle gates."

Her cousin had spent the last two years searching for a man he deemed worthy of her hand. Fortunately, Duncan's idea of a deserving husband did not exist. The man needed to be of proud birth and wealthy, yet capable of wielding both sword and pen. Fia had felt secure that she would never be shackled with a husband.

But lately, as the Scottish queen made error after error and the rumblings of war increased, Duncan had become more determined in his search. More determined and, Fia feared, much less exacting.

She grimaced. "Who needs a husband? Unless he could find a sponsor for my plays, I would be no better off than I am now." She plucked a ripe berry from the bush beside her and popped it into her mouth.

Already her venture had been blessed with an omen of success. How many other playwrights could boast of finding an Englishman so conveniently perched on their window ledge the very eve they set out to make their fortune?

It had been a lamentable mischance that she had knocked the poor man into the garden. A thought occurred, and she sat up straight. Perhaps the Sassenach came from London and was the envoy of some great lord. Or maybe . . .

The cold talons of reality struck. " 'Twouldn't help, Fia," she said aloud. " 'Tis not likely the man will forgive you for knocking him out of a window *and* stealing his purse."

She sighed wistfully. Lord Thomas the Handsome was probably a very pleasant companion when his head didn't ache and his coins were still safely tucked in his belt.

"Och, Fia, you've gone daft crazy mad, you have. For all you know, there could be a soul as black as the bottom of a kettle beneath that golden exterior."

She glanced up at the sky and straightened her shoulders. " 'Tis time to be going. If you wait much longer, you'll be eating breakfast with Duncan."

Hefting the bag, she walked toward the clearing.

A band of steel clamped about her arm.

"Where are you off to now, my little thief? Wandering about the forest looking for another fool to fleece?"

Her heart skidded to a thudding halt. *He had found her.*

"What? No sharp retort? No hidden knife?" The lazy voice was sharp enough to cut her to shreds.

Desperation whipped her into action. With all her might, Fia shoved her bag into Thomas's broad chest and whirled to make her escape.

She took fewer than two steps before his body crashed into hers, tumbling both of them to the ground. Her knife slid through the dirt and came to rest under a bush.

He lay atop her, his weight forcing the breath from her until black spots swam before her eyes.

"You disappoint me, little Fia. 'Tis way past time for fleeing."

Fia gasped. "Cannot . . . breathe . . ."

He gave a muffled curse and raised himself on his elbows. She gulped in the cool morning air, aware that his body still covered hers in a most intimate way.

She drew a shuddering breath, her mind racing to plan her escape. "You . . . you liked to . . . have killed me, you dumb ox!"

"Don't tempt me," Thomas hissed, his hands moving over her throat, pushing aside her hair in what seemed more a caress than a threat.

Her panting lessened. " 'Twould be a grievous error on your part, my lord. The women of my family have a tendency to go a-ghosting when we are done away with in such a foul manner."

"A-ghosting?"

"Aye. I'd be dressed in flowing white and keening at the top of my lungs. 'Tis not a sight you would favor." She couldn't help but give a wee grin at his expression.

To her surprise, he grinned in return. "I can do without the keening, comfit, though the thought of you dressed in a flowing white gown is quite another matter."

He scrutinized her from brow to chin and then went farther, lingering on the fullness of her breasts where they pulled the thin fabric of her dress taut. "Especially if your ghostly gown shows off your more impressive attributes."

Fia flushed at his bold gaze. She had bought this dress from the village laundress, thinking it the perfect disguise. She hadn't counted on the garment fitting so poorly.

Of course, the heavy purse nestled between her breasts did little to ease the strain on the small buttons. The thought of the Sassenach's gold brought her grin back in full measure.

"I'm sure I'd be a pleasing ghostie, dressing in a fashionable way just to tempt your fancy." She snorted inelegantly and wished he would rise. It was difficult to converse at such a close distance. " 'Tis more likely I'd be wearing dirty rags than a lacy chemise, so you can stop your wishful thinking."

"Rags might not be so unattractive on a wench like you." His breath was warm and sweet near her ear, and she shivered.

"A wench like me?"

His smile was suddenly not so pleasant. " 'Tis possible the Maclean may be on the verge of finding himself wed, but not to a common maid such as yourself. I think you are angered to be losing your protector, and thus you stole away with a small fortune in your sack."

"How wise you are, my Lord Lackwit." Had sarcasm been gold, she would have just made her fortune.

He ran a finger over the rough cloth of her dress where it stretched across her breasts. "This, milady thief, is neither silk nor brocade."

The sensations his wandering touch created were unbearable. Fia forced herself to keep her face as bland as possible, but her breasts were not so easily tamed. Her nipples hardened and peaked, as though eager for him to repeat the touch.

His grin widened. He captured one of her hands and pried it open, running his thumb over her callused palms and ink-stained fingers. "And this, as deft as it is, is not the hand of a lady."

She clenched her fist. "If you wait much longer, Duncan himself will come and tell you exactly who I am. Neither of us would benefit from that."

"I'd enjoy seeing Maclean's face when you explain how you came to possess a sack of his best candlesticks," he retorted. "A pity I don't plan on remaining that long. I came for my gold, little thief."

Yet for all his brash words, his eyes glimmered with the warmth of the sun-drenched moors. Fia couldn't let this go any further. As muddled as he made her feel, she'd not have the strength to refuse him. It had taken every bit of her resolve to halt his kiss in the garden. She didn't know if she could do it again.

Desperately, she began to chatter in reckless haste. "My great-grandmother is a ghost, you know. She flitters across Loch Buie, howling and a-moaning, scaring the people of the village nigh to death. She wears a gray gown, I think. Perhaps 'tis brown or—"

"How did she die?" The words seemed forced from

him. Fia could tell he wished them back as soon as he said them.

"Ah, 'twas rumored my grandfather killed her with his own hands. Grandmother was as demanding a woman as ever lived. Poor Grandfather could neither drink nor fight without her harping from dawn to dusk."

"A harpy, eh?" he murmured, tracing feather-light circles on her jaw with one thumb.

Fia steeled herself against his touch. "Aye. 'Twas said she had a voice as could freeze a running river in the height of summer. Grandfather finally lost his temper and felled her by a great blow with an ale mug. Then he was saddened beyond belief."

"He must have loved her," he said somberly, though Fia thought she beheld a distinct twinkle in his warm brown eyes.

She chuckled. "Och, nay! 'Twas just that he could never drink from a mug again, as it reminded him too much of her. He said 'twas enough to sour even good whiskey."

Thomas laughed. Fia felt her own breath catch in her throat. He was beautiful, all golden hair and smooth, tanned skin. A subtle heat began to build in her stomach.

He caught her gaze, and his laughter died. He regarded her through heavy-lidded eyes, a sensual smile curving his mouth. "You are nothing like your grandmother, my sweet. You have a voice like pure honey. Indeed, I would like to hear you moaning in pleasure with that luscious voice of yours."

It was all she could do not to twine her arms about his head and pull that firm mouth to hers. He was as delectable as fresh, warm bread. But the pressure of the bag of gold crushed between her breasts reminded her of her purpose.

"You should be worrying about the Maclean and nothing else," she admonished desperately. "We have no time for this."

23

His eyes gleamed golden, and he gave her a smile of such incredible sweetness that her heart lodged in her throat. Sweet Mother Mary, but 'twas almost a crime to make such a handsome man and then loose him on the world without warning.

The warmth of his hands as they slid to her breasts wiped all coherent thought from her mind.

"The laird be hanged," he murmured. "I begin to think you might well be worth the risk." His mouth lowered toward hers, and Fia felt herself drawn toward his lips— beautifully carved lips that would taste as warm and sweet as . . .

Fia frowned. He was not kissing her. She met his mocking expression and flushed.

"I will have my purse," he said with an irritatingly smug grin.

Fia forced a smile and hoped he couldn't hear her thudding heart. "I suppose I'll have to hand it over."

His gaze locked on her mouth, and she wondered for a mortified moment if she had berry stains on her chin.

"Perhaps," he mused, " 'twould be more enjoyable if I found it myself."

She stared in horror. Surely he would not.

"Aye, I would. But I fear you are right. I must be off, and were I to stay longer . . ." He sighed in regret.

Fia thought she would catch fire with the heat that rushed through her. Before she could frame a reply, he stood and pulled her to her feet.

"My purse, Fia. Now. Else I will come and get it."

He meant every word. Feigning nonchalance, Fia reached into the opening at her neck, halting as she saw his obvious interest. "Turn your back, Sassenach."

"What? Modesty?" *From a whore?* He didn't say it, but the words hung in the silence, loud and bruising.

Fia bared her teeth in the semblance of a smile. "Very well, *Lord* Thomas."

He was tall, handsome beyond belief, with a smile that could drop one's heart into one's shoes with no warning. Had she written this scene, Thomas the Handsome would have fallen to his knees and promised to take her to London. He would have found a sponsor for every one of her wonderful plays and fallen deeply and desperately in love with her.

Alas, this was not one of her plays.

She yanked open the front of her dress and removed his purse. Fia tossed it to the ground and closed her bodice.

In the quiet of the glen, his breath sounded almost labored. "You tempt me, wench, but I dare not tarry." He glanced about the clearing. "Where is your horse? Or were you going to steal one on the road?"

Fia shot him a baleful glare and picked up her bag and knife from where they lay all but forgotten. "Of course I have a horse, sirrah. 'Tis a fool who would travel by foot when a mount is available." She peered into the gloom behind him. "Where's *your* mount?"

"Now there's the rub, comfit." He flashed a rakish grin. "Some damned hound has chased my horse away. I need yours."

Some damned hound. *Sweet St. Catherine, let it not be* . . . She cleared her throat. "Ah, and just what kind of dog chased away your horse?"

His face mirrored suspicion. "A brown dog, with only half an ear. Why?"

"Was his tail slightly bent at the end?"

"Aye," he stated grimly.

"And was his left eye but half open?"

" 'Tis a dog well known to you, I see," he snapped.

"Och, no. I have never seen such a dog." She twirled a curl about her finger, not daring to meet his gaze. "Though I must admit he sounds like a poor, sad little beastie."

"Well, your damned mongrel chased off my horse." He sounded thoroughly disgusted. "You owe me a mount, milady thief."

"But the dog isn't mine!"

"No?"

Fia became intensely interested in rubbing an errant ink stain from her fingers. " 'Tis possible I may have seen him in the garden once or twice." She glanced at him from under her lashes. "And I may have fed him a mite now and again."

She could hear his teeth grinding even from this distance. By the saints, he would have naught but stubs left of his fine teeth if he made it a habit to abrade them so often.

"I will have your horse," he stated.

"Hmph. 'Tis unfortunate you are forced to become a horse thief because of a poor, abused pup. A good thing we have no wayward cows about, else you might commit murder or worse."

"I've had about enough of you for one day, mistress." His voice could have cut leather.

"La, how high and mighty! What are you, a prince?"

"Nay, I am but an earl." He gave an insultingly brief nod of his head. "The Earl of Rotherwood, at your service."

An earl. Fia cast her gaze heavenward and said a short prayer of thanks to the saints for sending her a real English earl. If she closed her eyes, she could almost see her name written in flowing script across a playbill.

"Why did you pray for an English earl?" Thomas demanded in an outraged tone.

Fia winced. 'Twas her greatest fault to speak her every thought out loud. She shrugged and said lamely, "I-I've always had a liking for earls. Duncan is one, and . . . I am used to having one . . . about."

He rubbed his temple. "Sweet Jesu, but you make my head ache. Just give me your mount."

"But Thunder is—"

He gripped her wrist.

"You'll not get far," she warned. "She's a Scottish horse, and she'll have naught to do with an Englishman."

"I can handle her. Where is she?"

Fia decided Lord Thomas's attractiveness faded even as they spoke. While blessed with beauty of face and form, 'twas obvious the good Lord had been forced to scrimp a bit when it came to molding the man's temperament. That was the real tragedy, she decided, for he would have made a wondrous character for one of her plays had he possessed but a measure more charm.

She cast one last glance at his determined face before nodding toward the clearing. "Thunder is tied to the big tree in the glen."

"Very well. I suggest you hie yourself back to yon house and replace the silver before it's discovered that both you and it are missing."

Fia looked at him, her head tilting to one side. She was loath to lose her horse, loath to lose her newfound gold, and, strangely enough, loath to see Thomas leave. "Where are you off to?"

He hesitated, and Fia could see him weighing the cost of telling her the truth. After a moment, he gave a lopsided smile. "It can cause no harm, I suppose. I return to London."

London. He goes to London. And he's an earl. Sweet Mother Mary, 'tis a sign from above.

Fia leaned forward eagerly. "You'll need a guide. I could—"

"Rob me the first time I look elsewhere than my pockets? I think not, my little Scot. Though the idea of having you warm my blankets makes the offer most attractive." One corner of his mouth curled into a blatantly sensual smile.

Fia sniffed loudly. *The pig.* "I'll be warming no man's blankets, Lord Thomas. 'Tis time you left." She wondered what Yolanda, the quick-witted slave girl from her play, *Miracle of Thebes,* would do in this instance. She gave a piteous smile. "I suppose I should return to the castle and wait for the Maclean to come."

His eyebrows rose, but no other expression crossed his face.

"He will probably beat me for daring to defy him." She leaned against a tree, her shoulders sagging as though weighted. Duncan would have lain on the ground and laughed until his sides hurt to see her so. The Sassenach looked singularly unimpressed.

She tried again.

She peered into the darkened woods and allowed a shiver to rack her body. "Do you think there are many wild beasties about?"

He chuckled. "Cease your playacting. 'Tis a lamentable performance, at best."

His eyes crinkled at the corners as he chuckled, and Fia gave a defeated sigh. How could she fight such a paragon of manly beauty?

"It doesn't matter what you do," she said. "Horse or no, I won't go back. I will get to London, whatever the cost."

He hesitated, then reached out and raised her face toward his with a gentle hand. "I was told this Duncan Maclean is a fair man. Do you fear him so?"

Until she met the sincere concern in Thomas's warm brown eyes, Fia had been willing to paint Duncan into the vilest character ever to grace a stage. Instead, she heard herself answer honestly, "Duncan is more like to toss me over his knee than beat me."

Thomas's hand dropped. "No doubt you have the laird wrapped around your little finger. I need have no fear for you, then."

Disapproval evident in his every move, Lord Thomas the Proud turned and strode into the shadows.

"Well, you'll not get far on Thunder," Fia muttered.

That fact alone should have brought a cheery smile to her face. Instead, she gazed toward the empty forest, her brow puckered in thought.

Chapter Three

Whatever image the name Thunder had conjured up, this was not it.

Thomas had never seen a more pitiful horse. Its dull, pale brown coat was rough and completely bare in places. A straggly mane hung in limp strands on a gaunt, bony neck. Some romantic fool had plaited the sparse mane with colorful wildflowers that drooped piteously, as though hanging their heads in shame.

He regarded the thin, knobby legs and the swollen belly with a disbelieving eye. 'Twas a wonder the horse could even stand, much less walk. "Excellent. I've stolen a horse not even fit for a tannery."

As though understanding his every word, the beast slowly turned her head and measured him with a look of acute dislike.

"Everything about that wench is cursed." Thomas wanted nothing more than to turn and walk away, but his head ached with a relentless throb. Much as he hated to admit it, he needed this ugly mount to reach his ship before nightfall.

"There, old girl," Thomas soothed, patting her neck. Encouraged, the mare attempted a spirited snort, only to end up wheezing and coughing so hard, Thomas felt obliged to thump her soundly on the back.

A relentless ache grew in the back of his head, increasing by the moment. He was only glad that Robert was not nearby. Though one of Thomas's closest companions, Robert MacQuarrie enjoyed a jest more than life itself, and he was not above exaggerating common circumstances into a tale of mirth. Thomas rubbed the lump on his head and reflected sourly that for once Robert wouldn't have to exaggerate to make a mockery of this particular foray. Everything had gone awry from the moment he had been shoved from the window by that fey Scottish wench.

Thomas found himself glancing back at the forest with a sharp sense of regret. He would have enjoyed teaching the chit a lesson or two. The image of her burned in his mind. Full lips and mysteriously dark eyes were indelibly etched in his memory. Worse yet, he feared her luscious breasts would haunt his dreams for many a night to come.

He reminded himself grimly that she was naught but a beautiful thief with a penchant for causing trouble. She had already shoved him from a window, stolen his money, and been indirectly responsible for the loss of his horse.

He tried to shrug off the sense of gloom that threatened to overtake him. At least he was not forced to cross this accursed land on foot.

" 'Tis just the two of us, Thunder." He almost choked on the name. "If you carry me well, I promise to put you out of your misery as quickly as possible and sell you to the first tanner we meet."

Thunder yanked her head about and glared at him. Thomas eyed her with growing unease. Surely the stupid horse hadn't understood him.

God's Blood, but I am becoming as fanciful as that Scottish wench. But as much as he tried to deny it, events had teetered precariously on the verge of disaster ever since he had met Fia.

He didn't relish the feeling. He was a Wentworth, and, as his father had reminded him countless times, Wentworths never failed. His father would have died alone and bootless before throwing a single leg over such a decrepit animal.

Thankfully, he wasn't his father. As much as Thomas hated to admit it, he was going to have to ride the pathetic beast. Gathering his resolve, he swung into the saddle and urged Thunder with a gentle nudge of his heels.

The mare twitched nary a muscle.

Thomas tightened the reins and dug in his heels. Thunder snorted and swung her head to glower balefully over her shoulder.

"So that's the game you play, eh?" Thomas smiled grimly. "You don't know who you're dealing with, do you, you scourge-ridden old nag?"

Thunder bared yellowed teeth, flattening her long ears.

That was it. Grasping the reins tightly, Thomas planted his heels into Thunder's bloated sides.

The mare hunched her shoulders and began to swell. Before Thomas could do more than mutter a curse, Thunder gave a snort of indignation, dropped to her knees, and threw herself onto her side.

Thomas went down, a bruising blow to his hip and an incredible pressure on his leg stifling his shout of alarm.

It took him a full moment to realize what had happened. He was trapped beneath a fat, hide-bare nag, his leg held as securely as though shackled in iron.

"Move, you ill-begotten, mangy bag of bones!" Thomas roared.

Thunder bared her teeth over her shoulder and then lunged. Thomas stared at his torn sleeve in amazement before bellowing in rage.

He placed his free foot squarely on the horse's back and pushed with all his might. The shaggy head didn't even move. He tried again, but his efforts elicited no response from the horse other than an insignificant grunt.

Thomas lay back panting, his struggles leaving him as breathless as the fall from the window had. It was unbelievable. He, Thomas Henry Wentworth, the fifth Earl of Rotherwood, scion of a long line of immaculately bred, impeccably comported, and extremely dignified English nobility, lay pinned in the cold mud beneath a fat, wheezing nag.

Things could get no worse.

A sudden noise in the woods had him straining to see over Thunder's heaving sides. Thomas found himself gazing at the mangiest, most flea-bitten mongrel ever to put four paws to earth. It was *that* dog. *Her* dog.

"Why, you filthy, rotten ba—"

"Och, imagine that! A horse just a-lying about the wood with nary a rider to be seen." Amusement laced Fia's every word.

He should have strangled her when he had the chance.

Fia peered over Thunder's side, her hair a riotous mass about her shoulders, her lips parted in feigned amazement. Peeking from the safety of her skirts stood the ugly dog. Half of one ear was gone, the jagged edge left to point straight into the air, while his narrow muzzle was adorned with a ridiculous grin.

Thomas looked about for a good-sized rock.

33

"Why, Zeus, 'tis Lord Thomas! Have you gone and hurt yourself yet again, you poor man?"

Thomas clamped his mouth shut. He'd be damned if he'd let her see how angry he was until he was in a position to do something about it. Something like putting his hands around her scrawny neck and slowly choking the smile off her face.

"Och, 'tis a pity, this. First you hit your head in the garden, and now your backside is like to be just as bruised." Husky and inviting, her voice quivered with laughter.

He had been wrong. Strangling was too quick. *First* he would lock her in a dungeon and starve her. *Then* he would strangle her.

"If you've come to gloat, be gone," he ground out. "I've no need of your company nor of that hell hound of yours."

"Sweet Mother Mary, is that the way you speak to someone who has come to help you? Aye, but you're a cold one, you are." She frowned at him, and he noticed how the morning sun lit her hair to a deep, rich brown. He reflected with satisfaction that he had never liked brown hair, especially unruly brown hair.

Thunder reached out and pushed her nose against her mistress's hand.

"There, you sweet beastie. You are the best horse in all of Scotland, are you not?" Fia crooned as she lovingly stroked the horse's nose.

"That is the most disgusting untruth I have ever heard," stated Thomas flatly.

Fia looked at him with lifted eyebrows before returning her attention to Thunder. "Don't mind the Sassenach. Some of his manners must have leaked from his head when he cracked it in the garden."

Scooting on the forest floor, Fia maneuvered herself so Thunder's head lay more comfortably in her lap. *Her* horse, Thomas reminded himself grimly. *Her* horse that was lying on *his* leg.

"Damn the horse, damn the dog, and damn you," he muttered.

He didn't care if he was ever rescued. Hell, he'd just make himself comfortable, and when his leg rotted off, he would be free of the whole lot of them—lackwits every one.

"You're not helping matters, Sassenach. She's had a rough life, the poor bairn. Her master beat her and made her work from dawn 'til night." Fia's silky voice crept into his ears and tried to lull his anger away, but Thomas would have none of it.

" 'Twould take a beating to get a slug like her to work at all," he grumbled and then clamped his mouth shut. Why had he allowed himself to say anything? She would just get him involved in one of her inane conversations, and then he would be even more tangled up in this venture than he already was.

"Do you always do that?" she asked.

"Do what?"

"Grind your teeth so."

"Only when I am in your presence."

"It can't be good for them. You'll lose them if you continue. I had an uncle once who had nary a tooth in his head. 'Twas a piteous sight. He could eat naught but pap." She frowned. "Or soup. He could eat soup, he could. Though to be sure, he did take bread soaked in milk for his Sunday supper. I once saw him try to eat a piece of manchet. It took him two hours just to gnaw down one bite. Even then he couldn't eat mo—"

"Forget your toothless uncle, and get this damned horse off my leg!" Thomas shouted.

The dog growled, and Thomas snarled back.

Fia raised her eyebrows. "You've the devil of a temper, haven't you? 'Twas a simple observation that you

35

seem addicted to grinding your teeth." She nodded wisely. "I think you should see a specialist when we get to Londontown."

"*We* are not going to London. *I* am going to London."

Fia shrugged. "Perhaps." She patted the horse lovingly. "You should know Thunder'll not get up 'til you apologize to her."

"Apologize?" Outrage, fury, shock all warred for expression. "I'll be damned first."

" 'Tis quite possible you will," she said. She leaned toward him, her smile full of sympathy and understanding. Even as uncomfortable and angry as he was, he was not immune to the stroking quality of her voice. "The Maclean may arrive any moment, and we have yet to make good our escape from the main grounds of the castle."

"I don't—"

"Meanwhile, Thunder here has quite a temper. I've seen her lie this way for hours when she gets into one of her moods, never moving a bit even though 'twas raining buckets. Didn't you, poor beastie?" Thunder rolled her eyes and snorted her agreement.

Thomas rubbed his pounding temple. Sweet Jesu, but he would give all he possessed to be gone from here.

Fia regarded him from beneath her lashes. "Of course, if you would be willing to assist me with one or two small efforts, I might be willing to get Thunder off your leg."

Thomas groaned loudly, but Fia continued undeterred.

"Come, now, Lord Thomas. Surely you would not mind some company on your way to London."

Try as he might to resist, the velvety voice laid a steady assault against his anger. With a great sense of unease, he inwardly admitted that he might indeed need Fia's help if he planned on reaching his ship before dark.

Some hint of his thoughts must have shown, for she

immediately rewarded him with a saucy grin. "I make a merry traveling companion, I do. I can even sing a wee bit."

"I'm sure I will regret it." He sighed deeply. "I've always heard it said 'tis better to be alone than in bad company."

Fia's eyes widened. "Sweet St. Catherine, but 'tis another sign. My mother used to say the same thing to me when I was child." A wistful smile curved her mouth. "She died when I was but eight."

"She had to warn you about the company you were keeping at age eight? I am not surprised," he said dryly.

She grinned. "I was forever sneaking off to play with the animals. I had a partiality for pigs. My mother would always find me in the barn, covered with hay and dirt."

He heard her confession with something akin to envy. His memories of his own childhood weren't nearly as happy.

Younger than his father by almost fifteen years, Thomas's mother had been undeniably beautiful, with golden hair and cool, distant brown eyes. When Thomas had been a small child of six, she had run away with a man of no fortune and less breeding. After that, Thomas's father had become obsessed with proving to everyone that the Wentworth luck still existed, that it was even stronger after she left.

"You look sad," Fia said softly.

" 'Tis having this damned horse on my leg," he snapped, irritated at her close scrutiny.

"Do you agree to our bargain?"

"What bargain?"

"You will take me to London and . . ." She stopped and regarded him uncertainly.

"And what?" he asked.

She paled, and a horrible suspicion crossed his mind.

37

"You aren't asking me to help you steal the crown jewels or the like, are you?"

"As though I would do such a thing!" she answered hotly.

"Then out with it, plague take you! My leg is likely to wither off before you speak a coherent sentence. Whatever duty you have for me, 'tis apparently so horrendous you cannot even ask it without stammering and blushing."

She drew herself up with regal pride. Thomas had to fight a sudden grin. Her queenly air was strikingly at odds with her appearance. Bits of straw stuck out from her wildly disordered hair, while the morning sun added a healthy golden glow to her skin. She had the look of a milkmaid just tumbled in the hay.

"There is nothing horrendous in my request at all. 'Tis just that I . . . well, I need a patron."

A patron. He couldn't say a word.

"I thought perhaps you could sponsor me." The voice was all forced unconcern, but the trembling of her hand as she stroked the horse's nose told another story.

For a moment, he was tempted to refuse her. Surely the horse would get up of its own accord. But Fia's eyes caught his attention. As dark as the rich peat that covered the forest floor, they burned with determination.

God's Wounds, she *wanted* a patron. His gaze wandered, lingering on her mouth and coming to rest on her tight bodice. Hell, he'd have been willing to fill that position without having been caught beneath this bloated excuse of a horse. The thought surprised him.

He met her anxious glance with a warm smile. As soon as he got her to London, he would take great pleasure in tying back that frustrating mass of hair with yards and yards of silk ribbon. "Don't fret, comfit. You had only to ask."

Her relief was evident. "Och, you'll not be sorry! I

was so worried you wouldn't like the idea. Though, to be sure, I'm surprised you didn't ask to see proof of my abilities."

Thomas burst out laughing.. "You're a forward piece, even for a Scot! If you'd like to show me some proof of your abilities, now is not the time for it, comfit. I can scarcely appreciate such a display while weighted down, now can I?"

He allowed his gaze to wander over her again, a feeling of great satisfaction warming him even in the cold. Perhaps he could salvage something from this muddle after all.

She chuckled. "You're not in a position to appreciate anything, are you?"

"The world looks vastly different from the underside of a horse," he agreed pleasantly. He was rewarded with such a laughing look, he began to tingle in places not being pressed into the dirt. "I hate to rush you, sweet, but my leg is numb."

"Of course," she agreed and stood. He admired her lithe, graceful movements with a new awareness.

"Up, Thunder," Fia commanded softly. Wheezing heavily, the horse clambered to its feet.

"That's it?" Thomas managed to get the words out through the rush of pain that flooded his leg. "You just say 'up,' and she gets up?"

Fia blinked. "What else should I say to her?"

He managed to swallow his irritation. "Nothing. Not a blasted thing."

"Good, then. 'Tis time to be on our way." She led the horse beside Thomas. "I had best mount first. She'll not act so unruly with me upon her. Can you put any weight on your leg?"

He nodded curtly. He would get out of this abhorrent land if it killed him.

Fia tied her bag to the saddle and nimbly climbed onto

the horse's back, her skirts sliding up to expose rounded calves, trim ankles, and small, muddy feet.

Despite his discomfort, his body responded instantly. *God's Wounds, but I must have injured my head to be so affected by the sight of a pair of ankles.* "Don't you own any shoes?" he asked quickly, hoping to hide his obvious arousal.

She regarded one dainty foot with a shrug. "I've shoes enough. I just hate to wear them." She chuckled, and Thomas's mouth went dry at the sound. "Duncan swears he'd nail them to my feet, would it do any good."

Thomas scowled at the mention of her old lover. *He* was her patron now, and as soon as he got up on the horse, he would remind her of that fact. He stifled a moan as he lifted his stiff leg to the stirrup. He doubted he would be able to move it at all before the day was over, but so long as he was gone from here, he would offer no complaint.

Thomas threw himself onto the horse, the pain shooting through his leg effectively wiping out every other ache in his abused body. "My ship is north of here. 'Twill take a full day's ride to reach her."

"We'd best hurry. Duncan is not known for wasting time, and we have to stop for Mary and Angus."

"Who are they?" he demanded.

"Mary has been working at Duart Castle since she was a child. Angus is her new husband." Fia looked over her shoulder, the trees casting long shadows across her silken cheek. "I couldn't leave them. Mary has been like a mother to me. 'Twill take no time at all."

Thomas looked into the uptilted face and heard himself answer, "Very well."

She smiled, and it was as if the sun had broken through a rain-blackened sky. "Come, Zeus!" Fia called. The ugly dog rolled to his feet and stretched out his legs, giving a wide yawn.

"Must he come with us?" Thomas grumbled.

"But of course. No one else would feed him."

He thought of a thousand answers, none worth repeating.

Thomas wrapped his arms more securely about Fia. He was a solid mass of bruises, aches, and lumps. The only thing that kept him upright in the saddle was the thought that if anything could speed his recovery, it would be Fia's lush, naked body lying in his bed, her incredible hair spread across his pillows. His loins tightened uncomfortably, and he called himself sharply to order. The last thing he needed was to spend the rest of the day fighting his own lust.

Safety beckoned. All they had to do was reach his ship before Duncan Maclean found them. Thomas glanced at the sun and estimated their arrival time. By late afternoon, he and Fia would be safely ensconced on the *Glorianna,* sailing to London and away from the nightmare of the last few hours.

As he relaxed in the saddle, Fia snuggled back against him with a contented sigh. The sweet scent of heather filled him with the inexplicable desire to grin like a complete lackwit. And for the briefest of moments, despite his aches and pains, Thomas knew he really was the luckiest man alive.

Chapter Four

"Och, Thunder, what have you done now?" Fia rubbed her cheek against the horse's rough mane.

Thunder's answering nicker rang through the clearing. It sounded suspiciously like a laugh.

"Lord Thomas was right about you," Fia chastised the mare. " 'Tis poor sport to pretend to be lame just as we were nearing the coastline. Mary will be wondering where we are."

Thunder hung her head and lifted one foreleg.

"Don't try that with me, you silly old nag. As soon as Thomas stomped off into the forest you forgot all about limping and started scrounging about for clover, as healthy and well as a young colt! I saw you myself."

The horse swished her tail and stared off into the distance with a bored expression.

Zeus whined by the small fire. Fia frowned at him. "Don't you play the innocent, either! 'Twas ill mannered of you to gobble up all our food as soon as our backs were turned."

The dog wagged his tail, and Thunder snickered again. Fia threw up her hands. "There's no speaking with either of you. 'Tis a wonder the Sassenach doesn't wash his hands of the lot of us."

And, oh, had he ever been angry. After cursing for an entire quarter of an hour, Thomas had finally stomped into the woods, determined to find his own supper.

Fia crouched by the fire. Her stomach made a noisy protest, and she cast a disparaging look at the dog curled up beside her. Zeus met Fia's condemning gaze and whined pathetically. Even stuffed with all their food, he managed to look ravenous.

"I hope you get a stomachache," she said. Zeus cocked his good ear and wagged his tail. "Don't try to cozen me, you silly lumpkin. I know your tricks, and I'm not about to fall for any of them now."

He sighed heavily and threw himself back onto Thunder's discarded saddle blanket. His sad eyes pleaded for forgiveness.

Fia patted him. He was such a sweet beastie, after all. She wrapped her arms about her knees, shivering slightly in the wind. 'Twas cold and damp this eve, the breeze carrying the veriest hint of rain. As the chill increased, Zeus dug deeper into the blanket, while Thunder huddled against the small stand of trees.

Fia wondered how Thomas was doing. He had been stiff and sore, favoring his leg even as he marched into the woods. His clothing hadn't fared well either, covered in mud, the fine cloth ripped thanks to Thunder's vicious teeth. The mare had taken great delight in snapping at Thomas every chance she'd gotten.

Fia stirred the fire and wondered how long it would

take Thomas to return. "I'm hungry," she announced. Thunder's ears flickered.

Fia rubbed Zeus's good ear, and he gave a heartfelt sigh. "Enjoy the heat whilst you can. Once Lord Thomas returns, 'tis back in the cold you'll be."

Zeus gave a disdainful yawn and rolled onto his side, promptly falling into a deep sleep.

Fia settled beside the fire and pulled out her knife, whittling aimlessly at a stick. Her gaze wandered to the blackness beyond the warm light of the fire. *Where was he?*

"He said he'd be back soon," she said loudly. The words sounded hollow in the darkness.

He would come back. He had to. *He promised,* she reminded herself. She wondered how much a vow was worth when it was made while one was pressed into the mud beneath a huge horse. The thought held her fast as she stared into the forest.

Darkness crept into the campsite inch by inch, bringing dampness and uncertainty. Thomas had warned her not to build the fire too large for fear Duncan might see the smoke and discover them. But now Thomas was gone.

An uncomfortable lump rose in her throat. Fia piled the remaining wood on the fire and moved closer to Zeus.

" 'Tis a wonder, I suppose, he stayed with us this long," she said, lifting her chin. "Well, I don't need the Sassenach's help to get to London. There'll be other patrons, and they'll all be better than his High and Mighty Lordship, won't they, Zeus?"

Zeus rolled over onto his back, his paws flopping nervelessly in the air, a deep snore emitting from his slack mouth.

Fia looked at him in disgust. "Some guard dog you are. Here I am, alone in the midst of the great forest, and there you lay, snoring fit to wake the dead. Lord Thomas was right about you being a la—"

The forest crackled to life. Thunder shied, prancing frantically as Fia whipped out her knife. Finally awakened, Zeus bounded to his feet and snarled viciously.

Thomas stumbled from the bushes.

"Damn thorn vines. Can't go anywhere in this land without stepping into a bog or getting ripped up by thorns. God only knows why anyone would want to conquer such an unsightly, ill-favored land. Once we get to London, I swear I'll never—"

Fia effectively stopped his tirade by launching herself into his arms.

Thomas stood completely still. Fia was plastered to him like wet silk, her body snug against his, her arms wrapped uncomfortably tight about his waist. He looked in amazement at her upturned face.

"I thought you weren't coming back." Her eyes were as black as the sea sky in the midst of a night storm, her long lashes tangled and luxuriant. Her skin glowed with vibrant color and health. And her body . . . he almost groaned. He was stirred beyond thought by the warmth of her curves pressed against him.

His eyes were drawn to her lush mouth. He already knew the taste of those lips, and nothing was going to stop him from tasting them again. Her face flushed rosily in the light of the roaring fire.

The fire.

The *roaring* fire.

Giving a shout, Thomas pushed Fia away and began kicking dirt onto the smoking logs. "God's Breath, woman! Didn't I tell you to keep the fire small? Is that *small?* Do you call that a *small* flame? What were you trying to do, alert the whole isle?"

No sharp reply halted his tirade. Fia stood, her head bowed, her arms crossed in front of her as though ward-ing off the chill breeze. Even without seeing her eyes, Thomas knew there were tears in them. He winced. Until he had run over her with his temper, she had been genuinely glad to see him.

Remorse washed away his anger, and he sighed in frustration, raking a hand through his hair. Today had lasted an eternity, for Fia as well as him. No doubt she was as weary as he.

A sudden movement at his shoulder reminded him of why he had left camp in the first place. Supper. He grinned. That was how he would make it up to his little Scottish thief.

Thomas sat down. Using his foot, he pushed Zeus off the saddle blanket. Heaving a disgruntled sigh, Zeus hauled himself to his feet and staggered to a spot nearer the fire, collapsing in a boneless heap.

Thomas pulled the blanket next to him and patted it. "Come and sit, Fia," he coaxed, flashing his most winsome smile. It was his best smile, one that rarely failed him.

It failed him now. Fia sniffed and turned her shoulder, going instead to stand beside Zeus. From across the fire Thomas met the dog's grin. 'Twas obvious the hound enjoyed his discomfort. Thunder snorted indignantly and shuffled around until her rump pointed directly at him.

He ignored them both and fixed his gaze on Fia. "Come and see what I've brought." He held up the bag. It shook as something struggled within. Fia's eyes widened in fascination.

" 'Tis a present," he said. He held the bag toward her. A small thing, wild and panicked, was trying desperately to get out. It had taken hours of laying traps and praying faithfully to catch dinner of some sort. He was as proud as if it had been his first successful hunt.

"Och, let me have it," she said. Her voice reached across the fire and settled about him like a cloak.

Every ache Thomas possessed melted into insignificance under the warmth of her smile. Sweet Jesu, but she was as lovely as a morning mist, even with leaves in her hair and her nose reddened by the cold.

He handed her the bag as she crossed to his side. "Open it, Mistress Impatience, and see what I've caught."

She sank to her knees and opened the bag eagerly. Her hands fumbled over the tie.

"Why, 'tis a rabbit!" she exclaimed. She held the animal aloft.

Thomas admired its plumpness. He could almost smell the roasting meat.

Just as he opened his mouth to ask Fia how she would suggest it be cooked, she cooed softly and kissed it on the nose. "You poor wee bunny. You have gone and hurt yourself, haven't you? Where did you find him?"

Across the soft brown fur, Fia's eyes met Thomas's, the softly glowing light telling him all he had to know. Swallowing convulsively, he forced a smile. "I . . . He was caught in a trap." Well, that much was true . . . more or less.

Fia's dark head bent over the rabbit, her delicate fingers carefully probing the injured leg. "I think he'll recover," she said with evident relief.

In the glow of the fire, Thomas thought he felt the rabbit's accusing gaze. He stared determinedly back at it. He would be damned if he would let a hare make him uneasy.

His mouth watered. It was difficult not to picture the animal as he had all the way into camp, neatly skewered on a stick, skin crisply roasted, meat succulent and tender. He was going to starve if he didn't get something to eat soon. He watched morosely as Fia made a soft bed for her new pet out of the blanket. The *only* blanket, Thomas reminded himself.

"Thank you, Sassenach."

The softly spoken words curled into the hollowness of his stomach and filled it. He found himself gazing into Fia's fathomless eyes. Drowning. That's what he was doing. He was drowning in the eyes of a wench who brought him the devil's own luck.

He had never been so beaten and weary in all his life. Every muscle he possessed ached through and through. But he ached even more for the taste of her, the sweet fragrance of her hair, and the lushness of her rounded body.

His gaze dropped to her lips. They were delectably moist. He couldn't look away from that tempting mouth. He had to have her.

He buried a hand in her hair and pulled her forward. With every ounce of the desire that streamed through his body, he kissed her. She returned his ardor as passionately as he could have wanted, her fingers tangling in the folds of his shirt. Her soft moans sent him spiraling toward heaven. God's Wounds, but she was a hot little piece.

The thought was barely coherent. Every time he was near her, he became as addlepated as a beardless youth.

He sank his hands deeper into the velvet length of her hair. He tasted the smoothness of her cheek and feathered sensual kisses over her face, her eyes, the sweetness of her neck. He pulled at the tight bodice impatiently. With a soft pop, the top button gave way, followed by the satisfying sound of another and then another button loosening.

He revealed one silken white shoulder and rained kisses down her throat to the hollow of her neck. He lightly bit her shoulder, and she sighed deeply. She moaned as his hands filled with the softness of her breasts.

"Duncan!" she said in a rush of breath.

Thomas stilled his assault on her neck. *No, she couldn't have.* His questing tongue focused on her delicate ear.

"Duncan," she said again. This time the name was accompanied by a definite moan.

Pulling back, Thomas looked at her, his anger plain. "*What* did you call me?" Here he was, on the verge of making love to her, and the wench had called him by the name of her old lover. Lips compressed, Thomas replied tightly, "Not Duncan, sweet. 'Tis Thomas. My name is Thomas Wentworth."

From behind him came the reply. Deep and rumbling, the masculine voice filled the small clearing. "Well, now, that is something useful to know. 'Twould bring my clan ill fortune were I to kill a nameless man."

Thomas met Fia's gaze. She gave a weak smile and pointed over his shoulder. " 'Tis Duncan. He's found us."

Chapter Five

"Where is he?" Fia demanded.

The guard remained solidly in front of the great oaken door. "Ye know where the laird is, lass, or ye wouldn't be a-standin' there tappin' yer foot."

"I wasn't speaking of Duncan. I want to know where the Sassenach has been taken."

MacKenna regarded her with a fond twinkle in his eye. "The Sassenach is with the laird, and the laird don't wish to be disturbed."

"He is about to be disturbed whether he wishes it or not," Fia stated.

"Now, ye settle down a mite, lassie. The Maclean is as mad as a bear with a sore paw. Ye had best wait until—"

The huge door slammed open, and Duncan glowered from the opening. "There you are," he growled, his dark eyes resting on Fia. "Get in here. We need to speak."

Fia nodded and stepped into the great hall, casting a

considering glance up at Duncan as she passed him. He was angered, there was no doubt of that. His mouth was a bleak slash across his face, and his eyes burned with suppressed fury.

Fia walked farther into the room and halted in her tracks.

Thomas was bound to a chair, his head bowed, a thin trickle of blood running down one cheek.

"What have you done to my Englishman?"

Duncan looked unimpressed. "Less than he deserved."

Fia smoothed back Thomas's thick, golden hair and carefully examined the large, purple lump on his forehead. His beautiful mouth was swollen and split in one corner. Worse yet, both his eyes had been thoroughly blackened.

"Och, you've gone and beaten him to a bloody pulp," she said, casting a stern frown at Duncan. "He's an English earl. You'd do well to remember that."

" 'Tis difficult to forget."

Fia ignored him. She gathered a pitcher of water and a cloth from the sideboard and returned to Thomas's side. She carefully bathed his bruised face.

"Let the man be," Duncan grumbled. "You'd think he was made of glass to be hurt by a few light taps."

Fia's mouth dropped open. "Light taps? And who among your men is given over to the practice of delivering light taps?"

Duncan scratched his bearded chin. "Well . . . young Fitzgerald has a light fist."

"I should hope so. He's all of twelve years of age." Fia pinned Duncan with an exasperated glare. "You had my Englishman trounced soundly and not by young Fitzgerald, either."

Duncan rubbed his ear, a sheepish look crossing his face. "Aye, but—"

51

"I'm ashamed of you, Duncan Maclean, for causing harm to an innocent man."

"Innocent, my ass."

Fia dabbed at the cut on Thomas's mouth. She hoped it wouldn't leave a scar.

Duncan sighed heavily and sank into a chair across from Thomas. "If you hadn't put yourself in the most damnable position, cousin, I wouldn't have been forced to take such an action."

"What do you mean by that?"

"You know very well what I mean," he returned. "Wandering about in the middle of the night with an Englishman like a common—" He snapped his mouth shut and glared. "What were you thinking?"

Fia rinsed out the cloth and dabbed at a briuse beneath Thomas's eye. "I was on my way to London," she said calmly.

"What?" Duncan shouted, jerking upright in his chair.

"Don't look so surprised. I told you I would go."

"So you just upped and traipsed to the coast with an English thief?"

"I'm not a child, Duncan. I had everything planned." Fia regarded Thomas's bent head for a moment. "I would have made it if you hadn't returned so early."

"What were you doing with the candlesticks?"

Fia rinsed out the cloth. She had hoped her bag of loot would have been overlooked in the general melee in the woods. Apparently, she had not been so fortunate.

"Cousin?" said Duncan grimly.

"I was going to pay you back."

He snorted his disbelief. "A house full of valuables and all you could think to steal were some paltry candlesticks?"

"Borrow," she corrected him absently. "I thought 'twould make it more difficult for you to find us. If I'd sold some of my jewels, you would have been sure to track us down."

"How did you propose to sell your loot? Just walk into some crofter's hut and flash it before his amazed eyes?"

"Nay. Angus's brother is a tinker. He was going to sell the silver and take us with him to London."

Duncan's brows lowered. "Us? Angus?"

"Angus Collins, the man who helps in the stables, He's Mary's new husband. They are waiting for me at Crenahan." Fia wondered if Thomas would need stitches for the wound on his cheek.

Duncan looked thunderous. "Mary knew about this?"

"Of course."

"By the rood, but I thought she had more sense than to encourage you toward such a fool course of action. Has she gone daft?"

"She thinks I am wasting away on this isle." Fia smiled. "She loves my plays, too."

Duncan groaned aloud, but Fia continued undeterred. "As Angus is her husband, it only made sense that once Mary agreed to come, he couldn't stay behind."

"Addlepated, the lot of you." Duncan scowled down at his boots before shooting her a sharp glance. "How did you plan on getting off the isle?"

"Tam MacCrea's father has a boat."

"Who's this MacCrea?"

"The sheepherder." She gave Duncan an admonitory frown. "You should make more of an effort to get to know the retainers, Duncan."

"Why should I bother? You know them all, and much too well from the sound of it."

"They are good people. Tam's father agreed to take us across the firth to Carnorvah. The tinker's cart is waiting for us there."

Duncan's shoulders sagged, and Fia grinned. " 'Twasn't such a foolish plan after all, was it?"

" 'Tis that which scares me more than anything else."
He frowned at Thomas's bent head. "Where did you find
the Sassenach?"

"Perched in the window like a great bird."

"What was he doing?"

"I'm not sure," she replied thoughtfully. "He said
'twas a wager, but I trow, 'tis a might odd to come this
distance for such a silly venture."

Duncan lifted his eyebrows. "So 'twas mere coincidence you met him at all?"

"Nay, Duncan, 'twas not coincidence. 'Twas fate." He
grunted, and she frowned. "Of course, none of this
would have occurred had you taken me to London as
you promised."

"Once you are married—"

"By the time I am married I will be a hundred years
old, too bent and gnarled to hold a pen in my hand, let
alone reach London."

Silence filled the room as Duncan glowered at her.
With a disgusted noise, Fia turned back to nursing Thomas. He looked like a prince, she thought wistfully, as
she traced the outline of a bruise on his cheek. A beaten
and muddy prince, but a prince nonetheless.

Duncan let out his breath in a long sigh. "Actually,
poppet, I *have* found you a husband."

Her hand froze, curled about a strand of Thomas's
hair.

Duncan leaned forward, resting his elbows on his
knees. "I had planned on giving this more thought, but
now . . ."

Fia clasped her trembling hands in her lap. "Who is
it?"

Duncan shifted in his chair. "Malcolm Davies."

"*Malcolm Davies?* He's naught but fourteen! Five
years younger than I!"

"Only four. He just turned fifteen."

"Four," she repeated.

"But he is mature beyond his years," said Duncan with an encouraging nod.

"Mature? When all he does is read books and translate ancient Greek writings? I don't think he's ever left the walls of Dunvena Castle."

"He's been ill," said Duncan bracingly.

"Ill? Faint of heart is more like."

" 'Tis not as easy as you think, Fia, trying to find a bridegroom who will allow you to write and take you to London, as well."

She favored him with a disbelieving gaze. "Malcolm the Maiden would leave Dunvena Castle and travel all the way to London?"

Duncan's color rose. "Who calls him Malcolm the Maiden?"

"You did. Just last year. After the gathering at Lochvie. You said—"

"That was before," Duncan interrupted hastily. "Let anyone else say such to me, and I'll have their liver in my haggis." Fia raised her eyebrows, and he waved a hand. "He will go to London. He has pledged it."

"With or without his mother?"

" 'Tis possible his mother will wish to accompany him on such a long journey," Duncan replied cautiously.

"Sweet Jesu, Duncan!"

"The lad is sickly!"

"From all accounts he is a babied lackwit. 'Tis said he's almost a hunchback from bending over his tomes until late at night." She looked at Thomas's fine broad shoulders. Why couldn't Duncan have chosen a man like this? One who was tall and handsome and—

"I thought a man of learning would appeal to you."

"A hunchback with the wit of a stone and a mother who cannot bring herself to allow the rain to dampen his brow is not an appealing sort of man, Duncan. His conversation is probably full of mysterious references to Greek deities."

Duncan looked away guiltily, and Fia snorted. She knew the estimable Malcolm's conversation couldn't hold a candle to that of her charming Englishman. She sighed and leaned her forehead against Thomas's arm, wondering why she suddenly felt so lonely.

Her cousin stood restlessly. "Malcolm has promised to take you to London after the wedding. He is an honorable lad, of a noble and wealthy house. You should be pleased I have found such a man."

"Perhaps I don't wish to marry at all."

"You've given me no choice. The next time I leave, you may well make it to London. I won't have you alone and unprotected in that hellish city."

She regarded him somberly, noticing for the first time the heaviness about his dark eyes. There was more to this than she had realized. "What has happened, Duncan?"

He leaned against the mantel and kicked aimlessly at the sputtering fire. "Queen Mary has escaped the Douglas stronghold and even now calls for those loyal to her. There will be war if something's not done, and quickly."

"Will you fight?"

"I can't let the queen tear Scotland asunder," Duncan said heavily. "Did she care for the land at all, she would step aside and let a regent rule for her infant son in her stead."

"She will choose war," Fia said.

Duncan shrugged, a gleam lighting his dark eyes. "If she's allowed a say, she will. Either way, I can't leave you here, alone and unprotected."

"I will—"

"No, you will not. I left for a mere three weeks, and look what happened! You snuck out of the castle in the dead of night and went jaunting about the isle with a strange Englishman."

"He's an earl."

Duncan crossed his arms. "I know what he is, cousin." He regarded her through half-closed eyes. "Thomas Wentworth is the earl of Rotherwood. The greatest of his estates marches the border between Scotland and England. He has lands in Northumberland, Devonshire and Yorkshire. He possesses a respected title and is of good birth. Furthermore, he is reputed to be one of Queen Elizabeth's favorites."

Fia looked from Duncan to Thomas. That, at least, explained the man's arrogance. She reached out and touched the ragged cloth of Thomas's shirt. Even in disrepair, the quality was evident. "What else do you know?"

Duncan's gaze rested on Thomas's bent head. "His closest companion is Robert MacQuarrie."

Fia raised her eyebrows. She knew the story of the missing laird of Balmanach. As a young man of sixteen, MacQuarrie had disappeared with his five sisters after the murder of their parents by a rival clan. At first it had been assumed that all of the children had been slain as well, and the young laird had been a figure of great sympathy—until rumors began to circulate that he had suddenly appeared at the English court and was well on his way to becoming a favorite of the English queen.

Few Scotsmen thought well of a laird who had slunk away in the dark of night and refused to accept his responsibilities.

" 'Tis hard to imagine the Sassenach having a friend like Robert MacQuarrie."

Duncan shrugged. "All I know is that the Coward of Balmanach is never far from your Sassenach."

Fia regarded Thomas's face for a moment. "What else do you know?"

"Wentworth works closely with Francis Walsingham, Elizabeth's most trusted counselor. Walsingham is reputed to be like a father to him. They say your Englishman dons the guise of spy on occasion."

"Spy?" Fia looked at Thomas as if she had never seen him before. "You think that's what he was doing here?"

Duncan pointed to a small table by the fire. A crumpled sheet of paper lay on the marbled surface. "I found that hidden in his tunic. 'Tis from my desk."

Fia swallowed with a throat gone dry. "What is it?"

Duncan shook his head.

She lifted her eyebrows, and he sighed loudly before crossing to pick up the letter. " 'Tis naught, I swear it. 'Twould interest none but a Sassenach." He slid the missive into his pocket as he spoke.

"Apparently the English would pay mightily for it if they sent an earl to filch it."

"Your Sassenach is known as the luckiest man in England. Perchance he came to try his fortune."

Fia frowned. "Duncan, how do you know so much about—"

Thomas stirred, and Fia dropped to her knees beside his chair. He moaned as he lifted his head.

At first, his blurry vision found nothing more remarkable than a nimbus of red-brown hair curling about a piquant face. He blinked rapidly, and soon a pair of fascinating dark eyes came into focus. He smiled, and a lush mouth parted in response.

Thomas sighed. Whatever dream he was having, it would be complete once this angel touched him.

"Welcome back, Sassenach," rumbled a voice as vast and hard as the ocean floor.

Thomas blinked and turned his head. There, leaning against the mantel, stood a giant. Though no small man himself, the giant would tower over him by a good half foot.

The giant grinned, white teeth flashing in a darkly bearded face. "Are you comfortable, my feeble little Englishman?"

Remembrance hit Thomas like the slam of a fist. The giant was Duncan Maclean, the earl of Duart. And the angel . . . he looked at Fia. The angel was Maclean's woman.

"Duncan, untie him," she said softly.

Thomas looked down at his arms. He was indeed tied. As many ropes and knots as held him, he wondered he was even able to move his head.

Fia whirled from him and marched to stand toe-to-toe with the laird. "Release him. He's done naught."

"His hands were inside your bodice. 'Tis a wonder he's even breathing," Maclean said firmly.

Thomas knew that had the laird not interrupted them, his hands would have traveled much farther than that.

Fia apparently thought the same thing, for her face glowed with color. "He's a guest in this house. All the poor man did was try to help me—"

"Aye, help you out of your dress."

"You are impossible." Fia crossed to Thomas and softly stroked his hair. "Can you not loosen his ties? At least until we have settled this?"

Thomas couldn't believe it. The wench was pleading with her lover for his life. He jerked his head away from the stroking hand. "I don't need your assistance!"

Fia patted his shoulder as though he were a petulant child. "You look a mite fevered. Pray, try to sit still." She turned an accusing expression on Maclean. "If he falls ill, 'twill be your fault, Duncan."

Thomas wondered if he could reach her from his trussed-up position. He would die for it, but, oh, what a satisfying way to end his life—with his foot firmly planted on her deserving backside.

Maclean scowled. "This is no wee puppy or sick horse but a live, breathing man. You should take more care, cousin."

The rumbling voice rang in Thomas's ears. *Cousin.*

Kim Bennet

He had been caught fondling the laird's cousin. Nay, he thought with startling clarity, it was worse. What had Fia told him when they first met? That Maclean was returning to marry her. Fia was Maclean's cousin *and* betrothed.

His irritation grew by leaps and bounds. Of course the wench hadn't seen fit to mention that the laird was her cousin. Not, Thomas reflected grimly, that he'd have believed her, seeing as how she was dressed in the veriest rags. Hell, he hadn't even believed her claims of an engagement. Heaven help the wench if he didn't toss her across his knee for being such a lackwit.

Fia shook her head sadly. "Duncan, you mistake what you saw. I was merely thanking the Sassenach for catching a sweet bunny for me. He's been nothing but fine and honorable since the beginning."

"Is it fine and honorable to take advantage of an innocent lass?"

"Is it honorable to attack an unarmed man?" She matched the huge man shout for shout, both so angry, it was as if Thomas did not exist. "You can't stand there with your cheeks all puffed out telling me of honor, Duncan Maclean!" She crossed her arms and frowned fiercely. "You owe him an apology. The man did nothing more than kiss me."

The laird looked at Thomas with an incredulous gaze. "You can't expect me to do such a fool thing!"

"Pray, do," Thomas said, grinning widely, though the gesture pulled painfully at his split lip. "I've a need for a good laugh."

Two pairs of wrathful eyes pinned him to his chair. Thomas's smile faded, the laughter dying in his dry throat.

Maclean spoke first, his disgust plain. "You're wrong, lassie, if you think that man had noble intentions. 'Twould take the sharp end of a claymore pricking his neck before he acted in an honorable way." His hand rested on his sword as he spoke. Thomas could tell the idea held an immeasurable appeal to Maclean.

Fia lifted her chin. "That just goes to show what a poor judge of men you are. The Sassenach is twice the man Malcolm the Maiden could ever hope to be."

"You leave young Davies out of this," growled Duncan.

"I'm more than willing to leave young Davies out of everything," Fia returned hotly.

Thomas stared from one to the other. What were they talking about? Walsingham would rub his hands in glee to find out what alliances were being offered to the powerful laird of Duart.

Fia placed a hand on Thomas's shoulder. "Duncan, 'tis not what you think. Thomas promised to become my sponsor once we were in London if I would but help him reach his ship."

Thomas stifled a groan. The wench was going to get him killed. Catching Maclean's black eyes on him, Thomas offered a vague shrug.

"If you don't believe me, ask him yourself," Fia said with determination.

Maclean rubbed his bearded chin. "You seem to have cast a spell over my cousin, Sassenach." He regarded Thomas for a long moment. "Well, speak up. Did you promise to sponsor her or not?"

Thomas swallowed. For better or worse, Fia was going to blurt out the whole. He had nothing to lose. "Aye, we agreed to some such arrangement."

Maclean looked puzzled. "Have you ever done such a thing before?"

Thomas's mouth went dry, and he shot an uneasy glance at Fia. "Once or twice," he managed to croak.

"I knew it!" Fia cried. " 'Twas fate that sent you to me!"

Maclean frowned, as though the answer to some puzzle still eluded his grasp. "What did you hope to gain?"

Thomas looked from Maclean to Fia and back again. What could he say? That the laird's cousin was an incredibly sensual and delectable woman? That there was something about her black eyes and the way she smiled that heated him beyond measure? That he lost what little sense he had whenever she pressed those full, silken lips to his?

Fia sighed. "Duncan, let the poor man be. Can't you see he is still befuddled? He agreed to sponsor my plays in exchange for help in getting to his ship."

"Plays?" Thomas asked. "What plays?"

Silence so thick it could have stood by itself filled the room.

Fia stared, her dark eyes widening. "B-but, Sassenach, if you didn't know about my plays, why did you agree to sponsor me?"

The voice curled its way around Thomas's neck and tightened into a noose.

Sweet Jesu, she writes plays.

It was the last thought he had before the hilt of a claymore slammed into his head and blessed darkness wiped out the sight of Fia's white face.

Chapter Six

The three men yanked Thomas's inert body from the chair, allowing his head to bang against the table edge. Fia winced when she heard the thud.

"Go gently with my Englishman," Fia said, glaring at the men. "He's suffered enough at the hands of the Macleans without bumping and thumping him all the way to the bedchamber."

Duncan looked thunderstruck. "Bedchamber?"

"Where else is he to go?"

"That . . . that pox-ridden swiver has done naught but offer our family insult!" Duncan's voice boomed, and the men halted. "He'll not be staying in a bedchamber like an honored guest! To the cellar he'll go, tightly trussed, 'til I've decided how to deal with him. Mac-Kenna, you, Berwick, and Talent see to it the Englishman is well bound. I'll not have the man escaping."

"But you can't!" Fia protested. She whirled to face

MacKenna. "Don't you dare take him to the cellar. The dampness will kill him."

MacKenna gave an apologetic shrug. "Sorry, lass, but the laird is the laird."

Fia crossed her arms. "Just who, Douglas MacKenna, nursed you back to health last winter when you were moaning and crying fit to shame a priest?"

He shifted uneasily. " 'Twas ye, mistress."

"And who sat by Katherine's side when she was giving birth to little David?"

The grizzled face softened at the mention of his youngest son. "Bless ye, mistress. Ye stayed with her the whole night, ye did."

"And who gave you the silver to buy that new horse you are so fond of?"

A dull red stole across MacKenna's cheeks. He cast a miserable look toward Duncan before replying. " 'Twas ye, mistress."

Fia raised her eyebrows. MacKenna swallowed noisily and laid down his burden. "Ah, if ye'll forgive me fer sayin' so, my lord, 'tis a bit cold in the cellar."

Thick black eyebrows rose slightly. "Cold?"

MacKenna nodded miserably. "Aye. And . . . and damp, my lord."

Duncan's anger could have burned holes through stone. He smiled with a terrible lack of humor. " 'Tis damp in the cellar. Well, by all means we can't have such for our wondrous guest, can we?"

MacKenna winced. "If 'twas a Scotsman, I wouldn't hesitate, my lord. But with an Englishman . . ." He shook his head. "Ye know the truth of it. The littlest thing could do him in."

Duncan's face darkened until Fia thought he would explode. She was relieved when he finally let out his breath in a long, drawn-out hiss. "Take the damned Sassenach and place him in a bedchamber. Post a guard.

And by the saints above, MacKenna, stop looking like a witless sheep!"

MacKenna sighed his relief and gestured to the men to resume carrying their burden from the room. As he passed Fia, she murmured, "I owe you."

His shrewd gray eyes twinkled somberly. "That ye do, mistress. Don't think I'll let ye be forgettin' it, either."

Fia grinned. "I won't." She slanted a challenge at Duncan from under her lashes before saying loudly, "Take him to the *best* chamber. I'll be up shortly with some medicines." The men moved with exaggerated caution as they maneuvered the Englishman out the doorway.

Fia followed them to the door.

"Hold, cousin! I'm not finished," Duncan growled.

She sighed. "I was afraid you'd say that."

"Sit."

She crossed to the nearest chair and perched on the edge. "Before we continue, I want to know what you plan on doing with the Sassenach."

He waved a hand. "I want to talk about you, not that damned Englishman."

"I want your word you'll not harm him."

"He's a spy, Fia. He crept into the castle to steal from me, from the clan. I can't let him just walk away."

"Duncan, let me—"

"I am sending for Mary. I don't want you near the Sassenach without a chaperone."

"For heaven's sake, Duncan! I'm not a child who—"

"Furthermore, I am inviting Malcolm Davies and his mother to attend us here at their earliest convenience."

"Duncan! 'Tis not fair!"

"You will marry as soon as Lady Davies and I agree on the contract."

"I don't want to marry."

Duncan's expression gave her no hope. " 'Tis for your

own safety, poppet. You will be married by Sunday. Earlier, if I can arrange it."

"And if I refuse? They say Lady Davies is as proud and haughty as a queen. What would she think to see me kicking and screaming all the way to the altar?"

Duncan's eyebrows lowered. "This is no laughing matter, Fia. 'Tis serious."

"I am serious," she returned.

He stared at her, his gaze black and hard. "If that's the way you wish to do this, then so be it." He stood and crossed to the door. "Fitzgerald!" he yelled.

A flurry of rushing footsteps answered him, and a red-headed lad slid into the room. "Ye called fer me?"

"Aye. Go and find MacKenna, and tell him to put that damned Sassenach into the cellar."

"Nay!" Fia cried. " 'Twill kill him!"

Duncan's flat gaze answered her. There was a tense pause as she struggled with her temper.

"Och, to the devil with you," she snapped. "Send Fitzgerald away. I'll meet this bridegroom of yours."

He arched an eyebrow. "You'll do more than that, lassie. You'll wed Malcolm if I say it. I can promise that."

"The laird will have me hide if he finds ye alone with the Sassenach," Mary warned from the doorway.

Fia frowned at her maid. "I don't need a chaperone."

"Whist, lassie. Ye'll get no argument from me on that score. I told the laird that if he truly wished to see ye married, then the less chaperonage ye had, the better."

"I don't wish to marry," said Fia sharply. She turned from Mary's disbelieving gaze and straightened Thomas's covers. The morning light from the mullioned window turned the dust motes to glittering sparkles of fairy dust. They wafted through the air, reflecting the warm gold of Thomas's hair.

Her Sassenach never stirred. She lightly traced the bruise on his cheek to the corner of his mouth. She should have been glad Mary's potions kept him in such a restful slumber, but she wanted him to waken and look at her as he had when he had kissed her in the forest. The passion in his brown eyes had melted her into a puddle of desire. Even now, just looking at his handsome profile made her stomach tighten uncomfortably.

"Are ye ill? Ye look a might heated."

Fia felt a blush rush into her cheeks. "Nay." Mary eyed her suspiciously, and Fia hurried to change the subject. "Duncan's angry."

The maid's round cheeks dimpled. "Aye, he's been bellowing like a bull all mornin'."

Fia winced. "He seemed determined to blame you that I had left the castle, though I told him 'twas the other way around."

"Och, don't ye worry 'bout me, my lady. Jenny Dow used to be Duncan's nurse when he was a babe. She's my third cousin, ye know." Mary grinned. "Nothing can hush a man quicker than a good memory, especially when it involves the changin' of his swaddlin'."

Despite the feeling of hopelessness that had begun to seep through her, Fia had to laugh.

Mary smoothed the bedclothes around Thomas. "The laird hushed quick enough, though he scowled fit to scare off a demon."

Fia could imagine. Though Duncan had always been stern, she had never seen him as implacable as he was yesterday. Something was bothering him. Something more than he admitted.

"Ye know, lassie, 'tis surprising the laird hasn't put a stop to these sickroom visits of yers," Mary said. "I suppose he is too busy to notice." She peered down at Thomas and squeezed one of his finely muscled arms. "Ye

67

caught quite an Englishman. Hale and hearty and as tasty as fresh-made pottage."

"He's an earl," Fia said proudly. "From London."

"Yer plays!" screeched Mary, clasping her hands to her broad bosom. "He can sponsor yer plays!"

"That's what I was hoping. 'Twas fate, Mary. I found an English earl sitting in the window right as I was leaving for London." She sighed. "You'd have to be daft not to see the hand of higher powers, but Duncan will hear nothing of it."

Mary planted her hands on her hips. "My second husband, James Brodie, used to say 'twas an ill wind as blows 'gainst a storm. If anyone would know of ill winds, 'twould be the Brodies. Horrible short on good fortune, they were."

Fia looked at Mary. "Duncan says war is coming."

"Pshaw," Mary scoffed, tossing her short red curls. "I've heard him say such before. There's naught but a thimbleful who'd support the queen. One or two bouts and they'll rout those scalpeens like the dogs they are." She reached over and smoothed a lock of Thomas's hair from his face. "Yer Sassenach is a hearty sleeper. The sign of a pure mind, milady. Note it well."

" 'Tis more the sign of one of your sleeping draughts."

Mary grinned. "Nothin' can cure an ill as quickly as a good rest. No doubt he was worn to the bone, what with the laird's men beating him so." She expertly examined Thomas's bruised face, running a hand over his head. "St. Christopher's sword, there's a knot the size of an egg on the man's brow."

Thomas stirred in his sleep, one long, beautifully muscled leg shoving aside the covers. Fia's breath caught in her throat.

Mary examined the huge bruise that covered his thigh.

"La, look at this. The laird's men must have used a tree branch to make such a mark."

Fia inwardly cringed at the colorful weal. It was a perfect imprint of Thunder's shoulder.

"Hmph. I wonder why they trounced him so thoroughly. Did he try to hurt ye, lassie?"

"Nay, he just kissed me."

The maid rolled her eyes heavenward. "What were ye thinkin'? There me and Angus sat, awaitin' on ye and wonderin' what had happened. And all the while ye were dallyin' about the forest with an English earl."

"He brought me a wee rabbit," Fia replied defensively.

"Ah, then 'tis yer rabbit I saw in the front hall. He's fallen in love with the laird's right shoe." Mary chuckled, her girth shaking like pudding. "I never saw Lord Duncan so discomfitted. There he was, meeting with an envoy from clan Davies, when the rabbit hopped up and started humpin' his foot like—"

"The Davies clan? What do they want?" Fia asked, her heart pounding so loudly, she could barely hear herself.

Mary eyed her curiously. "Caroline Davies, the iron fist of clan Davies, sent the message. She and that rat-faced son of hers are within a day's ride."

"Oh," Fia said, a band of fear tightening about her stomach. "What did Duncan say?"

Mary frowned. "Now that ye mention it, he looked a bit put out at first."

Fia felt a rush of hope. "Aye?"

"Then he seemed to think of something, fer he started laughin' and ordered Cook to prepare a banquet." Mary wrinkled her nose. " 'Tis a waste of good spice, if ye ask me, but the laird looked pleased enough to spit gold."

Fia scowled. Duncan might be pleased, but she was not. She had to find a way to end this farce of a wedding, and soon.

"What's toward, my lady? Ye look ready to fight a dragon."

Fia pasted a smile on her face. "Duncan has decided I am to wed Malcolm Davies."

"Malcolm the Maiden?"

Despite her own sinking heart, Fia had to laugh at · Mary's horrified expression. "Aye, none other."

"B-but he's only a boy!"

"He's fifteen. Old enough to wed."

"Aye, and a fumblin' fool to boot." Mary crossed her arms underneath her plump bosom. "Ye need a strong man, not some snivelin' boy who hides in his mother's skirts."

"Duncan says Malcolm's fluent in languages, philosophy, and history."

Mary snorted. "How wondrous fer his tutor."

"Duncan seemed impressed."

"Then let the laird wed the fool, I say."

Fia sighed. "I wish Duncan could be made to listen to reason."

"They say the boy's a hunchback, too. As bent as a stick in the wind," Mary added darkly.

"He's merely round-shouldered from reading so much," Fia said automatically.

Mary lifted an eyebrow.

"Duncan has made up his mind. Unless we can think of something, I will be wed whether I wish it or not."

Mary scowled. "What's he thinkin', to marry a headstrong lass like yerself to a sop-eared laddie with no more guts as have the slugs that crawl through the drains?"

Fia sighed and leaned against the bed. She absently patted Thomas's pillow. It was one of her favorites, colorfully embroidered with leaping unicorns. The fanciful cloth belonged on the bed of such a handsome man, she thought wistfully. They both looked as if they had sprung from an ancient fairy tale.

Mary regarded Thomas's sleeping face for a thoughtful moment. "Ye know, my lady, 'tis a pity the laird didn't catch ye and yer handsome Sassenach doin' more than kissin' in the forest."

"Mary!" said Fia, shocked.

"Don't look at me like that! He'd make a better husband fer ye than that spineless worm the laird has chosen."

"Duncan says clan Davies is powerful enough to avoid the upcoming conflict. They have promised to take me to London."

Mary snorted. "Aye, they'll take ye to London, but if ye think they'll sponsor yer plays, think again. Caroline Davies will allow no slight to her noble name. Havin' a playwright as a daughter-in-law will not sit well with her."

"Duncan is determined," Fia said, though everything Mary said confirmed her own thoughts.

"Your English earl, here, is another matter," continued Mary, undaunted. "Just look at him! A man of power, able to publish your plays, and from London. A pity ye can't get the laird to force him to wed ye."

"I don't think the Sassenach would take kindly to being forced to wed anyone," Fia said.

"He doesn't have to like it. As soon as ye reach London, ye can get an annulment." Mary turned the unconscious face toward her. "A pity he's so handsome. Handsome husbands have wanderin' eyes, they do."

"He's an honorable man."

"I've buried four husbands, lassie. If anyone would know about men, 'twould be me. He may look perfect, but likely he's far from it."

71

"He's not perfect. He just wants to be. You can see it in his eyes when something goes wrong." Fia smiled softly. "He wants to control everything and everyone."

Mary beamed her approval. "There ye have it. He's perfect fer ye."

Fia had to admit that marriage to Thomas would be better than marriage to sniveling Malcolm. After a moment, she sighed. " 'Twouldn't work. Duncan would no more let me marry a Sassenach than he'd let me travel to London without an armed guard."

Mary began tidying up the room. "I don't think ye know yer cousin as well as ye think ye do. He's had dealings with the English fer years. Angus tells me the laird gets more fer his wool than any other laird fer that very reason."

"Trade and marriage are not the same thing."

"They're not so far distant as ye would think." Mary looked thoughtfully at Thomas's still form. "Do ye know if the Sassenach's already married?"

Married? The idea roiled in Fia's stomach like a live coal. "I'm sure he isn't," she said stiffly.

The maid snorted. "A pity ye didn't take the time to find out before ye cavorted about the forest with him. Och, now, don't ye glare at me. We'll find a way out of this mess. Ye just wait and see if we don't."

Chapter Seven

" 'Tis time fer yer bath."

Thomas looked up at the maid standing in the doorway, her arms full of clothing. He had awakened early this morn to her wide, dimpled face, and she had graced his chambers almost constantly since.

He had never known until today how wearisome habitual cheerfulness could become.

Mary smiled brightly and laid the clothes in a chair. "Lady Fia thought ye might like a nice, hot bath."

Thomas suppressed an urge to ask about Fia. The thought lurked with annoying regularity in the back of his mind.

A bevy of men carried in a huge tub. More followed with buckets of steaming water. Mary bustled about the room, straightening as she went. "Ye won't believe what a flutter the whole castle's in, now that the Davies clan has arrived."

Thomas regarded the maid somberly. 'Twas obvious

he was supposed to ask about the importance of the Davies clan, but he simply shrugged. He was in no mood to chatter. Sore and stiff, his leg ached as if it were on fire. Worse yet, he was a prisoner.

At least, he *thought* he was a prisoner. He knew that the letter was gone. He had meticulously searched his ripped clothing where it lay in mutilated splendor on the floor by the bed. Nothing.

Some small, hopeful part of him wanted to believe it had been lost in the general melee with Duncan's men. But he knew better. He had carefully tucked the letter away. There was no way it could have been dislodged accidentally.

Thomas glanced around the pleasant room. Covered with thick carpets, the smooth flagstone floor was adorned with a large, ornate trunk and a pair of fine oak chairs. A cheery fire warmed the cold stone walls and lit the rich red velvet hangings that hung about the huge bed. Even the tub the men filled was large and finely made.

Never had he been confined to such luxurious surroundings.

Mary shooed away the men as the last of the water arrived. Chattering constantly, she helped Thomas from the bed. His legs shook, and every bruised muscle in his body screamed in agony, but he made it to the tub.

He slipped into the heated water with a thankful sigh, willing the warmth to soak away his aches and pains.

"I brought ye some clothes in case ye wanted to get dressed," the maid said breezily.

Thomas closed his eyes and hoped she would take the hint. She didn't.

"There's to be a banquet this eve. If ye'd like, I could come back and help ye down to the great hall."

Thomas opened his eyes. It would be interesting to see what he could discover if he were allowed to wander the castle, but the idea of seeing Fia with Duncan in-explicably soured him to the idea.

"I prefer to eat alone," he said curtly.

Mary lathered her hands as though getting ready to attack an especially greasy pan. " 'Tis a pity ye've had naught but thin porridge to eat. Perhaps, once ye've finished bathin', ye'd like some lamb stew to fill yer stomach."

He knew he was being bribed, but his mouth watered all the same. He swallowed. "Perhaps."

"There's a right tasty roast goose as well. Of course, that's all to be served at the banquet." Mary grinned, a dimple appearing by the side of her mouth. "I brought ye some of the laird's clothin' in case ye decided to join in the merriment."

A horrible suspicion crossed his mind. "What's the occasion?"

The permanent smile slipped from the round face. "A weddin'."

There it was. Fia was going to marry Duncan. A hollowness grew in Thomas's chest. Damn the fates. First they put that maddening Scottish wench in his path, with her tempting mouth and lush curves, and then they expected him to sit idly by while she married her giant cousin. "When's the wedding?" he asked, his voice harsh and cold.

"Ye sound a mite put out. Is aught wrong?"

"No," Thomas said tersely.

"Hm." Mary soaped a cloth and rubbed his shoulder. "Mistress Fia is to wed young Malcolm Davies on the morrow."

"But I thought Duncan and Fia were . . ." Thomas subsided into silence under Mary's sudden glare.

"Whist, now! Shame on ye fer thinkin' such a thing. The laird treats Fia like a sister, he does."

"Fia said Duncan was going to marry her," Thomas protested.

"He is. He's marryin' her to Malcolm Davies. The mistress is none too happy about it." The maid looked at Thomas speculatively. "Ye're both in a mite of a fix."

Thomas raised his eyebrows.

Mary must have taken that simple gesture as encouragement, for she patted his arm and leaned closer. "The mistress is bein' forced to wed the greatest dolt ever to walk upon the earth, and ye're a prisoner with no hope of escape."

"I haven't tried yet," Thomas said impatiently.

"Not yet," Mary agreed, rubbing his neck with a wonderfully warm cloth. "But ye will. Ye'll have to. And then ye'll be shot down like a dog."

She seemed entirely too cheerful, so he growled, "Not bloody likely."

"Ye're a proud one, aren't ye? Once the laird has married Fia to Malcolm and she's off with her new husband, there's no reason to keep ye alive. Lady Fia has saved yer life up 'til now. Once she's gone . . ." The maid gave an expressive shrug.

"Fia has such influence over Maclean?" Thomas asked. Strange, Walsingham had not mentioned that fact when he had sent Thomas to find the letter. Now that he thought about it, 'twas stranger still that Lord Walsingham, with his endless web of information, hadn't mentioned Fia at all.

"Och, ye don't know the half of it. The laird loves only two things: Scotland and his cousin. Fia has been his charge since she was a wee mite." A tear welled in her eye and spilled over her apple-round cheek. "Lord Maclean had just begun to scrape the whiskers from his chin when the little lass was brought here and placed in his care. I was a scrub maid at the time, but I took to her right away, as we all did." Mary sniffed and wiped her eyes. "Och, now. Look what ye've made me do! I was goin' to offer ye a way to escape from certain death, and instead ye got me weepin' like a babe."

Thomas didn't know what to do. The only rag he had to give her was soaped and lying across the edge of the tub.

The maid dabbed at her wet cheeks with her shirt-sleeve. "Ye have to escape, and soon. The laird wants the weddin' to take place as soon as the priest arrives. Ye'll be a dead man the minute Lady Fia sets foot outside the gates. I wish to help ye, Sassenach. If ye die, Lady Fia's heart will break. She can't stand to see any creature suffer."

Though Thomas wanted to deny it, Mary made sense. "I should escape immediately."

"Ye can't. Leastways, not the way ye're thinkin'. Ye couldn't get past the guards if ye tried. The laird put six of his best men to watchin' ye. If ye did get past them, the entire castle is ringed with the remainder of his men, not to mention the Davies clan. There's over two hundred of them campin' outside the walls even now."

It was worse than he had thought. "What do you suggest?"

"Marry the mistress."

Thomas sat straight up, sending a wave of water over the edge of the tub. "You must be jesting."

Mary looked down at her dress. Water drenched it from seam to seam. She scowled. "I'm not jestin'. Marry the mistress, and go to London. She's been wantin' to become a playwright, and ye're wantin' to get home. 'Tis the perfect solution."

"Maclean would kill me for even thinking such a thing," Thomas muttered. He sank back into the water.

"Not if ye'd already consummated the marriage. He couldn't do aught about it then except wish ye well," Mary said soothingly.

Thomas glared, and she patted his shoulder. "Think on it, my lord, but don't take too long. The weddin' is anon. The laird's not giving the mistress time to wheedle her way out of it."

"Lady, were I to spend from now unto eternity contemplating marriage with your mistress, it would still be too brief a time to settle my misgivings."

"Whist, now, don't be gettin' up on yer high horse with me! Lady Fia may be a mite different from the fancy skirts ye're accustomed to, but she's a rare one fer all that."

"Aye. Rarely properly clothed, rarely where she ought to be, rarely thinking before she speaks, rarely anything other than cursed infuriating," he muttered.

Mary's color rose, and she began scrubbing his shoulder with such effort that it brought a dull red to his skin. "The mistress is as proper a lady as any."

Thomas winced at the strength of her touch. God's Blood, if it were true that trials and trouble purified a soul, then his should by now be white as snow. "I'm in no hurry to shackle myself to any female," he stated firmly, just to set the matter to rest.

Mary sat back on her heels. "Ye'd rather die than marry? That's weak thinkin', even fer a Sassenach. Ye have to marry sooner or later. 'Tis only natural."

Thomas closed his eyes. He had thought so little of marriage, except for ways to avoid it, that he had never really put his mind to the question. He just knew Fia was not the vague, shadowy picture of perfect breeding and quiet prettiness he was destined to wed. She was too vivid, too passionate.

The very last thing he wanted was a woman of passion. Passion had led his own mother to betray his father. Thomas had no room for such a frivolous emotion in his life.

He opened one eye to find Mary regarding him with

a look of mulish determination. "Why don't ye want to marry Lady Fia?"

Thomas sighed. "There are certain qualities I seek in a wife. Lady Fia has none of them."

"Lady Fia's mother was the youngest daughter to the Earl of Arran. She's not only of good family but was as gently reared as a lamb."

Thomas choked. Fia was more like a black sheep than any innocent lamb he had ever encountered. He caught Mary's inflexible gaze and swallowed.

She was like a cat stalking a mouse, relentless and single-minded in her pursuit. Well, he would not give. He thought of the many women who languished about court. What accomplishments *did* such women possess, anyway?

"My wife must be well learned."

"The Lady Fia speaks four languages and writes in three." Mary seemed near to bursting with pride as she added triumphantly, "And she can do sums in her head. The laird says she's as good with figures as his man of business."

Thomas rubbed his forehead wearily. God save him from all Scots, be they young or old, diseased or clean, comely or naught. As far as he was able to tell, they were all cursed lackwits, every man, woman, and child. 'Twas a wonder the country existed at all.

"Lady Fia is an undisciplined chit with no notion of proper comportment." There. He'd said it.

Mary's lips thinned into a grim line. She lathered a cloth with a chilling determination. "'Tis time I scrubbed yer back."

"I'm not saying Lady Fia isn't a fine, lovely woman," Thomas said hastily, keeping a wary eye on the cloth. "Indeed, she is most beauteous."

Mary's thick eyebrows rose in answer, and he found

himself floundering. "And she is very good at . . . working with animals."

The snort of disbelief that met this statement killed his hopes of a comforting back rub. He was about to be severely scrubbed for his lack of enthusiasm.

Thomas wished he had the necessary charm to deal with this termagant of a servant. A pity Robert wasn't nearby. Robert MacQuarrie possessed the Scottish gift of glib speech. The queen often commented that her sweet Robin could charm the paint off a picture in less time than it took to observe one.

Thomas lifted his shoulders and winced in exaggerated pain. "My back is sore and stiff. I would appreciate some gentleness."

"Aye. That bruising would be from where the mistress knocked ye from yer perch on the window ledge."

"How did you know about that?" he demanded.

"Lady Fia told us all about it." Mary grinned with satisfaction. "Said ye fell like a sack of lard."

"Impertinent wench," Thomas muttered.

"She's been alone most of her life. When ye have such a lively mind as the Lady Fia and no one much to talk to but yerself, ye tend to take liberties when ye do." Mary blew a loose curl from her eyes. "My third husband, Magnus MacBean, did not hold with teachin' women. He said 'twas teachin' the cow to dance, so to speak."

" 'Cow to dance'?"

"Aye. 'Tis a pretty sight, that, but useless."

Thomas wondered what Queen Elizabeth would have said to such a homily and decided he would rather not know.

Mary rinsed the rag with an expert twist and began to scrub his back. "Not that I agreed with him, mind for he was not too swift of wit, himself. But Magnus was not one to listen to any thoughts other than his own."

She clicked her tongue and shook her bright curls. "God rest his soul, but he was not the merriest of men. My other husbands have all been of a merrier disposition."

"How many husbands have you had?" Thomas asked, wondering that Duncan had allowed such a woman to have free access to his cousin.

"I've been wed five times, I have." She beamed with pride. "They all died with happy grins on their faces, every one of them. All except my Angus. He's my current husband and as pleasant a man as ever lived."

She grasped Thomas's shoulders and shoved him forward until his head was but inches from the water. He managed to swallow his yelp of pain until it was no more than a muffled grunt. Then competent hands were kneading his back with exquisite thoroughness.

"Saints, but yer lordship is covered from head to toe with bruises! 'Tis a good thing the mistress is so good at tendin' the ill, seein' how ye seem to have such poor luck." Mary's voice was becoming lost in the pleasant sensations of her message.

Thomas struggled against the lassitude seeping through him. "You are washing away every ache."

" 'Tis more than aches and bruises ye'll have if ye do not marry the mistress like I told ye."

He cocked a half-opened eye at her. "Does Lady Fia know of this plan of yours?"

A flush of color mounted Mary's cheeks. "Sometimes the lassie doesn't know what's good for her."

"She's against it?" It should have brought him a measure of relief, but instead the realization that Fia had refused him rankled hotly.

"She doesn't wish to marry at all. She's her plays to see to, ye know. But the laird is givin' her no choice." Mary scowled. "She's doomed if she goes through with it. Malcolm's witch of a mother will see to it there's not a spark of life left in the child. She'll never allow Fia to be a playwright."

"Is that so important?"

Mary stopped rubbing and regarded him intently. "Have ye never wanted somethin' so badly ye were willin' to give up everythin' ye had to possess it?"

Thomas remembered the days after his mother had fled. His father had been like a madman, stalking about the house, snapping at everyone. In a matter of days, his calm, controlled father had become a gaunt stranger. Thomas became determined to make up for the loss of his mother. It had become an obsession for the six-year-old boy. He had stopped at nothing to please his father.

Not until much later did he realize it couldn't be done.

" 'Twould be best if she didn't attempt such foolishness," he said, his voice harsher than he intended.

Mary threw the cloth into the water, splattering soapy water into his eyes. "What do ye know of it? Mistress Fia has a gift fer writin'. 'Twould be folly not to pursue her dreams!"

Thomas rubbed his stinging eyes and wondered how many of Mary's husbands had jumped from the walls of the keep. "God's Patience, woman, I only meant she is ill equipped to deal with such a scandal."

With more dignity than grace, Mary clambered to her feet.

Thomas sighed in regret at the end of the wondrous back rub. Robert always said that the beauty of life lasted but seconds, while the rest took forever.

Right now there was no beauty, just a plump, homely maid who looked uncomfortably like a disgruntled fairy.

"I think ye should be considerin' that if ye don't marry the Lady Fia, the laird will end yer miserable life."

Turning on her heel, Mary stomped out of the chamber.

Thomas dropped his head back onto the rim of the tub and heaved a sigh. He was not about to offer marriage to any woman. Especially not a woman whose every movement made him harden and ache like an untried lad. That was exactly the type of marriage destined to end in disappointment.

He lay in the rapidly cooling water and wondered how he could find a way out of the castle, through the hordes of men Mary swore were encamped about the walls. He needed someone who knew the castle and the surrounding land.

Damn it, he thought. He needed Fia.

He looked about for a towel. A pity he couldn't just convince her to escape with him. Thomas straightened slowly.

He rubbed his chin thoughtfully. He had very little time to act. All he needed was a few moments of private speech with Fia. He knew he could convince her to help him win his way free of the castle and reach his ship. In exchange, he would take her to London and sponsor her plays.

He could almost imagine her excitement at reaching London. He had an impression of her body pressed against his. Even the rapidly cooling water couldn't tame his instant response.

Thomas grabbed a towel and heaved himself from the tub. He had no time for warm fancies. He had a wedding feast to attend.

Chapter Eight

"Ye'll pop right out of that dress if ye so much as sneeze."

Fia looked down. Mary was right. One little sneeze, even a hiccup, and Fia's entire chest would be completely exposed. She nodded her satisfaction. She hoped she looked like the loosest, most vile woman to ever grace the halls of Duart Castle. "It's perfect."

Mary pursed her lips. "Well, 'tis the best I could do. I didn't have much time to alter it, so the stitchin' is not what it should be."

"You did a wonderful job."

"Aye, ye look like a harlot. I hope ye don't catch yer death of the ague traipsin' through the castle like that. *If*, that is, the laird even lets ye enter the great hall."

Fia unfurled her wide, jeweled fan and held the stiff silk up to cover her neckline. "This will cover me until I'm seated. He'll be too busy fawning over the Davies clan to even notice me. When he does, 'twill be too late.

but he's got no more sense than your cousin. I pointed out how the laird was likely to kill him as soon as ye were wed, and how 'twould be a better thing fer everyone if he would just consent to wed ye himself."

"Mary! Pray, say you told him no such thing!" Heat burned Fia's cheeks. She could imagine Thomas's immediate refusal.

"Whist, now, don't look like that," Mary said. " 'Twas just an idea. I'm sure this plan will work out much better."

"Duncan would never have allowed such a thing, anyway," Fia said.

"The laird wouldn't say a thing if he thought ye might be with child."

"You didn't suggest that to Thomas!"

"Why shouldn't I? Someone needs to think of a way out of this mess." Mary seemed to notice Fia's discomfort, for she added, "There was no harm done. He refused, and that was that."

"Of course he refused," Fia managed to say. " 'Tis a ludicrous idea."

In fact, she decided, 'twas even more ludicrous than the one she was attempting now.

Mary's blue eyes sparkled with anger. "He's not the man I thought he was, I can tell ye. Nary a spark of adventure to him, and as pompous as they come."

Fia looked down at her dress and sighed. She wished she could speak with him, but she'd had no time. Preparing for Malcolm's arrival had taken every free moment.

Mary gave a final twitch to the bottom of Fia's skirt, adjusting the heavy folds into a graceful train. "There. Ye're dressed as near to a harlot as we can make ye."

Despite her misgivings, Fia had to laugh at Mary's satisfied expression. "Aye, I don't even recognize myself." She unfurled the fan and walked to the door, praying silently that her plan would work.

It had to, she reminded herself. It was all she had left.

It failed from the beginning.

Malcolm the Maiden might be immature and easily cowed by his domineering mother, but he was also a puberty-stricken youth. Instead of turning red and embarrassed at Fia's vulgar display, he leered ravenously. He lisped ribald compliments, staring down her dress until she yearned to box his ears.

She also discovered that Malcolm possessed a mean streak. Twice now he had cruelly pinched her beneath the table. Fia had repaid his last insult with a swift kick. When he had attempted to retaliate, she had allowed him a glimpse of her dirk.

She had every intention of protecting herself. His triumphant smirk had been lost in a sullen pout, but at least he was leaving her alone. For now.

For all Malcolm's pawing manners, Fia found him much less frightening than his mother. Lady Caroline sat stiffly, her cold, dead eyes fixed time and again on Fia with unwavering regard. Fia felt as if she were a horse being considered for purchase. She wouldn't have been surprised had Lady Caroline asked to see her teeth.

Fia had tried to put her brilliant plan into effect. She laughed loudly, made crude gestures, and had Duncan in a roaring black humor within a half hour. Lady Caroline remained unimpressed. Too late, Fia realized the Iron Lady of clan Davies was no fool.

The most horrible part of the evening was watching Lady Caroline's steady assault on Duncan. Older than Duncan by five years or more, Caroline Davies was still a very attractive woman. Her blond hair curled about her face, interwoven with pearls and sapphires. Her face was artfully painted, her brows thinly plucked. Even dressed in such revealing finery, Fia felt like a goose beside a swan.

Miserable, Fia toyed with the food on her plate and wondered what else she could do to halt Duncan's plan. Surely there had to be something. *Please, God,* she begged silently, *please help me out of this.*

"Lady Fia," said Malcolm softly into her ear. A shudder ran through her as his hand reached for her knee beneath the table. "If you would allow me, I vow I could bring a smile to your lips."

Fia leveled him a dark glance. "There is only one thing you could do to make me smile, Lord Malcolm."

"Aye," he said, his foul breath making her want to retch. "I know what you want." His hand crept up her thigh.

"Nay, I don't think you do," she returned and pricked the back of his hand with her knife.

Malcolm screamed and yanked his hand to his chest. Bright red drops of blood oozed from his fingers. "The bitch cut me!"

Every eye at the table turned toward them, and Fia felt her face glow red. Duncan's face blackened with rage. Since he had noted her dress, her cousin had refused to look her way. He was furious, and Fia knew it.

"What's the meaning of this?" Duncan demanded, his voice rumbling and harsh.

Malcolm held out his hand. A thin slice across the back of his fingers welled with blood. "Your cousin cut me," he said shrilly.

Duncan glowered at the boy for a fulminating moment before swinging his gaze to Fia. "Well, cousin?"

Fia frowned. By all that was holy, she had done nothing more than what Duncan had taught her. "He was stroking my leg under the table."

Duncan's face reddened. Lady Caroline placed her hand on his sleeve. "Malcolm deserved it," she said calmly. She turned to Fia and gave a cool, controlled smile. " 'Twas very well done of you, Lady Fia, to have addressed the child so firmly."

Duncan and Fia shared an amazed glance. "Pardon?" asked Duncan in a stunned voice.

Lady Caroline took a delicate sip of wine. Fia noted that the woman left her other hand resting possessively on Duncan's arm. "Malcolm is a strong-willed child. He will benefit from such firm handling." She cast a cool, triumphant smile at Fia. "You will deal well together."

"But, Mother . . . you c-cannot let—" Malcolm sputtered with rage.

"Silence," said Lady Caroline sharply.

Malcolm snapped his mouth shut and slumped sulkily in his chair.

Fia watched, her chest tightening as Lady Caroline said something to Duncan that made him nod reluctantly, the worry easing from his face.

Malcolm leaned forward until his face was uncomfortably close. "There will be no one in our bedchamber once we are wed. You had better treat me well, or I will make you very, very sorry."

Fia bared her teeth in the semblance of a smile. "If we wed at all, Lord Malcolm, 'twould make me very sorry indeed."

He gave a sly look and ran a hand through his greasy blond hair. "Mother said you would be difficult. But I like a challenge."

Fia ignored him. Her thoughts drifted to Thomas. Why hadn't they made a harder push to escape when they had the chance? Curse Thunder and her capricious whims.

All at once, Duncan burst out laughing in a loud guffaw that halted every conversation. Fia looked at him curiously and saw his attention fixed on the door leading into the hall. She turned, and her heart froze in her throat.

There, standing in the entry, stood Thomas.

A ripple of amusement grew and spread until the whole room was awash with it. Even Lady Caroline's cold, controlled face had lightened with humor. Only Fia didn't laugh. She contented herself with glaring at a snickering Malcolm until he subsided into an uneasy silence.

Thomas ground his teeth into a smile, willing himself to look away from Fia. He had never seen her dressed in anything other than a servant's ill-fitting clothing. Now she sat dressed in rich red brocade, her gown sewn over with silver thread that danced and played in the light and drew the eye unerringly toward her nearly exposed breasts.

He wondered what Fia was about, to so display herself. She had reddened her lips and piled her hair on her head in an attempt to appear older. Yet all she had managed was to look like a child dressed in her mother's finery. Except for her breasts. There was nothing childish about her bosom. His body hardened at the sight.

Thomas knew that if he continued to look at her, he would lose all power to speak. He forced his attention on Duncan. "I can see you're in excellent spirits, Lord Duart."

Duncan wiped his eyes, laughter choking his voice. "Aye, Sassenach. I'm feeling very fine indeed."

Thomas pushed up the cuffs that kept falling over his hands. The quality of the clothing was exceptional. The shirt and hose were finely made, crossed through with silk thread. The doublet was of rich amber silk heavy with colorful embroidery.

'Twas the size which made the outfit laughable.

Though Thomas stood over six feet, Duncan was taller by a good five inches and was made on a more massive scale. The lace-adorned sleeves flopped over Thomas's hands, and the doublet, stiff with decoration, rubbed his chin as he spoke.

Worse yet were the hose, which hung in baggy folds about his knees and gathered in ugly creases around each ankle. If Thomas didn't take care, they would slip completely off his hips, as they had done in the hallway outside his room.

Even now he could hear his guards chortling and giggling like a flock of geese behind his back. He suppressed the desire to turn and retreat to the bedchamber, for this might be his last chance to speak with Fia before the wedding. Surely she knew a way out of this stone fortress. All he had to do was convince her to escape with him.

Looking at Malcolm's sullen pout, Thomas felt a flicker of hope.

Duncan guffawed again. " 'Tis rude of me to laugh so openly." He waved Thomas to the dais. "Since you are here, come and join us. We are celebrating the upcoming wedding of my cousin to young Malcolm Davies."

Duncan thumped the boy on the shoulder as he spoke with false merriment. Thomas noted that the laird seemed pleased when Malcolm winced.

Fia sat silent and subdued, staring down at her plate. Thomas felt the kindling of hope burst into full flame. She looked miserable.

Thomas limped to the dais, holding his sagging hose up by the expediency of cocking a hand on his hip. He knew he looked like a braggart posturing about the room, but 'twas better than losing his hose before the entire assembly. He took the only empty chair and stared down the length of the table at Fia.

She looked up and caught his gaze. A tremulous smile crossed her lips, and he found himself smiling back.

Even dressed as she was, her mouth rouged to a deep red, she looked like an innocent in a pit of snakes.

"She is very beautiful."

Thomas looked at the woman who sat beside him, her long, jeweled fingers wrapped around the stem of her goblet. A slight resemblance to Malcolm identified her as Lady Caroline Davies.

Thomas nodded. "She's fair enough. Malcolm must be pleased to capture such a bride."

Caroline shrugged, her face hardening slightly. "Malcolm will be content with whatever wife I choose."

Thomas felt a wave of pity for the weak-chinned Malcolm. There were many women at court like Lady Caroline. Manipulative and hard, they used their silken hands and perfumed bodies to hide a grim determination to advance in position. They thought nothing of uttering a lie and even less of ruining lives to further their own endless ambition.

Mary had been right. Lady Caroline Davies would squeeze the joy from Fia as fast as she could.

"You look distressed, Lord Rotherwood," Lady Caroline said in her smooth, cultured voice.

Thomas raised his eyebrows. "You know me?"

She placed a hand on his arm. "We have never met. But everyone knows of the famous Wentworth luck." She leaned forward, her breasts pressed suggestively against his arm. " 'Tis said that everything you touch turns toward the good."

" 'Tis an exaggerated story," Thomas said.

"Nevertheless," she purred, "I would like to test it."

"The Sassenach is to be our guest but briefly," Duncan said curtly. His black gaze rested on Thomas over Lady Caroline's head. "He will be leaving as soon as the wedding occurs."

Thomas could almost hear Mary's voice. *"Ye'll be a*

dead man as soon as Lady Fia sets foot outside the gates."

"The Sassenach is *my* guest," Fia announced, glaring at Duncan. "He'll leave when he's well and not before."

Duncan shrugged. "As you say, cousin." But the dark eyes rested on Thomas, who felt the menace in that gaze.

Lady Caroline's slim fingers traveled down Thomas's sleeve until they grazed the back of his hand. "Perhaps we can speak later. I am very familiar with England." Her words were heavy with unspoken meaning. The tip of her tongue crossed her bottom lip.

"The Sassenach will *not* be joining you later," said Fia with deadly calm.

Thomas raised an eyebrow at the stern announcement. Fia glared at him, her prim, outraged expression at odd variance with her decadent dress.

"I don't think you have any say over this issue," said Lady Caroline after the tiniest of pauses.

"When I leave, the Sassenach will be going with me," said Fia, two bright spots on her cheeks.

"You can't take this man on our wedding journey," protested Malcolm.

Fia raised her eyebrows. "Why not? I found him. He's mine. If I want to take him with me, I can."

"Fia," said Duncan, "that's enough! The Sassenach is staying here. I'll not hear another word about it."

"I caught him. That makes him mine."

"That's true," said Thomas slowly. "She did catch me." He saw Caroline's startled glance and shrugged. "She shoved me out a window."

"That was an accident," Fia protested.

Thomas ignored her. "Then her dog chased off my horse. When I attempted to ride her mount, it threw me to the ground and laid on me until Fia arrived."

Malcolm's eyes widened as he regarded Fia. "I trow, but you are an evil female. I will not marry you."

"Fine," responded Fia instantly. She stood. "Since that is the case, I will retire."

"Sit down now!" thundered Duncan.

Reluctantly, Fia sank back into her chair. Duncan cast an apologetic glance at Lady Caroline. "They just need some time to themselves. Perhaps after we eat, they can stroll about the gardens."

Caroline nodded. "Of course. We should discuss the contract. I think—"

"There's the food," Duncan said with obvious relief as servants bearing trays entered the chamber.

Thomas spent the rest of the evening rebuffing Lady Caroline's unwelcome overtures and watching Fia deal with Malcolm's petty anger.

No one was more relieved than Thomas when the interminable meal finally came to an end. Fia was the first to leave, excusing herself quickly before Duncan could protest. Thomas caught her eye just as she swept from the hall.

"I need to see you," he mouthed silently. She hesitated, and he repeated it.

She gave a quick nod and left.

Thomas caught Lady Caroline's considering stare, and he silently cursed. Had she seen him? He set out to calm her suspicions. Yet even as he flirted and complimented Caroline, brushing his mouth over her wrist and smiling at her fulsome sallies, his thoughts were with Fia.

Soon, Thomas promised himself. Soon he and Fia would be on their way to his ship and safety once again. Only this time, Thomas vowed they would make it. They would make it if he had to toss the woman over his shoulder and run the whole way.

Chapter Nine

Thomas knew he was dreaming. All the same, he reveled in the vivid image.

Fia stood before him, wearing a flowing gown of foamy sea green. Strands and strands of smooth white pearls outlined her abundant breasts. Her luxurious red-brown hair curled and frothed about her shoulders like shimmering waves in a sun-tumbled sea.

Ignoring the presence of a scowling Duncan, she smiled at Thomas. Her eyes beckoned, as dark and mysterious as an evening storm.

He knew there would be dire consequences were he to reach for her. Yet it made little difference in the face of those warm eyes, soft bosom, and decadent cascade of hair. He could almost taste her full, soft mouth.

He reached to mingle his breath with hers. . . .

A soft curl tickled the back of his neck. The heat of the dream evaporated into the coolness of his dark chamber, the only light coming from the pale flicker of a candle and the dying embers of the fire. He became aware of the warmth of a body pressed snugly against his back.

For a moment, his mind floundered with the idea that Fia—sweet, delectable, maddening Fia—had slipped so wantonly into his bed. The softness of the hair against his neck belied his doubts.

Her hands tugged at his clothing, loosening ties and removing the binding cloth. She wanted him. He had known it all along. He turned over and gathered the warm, naked body closer.

The cloying smell of lilies crept into his senses. Pale blond hair spilled across the pillow like false gold.

Caroline Davies smiled at him, her pale blue eyes glittering with undisguised lust.

Thomas gave a muffled curse and pushed her away. "What are you doing here?" he demanded, sitting up.

Caroline regarded him through half-closed eyes, her tongue flickering out to wet her thin bottom lip. "I came for you," she said huskily. Her hands smoothed across his chest and down, under the sheet.

Thomas swung his legs over the edge of the bed. "I think you've made a mistake."

There was a moment of silence.

"No," she said carefully. "I don't think I have." She moved sinuously against his leg, her mouth hot and wet on his thigh. Her hair spilled across his lap with the cloying touch of a spider's web.

Irritation seeped through him. He had expected Fia, not this woman.

Fia. At the thought, he almost groaned. He had to get rid of Caroline Davies.

Thomas all but shoved her from the bed. "I didn't invite you here."

An ugly red flush mounted in her thin cheeks. "Didn't you?"

He gathered her gown from the floor and handed it to her. "No."

She ran her hands over her body. Her curves gleamed smooth and strong in the light. "I could make you very, very happy, my lord."

Thomas could think of nothing but the need for haste. He picked up her shoes and piled them in her arms.

"You fool," she spat, gathering her gown and tossing it about her. "You will regret this," she said stiffly.

Thomas opened the door. "Perhaps. But for now, I crave naught but sleep."

She turned and slammed the door behind her.

He raked a hand through his hair. Sweet Jesu, but that had bordered on disaster. He piled another log onto the fire and stood savoring the warmth.

The door opened, and Thomas turned toward it, ready to repudiate Lady Caroline yet again.

Zeus's muzzle appeared first. Fia peeked around the edge a second later. Her eyes widened when she saw Thomas standing by the fire. "You're naked," she said.

He sighed and crossed to the bed to pull the sheet free. He wrapped it about himself. It seemed his nocturnal visitors were opposites in their preferences. A pity, he thought.

Fia came into the room and held the door. "Stand guard," she told Zeus.

The dog cast a longing look at the fire and dropped onto the floor, whining pathetically.

Fia propped her fists on her hips. "Look at you, you silly dog. And after I gave you a whole plate of roasted lamb!"

Heaving a huge sigh, Zeus pulled himself to his feet and walked slowly out into the hall, his crooked tail sagging between his legs. Fia shut the door. "He'll bark if he sees anyone."

"I wouldn't count on it," Thomas said dryly. "Where are the guards?"

"Sleeping like babes. I gave them a wee dram of whiskey after the banquet. I mixed a good dose of sleeping draught in it."

She was once again dressed in servant's clothing. Thomas wondered if the dull brown dress would look so damnably attractive on someone else or if it was just Fia.

"Well, Sassenach? You wished to speak with me?"

He noted that she remained within easy reach of the door. One false move and she would bolt. "Aye, I wished to speak with you," he said easily. "But not from across the room. Pray, enter and have a seat." He gestured to the chairs by the fire.

"I'm fine where I am," she said quickly.

Thomas sighed. This was *very* different from Lady Caroline's visit. "I have no wish to yell across the room, and I can't as yet stand for any length of time. My leg is still sore."

Just as he hoped, she forgot her own fears in her worry. She crossed to stand by the chair, her eyes fixed on his leg. "I noticed you limped this eve. Did you let Mary look at it?"

"Aye, she said 'twas naught but bruised. Where is Mary?" he asked. He wondered if Maclean knew how much Mary allowed her charge to wander. The rotund maid was hardly a decent chaperone for such a high-spirited charge.

"She's down the hall, standing watch."

"Good. She'll be of more use than that foul-breathed dog."

That seemed to rankle. "Zeus is not as foul as the animal I caught trying to sneak into your room," Fia said stiffly. "It appears you have made quite a conquest with the Iron Lady of clan Davies."

Thomas sat on the edge of the bed and looked about for his hose. "It sounds as if the Duart hallways are busy this eve."

Fia sniffed. "She was trailing enough white lace to strangle an ordinary man."

"Who? Mary?"

Fia frowned. "Nay, Lady Caroline."

"Did she see you?"

"I should hope so. She almost stepped on poor Zeus's tail. I had to take her to task for being so clumsy." A sly smile crossed her lips. "She seemed a mite angered."

"She'll tell Maclean," Thomas warned, though he knew the real reason for Caroline's wrath was neither Fia nor her dog.

"I doubt it. I threatened to slit her gullet if she so much as blinked in the direction of Duncan's room. With any luck she's hunting in the stables for a warm bed." Fia gave him a pointed look. "She's poisonous."

Thomas silently agreed with her. He spied his hose lying across the trunk and stood to retrieve them.

She took a hasty step back, almost stumbling in her haste. Thomas found himself staring into the blackness of her eyes. The dream lingered, casting a sensual haze over the coolness of the night. It seemed as if the whole room was alive with a nameless heat.

"I've come to make you a bargain," she announced breathlessly.

This was what Thomas wanted to hear, yet his attention was irrevocably fixed on the curve of her lips. He stared at her mouth and ran a hand across his own, wondering if she remembered the kiss in the forest as well as he did.

She rushed on. "You need to escape. We can help each other the same as before, only this time 'twill be a bit different." She halted, a deep red suffusing her cheeks. "This time you will sponsor my plays and not me."

"More's the pity," he murmured. He reached out and captured a tendril of her hair. It curled about his palm as if alive. Thomas sank slowly to the edge of the bed, allowing the silken strand to slip through his fingers.

"Do you agree?" she asked huskily. The richness of her voice swirled through his stomach and below. He shifted restlessly. The sheet parted, and Fia stared at his bare leg.

Deliberately, Thomas flexed the muscle. Her lips parted, and she gave a deep sigh.

"I might agree," he said, "if . . ." He let the word hang in the darkness.

"If what?"

He reached out and took her unresisting hands and pulled her down to the bed beside him. "If you will seal the bargain with a kiss," he whispered. He brushed her hair from her face, marveling at the creaminess of her skin.

She shivered with desire. He could see it in the rapid rise and fall of her chest, feel it in the warmth that radiated from her skin. Thomas was fascinated beyond thought with her bottom lip. It was so full. So red.

He wanted—no, he *needed*—to kiss her, just once, to see if she tasted as sweet as he remembered. One kiss, he told himself. Just one.

He kissed her with a thoroughness that allowed for no reasoning, no thought beyond the feel and taste of her. All his earlier arousal returned in triple force, and he roughly caught her against him. She moaned and twined her arms about his neck.

He wanted more. He parted her lips and gently ran his tongue across the smooth edge of her teeth. She moaned into his mouth, pulling him closer. Thomas knew she was his.

Carefully, he moved from her mouth to taste the smoothness of her cheek, the delicate line of her jaw.

101

Fia tugged desperately at the sheet that separated them.
Her tongue encircled his ear. He had to have this
woman. Suddenly, *he* was the one tugging desperately.
Tugging at sturdy wool held in place with leather ties
and wooden buttons. *Damn!* He would see to it that she
dressed in naught but silk when they reached London.
Silk so soft and buttery that it slipped through your fingers and tore like proper fabric should.

With agonizing slowness her hand moved up his
thigh, the rough sheet only intensifying the tease of her
fingers as they came closer, ever closer to his straining
desire. The very thinness of the sheet added a piquant
danger.

Sweet Jesu, he thought desperately, if he didn't speak
now he wouldn't be able to say a word. He halted her
roaming hand and pulled her against him. Trailing the
wetness of his mouth to her ear, he whispered softly,
"Ah, Fia, if only we were now in London . . ."

She stilled, her hand lying motionless in his. Her
voice was like heavy cream, velvety and rich. "What if
we were in London?"

Thomas smiled and cupped her face, his fingers lost
in the silken mane of her hair, his thumbs running with
ease across the fullness of her bottom lip. "Were we in
London, comfit, I'd find you a sponsor for those plays
of yours. I swear it."

He brushed his mouth across her cheeks, the tip of
her nose, her forehead. "All we need to do is get to my
ship," he murmured softly.

She planted her hands against his chest and pushed.
Reluctantly, he allowed her to pull free. She looked de-
lightfully, sinfully mussed, her black eyes awash with
passion.

She put a trembling hand to her mouth. "So we have
a bargain, then?"

He wondered if he could ever refuse her anything. The

wavering candle lit the smoothness of her skin to molten gold. Her hair curled and frolicked in the flickering light as if begging for a taming hand. He reached out and captured a strand of her silken tresses and pressed it to his mouth. "I swear on my father's grave, I will help you publish your plays once we escape from this hellish isle."

Her eyes widened at the solemn vow. Never had Thomas seen eyes so dark. They were a deep, rich black with hints of amber lights.

She nodded slowly. "Thank you," she said, her voice itself a caress.

The luscious sound warmed him all the way to his toes. Sweet Jesu, but he was as taut and rigid as a mast. He bent his knee so she would not see his arousal through the sheet.

"Come," she said huskily, shaking her head as if just waking from a deep sleep. "We've no time to waste."

Before he could do more than utter a stifled protest, she slipped out of his reach, crossing the room and opening the door. "Come. The guards will awake at any moment."

He looked at his thinly covered lap. Her gaze followed his, and he was rewarded with the very faintest of blushes. She shut the door. "Dress. We've little time."

He stood, the sheet dropping away. His naked desire was there for all to see. Fia muttered something and turned away, her hands pressed against her hot cheeks. Thomas grinned at her back as he picked up his clothes from the chest at the foot of the bed. He found his hose and tugged them on.

She sighed impatiently. "Pray, hurry. We still have to gather Lord Thomas."

"Lord Thomas?"

" 'Tis the name of the wee rabbit you gave me. I named him for you."

Thomas shook his head. Of course she had named it for him. He sighed tiredly and wondered where his clothes had wandered to. Though an ill fit, Maclean's garb still afforded some protection from the cold of night. "We can't take your animals, comfit. 'Tis what got us captured last time."

"What do you mean?" she asked sharply.

Thomas stifled a wave of irritation. He still ached with pent-up desire, and nothing but the necessity of escape could have made him leave the bed so willingly. It was that same necessity that made him answer her now. "We can't take them. We have to travel as lightly as possible. They'll slow us down too much."

"I'm not leaving without them. I'll go down to the stables and saddle Thunder while you and Zeus—"

"We are not taking that ill-natured horse," Thomas interrupted firmly. "Nor will we stop for your insolent hound nor that cursed rabbit."

Fia stilled. "You gave your word."

He raked a hand through his hair. "I vowed to help *you,* not those decrepit animals."

"I am not leaving without them."

"And I am not leaving with them," he ground out.

She stood like a mast, straight and immovable.

Thomas spied the sleeve of his doublet peeping out from under a chair. His shirt lay with it. He bundled the clothing and stood. "Look, we'll send for them after we arrive in London. Surely Maclean will—"

"I'm not leaving without them," she repeated, a stubborn jut to her chin.

All of his frustrated desire pooled into anger, which streaked through him like an arrow. "If you won't leave those cursed animals, then I'll take my chances and escape without you." He gave her a brittle smile and shifted his clothing to one arm before yanking open the door. "After all, you have already removed the guards from the hall."

She stared at him, and he could see her mind working furiously. "You left your boots," she said, pointing behind him. He looked over his shoulder just as she snatched his clothing from his arms.

Thomas lunged for her, but Zeus lunged into the fray. Thomas stumbled over the dog as Fia flew out the door.

He cursed and bolted from the room, hanging on to his loose hose with one hand even as he ran. He caught a glimpse of Fia's skirt as it whisked out of sight. He ran down the hall and slid around the corner—right into Fia. Clothes flew into the air as arms and legs tangled in a tumbled heap.

When Thomas's breath returned to normal, he realized he was lying on the floor with Fia on top of him, her knees straddling his head, her skirt covering his face.

"Well, well, well. What have we here?"

Lifting the edge of Fia's skirt, Thomas looked up.

Mary's round face beamed at him. Behind her, Thomas saw Duncan Maclean, his broad shoulders lit by the gleam of torches from over a dozen men. And standing beside him, her blue eyes gleaming with triumph, was Caroline Davies.

Chapter Ten

Thomas urged his horse to a faster pace, ignoring Duncan's men when they did likewise. In a few minutes, he would be back at his ship, casting off from this cursed Scottish isle. He tried not to remember that he had failed in his mission and was now married to the most unconventional playwright to ever grasp a quill.

Lady Caroline's smug triumph still burned. He could have cheerfully strangled her. Fortunately, there were better ways of punishing such a spiteful cat. When Thomas had been called upon to kiss Fia at the end of the hurried ceremony, he had done so with deliberate passion, allowing his hands and mouth to roam at will.

Lady Caroline had spun on her heels and left the room, her color high. But he had spited himself as well. With Fia, he had no control. He had been overwhelmed with hot, burning lust, forgetting everyone and everything until Duncan had yanked him away from his bride.

It was like a sickness.

Thomas yearned for the sanity of London. Here, in the untrammeled countryside, he told himself Fia shone like a rare gem against a stream bed of pebbles. That would all change once they reached the English court. There, among the graceful women who surrounded the queen, Fia would fade to insignificance.

Duncan's laughter boomed through the morning haze. The laird rode in front of Fia's coach, jesting and singing ribald songs. Thomas decided he liked the dark and scowling Duncan better than this jovial lummox who couldn't meet his gaze without breaking into loud guffaws. It was a bewildering change.

Fia leaned out the window of the coach. The wind caught her hair and swirled it behind her, a banner of rich russet brown. Thomas could almost feel the silken curls and smell the heather that twined through the strands. Biting back a groan, he spurred his horse on. The sooner he reached London, the better.

Fia watched him as he galloped ahead. He had discarded the overly large doublet after the ceremony and now wore a billowing white shirt tucked into the ripped breeches he had first worn. The shirt flattened against his chest in the wind, and Fia noted the ripple of muscles across his shoulders. By the saints, but he was beautiful. Beautiful and angry, she reminded herself.

Each time she met his gaze, she was as scorched by his disdain as she had been by his passion. He had surprised her after the wedding with a lustful kiss. Even now, she could feel that demanding pressure against her lips.

She settled back on the hard leather seat, noting the blue ribbon that had fallen to the floor. It had been the only adornment she had worn to her wedding, and she had thought to keep it as a memento. Now, a scant hour later, it was as bedraggled and knotted as she felt.

Fia kicked at it. She had to acknowledge her own fault

107

in this entire debacle. If she hadn't allowed her anger to overcome her good sense, neither she nor Thomas would have been forced into this marriage. Her cheeks burned to think of the undignified arrangement in which Duncan had discovered them.

She picked up the ribbon and threaded it through her fingers. The strains of a vulgar song drifted through the spring air. Fia wondered at Duncan's unrestrained joy. He had been oddly triumphant since the priest had called the vows.

He had even gone so far as to make a jest about naked ghosts running about the castle. And his enthusiasm for the wedding seemed to increase by the minute. He had located yards and yards of fine brocade and silk for "bride clothes" and had arranged to have Zeus and Thunder taken to Thomas's ship with affable good humor.

Of course, Mary had been ecstatic. Even the servants had been caught up in a wave of excitement. Only Thomas had been solemn, his face carved in rebuke every time he looked at her.

The coach hit a rut in the road, and Mary tumbled across the seat. "If I could get my hands on MacKenna," she grumbled, "I'd match him bruise fer bruise, I would. He's drivin' the coach like a madman."

Fia grinned and leaned out the window. The sea-spiced air drew her attention. The sun warmed her face as the wind whipped through her hair.

She refused to dwell on the unfortunate events of her wedding. There was good in every occurrence, she reminded herself. She closed her eyes and imagined herself flying through the air on the back of a huge winged eagle. She clutched the image to her, dispelling her earlier gloom. No matter what else happened, she was going to London to make her fortune.

"Yer hair will be as tangled as a rat's nest if ye keep hangin' it out the window like that," Mary warned.

Fia turned to face her maid, ignoring the dust, the jolting of the coach, and the hardness of the leather seat. "Don't you enjoy the wind? We are finally on our way to London. 'Tis like a dream."

"Humph. I'd call it a nightmare, meself," grumped Mary as she rubbed a hand on her sore rump, almost losing her balance when the coach hit another deep rut.

Fia turned back to the window to hide a grin.

"Can ye see the harbor yet, lassie?"

"Not yet. I can smell the ocean, though, so it can't be far."

"Ye've got a tangle big enough for a flock of geese to nest in on this side of yer head."

"Aye," Fia agreed absently, her attention caught by her new husband. Thomas looked as handsome as a six-pence, even raggedly dressed.

Mary peered out the window past her. "He'd be a mite more handsome did he smile. I never saw a man more given to scowlin' in me whole life."

Fia bit her lip. "He blames me for everything."

Mary chuckled. "What a sight 'twas, ye sprawled across the Sassenach, yer skirts over his head and his face in yer—"

"I know," interrupted Fia hastily. "Mary, I have to convince him I didn't mean for that to happen."

"He'll come around. Anyone would have known ye wouldn't leave without yer animals. Ye saved the man's life, whether he realizes it or not. Now all we need to do is convince the Sassenach that ye'll be the perfect wife fer him."

"Mary, I'm not going to do any such thing! The Sassenach was forced to wed me. There has got to be some way out of this mess."

Mary's mouth dropped open. "Here ye are, married to

the perfect man, one who can sponsor yer plays and who looks like a prince, too. A man who can turn yer bones to butter just by touchin' ye—"

"I never said any such thing!"

"Ye didn't have to. Ye get all flushed and heated every time he enters a room," Mary said.

Fia thought she would catch fire with the heat of her embarrassment. If it was that plain to Mary, did others see it as well? Could Thomas know?

"God made only one man fer ye, mistress. Ye'd be a fool to walk away from him."

"Only one?" Fia had to laugh. "You've had five."

"Perhaps I should say 'one at a time,'" Mary amended cheerfully.

Fia shook her head. "I won't have a husband who doesn't want me."

Mary sighed. "Angus warned me how 'twould be. He said ye'd never be happy with the laird's maneuverin', but I disagreed. He laughed at me, he did."

"Angus laughed?"

"Aye. He near split a rib," affirmed Mary.

Fia leaned out the window to stare at Mary's dour husband. Angus possessed a very Scottish sense of humor, which meant he never smiled, especially when telling the most fanciful story. Even now, he looked for all the world as though he were on his way to the gallows.

Fia returned to her seat. "He doesn't look happy to me."

"Never ye mind about Angus, lassie. He's a mite dour but a fine man fer all that."

The coach swayed around a turn, and Mary grabbed the edge of the seat to keep from tumbling onto the floor. "Ye needn't worry, mistress. The Sassenach won't be happy 'til he convinces himself that 'twas his own idea to wed ye. And if he doesn't, well, then, ye can always seek an annulment. I can't imagine 'twould be too difficult to secure, seein' as how ye were forced to wed."

Fia remembered Thomas's frozen expression during the ceremony. "Perhaps that's what he wants," she said.

"Come, mistress," urged Mary. "Give the man some time. Why, my late husband, Lachlan MacQuire, no more wished to marry me than a stallion would wish to be gelded, but 'twere no time at all before he was as merry as a duck in a warm nest." She winked and nodded. " 'Twill be the same with his lordship. He'll come about once ye begin yer wifely duties."

"Wifely duties?"

"Whist, mistress, ye know what I mean."

"Mary, I have no intention of—"

" 'Tis but a wee hop from lust to love. Most men make the jump and never know it."

Fia had no doubt there was passion between her and Thomas. It flared like a spark in dried kindling every time they were together. But love was something else. She tried to imagine Thomas with a fistful of flowers, down on one knee quoting poetry, but no image would come.

She met Mary's expectant gaze with a faint smile. "I don't think the Sassenach is the kind to make a jump of any kind without carefully thinking it over."

Mary looked unconvinced. "Well, I suppose ye know him better." She brightened. "At least the Sassenach isn't a miserable scalpeen like Malcolm the Maiden."

Fia nodded. There was also the matter of fate, destiny, two souls who belonged together.

Mary patted her red curls. "If I do say so meself, yer husband is as bonny as Saint Christopher, with long, fine legs. And no need to stuff his codpiece with aught than what God gave him."

"Mary, please!" Fia choked.

"Well, if ye didn't want the whole world to know what he keeps in his codpiece, then ye shouldn't have been runnin' about the castle with him as naked as the day he was born."

"He wasn't naked!"

"Close enough," said Mary with unimpaired ebullience.

Fortunately, the coach lurched to a halt, and Fia didn't have to answer. Mary pushed past her to look out the window. "Och, 'tis a lovely ship. Will we be leavin' right off? Angus is not a patient man. There's your lordship now, marchin' to his ship as if he owned the whole of Scotland."

Fia crowded Mary for room at the small window and felt her breath catch in her throat. She was blind to the ship, her attention riveted on Thomas.

He looked wild and untamed as he strode to where the ship was moored. His long, muscular legs were outlined by his soft calf-skin boots, a span of muscular thigh showing through the rips in his breeches. The wind pulled his white shirt over the hard muscles of his arms and chest.

Thomas's face had always had a chiseled beauty that bespoke centuries of patrician breeding, but framed by his loosened hair, it became the face of a mythical god sent to earth. He was lean, strong, and incredibly virile. Just looking at him filled Fia's mouth with moisture and caused her breasts to tingle with awareness.

As Fia stared, he turned. His gaze locked with hers. The corners of his mouth turned upward, and Fia smiled back. His smile widened into something warm, and she shared his excitement at their impending departure.

For the space of a second, there was but the two of them. Then Duncan yelled to one of his men, and Thomas's smile froze.

He turned on his heel and walked away. Sweet Jesu, but he was as hot and randy for that woman as if he had been out to sea for a year.

Behind him, someone rudely belched and shouted at him in a gruff voice, "Time to quit dawdlin', ye lazy Sassenach. Crawl back into yer hole!"

Thomas turned on his heel, hands fisted to deliver a pertinent message to the rude dolt who dared speak to him in such a voice.

There, feet planted firmly apart, his hand resting casually on one hip, a fine Italian doublet of velvet complemented by exquisite woolen hose and ornate leather boots, stood Robert MacQuarrie.

Thomas had never been so joyful to see anyone in his life. "Robert!"

Robert grasped Thomas's hand, his eyes and voice intense. "How fare thee, *mon ami?*" The blue eyes took in every scratch and bruise.

Thomas grinned and thumped his friend on the back. "I prosper now you have come."

"Careful! You damage my ruff."

Thomas laughed. Few knew the quality of man that resided behind the foppish exterior of the lean and elegant Viscount Montley. "Your neckwear has always been in keeping with your person, Robert. 'Tis overdone and too damn frippery to stomach."

"As good to be out of the world as be out of fashion." Robert ran a critical eye over him in return. " 'Tis difficult to heed advice from a man dressed so . . ." He shuddered. "Pray, look to yourself, Rotherwood!"

Thomas waved a hand in dismissal. " 'Tis but clothing."

The corners of Robert's mouth twitched. "I would hesitate to call that clothing. God's Blood, what's afoot? I came prepared to fight my way through a welter of angry Scotsmen, only to find you escorted like an honored guest."

"I am no honored guest," Thomas responded.

"Aye. I can see it in the amount of lumps you have

113

acquired. Have no fear! I have a plan." Robert was all lofty superiority.

"There's naught to be done."

"Never say naught! I came to purchase your release."

"What?"

Robert smirked. "There's nothing a Scotsman prizes more than the yellow gleam of good Spanish gold. I am prepared to bargain for your release."

"Your own money? I am touched!"

Robert shrugged. "I'm sure Walsingham would repay any loss I suffer. After all, 'tis his arse I pull from the fire as much as yours."

"I'm surprised you thought to save Walsingham."

"I must admit 'twas a difficult decision. I would have enjoyed seeing that snake burn in the oils of Elizabeth's wrath." Robert removed a bit of dust from his sleeve. "So, ah, did you secure the letter?" he asked casually.

Thomas could not, would not, explain how a tiny mite of a Scottish wench had summarily disposed of the greatest instrument of Walsingham's secret network. He shrugged. " 'Tis a story for another time."

"Verily?"

Thomas frowned. "How did you find out I was here?"

Robert's smile was that of the cat with the cream. "When you failed to appear, Simmons came after me posthaste. You are lucky I was nearby."

"And why were you nearby?"

"I just happened to be rusticating. My health is never certain."

Thomas forbore to answer. "I assume you accidentally mentioned to Simmons that you would be nearby?"

"Oh, I may have mentioned it when we parted on the dock. You know, idle conversation." Robert looked up at the ship. "I trow, but I was glad for the chance to sail. She's as steady a vessel as they come. If you ever want to sell her, let me know."

Thomas cast an experienced gaze over the *Glorianna*. She did look magnificent.

"I hate to plague you with questions, Thomas, but Maclean sent a most curious missive this morning."

"Aye?"

"He sent us word that not only would the Earl of Rotherwood be gracing us with his presence, but the countess, as well."

Thomas grimaced. He had thought to escape explaining Fia until after they had set sail.

"Well? Speak up! Who is this mysterious maid?"

"There's naught to tell."

"Oh no! I smell a mystery. Is she short and fat, too plain to mention?"

Plain? Fia, plain? Infuriating, bothersome, maddening—yes. All that and more. But plain? He caught Robert's quizzical gaze and forced himself to shrug.

"She's an ill-dressed, ill-mannered ragamuffin of a chit."

"What? She wasn't mad to wed you?"

Thomas glowered. "Nay. She was not." It had galled him how silent and pale she had been during the wedding.

"Doesn't she sigh for your wondrous face, your handsome form, your incredible wealth, as do the ladies of the court?"

"Nay," Thomas answered curtly. "She cares more for her mongrel dog and ragged horse than anything else."

"Oh no! She rejects you out of hand! I vow, 'tis a first. But you will sway her! *Varium et mutabile semper femme.*"

Thomas looked at Robert.

He sighed. "I said, 'A fickle and changeable thing is a woman ever.' Your Latin is lamentable."

"Latin is for fools and priests. If you wish to make obscure references and put on such foppish airs, then

115

I suggest you go and search out the lady herself. She has aspirations to be a playwright and is ink-stained and bookish enough to suit even your high tastes."

"Ink-stained!" Robert's eyes widened to a ridiculous degree. "She is literate, then?" He smacked his forehead with an open palm. "That explains why she doesn't favor you."

Thomas closed his eyes. "You came merely to torment me?"

"I trow, this will make an excellent story for the telling."

The queen had always held that it would be easier to turn the Thames than to stop Robert MacQuarrie from being a useless fribble. Thomas regarded him through half-closed eyes. "I didn't have a choice, Robert. I was forced at the end of a claymore to take a wife."

"A wife or death. 'Tis a difficult decision," Robert mused. He stroked his trim beard. "I think, perhaps, a wife would be easier to ignore than the coldness of death."

"You have not yet met Fia."

"Fia?" Robert's eyebrows rose. " 'Tis a fine Scottish name. It means 'the dark peace.' "

Thomas choked. "Dark peace? God's Wounds, but the chit brings naught but mayhem and destruction in her wake!"

Robert grinned. "You have intrigued me. The lady is literate, a playwright, more difficult to ignore than the coldness of death, and she wishes to have no part of you. You are right. I don't like this woman. I love her."

Thomas scowled. He watched as Duncan strode to Fia's coach.

Robert followed his gaze. Duncan opened the door. Thomas looked away. Until he found a way to control his unbridled lust, he was determined to stay as far from Fia as possible.

"Sweet Jesu!" Robert murmured.

Thomas kept his gaze fixed on the *Glorianna*.

There was silence as Robert stared. Thomas shifted, irritation building. "Well?" he finally said.

"She's very, ah, pleasant."

Thomas glanced at the coach. There beside Duncan stood Mary, her broad face damp with perspiration, her round form shaking with laughter.

"That's not her," snapped Thomas.

Duncan turned and lifted a hand. Fia stepped from the coach.

"God's Wounds," Robert murmured.

Thomas felt a slight sense of relief. He was not the only one she affected. "She's comely," he said grudgingly.

"Comely? Only comely? Are you blind?" Robert clasped his hands over his heart. "I would have braved a thousand dangers for a glance from those dark eyes. I would have fought fire with my bare hands to receive a kiss from those dewy lips. I would have—"

"She is *my* wife," Thomas ground out.

"I can now see why 'twas so difficult to decide between death or marriage." He sighed heavily. "You have done it once again, *mon ami*. You have proven the Wentworth luck is stronger than ever."

Duncan strode up to the men, his arm about Fia's waist. His black eyes narrowed on seeing Robert. " 'Tis the Coward of Balmanach."

Robert made a graceful bow. Duncan ignored him, turning an ice-thin smile on Thomas. "You'll miss the tide do you tarry."

Thomas nodded. He itched to be at sea. "Come, Fia. We leave."

Fia swallowed a cold lump of fear. The brown eyes that met hers were impersonal. They held no emotion,

117

no welcome. They could have been the eyes of a stranger, not a husband.

Duncan took her hand. "Och, now, poppet. Don't look so saddened. We'll write often. At least once a week." His glared over her head at Thomas and spoke with a voice loud enough to be heard across the ocean. "If she's not happy, I'll come for her."

"Och, Duncan, don't shout in my ear," Fia protested. "I'll write, though I'll be hard pressed to think of something to say. I rarely see you more than once a month now." She stood on tiptoe to deliver her kiss, and he swooped down to hold her tight.

"Lassie," he whispered in a husky voice, "I've done what was best for you. But if you find you're not happy, you've just to tell Angus, and he'll bring you home."

She hugged him, not trusting herself to speak, and then she was set gently on the ground. Duncan cast a last glare at Thomas and held out a folded piece of parchment.

Thomas stared at the paper. Then, with a strange smile crossing his face, he tucked it into his waistband.

Duncan called to his men and stalked off, never sparing him a second glance.

Fia started to ask about the paper, but Mary came bustling up. She carried the few bundles she deemed too precious to let the men handle MacKenna was hard on her heels, his arms cradling a bundle of brown fur.

"Och,' said Fia. "I thought he was already on ship."

MacKenna grinned. "He's been on ship twice. He keeps escapin'. Thunder and Zeus are already sleepin' in the hold."

"Damned nuisance, the lot of them," Thomas said.

Fia started to argue, but Robert stepped into the fray. "Pray tell, gentle lady, where did you procure such a fine-looking rabbit?"

Fia eyed the man curiously. He didn't look like a coward. Indeed, there was a quiet merriment about him that made her want to smile. "Lord Thomas came from Mull. He's an islander."

"Lord Thomas?" Robert asked, a quiver of laughter in his voice.

"Aye. I named him after Thomas, as he is the one who saved him."

Robert turned an incredulous stare on his friend. "You saved a rabbit?"

"We have to leave," Thomas announced and took Fia's arm. He half dragged her onto the ship, leaving Robert to assist Mary. Before Fia could comprehend it, Thomas was roaring at his men to cast off.

And soon the Isle of Mull faded into the mist.

Chapter Eleven

"I'll be a loose-limbed Greek, Cap'n! Is that a salted pig?"

Thomas glanced up from the supply listing. Duncan had been generous in restocking the ship. "Aye, I believe it is."

"Praise St. Peter! Then 'twas not a wasted voyage after all," Henry Simmons declared as he rubbed his overstuffed belly.

Thomas raised his eyebrows. "Were we that short on supplies?"

The first mate's round face saddened. " 'Tain't me I was thinkin' of, Cap'n, but me li'l Meggie. It sets right hard on the missus when I comes home with nary a thing to show fer me absence."

Thomas grinned. "And you think a side of pork will satisfy her?"

"Li'l Meggie'd dance a jig with the devil fer a good slice of ham, Cap'n. There's no tellin' what she'd do fer a whole side of pork. It don't hardly bear thinkin' of."

As "li'l Meggie" was twice as wide and half as tall as Simmons, Thomas didn't doubt this. He handed the provisions list to the first mate. " 'Tis an interesting thought, your little Meggie dancing a jig."

"Aye." Simmons tucked the list into his waistband and gave a wistful sigh. " 'Tis a grand thought."

Thomas chuckled and leaned back against the mast, a feeling of deep satisfaction rising through him. The Isle of Mull was but a silver-hued mound of rock as it disappeared into the horizon. He could almost feel the fetters dropping off as the wind filled the sails and carried him home.

Watkins, a lanky, red-haired man, scrambled to the deck. "Cap'n! I brought ye word from me Lord Montley. He says to tell ye that he's seen to the women and they are resting comfortably in their cabins." The freckled brow puckered. "At least that's what I think he was sayin'. 'Tis hard to tell with Lord Montley."

Simmons muttered, "Montley is a coxcomb. He's destined for the gallows as sure as I was born on a long Sunday."

" 'Tis for exactly that reason I abide his presence on my ship," Thomas replied evenly. "If he's destined for the gallows, then I need have no fear of the ship sinking whilst he is aboard."

Simmons looked much struck by this observation. "Well, Cap'n! That is fine thinkin'." His face darkened in remembrance. "Though he was the devil of a trial to abide on the way to this Scottish pile of rocks."

"Full of spirits, was he?"

"He walked about spoutin' poetry enough to sicken a man." Simmons spat his distaste over the rail.

Thomas laughed. There was nothing like the anticipation of a good roust to liven up Robert's already high spirits.

121

Simmons cast a sardonic eye toward the bos'n, Watkins. "Don't mind the cap'n. He's been sort of giddy since he took hisself a wife."

All of Thomas's good humor fled. "Did you or did you not want that side of pork?"

The first mate gaped. "Surely ye wouldn't take the pork jus' 'cause I saw fit to warn ye 'bout the dangers of havin' women on board. 'Tis ill luck, as well ye knows. And ye've gone and invited two to sail with us all the way to London!"

Watkins's eyes grew rounder. He looked so like a startled bird that Thomas expected the man to sprout wings and begin cooing.

"What would you know of luck and women, Simmons?" Thomas asked.

Watkins interjected with haste, "If'n any was to know about bad luck and women, 'twould be Simmons. He's had his fair share of both."

Thomas cast a repressive stare at the bos'n, who promptly retracted his statement. " 'Less, of course, 'twas a Scottish wench. Simmons don't know as much about Scottish wenches."

Simmons puffed out his cheeks. "A Scottish wench is twice the ill luck of an English one. Everyone knows that, ye bloody loon!"

"Perhaps 'tis fortunate for both of you that the countess is not a Scottish wench," Thomas said.

Watkins frowned. "But she has to be, Cap'n, if she came from that isle."

"I think he was referrin' to ye callin' her a 'wench,' ye louthead," said Simmons.

"But ye was callin' her a—"

"Thank ye very much." Simmons glowered at Watkins. "Perhaps ye should be workin' whilst ye're standin' around. Coil up that length of rope." He pointed to a tangled hempen pile that lay a few feet away. Watkins shuffled to the pile and began unsnarling it.

Thomas shook his head. "I should confine the two of you belowdeck. I think the sun has mangled your brains."

Simmons drew himself up to his full five feet of portly manhood and hooked his thumbs in the rope that held up his coarse woolen breeches. "And who, I asks ye, would sail the ship fer ye?"

Thomas shrugged. "Robert MacQuarrie is a wondrous navigator. His men hold there is none better."

Watkins nodded reluctantly. "Aye, I heard it from his own bos'n when we was last in Londontown. He said Lord Montley could find his way out of hell in a full fog."

"Are ye through with that rope? No? Then cease yer prattlin'." After making sure the bos'n was adequately occupied, Simmons continued. "Beside that damn Scotsman, now we have to contend with a shipful of women. Women are the devil's own instrument, causing havoc and—"

"That's enough," Thomas interrupted, impatient to turn the topic. The weather was cool and clear, perfect for sailing. For just one moment, he wanted to think about nothing but the pleasures of being at sea.

"Ye'd do well to listen, Cap'n." Simmons nodded wisely. "I knows women, I do."

Watkins nodded in agreement as he untied a large knot.

"For the love of heaven!" Thomas burst out. "Neither one of you knows enough about women to fill the toe of my boot!"

"That may be true of me, Cap'n," said Watkins. "But Henry Simmons has the luck of Tom Shanty hisself when it comes to women. There's none as would know more about women and ill luck."

"Tom Shanty?" Simmons protested in an injured tone, rubbing his bald head with a pudgy hand. "Why, Tom Shanty had the angel Gabriel on his shoulder when it came to women compared to the luck I've had of 'em!"

Thomas ignored them, admiring the play of the sun across the glistening water. Henry Simmons was legendary among the sailing world for two reasons: one was his uncanny ability to organize a ship and maintain order even under the worst of conditions; the other was his long-standing and long-suffering relationship with a woman by the name of Leaky Meg, who was a character in her own right.

Thomas shoved himself away from the mast. 'Twas obvious that if he wished for peace, he would have to find it elsewhere than in the presence of his talkative first mate. "I'll be below."

Simmons opened his mouth to protest, but Thomas forestalled him with an upheld hand. "Hold, Simmons! I was of a mind to allow you to choose a gift for the redoubtable Meggie until you began to turn my stomach with your country proverbs."

"The side of pork, Cap'n?" Simmons leaned forward eagerly, his fat paunch resting on the deck railing.

"Consider it a reward for fetching Robert MacQuarrie when you did."

Simmons flushed. "Now, Cap'n, I can explain—"

"There's no need," Thomas interrupted. "Robert has already done so."

Simmons looked suspicious. "Just what did Lord Montley see fit to tell ye, Cap'n? I'd no sooner trust that—"

Thomas laughed. "Hold! If you think so little of him, then why did you fetch him when I didn't return as I had planned?"

"I went fer him because he was the closest thing to an Englishman I was like to find so far north." Simmons

124

scratched under one arm and added grudgingly, "Though I hate to say it, that Frenchified piece of lace does know his way around a sword."

Thomas grinned and headed belowdeck. "He'll be moved to tears by such a declaration."

Simmons sputtered and yelled after him. "Now, Cap'n! Don't ye be repeatin' what I said! Like as not he'll come spoutin' some nonsense at me, and I'll be right back to not likin' him again."

Thomas chuckled and strode across the deck. God's Blood, but it felt wondrous to be back at sea. He took a deep breath of the fresh salt air and turned toward his cabin. He could use a good sleep. He hadn't had much rest in the past twenty-four hours, and he was beginning to feel weary through to his bones. He would need to be at his best when next he came upon Fia.

He rubbed his neck wearily. He would have to deal with this improbable marriage. There had to be a way out of it. He would consult with Walsingham as soon as they arrived in London. Thomas touched the pocket that held the letter. The wily counselor would be pleased. What had Duncan been thinking to offer it? It held damaging proof of the Scottish queen's perfidy. That a Scotsman would just give it away was unthinkable.

Thomas wondered if Fia was aware of the letter. 'Twas obvious her cousin held her in his confidence. Perhaps he had spoken of it.

She was probably belowdeck at this very moment, looking after her ugly mutt or that damnable old nag. He had a brief image of her standing in the hay, her arms about Thunder's bony neck, the soft wool of her dress outlining her lush body. . . .

Thomas pulled himself together with a jerk. What was he doing, dreaming about that ill-fated wench? Serviceable wool was *not* seductive.

He rubbed his chin. Of course, it wasn't ordinary

wool. It couldn't be. It must be some special Scottish weave that was impossible for an English loom to create. This wool hugged and molded every delectable curve with a loving familiarity that made a man's mouth water.

In fact, now that he considered it, the thinness of her unsightly dresses merely drew attention to her shocking lack of underskirts. He would have bet his finest horse that she purposefully refused to wear proper clothing in order to vex him.

Well, he could deal with such wanton behavior. Once they were in London, he would see to it she possessed more petticoats than the queen. Aye, that was what he would do. He would purchase petticoats of green, blue, red, purple—every color imaginable. She would have an entire wardrobe devoted just to the underskirts he would buy her. And she would wear them or—

Jesu, but I am going stark, raving mad! Thomas stalked away from the railing where he had been standing, staring out to sea like a crack-brained fool. Thank God Robert had not seen him.

He swung himself down the ladder and strode the remaining few steps down the passageway. As he neared the door of his cabin, he began to unlace his shirt. His whole body ached with fatigue.

He stepped through his doorway and came to an abrupt halt. He was face to face with . . . *wool.*

Fia leaned over a huge trunk, her head and arms hidden from view as she dug through the contents.

"Och, now, where did I put that box? I know 'twas in here when we left," she muttered. She had burrowed so deeply into the trunk that her knees had inched off the floor, and all Thomas could see was her softly curved bottom. The ache of tiredness was lost in an immediate onslaught of pure lust.

"What in the hell are you doing in here?"

Fia's head hit the trunk lid as she jerked upright. The

rabbit scampered from behind the trunk and began to race wildly around the room in ever smaller circles until it veered and skidded under the bed. Zeus announced his presence by emitting a low growl.

Thomas ran a hand through his hair. He hadn't meant to shout quite so loudly, but his tortured body had demanded some sort of release. He glared at Fia.

She pressed a hand to her thudding heart. "By the saints, you scared the wind out of me!" She realized she was holding a swath of blazing red velvet to her like a shield. Heat rose in her cheeks, and she dropped the cloth with ill grace.

When Robert had first escorted her to this cabin, she had stood awkwardly, her rabbit clutched tightly to her, Zeus sitting at her feet. Before she could gather her scattered wits, he had left, calling for Angus to bring her trunks.

'Twas a beautiful room, warm with mellow wood and decorated with brass and leather. But 'twas clearly a man's lodgings. Nowhere could she find any sign that she belonged.

It was a lonely feeling. She had reminded herself that her heroines never balked at excitement, whether it was sailing into a storm, fighting with a drawn sword, or facing the devil himself. The thought had given her the resolution to make the cabin more her own.

So here she was, looking for her box of writing instruments. Of all her possessions, it was the most dear to her. Once they were placed in the cabin, she was sure she would feel more at home.

Hair fell over her eyes as she dug through the material for the precious box. "Och, Duncan is mad to think I would ever be able to wear such grand cloth," she muttered in irritation. "The brocade by itself weighs as much as an entire tapestry, it does. I'd not be able to stand with it."

She struggled to unwind herself from a length of velvet that seemed to have developed a mind of its own. Aye, this was working. She was not paying him the slightest bit of attention, and the pain in her throat had already eased somewhat.

But then he moved, and she found her attention caught by his hand as it raked through his golden hair. The ripple of muscles under his loose shirt made her mouth go dry.

He was her husband. The thought sang through her mind, and she stared at him with unabashed admiration. He stood in the opened door, one hand gripping the doorframe, the other fisted arrogantly on his hip. Somehow, his white shirt had come unlaced, and she noted with fascination the crisp curls of golden hair narrowing to a tantalizing trail that pointed straight to his belt. To her horror, Fia found that she couldn't look away from that muscular chest or those beckoning curls.

Sweet Jesu, she prayed, *please let the ocean swallow me before he sees me staring at his chest*. After what was surely an eternity, she managed to lift her gaze high enough to see his face.

His look of arrogant satisfaction told her that she might as well have spoken her every thought aloud, so well had he read her expression. Her cheeks flushed. She was hopelessly attracted to him.

" 'Tis quite large, your cabin. I didn't realize ships had big rooms." It was a stupid comment but all she could manage at the moment.

"Most don't."

"Oh." He wasn't going to make this easy. She offered a tentative smile.

"Well, 'tis huge all the same."

No answer. She found herself staring at his chest again until, with an exasperated sigh, he crossed his arms, obscuring the golden hairs from her view.

128

"You can't stay here," he said.

Fia nodded silently. She was suddenly aware of how tired she was, as taut and stretched as a sapling bent beneath a heavy snow.

"I've no wish to stay here," she said, struggling to her feet. " 'Tis dark as a priest's cell. I had an uncle once who had a study like this. My aunt couldn't walk into it without shivering as though entering a tomb. Once she entered the room to find that my uncle had died, and—"

"We need to talk." His words hit her heart like stones on a thinly iced pond, cracking the surface with every utterance.

Fia looked back into the trunk, her hands closing about a length of heavy red silk tucked into the bottom. "Aye?"

"I didn't seek this union," he said stiffly, as though the words burnt his lips.

"Neither did I," Fia answered, her anger flaring at his obvious distaste.

His face darkened. "This may not be a plot of your making, but neither did you discourage Maclean."

"There's no discouraging Duncan. Once he sets him mind to a path, he's like a great rock, rolling over everything and everybody."

His eyes narrowed in suspicion. Fia decided she didn't like his expression.

" 'Twas damned convenient your cousin caught us not once, but twice, both times in most compromising positions."

" 'Twas you, Lord Lackwit, who brought such a fine mount as was scared by a poor mite of a dog with no teeth! And 'twas you who ran through the castle with naught on but your hose!"

"I wouldn't have been without my clothes had you not stolen them," he growled.

Fia released the tortured silk and stood. They were

both speaking from pent-up emotions, but now unleashed, there was no calling them back. "If I hadn't married you, you dolt, your body would now be floating out to sea with fish a-nibbling at your toes!"

"If you'd wished it, you could have convinced Duncan to free me without this farce of a wedding."

"My cousin is laird first and foremost. Had he determined your presence was dangerous to the clan, there would have been nothing I could have done to save you."

"Liar!" he jeered. "You certainly were quick enough to agree."

"Fool! Duncan was determined that I wed, and soon. If it hadn't been you, I would have had to marry—" She stopped, realizing how damning the words were.

"Exactly," he sneered. "You would have had to wed that sniveling maltworm, Malcolm Davies. You and I both know Lady Caroline never would have allowed you to go to London."

Fia planted her fists on her hips. "London is my destiny."

"But I am not." His mouth was a straight slash. He looked like some furious god, all glorious anger at having been forced to wed a plain, commonplace urchin. The events of the day seemed to grow and fill her throat with a lump every bit the size of a pillow.

She wasn't surprised that he wanted to escape their marriage. So did she, she told herself resolutely. All she had ever wanted was to go to London for her plays. But somehow, having Thomas stand before her and tell her that he didn't want to be married to her was more painful than she had thought possible.

She knew the ball of pain in her throat was perilously close to unwinding itself into a torrent of tears, so she sat on the edge of the bunk and focused on the coldness of the air, the rough feel of her skirt against her legs, and the ache where her teeth were set firmly into the tender flesh of her lip.

Let him rant and rail. Let him decry their marriage and wish to be free of her. Let him do what he would. She could not, *would not* cry in front of him.

He heaved a sigh, one hand running through his hair. "Enough of this. We speak to no purpose. This marriage—"

"Can be annulled," she said quickly. Mary had been right. Whatever else happened, Fia would not allow Thomas to toss her out like a discarded shoe.

"What?" His voice was a sharp whip crack that echoed in the room. Zeus lifted his head and growled.

She bit the inside of her lip until she tasted blood. Despite his surprise, he looked . . . relieved. *Pretend you are Desdemonda, the warrior queen facing your worst enemy.*

She curled her hands into her lap. "Duncan said you were a favorite of Queen Elizabeth."

"Aye, but—"

"All we have to do is tell her the truth. You were forced. She will see to it that the marriage is annulled."

He was plainly dumbfounded.

The rabbit nudged her hand with its nose. Fia absently stroked the soft fur. "The marriage was never consummated. I will vow to it. All you have to do is find a sponsor for my plays."

Fia didn't dare look at him. The joy she knew she would see reflected in his eyes would wound her beyond repair.

Finally, after an eternity of silence, he spoke. "*I* will sponsor your plays."

"Nay," Fia said. She ached to feel his arms about her. She knew that if she didn't put some distance between them, she would be hopelessly, eternally in love. She wasn't about to make such a grave error. " 'Twould cast

131

suspicion if we continued to have a connection after the annulment."

His hands curled into fists at his side. Fia felt a wetness gather in her eyes. He was trying not to show his exuberance at her offer. Well, she would not disappoint him. "We will both get what we want. You will be free from an unwanted marriage, and I will get a sponsor for my plays."

Thomas wondered why he felt nothing but a strange hollowness. This was what he wanted—freedom.

She lifted her gaze to his and raised an eyebrow. "Well?"

There was nothing for it but to agree. "Agreed," he said shortly. Turning on his heel, he left the room and stalked back on deck.

It wasn't until much later that he realized he had forgotten to ask her what she knew about Queen Mary's missive.

Chapter Twelve

The door slammed, and Robert dropped his mug onto the table. He frowned at the spillage, slight though it was. He still had a Scotsman's dislike of wasting good drink. 'Twas but one of the many Scottish characteristics he seemed unable to remove, try though he might.

"Where in the hell have you been hiding, you perfidious cur?"

Robert winced at the belligerent tone. "Thomas, pray speak in a more moderate voice. I find I have a tender ear whenever I venture upon the sea."

Thomas strode into the room and threw himself into a chair. "I'll see to it that more than your ears are tender if you don't explain what mischief you are planning."

"Come and join me for a wee dram of Scottish whiskey. 'Tis the true elixir of life."

Thomas slammed his fist onto the wooden surface, causing Robert's empty mug to jump off the table in apparent fright. "Explain what ill-begotten thought made you put Fia in my cabin. And don't bother to act as if you thought I wouldn't mind, or you'd not have spent half the day hiding from me."

Robert eyed the bent mug now cowering on the floor. " 'Tis not an easy thing, to stay out of sight on a ship. I thought I had done rather well."

Thomas scowled.

"If you must know, I was being chivalrous. There are few enough places on this ship to house guests, and your cabin seemed the best suited to a female of Lady Fia's tender sensibilities. Besides, she is your wife."

"Not for long."

"Oho! Do you plan a murder? Shall I help you toss the body from the side of the ship?" Robert fished his mug from under the table by hooking a booted foot into the handle and dragging it toward him. "Before you carry out this nefarious plan, be sure you learn Lady Fia's handwriting. Duncan is expecting a letter every week."

Thomas splayed his hands on the table. "What Maclean expects and what Maclean gets may be quite different."

Robert lifted his eyebrows. "What was the letter he gave you on the dock?"

"The missive I was sent to find."

"He simply handed it to you?"

"Aye."

"Are you sure it's the same one?"

Thomas nodded. "Walsingham told me how to recognize Queen Mary's hand. 'Tis hers."

"I hope 'twas worth a wife."

"You're a fool," Thomas growled.

"So you say. Of course, 'tis not me who follows Walsingham's commands like a puppet."

Thomas frowned. "You know nothing of the matter."

"I know you think him better than he is. He's a maggot on the face of the earth, yet you are determined to think him well."

"He's done more for both me and the queen than you admit."

Robert kept silent. In the dark days after the death of Thomas's father, Walsingham had slipped into the young earl's good graces. Robert's stomach still roiled at the thought. Francis Walsingham was a snake, and he made little secret of the fact that he found Thomas's many talents of great use as he planned and plotted his little spying games. Thomas's loyalty never allowed him to see how the queen's minister used him.

Robert sighed. "Speaking of monsters, have you seen that thing Lady Fia has secured in the hold? I think 'tis a horse, though I wouldn't swear it." He poured whiskey into a tumbler and handed it to Thomas.

Thomas took a grateful drink. "Aye, I've seen it."

Robert shuddered. "I nigh screamed in terror when I beheld it." He lifted an arm, and a straggle of torn lace drooped from his sleeve. "I vow, but the creature attempted to eat me."

"You're fortunate it didn't get your arm, instead."

Robert smoothed his sleeve. "I'd have given up a finger ere I'd let that devil's mount eat my lace. 'Tis Italian, you know."

Thomas grunted.

Robert regarded him for a moment. "Well? Tell me by what foul manner you plan on ridding yourself of your wife. Though I must admit I'm at a loss as to why you would wish to."

"We are to get an annulment from Queen Elizabeth."

Robert lifted his eyebrows thoughtfully. "Hm. You think she'll grant it?"

"Why not? I was forced at knife's end to wed the chit."

"True. Queen Elizabeth is not like to enjoy hearing how one of her own was so cruelly abused. But what of Fia? She will have to agree to the petition as well."

" 'Twas her idea," Thomas said curtly.

"Oho! The web tangles!"

Thomas gazed at him with a considering look. "As usual, you act the virgin, yet there is something of the harlot in your gestures."

Robert laughed. "Pray liken me to no mewling virgin! If I must be a woman, then let it be one of robust and lusty abilities!"

Thomas rolled his eyes. "As usual, you take a comment and make it a mountain."

Robert waved a hand. "A minor talent. I have others."

"Such as?"

"They are too manifest to allow description." Robert took an appreciative swallow of the whiskey. "You know, *mon ami,* I can't help but notice you've lost what little humor you possessed. I wonder at the severity of torture you must have endured for it to have so altered your disposition. On the surface, I can see nothing more than a fading bruise or two. Perhaps you are wounded in other places?"

Thomas tossed off the whiskey, welcoming its burning warmth. " 'Tis true I was tortured." Robert shot a quick look of concern at him, and Thomas shook his head. "Nay, not like that. I was handled roughly at first but treated well enough afterward."

"Then what?"

Thomas considered the handle of his mug for a moment but said nothing.

"Ah, 'tis like that, eh?"

"Like what?" Thomas lifted a brow.

Robert tilted back in his chair. "You were tortured by love."

Thomas set his mug onto the table, sloshing a good

half of its contents onto the scarred surface. "Cease your jesting."

" 'Twas no jest," protested Robert. "You have all the symptoms."

"What symptoms?"

"Well." Robert held up a finger. "There is the fact that you find the Lady Fia to be an attractive woman."

Thomas scowled. "I'm lustful, I don't deny it."

Robert grinned. "Lust does not keep company with jealousy."

Thomas sat bolt upright, knocking his tankard from the table with a swipe of a hand.

"By the rood, Rotherwood, pray consider what you are about," said Robert. "That's good whiskey you have poured onto my floor."

"To hell with your whiskey! What do you mean, I'm *jealous?*"

Robert sniffed, his eyes lingering with disapproval on the stained floor. " 'Tis giving pearls to the sow, allowing an Englishman to drink whiskey."

"Montley!" Thomas ground out.

"Very well. You glare at everyone when she is about, including her cousin Duncan. I noticed it on the dock." Robert gave him a smug grin. " 'Twas the look of a jealous husband. I have witnessed it many a time."

Thomas was hard pressed not to answer Robert's grin with a fist. "I admit she has an effect on me."

"Aha!"

"I'll be well rid of such a troublesome wench. London cannot come too soon."

"And then?"

"And then the maid is free." He retrieved the mug and set it on the table with care, aware of Robert's sharp eye on him.

"Free to do what?"

"Whatever she wishes. All I have to do is find a sponsor for her plays."

Robert said nothing but stared at his boots, his brow drawn in thought. Thomas watched him over the rim of his mug.

Robert glanced up and caught Thomas's gaze. He grinned impishly. " 'Twill anger you, but I will say it anyway. I wonder why you feel so strongly against the Lady Fia as wife? Is she not of noble birth?"

"Aye."

"And quick of wit?"

"Aye." Thomas scowled.

"Is she not a woman of warmth and comfort?"

"She isn't the woman I would wed."

"Why?"

Thomas shoved his chair back and stood, pacing about the room. Must he explain this to every fool he met? "Just look at her! She wears her hair a-tumbled to her shoulders. She has no understanding of court life nor of proper comportment. The chit hates shoes and wants for manners. She doesn't even own a petticoat."

"That's a long list indeed." Robert took a considering drink. "Perhaps you are correct, and the ailment you suffer is not love but lust."

Thomas gave a bitter smile. "I can scarcely look at the maid without becoming as readied as a ship in a full wind."

Robert looked delighted. "She torments you, eh?"

Thomas nodded.

"She comes to you in your sleep, whispering warm words in your ear and stroking your body with her ardent hands until you awake, as stiff and eager as—"

"*Enough!*" Thomas snapped.

"I apologize, *mon ami.*"

Thomas scowled and sank back into his chair. There

might be no answers for him in Robert's company, but at least the whiskey was melting away some of his tension.

Robert tapped a finger to his chin. With a sudden nod, he announced, "There is only one thing to do in such a case as this."

"What?" Thomas looked at the bottom of his mug. 'Twas already empty. He poured some more whiskey and gulped it. At this rate, he would be unable to stand. Part of him welcomed the idea of a few hours of blissful unawareness.

"You must take her. Make her yours. Woo her and—"

"How am I to do that and leave her a maid?" Thomas demanded. "Elizabeth will not grant an annulment if I so much as touch the wench."

"Ah, I had forgotten that." Robert shook his head and poured more whiskey into Thomas's mug. "Then there is no hope. I fear you are lost."

Thomas frowned. There must be something he could do to lessen the tension he felt around Fia during the time they had left on the ship. Seeing her walk about, her silken hair flying, her mouth soft and begging for kisses . . . He shifted in his chair. By the saints, but the chit stirred his blood. And if he was not mistaken, she lusted for him as well. She had scarce been able to look away from his bared chest today.

All he had to do was keep his hands from her until they arrived in London, he reminded himself. Once they were there, he would leave her in his house while he removed to court and allowed the perfumed wiles of the court beauties to douse his inexplicable lust. If only there were some diversion here, aboard ship. For him and for Fia.

He sat upright. "Robert, perhaps there is something you can do."

Robert had tilted his chair back and was examining the sheen of his boots. He arched an eyebrow.

"The queen herself says you'd as soon talk a woman out of her petticoats as pull the laces yourself."

Robert beamed. "I must admit to owning some address, immodest though the words be."

"You can talk to Fia for me, convince her to attach her affections elsewhere."

"What?" The legs of Robert's chair banged onto the wooden floor. "Nay."

"Nay? Is that all you've to say?"

"I can't."

"Why not?"

"The MacQuarries are pledged to the Macleans. I can't forget the allegiance of my clan," declared Robert, waving his hand as though it were a banner. " 'Tis a matter of honor."

Thomas scowled. "Honor? Since when has honor been a concern of yours? You would as soon cheat at cards as take an honest loan."

"Cheating a Sassenach at cards *is* a matter of honor among the Scots," said Robert gently.

"I never realized 'til now just how Scottish you are, Robert. I'll not soon forget it."

"I've no doubt you'll be throwing it in my face every chance you get. I'll stand at your side on any venture you care to undertake, Thomas, be it pirating, fighting, or else. But I'll not lift a hand against a Maclean."

"I never said anything about lifting a hand." Thomas was thoroughly revolted by Robert's theatrics. "I merely suggested that you convince Fia that she would be better matched with you. Then she would leave off taunting me."

"She taunts you?"

"Ceaselessly," Thomas ground out. "All you have to

do is act a small lie. You have ever been good at weaving stories."

"I'm not denying I've a silvered tongue," returned Robert with a grin.

"To hear you tell it, 'tis almost golden." Thomas sighed. "However, Fia is a very intelligent woman."

"Aye, she is. Intelligent and as fey as they come. Ah, that hair, those eyes, that skin, that—"

Thomas cut Robert off with a glare that would have caused any other person to swallow his own tongue. He had no need to be reminded of anything about Fia. He saw enough of her in his sleep to do him for a lifetime. "She is attractive." His scowl dared Robert to say else.

"She is a veritable goddess, all rounded curves and sweet light." Robert sighed soulfully.

Thomas wondered that someone had not yet put an end to Robert's annoying life. "You have the ability to try the patience of a saint, you pestilent cur. 'Tis a simple request."

"Not when you consider the history of the MacQuarries and the Macleans. 'Tis a sad story, that." Robert's face became mournful. "You see, once there was nothing but love between clan MacQuarrie and clan Maclean. Love and brotherhood. But all fell afoul when a certain Maclean prince played ill with a MacQuarrie lad over a woman—"

"Is this going to take long?"

"Nay. 'Tis a brief story, though poignant."

Thomas helped himself to more whiskey. Robert MacQuarrie did not know the meaning of the word *brief*.

"The MacQuarries requested retribution for the wrong played their kinsman, but the Macleans were resolute in defending the base actions of their prince. In retribution,

141

the MacQuarries were forced to steal all the Maclean sheep."

"Sheep thieves, eh? I can believe it."

"Forced by honor." Robert sighed. "A noble thing is honor. What happened next is recorded in the annals of history. The Maclean men sent all their bonny and fey women to the MacQuarrie camp." He stared blissfully off into the distance. "I must acknowledge that there are few with the beauty of the Maclean women, a fact you can see for yourself when beholding the fair Fia."

"What has this to do wi—"

"At first there was suspicion among the MacQuarrie men. But with much pleading and soft words, the Maclean women managed to convince the MacQuarries that they were angered at the stubbornness of their men and were forsaking the clan Maclean. Needless to say, there was much singing and rejoicing. So 'twas that after an evening of whiskey, ale, and much merriment, the MacQuarrie men awoke to find . . ." Robert paused dramatically.

"What? What did they find?"

"All their hair had disappeared." Robert's eyes were wide.

Thomas blinked. "*All* of it?"

Robert nodded. "Even from their most private areas. Thus MacQuarrie men *never* cross Maclean women and, of course, refuse to doff their hats in their presence."

Thomas blinked yet again. The room was fuzzy. He regarded the whiskey in his mug with suspicion. "Your whiskey is too strong, and that story is foolish."

Robert said nothing.

"God's Blood! You can't believe such a ridiculous tale."

" 'Tis a known fact that all great myths have a kernel

142

of truth in their telling. I'm afraid of what *other* than hair may have been missing."

Thomas was astounded. Somehow, he found himself gazing down at his codpiece while Robert laughed uproariously.

"You are the greatest fool to have ever graced the earth," Thomas muttered in disgust.

"Compliments will catch you no fish. I still refuse to help you. Furthermore," he added with a serious expression, "I think you would change your mind were you to actually see me or anyone else paying their addresses to your lovely bride."

Thomas stood. "You have been as useful as ever. However, I must now request that you leave me to the comforts of my bunk."

Robert looked around. "But this is my cabin."

Thomas grinned. "Nay, lackwit. You gave your cabin to me when you put that wench in mine." He lumbered to the bunk and sat upon the mattress, making a great show of testing its firmness.

Robert corked the whiskey bottle and gathered the mugs with an offended air. "I plan and plot to help you, and this is the thanks I receive. Very well. I'll share the cabin with you, but—"

"Nay," interrupted Thomas as he made himself comfortable on the small bunk. It was not the proper length, but he would make do.

"What do you mean, 'nay'?" asked Robert, his tone injured.

Thomas smiled, his eyes already closing. "I mean that we won't be sharing anything. You will bed below with the crew, or with Simmons in his cabin. In the meantime, I wish you well in keeping a hat on your pointed head during our voyage. 'Twill be difficult if the wind remains full."

After a great deal of huffing, Robert slammed the door behind him. Thomas smiled and slipped immediately off to sleep, his peace interrupted only once, when he dreamed of a black-eyed Scottish wench carrying a razor and looking with longing at the hair on his chest.

Chapter Thirteen

"Ye lazy mongrel! What if I had been a pirate or some-one as come to hurt the mistress?" Mary set a pan of water down on the table with a thump and eyed the dog that lay sprawled across the floor.

Zeus displayed his gums with a jaw-popping yawn.

Fia sat up on the bed and rubbed a weary hand over her brow. "I've a bit of a headache."

Mary regarded her narrowly. "What has his high-and-mighty lordship done to ye now?"

"Nothing. 'Tis just the motion of the sea."

"Hmph." Mary unhooked a worn leather bag from the crook of her arm and pulled out a small stack of soft woolen cloths. "I'll not believe a word of that tale. Ye've been asleep this past hour and more. I know because I looked in on ye three times, I did."

Fia sighed and stood, stretching the knots from her back. "Is it dark yet?"

"Nay." Mary hesitated, then reached for Fia's hand.

"Whist, now, lassie. Tell me what's the matter, what's a-hurtin' yer heart."

Fia swallowed the lump that rose in her throat. She had cried her last tear for that wretched, vexatious, addlepated fool, Thomas Wentworth. She'd not start again merely because someone showed her a bit of sympathy. "Nothing is hurting my heart, Mary. I've a headache, 'tis all." That, at least, was no lie.

Mary patted her hand. "Very well." She took a cloth and dipped it in the pan, wringing it out with a quick, practiced motion. She held it out to Fia and gave an admonitory frown. "Here, put this over yer eyes. They look as puffed up as pastries."

There was no arguing with Mary when she was determined. Fia slipped into a chair and applied the soft rag. The coolness soothed her swollen eyes, though it did nothing to diminish the inexplicable ache in her heart.

What was wrong with her? No matter what, she was on her way to London. Her dream was coming true. But she felt empty. Empty and bereft.

After a moment of silence, she peeped from under the rag. "Thank you, Mary. This feels wonderful."

Mary's cheeks creased into a smile as she marched to the door. " 'Twas nothin', lassie. I'll just go and fix ye up somethin' warm to drink. Ye sit quiet 'til I come back."

Fia nodded. She felt as weak as water. There weren't enough cool cloths or hot possets in the world to mend her.

Zeus roused himself enough to lumber across the room and throw himself in a boneless heap on Fia's feet. Fia wiggled her toes to massage his chest. After a moment, the dog gave a soft snore. Surely there was no other canine in the world so nerveless as her dear, beloved Zeus.

Mary marched back into the room, her energetic tread causing Zeus to whimper in his sleep. Fia could sympathize with him. She herself felt unequal to facing the maid's vigorous cheerfulness.

"There now, drink your posset." Mary set a steaming mug down before Fia. "The cook already had a pot of water boilin' away on the stove, he did. I told him as how 'twas fer ye, and he found a mug right swiftlike. Now drink that up afore ye go a-swoonin' away like that servant girl in one of yer stories."

Fia gave a reluctant grin. "Esmerelda in *The Isle of Witches*?"

"Aye." A wistful smile unfolded across Mary's plump face. "I do so love that one." She reopened her bag and dug into the very bottom. "That reminds me, lassie, where do ye wish me to put this?"

Fia stared at the narrow wooden box Mary held out to her. "My quills! I was looking for them."

"I didn't trust them to the laird's men fer safekeeping. Those louts would as soon break a thing as look at it." Mary glanced around and then headed for the table by the window. "I think I'd best put them here. Ye'll be wantin' to write soon. They'll be ready when ye're up to it."

Fia doubted she would be ready to write for a long time yet. She took a sip of the posset and welcomed the warmth that stole through her. The maid began to bustle about the room, seemingly intent on moving every item that was not nailed down.

Mary stopped by the trunk and pointed to the fabric trailing from it. "Is this the cloth from Duncan?"

"Aye." Fia smiled in wistful remembrance. She ached for his familiar face. "He sent enough to make twenty dresses."

Mary fingered the red silk with an appreciative nod. "It'll surprise ye how few dresses this'll make. And ye'll need more than a few so as to have proper clothin' fer the court. I hear tell the English change their clothes ever' time the clock chimes. As ye're a countess now, ye can't be runnin' about without the proper clothes."

Fia felt her throat tighten. Her knuckles clamped about the mug. "I won't be a countess for long, Mary."

Mary turned an incredulous look toward her. "Won't be a countess fer long? Why not?"

"Thomas and I talked, and we decided . . ." *To part.* The words stuck in her throat as painfully as a lump of cold, congealed pudding.

"Decided what?" Mary frowned. "Ye haven't gone and wrecked what yer cousin worked so hard fer, have ye?"

Fia gave a weak smile at the mention of Duncan's efforts to marry her off. For a moment, she wanted nothing more than to throw herself into his arms and cry like a wee lassie. But she was no longer a wee lassie, and Duncan was far away. She took a gulp of the steaming posset, blinking away the tears caused by the scalding liquid.

Mary looked from the mug to Fia's face and frowned. "Ye know, lassie, 'tis unladylike to suck down yer drink in one big swallow as though ye were a tavern wench."

Fia gave a watery chuckle. "Duncan was never one to notice such."

"Nay, he wasn't. Though 'tis not my place to say such, the laird was not always the proper guardian fer a lassie. Especially seein' as how he told ye there was no such thing as a good Englishman and then went and married ye off to the first one as fell into his hands."

"No matter what, Thomas was better than Malcolm Davies," Fia said.

"That's another thing. Why would the laird wish ye to marry a whey-faced measle like Malcolm the Maiden? I've been thinkin' about it, and I can't reconcile the idea of Duncan Maclean welcomin' that scalpeen into the family."

Fia nodded. It had seemed strange to her, too.

Mary leaned across the table. "Are ye goin' to tell me what the Sassenach said to make ye so sad?"

" 'Twas naught."

Mary sighed. "Would ye like a word of advice from an old hand at dealin' with menfolk?"

Before Fia could reply, Mary continued. "Have a talk with his high and mighty lordship about what'll happen to him when the laird finds out he has not treated ye with proper respect. That should take care of whatever problem it is ye're havin' with him."

Fia shook her head. "It wouldn't work, Mary. We have decided to have the marriage annulled."

"What?"

Fia winced and tried to pry her hand from Mary's rigid grip. "We have decided to—"

"I heard you the first time, I did." Mary slapped the surface of the table with a crack. "Well! We'll just see about this! If his high and mighty lordship thinks the laird will let him discard ye like unwanted baggage, then he has another thing comin' to him, and I, fer one, intend to see that he knows it." She started for the door, her back stiff and unyielding.

Fia jumped to her feet and rushed to head off the furious maid. "Nay! You'll do no such thing!" She planted herself between Mary and the door, her arms outstretched to either side. " 'Twas my suggestion!"

Mary rested her hands on her broad hips. "Why did ye suggest such a fool thing?"

"I don't know," said Fia miserably.

Mary regarded her for a moment. "Hmm. I see what 'tis now." She sighed and returned to the table, shaking her head. "Ye think ye're doin' him a favor by givin' him his freedom. But ye don't seem to realize that men don't always know what's good fer them. 'Tis up to women to tell them."

Fia sank into a chair across from Mary. "Thomas knows what he wants."

"They all think they do. My first husband, John MacAllister, the poor saint, was the richest man in Dalrie. He had over twenty cows, he did. And the biggest bull as ever lumbered across a field. Just about half the village paid rent to him, too."

Mary dampened a rag and began to scrub the table top with vigor. "He was properly set even without my bride price, which was no small amount. Why, I was so in awe of the man and his property, thinkin' I wasn't really bringin' much to the match meself, that I barely spoke a word to him fer the first three months of our marriage."

Fia had heard this story before, and it amazed her how much wealthier John MacAllister became with each telling.

"You can look at me like that if you wish, lassie, but 'tis God's truth. I didn't feel myself to be worth spit in a hot pan compared to the likes of John. But then, one day, I noticed his bull had wandered out the gate and was meanderin' toward town. So I mentioned it to him, sort of tentativelike." Mary planted her fists on her hips. "Do you know what he said to me?"

Fia knew no reply was expected.

"He said to me, 'Mary, now that's the reason I married ye.' And I never held my tongue again."

Fia grinned. She doubted the poor man ever had a chance to speak another word.

"Of course, that is neither here nor there. Ye need to think of a way to make his lordship realize how much he needs ye."

"But he doesn't need me. And I don't need him," Fia replied staunchly.

Mary threw her hands up in the air. "Och, now ye're speakin' like a crazed woman. Of course he needs ye!"

"For what?"

"How would I know? Use that head ye got on yer shoulders! By St. Peter, if'n ye can write them plays and such, then ye can figure out what use his lordship'll have fer ye. Ye never had to ask how to deal with the laird, now, did ye?"

Fia frowned. "Duncan was another matter."

"Aye, ye weren't in love with Duncan."

Fia felt her cheeks redden. "I'm not in love with Thomas." *Yet,* she silently added.

Mary arched her eyebrows. "Hmph. Well, either way, the road would be a mite easier if the Sassenach was with ye and not against ye."

"He's not against me. He's going to find a sponsor for my plays."

"How did ye wheedle that out of him?"

"I promised to testify to the queen that we hadn't consummated the marriage."

Mary rolled her eyes. "Lassie, if ye was dyin', I do believe ye'd offer to shovel yer own grave." She reached out and took one of Fia's hands between her own rough ones. "Ye know, lassie, ye mentioned before that 'twas fate as brought the Sassenach to the windowsill. If 'tis fate, then ye can't fight it."

Was she fighting fate? Was that why Thomas' promise to help with her plays now seemed a hollow victory?

"Fortunate fer ye, no one can be around ye long and not fall in love with ye. I've seen it many times, I have. Ye and his lordship need to spend some time together. If he's the one fer ye, ye'll know it soon enough."

Fia sighed. Perhaps there was something in what Mary said. So far the time she and Thomas had spent together had been heavily shadowed by Duncan's looming presence.

Mary patted her hand. "What do ye mean to do, lassie?"

"I need a plan."

"Hmph. I was never one as held with thinkin' overlong, but I'll do my best." There was silence as Mary settled her mind on the problem at hand. After a moment, her beefy fingers drummed a steady tattoo on the table.

Fia idly folded and refolded the damp rag Mary had used to scrub the table. The cloth was a soft wool, not unlike her own dresses. She grimaced at the thought and pushed it from her. Her clothing was fine for the cold, drafty confines of Duart Castle but not for the English court.

She wondered what attire Thomas would think appropriate. Probably gold brocade and red silk with enough jewels and embroidery to feed the entire clan for a whole year. Her gaze fell on her trunk, still opened, its contents spilling onto the floor.

She tilted her head to one side, considering the sweep of the red silk.

Mary's gaze followed hers to the trunk. " 'Twould be a start. We can make ye dresses fit fer a queen with such material." Her fingers drummed on the table with more rapidity. "In fact, with a little time and some proper thread, we can make ye some gowns as will have the entire court at yer feet."

Fia rested her chin in her hand. "Aye. I need to have more than rich clothing. Merely dressing like an English lady won't help if I don't know how to act."

She imagined herself sweeping into the English court, dressed in the red silk, gold dangling from her ears and neck. Everyone would be whispering about her, wondering who she was. A man, perhaps a prince, would come forward to ask her to dance. Thomas, at first astounded by her glowing presence, would turn crimson with jealousy. Fia smiled sweetly at the image. "I must *become* an English lady."

Mary's face fell. "Whyever would ye want to do that?"

" 'So I can prove to Thomas that I can find my own sponsor." She made a face. "I haven't exactly been at my best since he arrived."

"Aye, I suppose ye have something there," Mary said grudgingly. "What with shovin' him from the window and then thievin' from him at knifepoint, well, 'tis a wonder he'll stand in the same room with ye at all."

Fia rolled the damp rag into a ball. "That isn't the worst of it, Mary."

"What else is there?"

"He believes I enticed him into the hall without his clothing in order to let Duncan catch us."

There was a moment of stunned disbelief as Mary tried to comprehend this. "Why does he think you would do such a thing as that?"

"To force him to marry me."

"By havin' him chase ye through the castle without his clothes?" Mary's eyes seemed to start out of her head.

Fia gave a reluctant smile at Mary's exaggeration.

Mary rubbed the bridge of her nose with a thick finger. " 'Tis said a lack of roasted meat fer a prolonged time can cause a man to lose his ability to reason. I had thought 'twas an old wives' tale, but I'm beginnin' to see some truth in it." She heaved a sigh. "So what now, lassie?"

Fia smiled. "We'll begin to work on the dresses."

"And?" Mary urged.

"I think I'll go and have a word with Robert Mac-Quarrie." Fia nodded decisively and stood.

"That wastrel? What would ye be wantin' with him?"

Fia stopped by Mary's chair and gave the woman a

swift hug. "Because, Mary, if anyone can tell me how I should comport myself, it will be the dashing Robert. You saw him on the dock."

"Aye, he looked like an overdressed popinjay, if ye was to ask me."

"He was the very picture of an English gentleman. I've an idea he knows more about the English queen's court than the queen herself."

Mary returned the hug and gently shoved Fia toward the door. "Very well, then, off with ye! Take care speakin' to Lord Montley. He's got a tongue as sweet as honey, he does. Don't let him talk ye into doin' anything ye shouldn't."

"Nay. 'Tis Lord Montley as should have a care." Fia straightened her gown. It was one of her favorites but woefully plain. "Let's hope he's as willing to make a wager as I think him."

"A wager? A wager on what?"

Fia tucked a few strands of her hair back into place and wished it wouldn't curl so. There was no containing it.

"Well?" asked Mary impatiently.

Fia grinned. "On me, Mary. Lord Montley is going to place a wager on me."

Chapter Fourteen

Robert squinted, slowly lowering the mug to the top of the leaning stack. He had managed to pile no fewer than fourteen mugs of varying sizes into a complex tower. 'Twas a record, he was sure, though Simmons refused to say anything other than that it could not be done.

The most difficult part was adjusting for the constant shifting of the deck. He would swear that the first mate was sailing against the wind just to make his task more difficult.

As his hand lowered with the fifteenth and final vessel, he became aware of someone standing just beyond his range of vision. He forced himself to stay focused on his task. If he could just get this mug atop the pile without it falling over, Simmons would have to pay up. And as there was little else to do for entertainment than taunt the first mate, the building of this tower offered considerable amusement for Robert and discomfort for the doubting Simmons.

The person moved, and Robert became aware of a softly rounded bosom.

Such a bosom could not be ignored.

The mug tower wavered and then toppled to the deck with a rousing chorus of thunks and thuds.

Simmons gave a shout of laughter from the foredeck. Robert sighed. Well, it had been worth it. 'Twas a truly magnificent bosom.

"Lord Montley."

The voice drew a shiver from him. God's Breath, but as soon as they landed he would write a sonnet to that voice.

"Lady Fia." He rose to his feet and made an elaborate if unsteady bow. 'Twas perhaps unfortunate that he had felt the need to drink out of each mug before adding it to the stack. It hadn't been precisely necessary to win the wager; 'twas more a question of style. He quickly lowered himself to sit upon a barrel.

"You've been drinking." The lush voice carried a touch of reproof, and he was instantly apologetic.

"Aye. Perhaps we should wait to speak until—"

"Nay," she interrupted.

Robert arched his eyebrows. "Very well, then." He looked about and then gestured toward another barrel. "May I offer you a seat?"

"Nay, I would prefer to stand."

She looked magnificent on the open deck, the wind tugging at her skirts and hair.

He would have kissed her had he not been so lamentably drunk and she so damnably innocent. Innocent . . . and married to his best friend, of course. He grinned. How could he have forgotten *that?*

"If you remain standing, then I shall have to stand as well, and I fear I'm not capable of maintaining my balance for a prolonged period just now," Robert said.

He dusted off the barrel beside his and patted it.

"Come and sit. 'Twould crumple my ruff should I lift my chin to such a height."

She laughed and hopped easily onto the barrel. He noted she was innately graceful doing even the most awkward of things. The swaying of the deck hardly affected her, either. She seemed a born sailor.

"Lord Montley, I—"

"Pray, call me Robert. There is no need for formality between us, as we are nearly family. Thomas is as a brother to me."

"I see." She smoothed her skirts over her knees. "You must know his lordship very well then."

Robert wondered what she wanted. If there was one thing his sisters had taught him, it was to beware a woman who wanted something. Like a small but steady dripping of water, they could wear away stone did they deem it worth the effort.

With the wariness of experience, he answered, "We've been close these past six years."

"Six years?" She slanted him a look redolent with doubt. "That's all? Then there is probably much you do not know."

Her eyes were the velvet black of midnight with the veriest tinge of amber in their depths, Robert noted.

"Lord Robert? You don't answer."

He blinked. She was speaking, and he sat as witless as a bag of pudding, staring into her eyes. "Forgive me, fair damsel. I was lost in wonder at thy beauty."

She frowned impatiently. "Pray, listen."

Robert's lips twitched, but he replied meekly, "Forgive my impertinence. What is it you wish of me?"

Fia spoke plainly. "I wish to know what Lord Wentworth would require of a wife."

A faint pink brushed her cheeks, and Robert was hard pressed not to run a hand over their heated smoothness.

Sweet Jesu, but Thomas must be mad to want to be rid of such a comely maid.

He called himself to order with an effort. "That's a difficult question."

She stared at him, her heart bared for him to see. She was fond of Thomas—more than fond, if the sincerity of her gaze held any meaning. Robert was aware of a sudden and surprising pang. 'Twas an intoxicating madness, made worse by his drunken state.

He leaned forward, pulling her toward him by the simple expediency of capturing her hands and gathering them to his chest. He smiled into her eyes with his best, most winsome smile. "Forsooth, 'tis rare that a maid I hold so close can think of any other than me."

Her dark eyes met his squarely. "I think it more rare that you, Lord Montley, think aught of any other than yourself, whether holding a maid or not."

He was left like a ship in the midst of a great lull, with nary a breath of wind.

She chuckled, and he found himself laughing with her. She reminded him of his sister, Aindrea. Like Fia, Aindrea was a dreamer, yet very practical when occasion demanded.

He opened his arms. "I cede victory to you! Ask what you will."

Fia grinned and pulled her hands free. "What does Thomas look for in a wife?"

"You seem particularly fond of that question. May I sell you another?" He blinked owlishly at her, and she had to fight the urge to grin. He really was a charming scamp.

"Thomas has made it plain that I'm not at all what he desires. I wish to know what type of a wife would suit him." The words pained her, yet she thought she had done well in speaking them so lightly.

Robert shrugged. "A small question with an answer

as big as the sea. Perhaps 'twould be best answered by the man himself."

She plucked at her skirt with nervous fingers. " 'Tis not a question one can easily ask."

"Hmm. I can see where 'twould be awkward." He stroked his trim beard thoughtfully. "You're mistaken if you think he has some mystery list of qualities he would seek in a wife. In truth, I don't think he's ever really considered it."

"But if he had no expectations, why is he so opposed to me?"

"Ah, now we approach the heart of the matter. The problem lies not so much in what you aren't but in what you are."

"And I am?" she prompted.

"Perfect for him," he said simply.

"Nay. He's made it abundantly plain that's not true."

"He's not sure how to take you. You're different from the ladies who languish about court."

"How?"

"Well, you don't lie through your pretty teeth, nor disguise a prickly heart in rustling satins. Fie on them all, Fia! You've much more to offer than they."

Fia's heart lifted a little. "You flatter me shamelessly, but I don't think Thomas agrees."

"Thomas doesn't believe good can come from any marriage. His father soured him to the idea long before you appeared."

"It doesn't help that he believes I trapped him into wedding me." She caught a quizzical gleam in Robert's gaze and hurriedly added, "Which I would never do."

Robert shrugged. "Did he love you, it wouldn't matter."

"Did he love you . . ." To her surprise, a shaft of pain

159

shot through her as surely as if he had drawn an arrow and loosed it at her heart. She cast a furtive glance at Robert, afraid he would see her reaction, but he was staring off at the blue horizon, his eyes unfocused, unseeing.

After a moment, he began to speak in a low voice. "Thomas Wentworth is a man who has known nothing but wealth and success. 'Tis a family inheritance of a sort." He pursed his lips thoughtfully. "You could call it a curse and not be far wrong."

"Being blessed with success is a curse?"

Robert turned to look at her, seeming to measure her sincerity before he answered. When he spoke, his voice was quiet. "Do you know what it's like to be known as the luckiest man alive? 'Tis the most damnable thing. The whole world begins to plan your downfall. Oh, not intentionally." He shrugged. " 'Tis just that one success must lead to another. Thus, the more luck you have, the more daring the wager you are expected to take. The more successful you are, the more dangerous your next assignment."

"Assignment?"

Robert hesitated, a shadow crossing his face. "Assignment, or wager, or queenly request—it matters naught. It matters only that you win yet again. Thomas has worked since childhood to become an excellent rider, a master tactician, an outstanding swordsman, a sea captain without rival."

"By the saints, is there anything he can't do?"

Robert shook his head. "Not much. Such accomplishments would earn any other man esteem and praise. Yet with all this, he is only doing what is expected of him. He is a Wentworth, you see, and Wentworths never fail." His smile twisted with bitterness. "His father saw to it that he would never forget."

"Thomas has never mentioned his father. He did say something about his mother once."

"Nothing good, I'd wager," said Robert. "He was raised to believe the worst of his mother—of all women, really. She's the blight on the family name, the one proof that the Wentworth luck may not be what all believe it."

"What did she do?"

Robert leaned back, staring out at the endless ocean. "She left them both, Thomas and his father. Ran off with a stable hand. Thomas's father was livid. Not because she had left, but because she had done it in a manner that tarnished the perfection of the Wentworth name."

"How sad for Thomas."

"Exactly. His father became an embittered man. He was determined that no Wentworth would ever be subjected to such humiliation again. He taught Thomas to trust no one."

"Especially women."

Robert's blue gaze rested on her gently for a moment. "Can you understand now why he has never thought of marriage?"

Fia nodded, a lump in her throat. She could almost see the bereft young boy as he lost both his mother and the love of his father in one fell swoop.

"Surely he trusts someone," she said. "He must trust you."

Robert smoothed a hand over his sleeve. "He tries."

Fia wondered at the emotion in Robert's voice.

His eyes darkened. "I owe him more than I can ever repay." He stared back out at the ocean. Fia thought he looked beyond the white-capped swells. After a moment, he turned to her. "Do you know why some call me the coward of Balmanach?"

Though she had heard tales, she shook her head.

He read the truth in her face. "Aye, you do. Yet you know only half the story." He brushed at the fine lace

161

on his cuff, seeming intent on adjusting it across his elegant hands. "My parents were murdered while returning from my uncle's house. My uncle himself gave me the news. He could scarcely contain his triumph. Their blood still glistened on his sword."

"But I thought the MacDonald clan had ambushed them."

Thin white lines of tension bracketed his mouth. "That's what my uncle wanted everyone to think."

"Was there no one to help you?"

He gave a mirthless smile. "He told me of his deed, bragged of it in front of three of the clan leaders. No one would take my part against him. I was given a choice. I could either stay and fight for my right as laird, or I could run as far from Mull as my feet could carry me."

There was a pause, then he said, "I chose to run. I had five sisters who looked to me. I couldn't let them down, let them die in a contest I would surely lose."

Fia felt tears prick her eyelids. "How old were you?"

"Just sixteen. Man enough to know when I was beaten, yet child enough to taste the full bitterness of defeat. I knew my duty."

"You saved your sisters."

He nodded. "The oldest, Aindrea, was only eleven. The rest were babes, the twins just turned two. Had I stayed, it would have been the death of my sisters and any who sided with me." His face hardened, and Fia caught a glimpse of the iron hidden beneath Robert's silks and laces. "My uncle never intended for us to survive. If he did not kill us, he fully expected the winter cold to do so on our flight. And, indeed, we would have died a miserable death if not for Thomas."

"What did he do?"

"We made it as far as the border, begging for food and stealing what we could. Snow began to fall, and we were desperate for shelter. Though we didn't know it, we were on Wentworth land. We crawled into the stables and huddled in the hay, thankful for the warmth."

"And Thomas found you."

"Aye. He brought us to his house and treated us as guests. His father ranted and raved about how we would take advantage of him, how we would use him and his good fortune and then desert him."

"Like his mother."

Robert nodded. "Thomas wouldn't listen. I think he has always wanted someone or something to prove that his father was wrong." He sighed and raked a hand through his hair. "Thomas is caught between what he was taught and what he wants to learn."

Fia looked down at her hands. They were clenched in front of her, the knuckles white. "I need your help, Robert. I have a plan."

She thought he'd refuse. Instead, he leveled a gaze at her. "Does it involve helping Thomas to trust?"

She hesitated, then nodded. Robert deserved the truth. "Aye. I believe it does. Though it might require a bit of harmless trickery first."

His smile dawned slowly, his eyes crinkling with mirth. "Then I am yours, milady. What do you require of me?"

"Teach me what I need to know to win over the English court."

"All of it?"

"All of it."

He gave a low whistle. "Well, if anyone could teach you, 'twould be me. The queen herself has noted the elegance of my dancing, the sharpness of my wit, the grace of my manners."

"Good." She stood. "We've less than two weeks."

"Two weeks?" He looked as if his ruff had suddenly been drawn too tight.

"Aye. I want to be prepared when we reach London. Of course, if you cannot do it, I will understand. I'm sure there are limits to even your abilities."

His eyes gleamed in appreciation. "I've never backed away from a challenge in my life."

" 'Tis done, then. I wager you can't teach me all I need to know to become a lady of the English court by the time we meet the queen."

He smoothed his trim beard and regarded her narrowly. "What are you up to, I wonder?" he murmured.

She met his gaze squarely. "There are times when even fate needs a bit of a hand."

His eyes twinkled like a rising star. "You'll have to promise to work hard. There are dances to learn, titles to memorize, and all manner of other things."

She nodded, excitement pooling in her stomach. "I will work night and day."

"Daytime should be sufficient. Were we to continue at night, I fear my life would be forfeit to the strong hands of your husband."

"Do you think he'll mind?"

Robert said nothing. He merely looked at her with such a knowing expression, she felt her whole intent must be writ across her face for all the world to see.

Suddenly, he gave a crack of laughter. "Saints, I *will* do it! 'Twill madden Thomas no end, but I'll teach you. When I'm finished, you'll have manners fit for a queen. What will be our wager?"

Fia bit her lip. "If you fail, then you will find me a sponsor for my plays from among your friends at court." If this plan didn't work, at least she would have the satisfaction of having her plays published.

He pursed his lips. "Are they of any merit, these plays of yours?"

"Aye," she returned smartly. "They are excellent!"

"By whose report?"

She blushed. In truth, they hadn't been read by any she would call knowledgeable. "By mine. You may read them if you wish."

He burst out laughing, grabbing her hands and pulling her back onto the barrel. "Softly! I was but torturing you. I will find a sponsor for your plays and gladly."

"Very well. Then we have a wager."

"Hold, lady! There are two parts to any wager. We have settled yours. Now we will settle mine."

She eyed him warily. "Well?"

He grinned. "I'll not tell you as of yet. Just know that you owe it to me, and you are pledged to pay when this scene is played out."

"You won't tell me more?" she asked incredulously.

"I promise it won't compromise either your virtue or your honor."

She bit her lip and looked at him uncertainly. "I don't know."

"The things I could teach you!" He leaned close and whispered, "You will be the desire of every man at court, the most accomplished woman since Elizabeth to walk through Hampton Palace! Thomas will be awed by your grace and talents. How can you say nay?"

She considered him from under lowered eyelashes. The picture he painted was almost too appealing. His confident words combined with the absurdity of his grin reassured her. He was as impish as a child, but there was no harm to him.

"Very well," she agreed. "I pledge, but only on the understanding that if your wager seems too harsh, I have the right to forfeit."

"Done!" He stood and pulled her to her feet. "Come. We've no time to waste. You must learn the most important skill of a lady in the queen's court."

"Aye? And what would that be?"

"Use of a fan."

"A fan?" She blinked. What use would she have of a fan?

"Aye. And once you have mastered the rudiments of the fan, we dance!"

Fia allowed herself to be swept along by Robert's enthusiasm, her excitement building. 'Twas a gamble, but then, this had been a chancy venture since the beginning. Only now there was much more at stake than mere dreams. Now there was the little matter of her heart.

Chapter Fifteen

Everywhere he looked, there they were. Thomas couldn't decide which would relieve his torment the quicker, knocking that damned knowing look from Robert's face or locking Fia in the safe confines of the hold.

Either the pair was in the comfort of his own cabin, exchanging exaggerated compliments and sallies with enough wit and archness to mock the most jaded of the queen's court, or else they were seated on deck, discussing for hours the merits of linen to silk, of silk to lace, of lace to brocade. And all with enough laughter and merriment to lead Thomas to believe they spoke of some scandalously naughty topic other than fashion.

Despite his best intentions, he found himself hovering nearby, straining his ears for the nature of their conversation. Robert was evidently beside himself with joy, and Thomas could have cheerfully killed him.

The music from a lone flute drifted through the air to tickle his eardrums. He frowned, waving a hand as though to shoo the strands of music away. A barrage of rhythmic clapping told him the likely location of his entire crew.

Fia had bewitched them all. No doubt every man on ship was at this moment admiring her trim ankles as she whirled about on Robert's arm, learning the latest Italianate dances so favored by Queen Elizabeth.

Thomas ground his teeth. The sooner he put a stop to this nonsense, the better. The only problem was how to do it without appearing a fool. Every time he attempted to complain to Robert of Fia's sudden, indecorous frivolity, the handsome wag would expound on the sin of envy until Thomas was ready to explode.

He was not jealous. He was merely concerned about the spectacle Robert was making of an innocent maid.

And that was what she was, Thomas decided with conviction. An innocent maid unaware of the dangers represented by a frippery knave like Robert. For a moment Thomas heard his own voice, harshly accusing Fia of slyly tricking him into this marriage, and a distinct feeling of guilt nipped him.

He winced and ran a hand through his hair. Upon being forced to wed, he had been angry with the world. He knew Fia was innocent of that deception, as much a victim in Duncan Maclean's plans as was Thomas. 'Twas for that reason she should be warned of Robert's low purposes.

Thomas hoped Fia hadn't already fallen for Robert's smooth, idle ways. Surely she didn't mistake his overblown gallantry for anything more than the impulse of a moment. Thomas stared down over the rail at the dancing couple, noticing the way Fia's hand rested so trustingly on Robert's arm.

A thought assailed him. If Fia could lavish affection on a broken-down nag and a half-blind dog, 'twasn't difficult to imagine her response to Robert's oft-delicate but decidedly worldly wit. Thomas swore long and eloquently under his breath.

He must save her. He must save his wife.

His wife? How easily the thought had come to his mind! Sweet Jesu, but he would find a way to separate Robert from Fia if it took sailing through hell to do it. 'Twas becoming painfully obvious that Robert was the most determined seducer of women to ever step onto English soil, and Thomas wondered what madness had possessed him to ask such a feckless bounder to woo his own wife.

Fia's laughter drifted above the clamor, and Thomas was as drawn to the sound as a moth was to flame. He glared down at the dancing duo. Fia's skirts flew higher and higher with every turn she made on Robert's arm, and the sight made Thomas as queasy as a cabin boy on his first voyage.

He would make haste to reach London. The less time the chit spent in Robert's presence, the better.

Thomas looked about for Simmons. The portly first mate was nowhere to be seen. In fact, Thomas was completely alone on the foredeck. He leaned farther over the railing.

Simmons, his stomach peeping from beneath his too-tight shirt, was now holding Fia's hands. Under Robert's tutelage, Simmons pranced through the intricate steps of a whimsical French dance. His round face perspired freely, his chin to his chest as he stared at his feet. Robert stood to one side and shouted instructions as the couple passed near.

"Simmons!" Thomas bellowed.

There was a satisfying and abrupt halt to the mewl of the flute. Simmons made a quick, awkward bow to Fia and scurried to the ladder.

Thomas was about to order the men back to their tasks when the fluting began again. There was an immediate

169

resumption of merriment as Fia began to whirl about on Robert's arm, her skirts flying once again, her bare feet skimming over the weathered planks. Thomas dropped his head into his hands. *God grant I live long enough to buy that Scottish hoyden a decent number of petticoats and at least one pair of slippers.*

He lifted his head just in time to see Fia raise her face to Robert. There was such joy, such happiness in her expression that Thomas held his breath. *By the saints, but she is lovely.*

"Cap'n?"

"What?" he snapped, glaring at Simmons.

"Ye yelled fer me?" The first mate's face was red from his exertion.

"Call the crew and turn eastward. We'll draw more sail and be well sped along our course."

Simmons squinted up at the rigging, doubt plain on his face. He scratched the seat of his loose britches thoughtfully. "I'll turn her if ye wish it, though I doubt we'll catch a swifter wind than we've got."

Thomas raised his eyebrows, and Simmons's face turned purple. "Not that I'm questionin' yer orders, Cap'n! 'Tis just that we're making right smart time as 'tis."

"Trim the sail and turn her, Simmons. Now."

"Aye, Cap'n." Simmons bawled the orders, and the flute once again ceased. Thomas eyed his crew as they scrambled to obey. He would keep them all scrubbing and cleaning and so tired that not a one would remember having seen his wife's ankles. He strode from the deck with a feeling of satisfaction.

"Amazing the effect marriage has on some men."

Thomas turned on his heel to face Robert.

The Scotsman pursed his lips. "Strange how you seem to resent anything that might bring Fia pleasure."

Thomas's eyes narrowed. There was tension beneath

Robert's polished veneer, and 'twas obvious the fool was spoiling for a fight. The idea had some merit. A good thumping might very well turn Robert's thoughts away from Fia.

If nothing else, Thomas could make sure the libertine was in no condition to dance for the rest of the voyage.

"If we turn with the wind, we'll make London by midweek." Thomas cocked an eyebrow at Robert. "We have a missive to deliver, remember? Lord Walsingham will expect us to use all possible speed."

"You weren't thinking of that damned letter, and you know it. You ordered the men back to work to keep them from looking upon the fair Fia."

Thomas closed the space between them until they stood toe to toe. "Do not speak so freely of my wife."

"Oho! Your wife, eh? She's only yours until you gain an audience with the queen. After that . . ." Robert shrugged. "After that, she's fair game to anyone who wishes to pursue her."

"What do you mean by that?"

Robert's smile mocked. "Once you cast her aside, she won't be alone for long. There will be others hard upon your heels. Best you get used to the idea now."

Thomas seized Robert's doublet and hauled him forward until but a hair's breadth separated them. "Fia is my wife until the queen says otherwise. Keep your distance, do you hear?"

"But 'twas by *your* insistence that I spent time with her!"

Thomas frowned. He hadn't meant for Robert to charm Fia into insensibility, dancing about the ship for all to see. At no time had he suggested such a vulgar display. He shoved Robert away. "It doesn't matter. Leave her."

Robert laughed. "I vow, Thomas, you are a jealous husband. I'd not have credited it."

"I am not jealous."

"Of course you aren't. You merely hate to see another man look upon her, speak with her, or smile at her. If that doesn't sound like jeal—"

"Don't say it," Thomas snapped.

Robert shrugged. "As you wish. I will cease to mention how similar your outbursts are to those of a man deeply in love. My lips shall remain locked against—"

With a furious curse, Thomas stalked away. He *was* jealous. Jealous beyond reason over a wife he didn't even want.

"I said," Robert repeated with exaggerated loudness, " 'tis yet your turn. But should you need more time to stare out at yonder hostile sea, I will continue to await your pleasure."

"Och, now, ye leave the mistress be," said Mary, her red curls ruffled by the brisk wind. "She's thinkin', she is. Ye wouldn't have her play the wrong card, would ye?"

"The wrong card would be better than none at all," grumbled Robert. "I age as we sit."

Fia forced her attention back to the game. She selected a card at random and tucked it under the mug that weighted the loose discards. She couldn't help it. She had never been on a ship before, and she found the view ever exhilarating. Besides, watching the waves kept her from thinking about Thomas, something the slowness of the card game did not.

The sea surged green and blue as white caps rocked the ship. The wind licked at the cards on the barrel, trying to pull them free. Fia lifted her face to the sun. She would write a play about a pirate, she decided. A pirate with golden hair and honey-brown eyes.

Mary plucked a card from her own hand and started to lay it down. She halted, her fingers hovering a scant inch above the barrel, her face puckered in thought.

"Are you playing that godforsaken card, or aren't you?" Robert demanded, his gaze now fixed on Mary's hand.

"I'm puttin' it down now, ye cankerous maw worm!" Mary slapped the card onto the barrel.

"Praise St. Peter," said Robert. He stared at his own cards, absently chewing his lip.

"Don't ye just sit there like a lump! If 'tis against the rules fer me to take a second to look at me cards, then 'tis against the rules fer ye."

Fia swallowed a giggle. Had the game not needed at least three persons, she knew Robert would have forgone Mary's company with pleasure. Fia wondered that he hadn't called Thomas to play. She had been part hopeful, part fearful, he would do just that. But instead, he had cajoled a reluctant Mary to join them.

Fia regarded Robert from under her lashes. Since their conversation, he had been true to his word, working ceaselessly to teach her the ways of the court. He had shown her the proper way to curtsey and address the queen. He had talked to Mary about clothing and how best to use the fabric sent by Duncan.

Mary had favored the man with her own form of approval. "He's a mite too French fer my taste, but he does know his way with fashion," she had explained to Fia.

From Mary, that was high praise indeed.

Robert pulled a card from his hand and slid it under the mug. "Your turn, Fia, my sweet."

She blinked at the makeshift table. What, exactly, were they playing? She could scarce remember.

Robert sighed. "For the love of . . ." He crossed his arms and stared at her like a stern tutor. "I think you've a touch of ague."

"Now, you leave the lassie alone," admonished Mary. "She's a lot on her mind."

Fia stared at her cards. She had lain awake most of the night, her mind full of plans revolving around her triumphant appearance in court and the successful reception of her plays.

And Thomas. Especially Thomas.

She plucked a card from her hand and placed it on the barrel.

"I win," said Robert.

"Ye do not!" protested Mary.

"I do, too." He waved at the cards. "Look."

Mary looked. "Who played the knave?"

Fia bit her lip. " 'Twas me."

"Surely ye didn't! I think he's cheatin'."

Robert clutched at his heart. "I would never cheat such beauteous women!"

"Don't waste yer airs on me, Robert MacQuarrie. A no-good lazy wastrel is what ye are."

Robert gave a roguish grin. "Words fall from thy lips like rubies, sparkling in the sun with blinding truth."

Mary nodded at Fia. "He's a blithering idiot, but he has the MacQuarrie charm." She placed her cards on the barrel and stood. "As much as I'd like to stay and waste away the mornin', I need to get to work makin' yer dresses. Don't stay too long, lassie. I'll need yer help once I get ready to pin the material." She patted Fia's arm before she left.

Robert gathered the cards and shuffled them with an elegant twist of his wrists. "Come! There's another game I would teach you."

Fia looked at the cards Robert dealt, listening with half an ear as he explained the rules. 'Twas difficult concentrating on such a glorious day. Though the ocean was rough, the sky was a clear, cerulean blue.

"Are you well, my lady?"

Fia glanced up and caught Robert's concerned gaze.

"Aye, I'm just a mite weary. I haven't been able to sleep much of late."

"Hmm. Thomas seems to suffer the same ailment. It's made him most ill-natured. Twice now he has threatened to toss me overboard, and for no fault of mine." Robert cast a furtive glance over his shoulder before whispering, "I think your plan is working."

Fia raised her eyebrows. "We haven't been to court yet. How can you tell?"

Robert gave a knowing smile. "Not that plan. The other one."

"There was no other plan," she said stiffly.

"No?" His gaze focused over her shoulder. "Here cometh the mighty earl now."

Thomas strode across the deck. His white linen shirt hung in graceful folds over his powerful chest.

Fia swallowed. Images from her dreams flashed before her eyes, making her stomach tighten and her breasts tingle in an alarming fashion.

Robert waited until Thomas was almost upon them before saying loudly, "While 'tis true, Lady Fia, that the married women of the court are not the most discreet of lovers, 'twould be an error to allow the queen to become aware of your dalliances."

Fia heard a choked exclamation from Thomas. It was all she could do to keep from laughing at Robert's ever so guileless expression. No one knew better than Robert how to tweak Thomas's temper.

The Scotsman laid a card on the barrel and gave her a singularly sweet smile. " 'Tis your draw, beauteous maid."

Fia drew a card, biting her lip to stifle her laughter.

"Montley, I have been looking for you," Thomas said sharply.

"And you have found me. I trow, 'tis a wondrous life."

Thomas scowled. "You are needed on the foredeck."

"I fear I cannot leave, bold captain of the seas."

"Why not?"

"I'm pledged to Lady Fia."

Fia knew they both looked at her, but she kept her gaze firmly fixed on her cards.

"She'll survive without your presence. 'Tis time you ceased this foolishness and earned your keep. Simmons thinks there's a storm brewing. We need to ready the ship before nightfall."

"But I am a guest," Robert protested.

"If you don't like it, then leave."

"How could he leave?" Fia asked. "We're at sea."

Thomas's eyes glinted with amusement. "Precisely."

Robert shook his head sadly. "Whilst a swim would be pleasant, I fear 'twould ruin my new doublet."

"Most likely," said Thomas, devoid of sympathy.

"I vow, but you're unreasonable," huffed Robert.

"And you are late. Simmons awaits you."

Robert sighed heavily. "Very well. As soon as Lady Fia and I finish this hand, I will go."

"For the love of God, Montley! Give you a deck of cards, and all the world may go to hell with your blessing."

Thomas raked a hand through his hair, and Fia yearned to smooth it back into place.

"Just one hand, Thomas. Come and watch." Robert patted the barrel next to his invitingly.

After a long moment, Thomas sighed. "Very well, though I'm sure I'll regret this." He sat and crossed his arms with the air of a man determined to see some unpleasant business through to its inevitable end. "Make haste. We've work to do."

Fia noted how tired Thomas appeared. Fatigue brought a sharpness to his face that only increased its handsomeness. She wondered if he had been as disturbed by dreams as she had. A bubble of hope filled her.

"My sweet, do you discard?"

Fia dragged her gaze back to her cards. She chose one at random and slid it under the mug.

Robert clucked his tongue. "Ah, Lady Fia. I begin to suspicion you harbor unexpected depths. *Gutta cavat lapidem non vi sed saepe cadenda.*"

When Thomas's eyebrows lowered, Fia leaned forward to explain. "He said, 'The drop hollows the stone not by force but by falling often.' "

"I know what he said," Thomas replied defensively. "I just didn't see how it applied."

"He thinks I'm pretending to lose merely to catch him unawares."

Robert blew her a kiss. "*Bien, mon amour!* You have explained me better than I could have myself. Ah, the burdens of genius! Understood by so few." He sighed and stared at the sea, as if beholding some invisible sign of his greatness.

Thomas snorted. "Crack-brained fool."

"You see what I have to contend with?" Robert asked Fia.

"Play the damned game or be done," said Thomas.

Robert made a great show of choosing a card. "I trow, 'tis a difficult decision when there's so much at stake."

"At stake? There's a wager?" asked Thomas.

"Aye," said Robert sweetly. "We play for kisses."

"*What?*" Thomas roared. He stood, pulling Fia with him, heedless of the damage he inflicted on the cards she held. "Enough of this nonsense. Robert has duties to attend to. Return to the cabin."

Fia pulled her hands free and dropped back onto her seat. "I'm staying where I am. Robert and I have a game to play." She smoothed a crumpled card and tossed it onto the barrel. She hated being ordered about like the veriest drudge, and the sooner he realized it, the better.

"Fine," Thomas said. He sat. "Deal me in."

Fia and Robert exchanged a glance.

Robert gave an elegant shrug and gathered the cards. She cleared her throat. "But . . . if you win . . ."

"If I win," Thomas said calmly, "then the kiss is mine."

Her stomach gave a strange lurch of excitement. "What if I win?"

"Then you, comfit, can kiss me."

She felt as if he caressed her with his smile.

"Hold!" Robert's voice intruded. "What of me? I may yet win the kiss for myself."

Thomas gathered his cards. " 'Twould be unfortunate if you did."

Robert smirked. "For whom?"

"For you."

"Sweet Jesu, Thomas! 'Tis ill-mannered to threaten a man whilst he is playing cards. You break my concentration."

"Good."

"Fortunately for you, I thrive on challenges. Shall we sweeten the pot?"

Thomas's gaze lingered on Fia. "I think the pot sweet enough."

It was the most agonizing game she had ever played. Not because of the tension between the two men, but because in their determination to win the game, they completely ignored her.

When they twice missed her turn without noticing, Fia threw her cards down on the barrel. Neither did more than glance up until the wind tried to carry the thin placards away. For a moment, they were occupied in gathering and placing the lost cards into the discard pile. Then, with the air of men achieving greatness, they settled back on their respective seats and lost themselves to the delicious game of strategy and counter strategy.

She was utterly forgotten while the two fools competed for her. 'Twas ludicrous. With a muffled exclamation, she rose. "I'll take my leave. Mary needs me below."

"Very well, my sweet," answered Robert absently.

"Anon," answered Thomas, his regard solely for the card Robert slid under the edge of the mug. "Aha! Now I have you! You play like a damned novice, Montley."

Fia turned on her heel and marched away. Only once, as she reached the steps to descend into the hold, did she look back.

Robert stared at his cards with a rapt expression, lost to everything but the game. But Thomas's gaze met Fia's. His knowing smile confirmed her growing suspicion.

The bounder had done it apurpose. He had cut her out of the game as cleanly as a knife slid through warm butter.

Chapter Sixteen

Fia flipped the fan open and turned it toward her, admiring the rich colors of the painted silk. A pastoral scene decorated one panel. It presented a man asleep in the golden grasses of a sun-drenched field, his long, bare legs peeping through the wheat. A covey of young, buxom nymphs admired him with wandering hands, their nudity barely covered with garlands of flowers.

She held the fan before the window and examined it more closely. The man lay naked, and the grass was very inadequate to cover his nether areas. She gazed anew at his face. "Sweet St. Catherine, 'tis Robert MacQuarrie."

She shut the fan with a snap. Only Robert would own such a fan so daringly painted with his likeness. She grinned. Perhaps she should wonder aloud to him why the nymphs were so enthralled with such a plump little man. Aye, that should tease him well enough. Of all things Robert abhorred, to be thought plain or ordinary burned him the most.

Fia danced around the cabin, an imaginary partner clasped in her arms. It had been pleasant to whirl around the deck, her feet moving with the music. It had been even more pleasant to have Thomas staring at her with such interest.

'Twas a pity he hadn't won the card game, she thought. She had waited impatiently for the outcome, pacing the cabin until Mary had sent her away. Robert had met her in the corridor. There was no mistaking the triumph in his blue eyes. Fortunately, before he could claim his kiss, Thomas had appeared and demanded his presence on deck.

Fia sniffed. Her husband was a mite high-handed. 'Twas probably for the best he'd lost the game.

Mary had been right. Fate was what you made it.

Fia marched out the door of the cabin. She would just practice her wiles on some of the sailors on deck. Simmons would be good for a beginning.

She approached the ladder leading up to the deck just as a shadow darkened the opening. She fluttered the fan. Robert had vowed there was little so entrancing as a pair of feminine eyes peering over the edge of a fan. Not only did it draw attention to the beauty of one's eyes, he had explained, but it screened the rest of the face from view, and there was not a man alive as could withstand a mystery.

She peeped over the edge, lowering her lids to give a sultry expression. Robert had specifically taught her this trick. He swore such a look would render her admirer speechless. She glanced up through her lashes at her intended victim.

"God's Blood! Where did you get that?" Thomas's voice dripped with disgust.

Her smile froze into a grimace behind the fan. " 'Tis a thing of beauty, isn't it? Milord Robert was most kind in allowing me the use of it."

181

"Then return it to him. You look a fool."

Behind the fan her lips pressed into a straight line. "Nay, I am told 'tis all the fashion."

His hand shot out and gripped her wrist, forcing the fan down. "To the devil with fashion," he said. "I wish to speak with you."

"Och, my lord, I am greatly honored," she said, curling her lip. She retrieved her captured hand with an awkward jerk of her arm.

This was not going the way she had imagined. He was supposed to smile and respond in turn, as Robert did, not glare at her as though she were some disagreeable child. Or, at the least, he should look at her with more interest. Nothing in her brief time with Robert had informed her what to do if her partner began to eye her as though she were a two-headed snake.

Perhaps she had not plied the fan correctly. She tried again.

"I look forward to hearing what you have to say. May I suggest that we go somewhere . . . more private?" She gave him a languishing glance through her lashes.

"Sweet Jesu, what has that devil's spawn been teaching you? You sound and look like a—" His mouth opened and shut, but he seemed unable to continue.

"Robert has been showing me your English ways." She didn't mean to sound so defiant, but it irked that he did not recognize her grand new manners and beautiful fan for what they were.

" 'Tis absurd. I'll not have you wandering about the deck acting like an addlepated fool." Thomas scowled.

"I will wander where I wish and act as I wish. You have no claim over me."

"For as long as you carry my name, you will do as I say."

Before she could frame a reply, he grabbed her wrist and stalked toward his cabin, pulling her behind him like an unruly horse. He hauled her through the doorway and then kicked it shut with a firmness that denied argument.

Fia's heart pounded. This was not the reaction she had expected. She stared pointedly at his hand where it gripped her wrist. With an impatient noise, he let her go and began pacing the short length of the room with huge, restless strides.

Fia tapped the palm of her hand with the closed fan. By the saints, but the man was spoiling for a fight. Well, she would give it to him. She was a Maclean, after all, and the Macleans never walked away from a good argument.

With all the hauteur she could muster, she announced, "As much as I enjoyed yon display of rudeness, I must beg your leave. Robert awaits me on deck."

"Why? Are there, perhaps, some few of my crew who have yet to see under your skirts?" he sneered.

Fia felt her own anger rise to meet his. She managed a grimacing smile. "Well, now, as to your crew, I cannot be too sure. I *think* there may be one or two I've missed. I'll have to check the list to be sure."

For a moment, she thought he would lunge for her, so enraged did he seem. She backed warily behind the table.

He took a long, controlled breath. "You will cease your association with Lord Montley immediately."

Fia stared at him. "Surely you jest."

"Nay, lady. I will not have you bringing dishonor to the Wentworth name."

She unfurled the fan and gently wafted it. This, according to Robert, indicated indifference. 'Twas a pathetic ploy but all she had. "And how, pray tell, do you think I am causing you dishonor?"

His nostrils flared, and a muscle clenched in his jaw. With a savage snarl, he resumed his wild pacing. He halted after several turns and whirled to face her. "Your behavior is inexcusable. You are my wife and will act with the decorum as befits the position."

"And how, my lord, should your wife act?"

He ran a hand through his hair with a quick gesture. "I don't know. You should . . . stay in the cabin more. Be on deck less. Just . . . don't be seen quite as much." He thrust his shoulder against the farthest wall and stuffed his hands into his pockets.

"Not be seen as much? Have you lost your reason?" The beginning of a smile tugged at her mouth.

"You should stop dancing, too," he said severely. "Your skirts were flying about, your legs exposed to one and all. 'Twas indecent."

"My skirts were flying?"

"All could see," he said, white lines about his mouth.

She settled the fan in front of her and threw him a look over the edge. "I care not for *all,* my lord. What did *you* see?"

She could hear his teeth grinding even from this distance.

"A wife does not encourage the attentions of a known bounder." He spat out the words as though they tasted of burnt ashes.

"Nay?"

"Nor does she display her legs in such unskilled dancing before an entire ship of men."

" 'Tis nigh impossible to dance in an unskilled manner with such a partner as Lord Montley."

"God's Patience, but I will pluck every feather from that overgrown peacock if it takes me until the end of eternity. He is making a fool of you!"

Fia shut the fan with a snap. "He is doing no such thing. Robert has been quite kind to me." 'Twas just like the scene she had written in her play *The Merry Maids of Azure.* Ramonda, the warrior queen, had been accused of treachery by Thelius, the handsome hero. What was it Ramonda had said? Oh, yes . . .

Fia tossed back her head and held her hands out to her sides as though they were encased in the iron shackles that had held the defiant Ramonda. "Aye! I am loyal to those who are loyal to me. Come death, war, famine, tortures of the worst and most unspeakable kind, I will not turn from—" She paused. *My people* didn't exactly fit. ". . . my friend."

His anger faded into a look of absolute bewilderment. "Where in the hell did that come from?"

She grinned, pleased she had remembered the whole passage. "From Ramonda."

"Who?"

"Ramonda. She's a character in one of my plays."

He looked at her as though she had spoken in a foreign language. "I ask you to behave with more modesty, and you quote poetry."

"Och, 'tis not poetry. 'Tis her farewell speech. Her lover had—"

"Halt!" he snapped, clasping his head with both hands. "You're just trying to escape from explaining your shameful behavior."

"Explain?" Fia said with an incredulous laugh. "As I am your wife only for the length of time it takes you to be rid of me, I owe you no explanation for anything I may do or say." She unfurled the fan and wafted it through the air with determined boredom, hoping the slight stir would cool her cheeks. " 'Tis a paltry marriage we have, at best."

"Paltry? You would call our marriage paltry?" He seemed unable to do more than gape at her.

"Less than that."

"I'll have you know I am the wealthiest man in England," he snapped.

"Is that so? Well, you've also the distinction of having

185

the least imagination of any man to have ever lived. Aye, that and you possess a total lack of feeling."

He closed his eyes and pinched the bridge of his nose in a look of acute suffering. She marveled at the gesture. It was one she had seen Duncan use a hundred times before.

Thomas heaved a deep sigh. "All I want is for you to cease dallying with Montley in full view of my entire crew."

"We're getting an annulment as soon as we reach London. Why do you care what I do?"

"I don't," he replied stiffly. "I merely thought to warn you about Robert, 'tis all."

"Robert?" Fia asked, genuinely perplexed.

"He is a bounder and a knave. You may think he's earnest in his attentions, but he's merely amusing himself with the only woman available. It means naught to him. He will feed on your regard and then cast you to the floor like a worn bone."

A wave of hope flared through her like a light in a dark cave, illuminating and warming at the same time. "You are worried he will discard me?"

"Aye," he answered reluctantly. His eyes met hers, so deep and rich a brown that she felt an instant flush of desire. It seemed as if it had been years and not days since he had last kissed her. But the memory was fresh. She swallowed convulsively.

"Why?" she asked. "Why are you worried?"

"You will not make a fool of me." He spoke with quiet conviction, more to himself than to her.

She knew he was thinking of his father's bitterness, of his mother's abandonment, but she didn't know how to reassure him. She dropped her gaze to the painted fan still gripped in her hands. " 'Twas not my design to make a fool of anyone," she said quietly. "Lord Robert kindly consented to teach me the manners of your English ladies. I just wanted to learn."

His brows lowered in puzzlement. "Robert is teaching you *what?*"

She forced herself to meet his questioning gaze. "He's teaching me all I need to know to be presented to the English court. I wagered him that he couldn't do it, and he accepted."

His eyebrows lowered until his eyes appeared almost black. " 'Tis a ploy. He's just trying to get you into his bed, and you are naive enough to let him."

Fia dropped her gaze to the crushed fan. With fumbling fingers she attempted to open the delicate silk, but the bent and wounded spines refused to part. The once glorious fan lay like a broken bird in her hands.

To her horror, Fia felt her lip quiver. She struggled to get the fan open. She could hide behind it if it would just . . . With a snap, the mangled fan broke cleanly in two. There was a moment of deep silence. She forced herself to look at him.

Thomas's gaze moved from the fan to her face. He groaned and pulled her against him, sinking his hands into her hair. "Ah, comfit, don't look at me that way."

His voice was ragged against her hair, and she clung to him, lost in a wave of longing so intense she could no more move than she could stop loving him.

Fia closed her eyes and turned her face into the protective warmth of Thomas's shoulder. She couldn't say how long she'd loved him. She only knew she would trade everything to stay within his arms.

One of his hands carefully cupped her cheek, his thumb rubbing behind her ear. His other hand trailed lightly down her back to rest on the slope of her hip. She was a mass of unbearable tingles.

Just when she thought she could stand it no more, he

heaved a sigh and ran his hands down her arms, holding her away from him.

He gave her a lopsided smile that made her heart lodge in her throat. "I came to warn you about Robert, and I've done nothing but prove I'm the one you should beware of."

She returned his smile, all her feelings displayed for him to read. His smile faded before her gaze, and he stepped away, his eyes suddenly hooded.

"What we need, milady, are some rules."

Fia wondered if she'd heard him aright. "Rules?"

He nodded and motioned her to sit, and she sank into the chair.

"If we know what we expect of each other, then there won't be any more misunderstandings. Just a few simple rules will suffice."

"How few?" she asked, her mind racing over the possibilities.

"Six," he blurted.

That he had some specific rules already in mind was obvious. She regarded him narrowly. Perhaps there was a way to turn this to her advantage after all.

"Four," she decided.

"Four? Nay. Four is too few. I insist on six."

She shrugged and smoothed out some of the wrinkles in the abused fan. "Four or none."

He glowered, but she affected not to notice. "Very well," he said grudgingly. "Four."

Fia rewarded him with a brilliant smile. "Wonderful! Then there will be two for you and two for me."

For a moment, she thought he had choked on something. Fia jumped up and pounded his back.

He gestured her back to her seat and took a shuddering breath, his color returning to a more normal shade. "I see you are determined to be disagreeable," he said hoarsely.

"Nay," she countered gently. "I am determined to make this fair."

Amusement glinted in his eyes. " 'Twould be easier were you less fair and more agreeable."

"I'll get pen and paper. We will need a record." She scrambled to the desk and pulled out her writing box and paper.

Thomas raised his eyebrows in surprise. " 'Tis almost formal, this. Perhaps we need a witness to sign it?"

Fia returned to the table and opened the inkwell. "Nay. If there's a problem, we shall have Lord Thomas the Rabbit to serve as a witness."

He cast a doubtful eye at the fluffed tail, which was all that could be seen of the rabbit where it burrowed beneath the sheets on his bed. "I don't think he'd be much of a witness for me."

"He's an impartial rabbit." Fia grinned. "Unless one has a bit of greenery for him. 'Tis the only thing that might sway his judgement." She held her pen over the paper. "Begin!"

He laughed, his eyes crinkling with devastating humor. "God's Wounds, but you are eager. I begin to fear what rules you have in mind."

"If they are not to your liking, perhaps we can bargain."

He lifted his eyebrows and leaned back in the chair, more at ease than Fia could remember seeing him. "Write this," he said. "*Rule one: No dancing on the deck.*"

"None?" she asked, startled.

"Nay."

She nibbled on the end of the quill. "What if we just write *No Italian dances*. Robert says they are more lively than the others."

"None." His tone brooked no argument. " 'Tis unseemly."

She sighed. 'Twas inconvenient to her plans, but she supposed she could work with Robert on some other area of her instruction. "Very well."

"Rule number two: *No com*—"

"Nay!" she interrupted. " 'Tis my turn to make a rule."

He gave a slight smile. "So speak, Mistress Impatience."

"No more shouting."

"Shouting? I don't shout," he protested, his voice rising with each word.

She arched an eyebrow and waited. He bared his teeth in the semblance of a smile. "Very well. But I don't shout. I merely make my requests in a loud voice."

She chuckled and carefully wrote *No more shouting* on the paper. "We are now to rule three. 'Tis your turn."

"No more conversing with Lord Montley," he answered promptly.

That stunned her. "I'm to avoid him altogether?"

"Well, during the morning and afternoon and evening hours."

"That leaves only the nights."

"No nights," he snapped, glowering.

Fia sighed. "And just what would I tell him?"

"I know what I want to tell that lackwit," he muttered. "But I suppose you have the right of it. Were he to discover that I asked you not to speak with him, he would tease me unto death." He sighed heavily and drummed his fingers on the table.

"Very well," he allowed, "you may change it to *No more whispering with Lord Montley.*"

She rolled her eyes but wrote it in careful script across the page.

"Now 'tis my turn," she pronounced.

He nodded and eyed her warily. She rested her chin on her hand and stared out the window. What she would

190

like to add was *More kisses*. She wanted to feel the pressure of his lips sliding across hers. She cast a quick glance at him from under her lashes only to see those warm brown eyes fixed on her with unnerving regard. She blushed and hurriedly dipped her quill into the ink once more.

"What have you decided?"

She flashed a grin and wrote in a large, firm hand, *More smiles*.

"What in the hell does that mean?"

"I'd like to see a bit of merriment from you." She shook her head. " 'Tis unnatural, the way you glump about. Mary says 'tis a sign of an ill liver, but I'm more inclined to think 'tis a soured stomach."

"Neither my stomach nor my liver are ill," he said, his brow furrowed.

Fia looked at him and pointed to the fourth rule. He bared his teeth in a false smile.

"There, now. That didn't hurt, did it?"

The stiff smile softened into one of genuine amusement. "You are an impossible chit."

"Och, now, that is exactly what Duncan said, too." She examined the paper. "Should we sign this to make it official?"

She held out the quill.

He took it and signed his name with a flourish. " 'Tis your turn." He handed her the pen.

She took it but didn't sign her name. The end of the quill wavered over the paper, dripping ink into a heedless puddle.

Fia raised her gaze to his. "We've not listed a forfeit. What if we don't follow this agreement, Sassenach? What will we do then?"

He smiled. Then, with the grace of a cat, he rose and stood behind her. Leaning over, he closed his large, warm hand over hers and guided the quill slowly through seemingly endless loops. She stared in wonder where he had written her name in an exaggerated script: *Lady Fia Wentworth, Countess of Rotherwood.*

She was still staring at her name when he whispered into her ear, his breath light against her cheek. "You had better pray, my little Scottish thief, that you never find out."

Chapter Seventeen

The storm blew in with rude suddenness. Thomas had appeared briefly in the cabin to lash Fia's trunks to the huge iron rings that decorated the walls. After admonishing her to remain within, he had left.

Fia spent hours hanging on to the edge of her bunk, wishing she dared get up and retrieve her writing materials from the desk. Not that she could pen anything with the ship rising on the crest of one wave, only to slam down into the base of another, but having her writing box within reach would have been comforting.

After the first hour, Fia decided that being confined while wondering if the ship could withstand the fury that pounded outside was fairly boring. She wondered if Robert was on deck, assisting Thomas. Earlier, Robert had helped her secure Zeus and Thomas the Rabbit in the hold with Thunder. She had piled up a mound of hay so that all were snugly ensconced in a comfortable nest.

She wondered that he hadn't yet claimed his wagered kiss. Of course, he had been kept busy all afternoon. Even during the brief time he had assisted her with her animals, Simmons had come running to fetch him. Fia wished she could talk to Mary about it, but Angus was suffering from the violent seas, and so the maid was engaged elsewhere.

There was nothing to do but lie on the bunk and wait.

Well after midnight, the seas finally calmed, though the howling wind indicated that the storm had not yet spent itself. Fia found herself wide awake and ready for a new adventure. How she wished she could have been on deck to see the ocean come alive like an infuriated dragon, thrashing and writhing enough to sink an entire ship. The thought thrilled her.

She stumbled to the desk and found her writing materials, staggering back to the bunk. She would put a violent storm in a play.

Fia looked about the cabin for further inspiration. This would do for a pirate's cabin, she decided. The stark furnishings would serve well. Aye, with just a few embellishments, it would do nicely.

She looked at the desk. Would a pirate have a desk? Aye, Thomas the Pirate would. No doubt he would be the type of pirate as would keep detailed records of his exploits. She would put a desk in the cabin of her pirate, a desk with a big lock on it to keep all his maps, charts, and treasure inventories safe from prying eyes.

Perhaps, she thought, nibbling on the end of her quill, she should put a secret drawer in it. For the next several moments, only the retreating howl of the wind and the scratch of her quill made any noise in the room.

Sighing with satisfaction, she finished her description of the desk and looked about the room. Her eyes fell on the intricately carved chest at the foot of the bunk. She scooted over to regard it. As it was rather small, she had scarce noticed it before.

There was no need to embellish the description of the trunk. It looked for all the world like a pirate's possession, of sinister, dark, carved wood. She glanced about the rest of the room and then returned her gaze to the elaborate trunk.

Within minutes, she was on her knees, the end of her knife in the lock. It took but a few twists before the lock gave and the chest opened with a satisfyingly gruesome creak.

Taking a deep breath, Fia opened the lid and saw . . . folds and folds of pale blue silk. It shimmered like water as it rippled through her hands. 'Twas of such a light, pale color that it was obviously meant for someone of a fair complexion. Perhaps Thomas meant it for himself?

Fia could more easily imagine Thomas dressed as a pirate than she could see him in such a pale, feminine color.

She looked at the material thoughtfully and pulled it from the trunk. She would ask him about it later. As she pulled on the silk, a small leather pouch fell into her lap. For a moment, she could only stare at it. "Gold," she whispered to herself. "Or jewels?" Her heart pounded as she lifted the bag. 'Twas light . . . too light to be either.

She untied the lavender ribbon that cinched the pouch, opened the bag, and poured the contents into her lap. Colors flew everywhere. Light yellow, deep purple and amethyst, blood red, pale blue, azure, and every shade of green imaginable lay twined across her lap. "Embroidery thread. He keeps blue silk and embroidery thread locked in a trunk."

Like a woman possessed, she dug into the chest, heedless of disarranging the contents. A pair of women's shoes, the heels painted a pale blue to match the silk, flashed into view, and Fia halted long enough to compare one shoe to her foot. It was inches too long. "Och, Thomas, so you are dressing a giant."

Fia could almost see the mystery woman encased in pale blue silk and lumbering about in the blue heels. The troll-like image somehow faded into that of a beautiful lady more like a fairy queen.

Aye, a man of Thomas's looks and position would have a woman with long blond hair and pale blue eyes to match the carefully stored silk. She would be tall and beautiful and practiced in all the feminine arts. No doubt such an accomplished woman already resided at court and was fully accepted within that closed circle. Perhaps that was why Thomas was so eager to return to London.

The thoughts crashed in, one after the other. Fia slumped against the trunk, a shoe clutched in one hand and the packet of tangled embroidery threads in the other.

She was so lost in her unpleasant reverie, she almost didn't hear the footsteps coming down the hallway. With a startled gasp, she leapt to her feet and shoved the fabric and scattered threads into the trunk. She slammed the lid shut only to see the tip of a pale blue shoe peeking from beneath the bunk. With a desperate kick, she sent the shoe sliding under the bunk just as the door opened.

Thomas took a quick step across the room. "You're awake. Have you been ill?"

He was wet from head to toe, as if he had been swimming in the ocean and not sailing upon it. His clothing clung to him as lovingly as ever ivy had clung to a castle wall.

Fia found her voice with difficulty. "Do they let the captain of the ship go wandering about during a storm? Shouldn't you be on deck?" Her voice was breathless with her need to keep his attention away from the trunk. The loosened lock creaked with every move of the ship, and she was sure the sound was loud enough to be heard all the way to shore.

Yet by some miracle, he didn't seem to hear the unnerving creaking of iron. He leaned against the table, a mere arm's length from her. Fia decided he was too close by far.

" 'Twas more a squall than a storm." He grinned, and she felt the force of that devastating smile all the way to her knees. "Simmons will send for me if things grow worse. I wanted to dry off. The rain has ceased, and I've no wish to catch my death."

She found herself looking at his drenched shirt where it hung in almost transparent folds about him, the golden curls on his broad chest glistening with wetness. She wanted nothing more than to run her fingers through those crisp hairs and watch the water drip down his chest, past the flatness of his stomach and on to—

"I don't know what you are staring at, comfit, but perhaps you'd like to come and help me into a dry shirt." His smile was both wicked and angelic at the same time.

Her breasts tightened at the images all too quickly forming in her mind. "Ah, no, thank you. Surely you aren't changing your clothing here?"

His hands were already unfastening his few remaining shirt ties. "And why not? 'Tis my cabin."

She tried to swallow, but her throat would not allow it. "Y-you've been using Robert's cabin."

"Aye. Unfortunately, Robert is sound asleep in his own bunk. Simmons said the fool talked too much, and he kicked him belowdeck." A smile slipped across his face, his eyes softening to amber. "Don't look so discomforted, sweet. I'll find accommodation elsewhere. I prefer you here, in my bed."

There was no mistaking the blatant sensuality of his voice. Fia swallowed. "Ah, well, thank you. I feel as if I should repay you for the inconvenience."

"You already owe me a kiss."

"A kiss? You won the card game?"

He nodded, his gaze flickering over her. "I've thought about nothing else today," he said huskily. "Perhaps I should claim it now."

Fia shook her head. The way his presence was playing havoc with her senses, she wasn't about to let him come any nearer.

His frown was as fierce as it was sudden. "You seemed eager enough to wager a kiss with Robert."

"We weren't playing for kisses. He just said that because he knew 'twould anger you."

Thomas scowled. "Wretched lackwit. I should've known."

" 'Tis against the rules to frown."

"So 'tis." He spoke softly, his voice as caressing as a touch. "I owe penance for my error. I always pay my debts. What would you have? Some emeralds for those pretty ears?" His eyes went to her bare lobes, then dropped to her neck. "Or perhaps a strand of pearls."

He was nigh undressing her with his eyes. Fia could do nothing but stand there, her mouth opening and closing with the effort to think of something quick and witty to reply in turn. Nothing came.

He laughed softly, and Fia felt a wave of longing sweep through her with such intensity that she nearly sank to the floor. She needed to look away from those torturing eyes and bared chest. With a supreme effort she dropped her gaze to the floor and saw . . . the lavender ribbon.

A cold hand clutched at her heart. Robert had told her how Thomas needed to learn to trust. If he saw evidence of her spying, mild though it was, gone would be the warm tone, the heated gaze, and the playful smile.

Fia took a casual step toward the ribbon. If she could just keep his attention off the floor . . .

"I'll take the necklace," she heard herself say in a breathless voice. "Robert says all women need at least one good length of pearls for adornment."

His brow furrowed, and she wished she hadn't mentioned Robert's name. She was at a loss to know how to keep his attention away from the movement of her feet. What would Argyll, the great seducer of men, do?

Fia allowed her fingers to trail lightly down the high neckline of her dress. Thomas's eyes followed the slow movement until her fingers reached the cleft between her breasts. His breath quickened to match her own.

The tension in the room was nigh unbearable. The air was storm-moist and heavy, like a warm, wet cloth. Fia took another casual step toward the center of the room. Thomas's heated gaze followed her. He seemed to have forgotten about changing his wet clothing. Just one more step and the ribbon would be safely hidden by her skirts.

She lifted her foot but couldn't move. Her skirt held her as securely as if it were nailed to the floor. She pulled on it, but to no avail. She looked back and winced. Her skirt was caught in the hastily shut trunk.

Fia swallowed and thought as quickly as sheer panic allowed. "Och, now, will you look at that? My skirt has caught on the trunk." She tugged at it with a desperate hand, but it didn't budge. It was clear it was caught *in*, not *on*, the trunk.

Fia expected anger, outrage, a loud and violent reaction. What she saw was Thomas's beautiful mouth curve into a humorless smile. It was a chilling sight.

"What were you doing?" He spoke softly, his suspicion burning as brightly as had his desire but a moment prior.

She didn't want to lie to him, but the need to keep him close was strong. "I was just looking for a . . . a blanket for the bunk. 'Twas cold during the storm."

His gaze narrowed, and it was suddenly very easy to

imagine him as a pirate. "What else were you seeking?"

"Nothing," she said. "I was just looking for a blanket." She prayed the slight pitch of the ship wouldn't send the blue shoe sliding into view.

Thomas crossed to her, his gaze trailing a heated path down her body. "Can I trust you, little thief?" he murmured, his eyes searching hers.

"Aye. With your life," she answered. Where the words came from, she didn't know. She only knew that she loved him and wanted him to love her more than anything in the world.

"With my life," he repeated. He raised a hand to her face. "I wonder," he said slowly, as if he had been asleep for a long time. She closed her eyes and leaned her cheek against his hand. She couldn't think for the passions that stirred within her.

He pulled her against the very chest she had stared at so shamelessly mere moments before. She expected to feel the coldness of his wet shirt through the front of her dress. But the water that seeped through her bodice was heated, as heated as he. It soaked through the thin wool, causing the material to cling to her peaked breasts.

He moved his mouth to her ear. "I am near desperate with wanting you." His voice dropped to a whisper, wonder mixing with passion. "So desperate that I don't even care if you did try to rob me yet again. You could steal everything I have, and I wouldn't care. You can have the damned letter."

She wondered hazily what letter he was talking about. But when he brushed his lips across hers, she forgot all else. She felt the sweet warmth of his breath on her cheek. It was maddening to be so close to those carved lips and not have them on her, kissing her, tasting her. . . . With a groan, she threw her arms around his neck and pulled his mouth to hers.

He stilled in surprise, but she tightened her arms and

opened her mouth under his. The roughness of his unshaven face both burned and excited her. She slipped the tip of her tongue past his lips. He tasted of the sea and the heat of desire. She tangled her hands in his hair and moaned her passion into his mouth.

He gave a muffled groan and caught her against him. His hands slid over her back and lower, grinding her against the hardness of his desire. He molded her to him, refusing to allow her to part from him.

She was lost, spiraling in a world of pleasure. She threaded her hands through the thickness of his hair. How she had longed to do that. She ran her tongue over his jaw, reveling in the scrape of his unshaven skin. She wanted this man now and forever. They were meant to be. The signs were all there. She wanted the feel of him, the taste of him. He might regret this moment come morning, but she never would.

Thomas was awash in a welter of hot desire. It ran through his veins like burning oil, sweeping every thought away in a torrent of passion. It was madness. He had come to the cabin worried that Fia was frightened by the storm, only to find her blithely pilfering his trunk. For a brief moment, anger had raced through him like a living thing. But then he had made the mistake of touching her.

The smoothness of her skin, the delicate hollows of her neck, the silken mass of her hair, all lured him until he could no more quit touching her, tasting her, than he could think. He wanted this woman. She was his, and by the saints he would have her.

He trailed his lips over the sweetness of her mouth, nipping and teasing the lush lips until they parted and welcomed him into their honeyed depths. He plundered her mouth again and again until she was moaning with unnamed need. He left her lips to taste the delicate line of her jaw, and she clutched at his arms.

Her head fell back, revealing the white column of her neck, and he was afire anew. Thomas trailed his mouth to her shoulder and farther still, to where her dress pressed her breasts into a fascinating cleft. He was determined to free those lovely mounds from their prison of gray wool.

With eager fingers, he undid clasp after clasp. The wool parted slowly to reveal dazzling white skin. As the last clasp released, her dress dropped to the ground in a swirl, its hem still firmly caught in the trunk.

Fia's plain linen shift clung to every curve, every hollow. Thomas thought he had never seen a garment more beguiling in his whole life. He tugged on the ties and was rewarded with a satisfying ripping sound.

Within seconds, she was naked, nothing between them but his wet clothing. Thomas ran his tongue around the delicate swirl of her ear as he let his hands roam freely, wildly across her bared back. His mouth trailed down her neck to her shoulder and then to her breasts.

He laid her carefully on the bunk, his mouth never breaking contact with her breasts. Full, lush breasts tipped with large, rose-hued nipples that begged to be tasted. They were magnificent. They were perfect.

His mouth trailed farther down to the flatness of her stomach, to the tangle of fine, tight curls. She gasped with pleasure, her back arching convulsively as his tongue found her wetness. He worshipped her with his mouth as he frantically ripped off his own clothing.

He could tell from her gasps of pleasure and the clutching insistence of her hands that she was as lost in wonder as he. Sweet Jesu help them both, but they were drowning in this wild passion.

He wanted to take his time, initiate her in the pleasures of lovemaking. But the demands of his body and hers were too much. Within seconds, he was positioned between her thighs, his body tense with the effort to control his passion.

He halted, knowing this would bring her pain, yet even as he hesitated, she surged up to meet him with eager hips and clutching thighs. She whimpered for a moment, but he continued to stroke, murmuring he knew not what into the silk of her hair. He was lost, lost in her wet warmth. Again and again he thrust into her, each stroke an agonizing feat of delicious exhilaration.

She gasped, and her hands tightened on his shoulders. He paused, taking in the sight of her on the crest of her pleasure. Her face was flushed, her eyes closed, the lashes fanning in thick crescents, her lips parted and swollen. His mouth covered hers, and she tensed, gasping as waves of intense sensation rippled through her. Moisture beaded on her lip, and as he bent to taste the salty sweetness, a surge of exultation pulsed through him and carried him on a wave of passion.

His breathing was harsh in the silence of the room, only the faint howl of the wind and the lazy rocking of the ship reminding him where he was. He pulled her to him and wrapped her in his arms, refusing to think of anything other than how perfectly made she was for him. And she was his. He smiled and rested his chin on her hair, lazily admiring the way the curls seemed to have a life of their own.

He sighed. As pleasant as this was, they needed to talk. "Comfit?" he asked softly. But there was no answer. He raised his head and looked at her. Fia was sound asleep. Thomas smiled and placed a lingering kiss on her forehead.

It would wait. He pulled her closer and then lay listening to the steady, even rhythm of her breathing until it lulled him to sleep.

Chapter Eighteen

She awoke slowly, aware of a pleasant warmth between her shoulders where the sun lay hot on her naked skin. Fia smiled drowsily and snuggled deeper into the rumpled bed, her bared breasts gently abraded by the rough blanket.

Bared breasts? Where was her shift?

Remembrance flooded through her in hot, vivid detail. She sat upright, clutching the blanket to her chest.

Sweet St. Catherine, but I have . . . we have . . . he . . . Fia clapped a hand across her brow and sank back on the bunk. 'Twas too difficult to even think of.

She trailed an uncertain hand over her mouth and neck where Thomas's roughened cheek had left its mark. Her hand dropped lower still to the tenderness of her breasts. The sensation sparked a thousand memories of his roaming hands, the warmth of his lips, and the feel of his body against and inside hers. A faint smile tugged at her mouth as she tossed the blanket aside and turned over, stretching out in the pool of sunlight like a contented cat.

Last night he had been hot and passionate. This morning he had awakened her with the dawn by placing soft, featherlight kisses along her shoulder and down the center of her back to the curve of her hip. His tongue teasing, his teeth scraping the sensitive skin until she writhed in need, he had made love to her with a tenderness that brought tears to her eyes even as it drove her mad with passion.

In his desire, he had murmured a thousand lies into her ear, each one sweeter than the one before. And she had let him. She had wanted him to say she was beautiful and perfect, that she was made for him.

Afterward, she had wrapped her arms around him and smiled in wonder as he drifted off to sleep with his head nestled on her shoulder, his breath warm against her neck.

And now, 'twas a glorious day with bright, streaming sunlight and a blue, blue sky. Fia grinned happily. She and Thomas were man and wife in the truest sense. He could no more deny her now than a fish could ride a horse. She sat upright, scooping the blanket to her. Perhaps he had already begun to realize they were together as fate intended them to be.

"Och, Fia," she murmured, " 'tis better than a play." She hugged the blanket and closed her eyes. She could almost imagine him waking to find her in his arms, his face softening in reverence at the realization that she and only she was the woman of his dreams.

She wiped a lone, joyful tear from her cheek. Soon, he would return and throw the door wide. He would stride across the room like a hero in a play to kneel at her feet. She scooted to the edge of the bunk, her eyes fastened on the door.

A long, swirling cape of blue would be thrown over

his shoulders, his golden hair would glint in the sun, and his white shirt would be unlaced to reveal his strength. Pure, hot desire would smolder in his velvety brown eyes as he placed a lingering kiss on her hand and told her of his love.

She heaved a deep sigh. 'Twas almost as good as when Nicoli the Unruly had swept the lovely Rosalind from the bower in her play *The Lady of Ghent*. Fia stretched her bare legs and wiggled her toes in anticipation. He loved her! He would be here at any moment to tell her th—

The blue shoe sat on the corner of the table, the lavender ribbon draped across it. Beside it lay her clothing, no longer caught in the mouth of the trunk but folded in a neat pile.

Cold fear sucked every bit of air from the room. Fia cringed as the truth flooded her: he knew she had lied about seeking a blanket in the trunk, that she had indeed been rummaging through his belongings.

Her earlier euphoria washed away as completely as a summer downpour on a dusty lowland road left naught but brown desolation in its wake.

Images of Thomas flashed before her. Thomas standing before the queen, his cold voice demanding an annulment, accusing her of theft and deception before a roomful of smirking courtiers and elegant women. Thomas banishing her to some horrendous place while Mary cried helplessly in the background. Thomas looking at her with distrust and hatred in his eyes, telling her that he never wanted to see her again.

Fia groaned and pressed cold, damp hands to her pounding temples. Sweet Mother, but she was lost.

"Can I trust you?" he had asked. And she had answered him with a lie. A wee lie, but a lie. Robert had told her of Thomas's lack of trust, and she hadn't listened. Now all was lost. She dropped back onto the bunk, unable to tear her eyes from the damning shoe.

"Och, Fia," she whispered, "you've lost him for sure." She curled into a ball and drew the blanket up over her head. Maybe 'twas all a nightmare. Maybe she'd wake and the shoe would still be safely tucked under the bunk.

The door opened.

"What do ye think ye're doin' to be lyin' abed so late, I'd like to know?"

Fia peeked from under the blanket as Mary dropped a fat ball of fur onto the table. Thomas the Rabbit immediately hopped to the blue shoe and sniffed suspiciously at the painted leather. "I expected ye up at the crack of dawn, considerin' everythin'."

"C-considering what?" Fia stammered. Surely Mary didn't know.

"Considerin' we've arrived in London, of course!" Mary shut the door with an expert shove of her elbow. "I had Angus take Zeus fer a bit of a walk. The hound was beggin' to come into yer room, bound and determined to wake ye, the unruly beastie."

London. So she was finally in London. And no closer to having a sponsor than when she had first stolen out of Duart Castle in the middle of the night. If anything, her situation had worsened, for she'd be fortunate if Lord Thomas allowed her to stay in the city long enough to blink an eye. As soon as he was released from their marriage, no doubt he would cast her out into the streets with neither food nor clothing. Her lower lip trembled.

Ignoring the warmth of the sun streaming through the window, she pictured herself huddled against the outer gates of a huge manor, the wind and snow swirling about her as she tried piteously to start a fire with nothing but a broken piece of flint and a small stack of damp twigs.

Her dress would be torn and shabby, and her feet would be wrapped with dirty rags. Eventually she would die from the cold, and they would find her wasted figure

Kim Bennet

in the snow, her fingers clutched about her brilliant plays.

She'd bet her best quill he'd be sorry then. Aye, he would come to her deathbed and kneel, his head bowed over her lifeless form as he realized his errors and—

"What are ye pretendin' now, lassie? Ye look as though ye've gone and died right there on the poor master's bunk."

Fia became aware that she was draped across the bed, her head and arm hanging dramatically over the edge, the very picture of an innocent maid dying wrongly accused. A self-conscious blush spread across her face, and she sat up and tugged on the blanket so that it covered her from head to foot.

She met Mary's amused gaze and lifted her chin. "I was just thinking about a play I am writing."

Mary's eyes brightened. "A new play? Well, as soon as ye're out of yer bath, ye can tell me all about it."

"Bath?"

"Aye, lassie, so no more dallyin' with ye," Mary said briskly. " 'Tis nigh on noon, and I've asked some of his lordship's men to bring ye a bathin' tub and some nice fresh water. Seems we are not to be allowed to step foot on land until some messenger arrives. But that'll give us time fer ye to have a nice long soak. I'm sure ye'll be feelin' a mite less sore after some soothing hot water and some nice scented soap."

"Sore? Why would I be sore?" Fia blurted out the question.

Mary's heightened color answered her. *Sweet St. Catherine, but Mary knows.*

A brief knock sounded on the door before it was thrown open and Simmons beamed into the room. "Good mornin' to ye, milady!" His ruddy cheeks stretched into a wide, knowing smile as he nodded to Fia.

Thrill to the most sensual, adventure-filled Romances on the market today...

FROM  LOVE SPELL BOOKS

As a home subscriber to the Love Spell Romance Book Club, you'll enjoy the best in today's BRAND-NEW Time Travel, Futuristic, Legendary Lovers, Perfect Heroes and other genre romance fiction. For five years, Love Spell has brought you the award-winning, high-quality authors you know and love to read. Each Love Spell romance will sweep you away to a world of high adventure...and intimate romance. Discover for yourself all the passion and excitement millions of readers thrill to each and every month.

Save $5.00 Each Time You Buy!

Every other month, the Love Spell Romance Book Club brings you four brand-new titles from Love Spell Books. EACH PACKAGE WILL SAVE YOU AT LEAST $5.00 FROM THE BOOK-STORE PRICE! And you'll never miss a new title with our convenient home delivery service.

Here's how we do it: Each package will carry a FREE 10-DAY EXAMINATION privilege. At the end of that time, if you decide to keep your books, simply pay the low invoice price of $17.96, no shipping or handling charges added. HOME DELIVERY IS ALWAYS FREE. With today's top romance novels selling for $5.99 and higher, our price SAVES YOU AT LEAST $5.00 with each shipment.

AND YOUR FIRST TWO-BOOK SHIP-MENT IS TOTALLY FREE!

IT'S A BARGAIN YOU CAN'T BEAT! A SUPER $11.48 Value!

Love Spell ✦ A Division of Dorchester Publishing Co., Inc.

Get Two Books Totally
FREE—
An $11.48 Value!

▼ Tear Here and Mail Your FREE Book Card Today! ▼

PLEASE RUSH
MY TWO FREE
BOOKS TO ME
RIGHT AWAY!

Love Spell Romance Book Club
P.O. Box 6613
Edison, NJ 08818-6613

AFFIX
STAMP
HERE

She almost groaned at the archness of that look. *By the saints, was there no one on the ship who did not know of last night?* She managed a faint answering smile and waved her fingers at him. His grin widened.

Mary moved to stand before Simmons, her pale blue eyes raking the first mate up and down, her mouth prim with disdain. "Och, now, and what do ye think ye're about, boltin' into her ladyship's room without so much as a by-yer-leave?"

Simmons regarded the maid's rounded frame with admiration. "Bringin' ye the tub like ye requested, Mistress Mary." He stepped aside and waved in what seemed to be the entire crew, carrying pails of hot water and a half cask that could only be a washtub.

Fia couldn't decide if the men were all sporting identical knowing smirks or if her imagination had finally run utterly amok.

"What, I'd like to know, do ye call that?" Mary's voice was sharp with disbelief.

Simmons scratched absently at his stained shirt, his face showing mild surprise. " 'Tis a tub."

The man carrying the round bin dropped it with a bang. Thomas the Rabbit made a mad, scrambling leap, his chubby paws clawing the air before he landed squarely in Fia's lap. Without further ado, he began to burrow into the blankets until only the white, trembling tip of his tail was visible.

Mary stared at the makeshift tub. "Hmph. 'Tis more an oversized mug than aught. Have ye nothin' larger on this godforsaken ship?"

"We weren't on a pleasure trip, missus, but on a mission to save the cap'n. We'd no intention of bein' out more'n a week or two at most. Besides, her ladyship here is no bigger'n a flea. I reckon she'll fit."

Simmons motioned for the men to fill the tub. When

the last drop of water was poured, he waved the crew out of the cabin as though chasing chickens.

He halted near the door and scratched absently under one arm. "I don't hold much with bathin' so oft. The cap'n is forever washin' this and washin' that. So much scrubbin' will thin the skin, as I've told him many a time."

Mary advanced on the sanguine first mate and pushed him toward the hall. "When her ladyship needs yer opinion of bathin' or anythin' else, I'll let ye know, ye lack-witted fool. Now leave before I call his lordship and tell him as how ye would not allow Lady Fia to have her bath in privacy."

Simmons backed away, obviously bewildered by such treatment. "But I was jus'—"

"Out!" She pointed with a plump finger.

The first mate headed out the door, muttering loudly about women as needed a strong hand.

Mary snorted, then yelled down the hallway after his retreating form, "Weak-livered, snivelin' cur!" There was no answer other than Simmons's loud stomping as he made his way to the deck. Giving a vindicated nod of her head, Mary slammed the door closed and went to check the water.

She dipped an elbow into the tub. "Well, 'tis not much of a tub, but the water's good and hot."

Mary shot Fia a quick, assessing gaze. "Och, now, lassie, I've no doubt but what ye feel a mite strange this morn. But there's little wrong with ye that a nice soak in the tub won't fix." She bustled to the door. "See to it that ye waste no more time. Get yourself in the water afore it cools. I'll fetch ye up some drying cloths." And with that, she was gone.

Fia stared after her. "A bath. Aye, all I need is a hot bath, and all my problems will float away. Ha!"

Thomas the Rabbit wriggled his way farther into her

lap. He tugged and pushed at the blanket until he made a little nest.

Fia smiled reluctantly. "Och, now, you are an insistent beastie, are you not?"

He gave a final nudge at a particularly resistant fold and then flopped into his new bed and closed his eyes in apparent contentment.

Fia scratched his head approvingly. "Aye. You aren't waiting for anyone to help you, are you? I suppose you have the right of it. There's no waiting for fortune to come to you." She sighed. "If I want Thomas to see me as something other than a test of his luck and honor, then I'm going to have to prove myself."

She lifted the rabbit, planted a quick kiss on his quivering nose, and deposited him, blanket and all, on the table. "But fortune will have to wait 'til I've had a hot bath."

Chapter Nineteen

Thomas halted outside the door to his cabin, one hand holding the towel he had managed to secure from the overprotective Mary, the other resting uncertainly on the brass handle.

There was no longer a possibility of an annulment. He had crossed that line last night. Even now Fia could be carrying his child. The idea didn't cast fear into him as he had thought it would. In fact, he felt strangely pleased.

Sweet Jesu, but it had been a short night. He had fallen asleep with Fia in his arms only to awaken in the still of morning, his body already taut with desire. She had been sleeping so peacefully, he had hated to awaken her. Instead he had lain with her in his arms for an agonizing hour before his unbridled lust had taken over.

He closed his eyes against the heat that rose at the remembrance of those early morning hours. He had taken her again and yet again, and still he lusted for her.

Even now, merely hearing her splashing in her bath through the oak door was an exquisite torture.

Thomas could almost see her white shoulders rising above the water, her hair floating around her like a mermaid's. His loins tightened painfully. By the saints, but he was as besotted as a stripling.

He reminded himself that he would still be with her now had he not found that damnable blue shoe. He leaned his forehead against the door. Some part of him that had loosened under her sensuous touch had curled back into a tight knot when he had found that shoe.

Evidence that she had lied to him.

He had torn into the chest, expecting to find the letter gone. But it was still tucked in the bottom, wrapped securely in a leather pouch. And, like a fool, he wanted to give Fia a chance to tell him the truth, whatever it was.

With a determined grip on the brass handle, he opened the door.

Fia sat with her back to the door, her arms and legs inelegantly sprawled over the edges of a very small tub. Her wet hair hung in a black curtain down her back and pooled into a wet puddle on the floor. She looked more like a sodden puppy than the mythical mermaid of his inspiration.

She turned at the sound of the door closing, and Thomas caught a glimpse of her profile, her eyes tightly shut to ward off the soapy water dripping from her hair down her neck and arms into the water.

"Could you hand me a towel, Mary? I've soap in my eyes."

If ever a woman had a voice that whispered of wanton pleasures, it had to be hers, Thomas thought with a grimace. He tried to ignore the rise of her breasts as she reached blindly toward him. He was struck with an almost overwhelming urge to pull her into his arms and taste that bath-sweetened skin.

"Mary?" Fia repeated.

Thomas dropped the towel into her outstretched hand.

"Thank you, Mary," Fia said, wiping her eyes. She lowered the towel to the floor. "I can't believe this is all the tub that's to be had on the Sassenach's ship," she grumbled. " 'Tis more a tankard than else." She leaned back in the tub and began to scrub at her arms with a cloth. After a moment, her motions stilled, and she sat staring off into the distance, her lips parted and her eyes unfocused.

Thomas leaned against the door frame and watched her, noticing with amusement the puddle forming under the wet rag that now hung from nerveless fingers over the edge of the tub. He grinned and wondered if she had any idea how appealing she looked, arms and legs sprawled awkwardly, surrounded by a puddle larger than the tub in which she sat. What were the thoughts she had become so lost in, he wondered. He fished in his pocket for a coin.

A glimmer of gold flashed through the air, and Fia blinked, then stared in amazement as a glistening coin landed with a splash in her bath water, coming to rest on the curve of her stomach. Before she could speak, another coin glittered through the air. Fia gasped as it plopped onto the damp slope of her breast.

"Normally I'd offer only a half penny for a thought, but yours always seem to be worth more than most."

The deep male voice reverberated with humor, and Thomas walked into her line of vision, a faint smile on his lips.

In an attempt to gather her poor wits, she stammered, "I-I fear you're throwing away good money. My thoughts were hardly worth a penny, much less gold."

"Nay?" he said in apparent disbelief. His eyes held

hers for a moment, a disturbing flicker in the brown depths. Then his gaze dropped lower, and Fia instantly became aware of both her lack of clothing and her less than graceful position.

With a mad scramble, she closed her legs and tried to cover her breasts and reach for the towel at the same time. Her hand closed about the towel, but one of Thomas's booted feet held it firmly to the floor. His smile widened when she looked up at him.

Fia wished she could at least pull her legs into the tub, but the most she could do was cross one over the other, fold her arms over her chest, and hope the soapy water hid the rest.

"What . . . why are you here?" She tried to pretend that she was neither naked nor ill at ease.

He leaned against the desk and lazily pulled the towel toward him with his foot. "I just came to watch you bathe."

"Well, 'tis rude of you to deny me a towel," she huffed, confused by the playfulness of his grin. He was supposed to be angry with her for rifling through his trunk. Her eyes strayed toward the table, where Thomas the Rabbit sat nibbling on the offensive blue shoe.

Thomas's eyes had apparently followed hers, for he said, "Ah, the shoe. Yes, I meant to ask you about that, comfit." His gaze returned to hers, the humor fading. "Was there something you needed to tell me?"

Here was her chance. She tried to think of a way to put the words *I used my dirk to open the lock on your chest because I thought you might be a pirate* in such a way as to keep her from sounding like the biggest lackwit to ever walk the earth. No brilliant ideas came.

He raised his eyebrows.

Fia flushed slightly. "I merely peeked. There are so many things that could be hidden in a trunk. I didn't take anything, and—"

215

"Hold!" he said, throwing up a hand as though to ward off her words. "I know you didn't take it. I looked this morning."

"It?"

He frowned. "You know what I'm talking about."

She shook her head. "Nay. All I saw was some embroidery thread, silk, and shoes. Who are they for?"

He regarded her silently, then shrugged. "If they're to your liking, they're yours. I can find other gifts for the queen."

Relief swept through her. The shoes were for the queen. And he wasn't angry with her at all. At least, she amended, he didn't seem angry, though some of the warm humor had left him.

Perhaps they could still begin anew, start their marriage as it should be. In her relief, she lowered her arms, forgetting to cover her breasts.

Hot desire wiped the last vestige of amusement from Thomas's face, and Fia hurriedly crossed her arms across her breasts. Her face flamed, and she fixed her gaze on the edge of the tub.

He laughed softly, the sound tingling down her back. "Don't think, comfit, that I won't still give you what you deserve," he said.

Fia fought the impulse to stand up and throw herself against him. Sweet Mary, but she could fight anything but his sweetness. "I meant you no harm." Her voice was breathless, hurried.

He regarded her silently before shrugging. "Harm me by breaking into my trunk? Robert has done as much and worse."

"Robert? But I thought he was . . . that you were friends."

"Aye. For that reason he feels the need to keep abreast of my every move, even if it means picking the locks on my trunks, opening missives clearly addressed to me, following me wherever I go, and in general playing the part of an overeager personal guard."

"He's a good friend."

Thomas shrugged. "He feels he owes me a debt for something he has already repaid many times."

He looked so handsome, standing there smiling at her, that she was achingly aware of him. She wanted to press herself against him, pull his loose shirt from his broad shoulders, and run her fingers through the crisp hair on his chest.

Sweet St. Catherine, but I need to maintain some dignity, she reminded herself. It took all her resolve to gather her wits, but she did. "Robert's a rare one. 'Tis as easy to teach manners to a pig as 'tis to get him to speak sensibly. I had a pig once who—"

"Is this from one of your plays?"

"Nay! Why would I write a play about a pig? Arthur was—"

"Arthur?"

"Aye, *King* Arthur."

"I was afraid of that," he muttered, rubbing a hand across the back of his neck.

She frowned at his interruption. "As I was saying, I could never convince Arthur to let me rescue him. He refused to leave his pen. Every time I tried to help him escape from the keep, he would squeal and cry enough to wake the dead."

Thomas tried to tear his gaze from her mouth long enough to follow her recital. "Rescue?"

"Aye," she responded with an ominous look. "Duncan, you know, is very fond of roasted pig." Having said this, she sat staring into the distance, silently musing over this apparent failing of her cousin's.

Thomas sighed. He could either let her finish her story or wonder for the next several weeks what had become of the hapless pig, King Arthur. He was caught despite himself. "What did you do?"

She frowned, and he was captivated by the slight crease that appeared between her eyes. He wondered what she would do if he kissed it.

"Och, well, it took me no time at all to discover what the problem was. Arthur wouldn't leave his trough. He near slept in the thing, so attached to it he was. Duncan just laughed and said 'twas a sign Arthur was meant for the table, but I don't believe such a thing. Do you?" Black eyes fixed on him in silent appeal.

He heard himself reply with all the assurance of a professional swineherd, "Nay. All pigs sleep in their troughs."

She rewarded him with so sweet a smile, he found himself grinning like a besotted half-wit.

"So I thought, too." Her brow creased again. "But Duncan was determined to eat him, and I knew 'twas just a matter of time. One night, I got the kitchen maids to help me heft Arthur's trough up onto an old wagon, and then we coaxed Arthur into following it."

"And did he?" He was enthralled with the picture of a pig lumbering after a trough perched on the back of a rickety cart. Knowing Fia's flair for the dramatic, he had no doubt that all was accomplished in the dark of night, with carefully chosen disguises for the lot of them.

"Aye. It worked like a charm. He trotted after the wagon like a hound on the scent of a fox, his nose twitching the whole way."

"So you saved him."

"Well, I think so," she answered cautiously, her even white teeth catching at her lower lip.

"But?" he prompted, wishing he could release her tortured lip with a kiss of his own.

She shrugged, the movement causing her breasts to peek through the curtain of her hair. Thomas gripped the edge of the desk with both hands and willed himself to look into her eyes.

Fia continued, blithely unaware of Thomas's valorous struggle. " 'Twas just that several months later an uncommon amount of sausage appeared at the keep. I was a mite suspicious that perhaps Duncan had found poor Arthur, though he never would say."

She was lost in a reverie as she contemplated the probable outcome of King Arthur. Thomas noted that her lip quivered slightly, and he hurriedly changed the subject.

"We need to speak of last night."

She cast a startled glance at him. "Aye?"

A fist pounded on the door. "Cap'n!" Simmons's muffled voice was raised in alarm. "Ye had best come quick, fer Lord Walsingham's messenger has arrived, and that damn Frenchified Scotsman has done angered him 'til he swears he'll not wait another minute fer ye!"

Thomas swore under his breath. "Very well, Simmons," he called out. "I'll be there in a moment."

There was a doubtful silence, and then Simmons urged, "Aye, Cap'n. But ye'd better make haste. There's not a jack one o' us as can keep that Scot's mouth from flappin'." His heavy footsteps sounded down the corridor.

Thomas's eyes met hers. "I've got to leave. I came to say that I've given some thought to our situation."

Fia nodded. "As have I."

"We can no longer seek an annulment."

Fia stared at him, hope rising wildly within her. She waited, willing him to admit to some feeling, even affection. That's all she needed—for now.

There was a mad scramble down the hall and then a frenzied banging on the door. "Pray come above, Cap'n!" Simmons pleaded. "Lord Robert's gone mad, he has! He has insulted the queen's man in every way but callin' his mother a lightskirt! The messenger is lookin' as dark as a thundercloud! By the seas, Cap'n, ye had best hurry!"

Thomas cursed and took a step toward the door. He halted abruptly and turned. "When I return, we'll speak some more. In case there is a child, we must—"

"In case there is a child?" she repeated. Sweet Mother Mary, but she hadn't even considered that.

"Of course."

She searched his face. "Is that why you've decided our marriage should stand?"

"What else could it be?"

He sounded defiant, almost as if he expected her to try to convince him that he had other reasons. Fia trembled with the coldness that settled in her stomach. But she wouldn't lose what little dignity she had left. "My answer is nay. I want the annulment."

"What?" He seemed unable to comprehend her.

"Last night makes no difference. I came to London to publish my plays and for no other reason."

Thomas's face went white. "And if there's a child?"

"Then 'tis my concern and not yours," she returned hotly. "I'll not be married just to provide a name for a babe."

"May I remind you, madam, you are already married. To me. And you will stay so if I decide it." He was shouting, but she didn't flinch.

There was the sound of running feet, and then yet another voice joined Simmons's, entreating the captain to hurry aboveboard.

With an audible grinding of his teeth, Thomas stared down at her. "I must go. We will finish this later."

She shrugged, not seeming to notice what her gesture did to the wet hair that clung lovingly to her curves, though its effect on him was instantaneous and painful.

"We have nothing more to discuss, my lord. I have

no wish to be wed to you now or ever. Go and take care of your guests."

He had been prepared to offer her a place in his life, and she had the effrontery to refuse him without so much as a wince. His father's voice sounded in his head. *Trust no one.*

Simmons pounded once again, and Thomas turned blindly. Fists clenched, he left, slamming the door behind him.

"Simmons!" he snapped.

"Aye, Cap'n?"

"I must leave to meet with Lord Walsingham. I want you to take Lady Fia to Rotherwood House."

"But, Cap'n! Me li'l Meggie'll be waitin' on me! And ye did promise me a side of that pork."

Thomas managed to swallow his temper. "Take Lady Fia to Rotherwood House, and see to it that she does not leave until I arrive," he said slowly.

Simmons blew out his breath in a long hiss. " 'Tis like that, eh? Well, ye can count on me, Cap'n. If anyone knows about women, 'tis me."

As the first mate expounded on his experience with women, Thomas rubbed his forehead.

The day could get no worse.

Chapter Twenty

The tavern was like a hundred others along the waterfront. The Blue Stag sported a dark and dirty taproom enshrouded in the stale odor of rotting timbers and unwashed bodies. A jumble of uneven tables and broken chairs littered the chamber. Though the hour was early, several of the more hardy patrons already sat hunched with bleary-eyed hostility over bent pewter mugs.

Thomas made his way past the scarred tables. A gaunt dog bared his teeth, protecting a sliver of bone he had managed to steal from the kitchen. Thomas was glad Fia wasn't there. He knew she'd want to adopt the mangy beast.

He resolutely pushed away any other thoughts of Fia. He couldn't afford to be distracted here. At the back of the room sat an immense man, his boots worn and cracked with age, his black leather tunic marred by an array of unidentifiable stains. Small, piglike eyes glowered at Thomas from under heavy, scraggly brows.

"Hail, Goliath," Thomas called, feigning a merriment he was far from feeling. "I come to see Leticia."

"What 'ave ye got to give fer it?"

Thomas winked. "That, my good man, is between me and the lady herself."

Goliath snorted.

Thomas pulled a coin from his purse. "Here." He flipped it into the air. The coin disappeared into the greasy tunic, but the giant remained blocking the door.

"Let me by," Thomas said impatiently.

The man shook his head slowly, his gaze moving from Thomas to beyond his shoulder, then back again. "It's two coins if'n Letty's to take on both ye and yer fancy friend."

Thomas looked over his shoulder and swore. "By the saints, Robert, what are you doing here?"

"I've also come to see the wondrous Letty. Verily, I apologize for my lateness, but I found myself with naught but rags to wear." Robert was even more elaborately dressed than usual. His velvet doublet glimmered, the deep purple shot through with gold threads that caught the dim light and made him almost iridescent.

Thomas noted sourly that every eye in the room was now transfixed on Robert, each face reflecting varying degrees of amazement.

With a flourish, Robert tossed a coin to Goliath.

The giant grunted and lumbered to his feet. "I'll send Letty in to ye as soon as she's able."

Thomas threw the door open and stalked into the room, Robert's measured tread behind him.

"Sweet Jesu, Robert! Why must you insist on following me?"

Robert tossed his cloak onto a chair. "I owe you. 'Tis no secret."

"You owe me naught but peace. Now leave."

223

"I can't."

"Why not? You managed to get here without an invitation, 'twould seem a thing of ease to leave with one."

"I fear for my life." Robert lowered his voice to a whisper. "The streets are narrow and fraught with dangers."

Thomas made a disgusted sound. "You arrived without mishap."

"I followed you. None would dare harm me so long as I remained within the safety of your shadow." Robert dusted off a rickety chair. "So here I remain until you leave, safe and sound."

Thomas shook his head. If he didn't know Robert better, he might believe his coxcomb mannerisms. But Thomas knew that while Robert's sword might gleam golden, the handle set with rubies, it was deadly. He sighed heavily. There was naught for it now but to make do.

He pulled out the closest chair and dropped into it, stretching his legs. The room was little better than the taproom, with the surprising exception of a small fire sputtering in the grate and a bowl of apples sitting upon the crooked table. A small pot slowly steamed over the gasping blaze as though in defiance of the chill wind that whistled occasionally through the plank walls.

All in all, the chamber was cold, damp, and foul. Thomas frowned and wished he could leave this matter to Robert. He needed to see Fia and finish their conversation, make her understand . . . what? He rubbed his neck wearily. What had he been thinking to make her his wife in truth? She was a woman who lied as easily as she breathed.

The door swung open, and a barmaid sauntered in, her russet hair contained beneath a dirty scrap of lace. She flashed a pouting smile and clunked two mugs of ale onto the scarred table. Her overflowing breasts pressed against the inadequate scrap of muslin tucked into her open bodice.

Robert drained his mug with startling quickness.

"I can see yer lordship is the thirstin' kind." The maid flashed a saucy smile at Robert, her eyes glinting hazel in the dim light. "Perhaps ye're wishful fer some more ale?"

He captured her hand, murmuring soulfully, "Forget thy ale, Sweet Maid Leticia! Do but reside within mine heart, there to warm it until the coldness of death shall overtake it."

She pulled her hand free with a brisk tug. "Me name is Annie, no' Leticia. Letty's on her way, so I wouldn't be wastin' no time if'n I was ye. Me duties don't include entertainin' the customers in no way other than servin' ale."

Robert clutched at his chest. "Fair cruelty! You have wounded me with thy words! I seek but to please thee, and instead I am sent away, sore and rejected as a beaten dog from the beckoning warmth of a hearth."

Thomas's attention drifted from the all-too-familiar sight of Robert flirting with a barmaid. He wondered what Fia thought of Rotherwood House. She would have arrived by now and doubtless would be wandering from room to room. She was probably too busy searching through his belongings to note the quality of the lodging.

He stirred restlessly. God's Blood, but he ached to be gone.

A shadow darkened the doorway as an old man stood within the opening, his dirty face shadowed by a ragged cloak.

"I come to beg a word with me daughter." The voice cracked with weariness; the thin, dirty hand gripping the cloak shook with the palsy of age.

"Da!" The barmaid forgot about the pursuing Robert and bustled to the door. "What are ye thinkin,' t' be comin' down here wi' so little coverin' on ye? 'Tis in bed ye should be, not wanderin' about!"

"Let me be, daughter! Do I look t' be dead yet?" Even as the old man spoke, he began to cough, swaying dangerously on his feet.

"Come, Da!" Annie pulled the old man from the doorway and fixed a pleading gaze on Robert. "There's no fire in the grate in the taproom. Do ye mind if me da sits a spell here in yer room? He won't be no trouble t' ye, I promise. And he can spin a tale fer ye once he catches his breath. He's a right fine tale-spinner, he is. He can leave as soon as Letty comes fer ye."

Robert ignored Thomas's frowned warning. "Of course. Pray, bring the good man something to eat as well. He'll feel better once he's had some food."

The girl flashed a grateful smile as she pulled out a chair for her father. Thomas felt his jaw tighten. Robert would think nothing of adopting the girl's entire family ere they left the tavern.

The old man's wheezing lessened, and he motioned to the girl. Annie leaned over, and Thomas watched incuriously as the man whispered into her ear. She nodded once, then grinned widely at Thomas and Robert. "I'll jes' leave you wi' me da fer a time."

She looked at the old man and spoke softly, her broad accent disappearing altogether. "We await your signal."

The old man nodded once, and Annie slipped from the room, sparing no glance for Robert. As she carefully closed the door behind her, Goliath resumed his position guarding the chamber, his chair scraping against the door.

Thomas watched in amusement as the old man pushed the tattered hood from his head.

"How fared your adventure, my fine young buck?"

Robert scowled with gathering wrath at the thin, patrician face of Francis Walsingham, chief counselor to

Queen Elizabeth. "You bounding knave! Of all the perfidious tricks!"

Walsingham's mouth thinned. "I have gone to great trouble to arrange this meeting. Don't endanger us all with your brash foolery!"

Robert's face flushed a deep red as he started from his chair, his fist about his sword.

Thomas threw an arm between the two. "Hold, Robert!"

Robert's eyes blazed, but he subsided into his chair. "Do not heed him, Thomas, for I swear his tongue is as forked as the devil's."

"I'm not so newly breached that I'm in danger of falling for soft words and the promise of riches," Thomas admonished his friend. "Now hold your tongue, and let's find out what our ragged visitor has to say."

Walsingham's eyebrows rose delicately. "I have much to tell you. But first I must wash off some of this dirt." He rose and walked to the small pot that steamed over the fire. He pulled a small cloth from the folds of his clothing, dipping the cloth into the water. "I've no liking for filth."

"And yet it becomes you," Robert said in a deliberately goading tone.

The minister gave a thin smile. "Amusing," he said in a dry tone. He rubbed at the dirt on his hands, grimacing at the blackened rag. "It seems you had some difficulties securing the letter."

"Aye, he was nigh well killed," Robert said.

" 'Twas my own decision to go," Thomas stated firmly.

"True," said Walsingham. "I did but mention to Thomas that the queen would benefit from the possession of such a letter. What Lord Rotherwood decided to do with that information was quite beyond my power."

227

Robert glowered. "There is very little that is beyond your power."

Thomas shoved his mug toward Robert. "Here, pup, drink that. 'Twill mellow your tongue. I vow you are quick to show your teeth this morn. No doubt you are still stung by the treachery of the lovely Annie." He turned to Walsingham. "I must admit, I was taken in by your new recruit. She was quite unexpected."

Walsingham sat with a controlled grace that was peculiarly his own. "The lovely Annie is as unique as she is useful. She is also very, very adept at what she does."

" 'Tis unfortunate she ever fell into your clutches," jibed Robert. "Have you told her how you will use her to lay your little traps until she herself is caught in one, and then you will walk away congratulating yourself on her 'usefulness'?"

The minister turned a cool gaze to Thomas. "How do you stand such a constant barrage of nonsense? I, for one, would find it most wearisome."

Thomas grinned. "I drink a lot."

"Ah. That would explain it. Though I must admit, it's very touching, this affection you have for one another. And, though I am loath to say it, the concern on the part of our poor Scotsman is at times rather on the mark." He carefully selected an apple from the bowl and gave Thomas a mirthless smile. "I despair that you will ever learn the value of caution. You tend to test the limits of your good fortune more than necessary."

Thomas pulled out a leather-wrapped packet and tossed it to the minister. "Only when circumstances warrant. It seemed to me that they did in this instance." He frowned. "Though there is not as much to this missive as you hoped."

" 'Tis not the ultimate proof, but 'tis enough for now." The thin lips curved into a satisfied smile. "We must raise Elizabeth's doubts about Mary gradually."

"It's definitely enough to do that."

The packet disappeared into the folds of Walsingham's cloak.

Robert leaned forward. "Aren't you going to read it?"

"I know what it contains. 'Tis a letter from Queen Mary, writ in her own elegant hand, suggesting that she may have known a bit more about the death of her husband than she testified."

"Suggests? Just suggests?" Robert's voice rose with each word. "You would risk Thomas's life for a letter that merely *suggests*?"

"Cease, Robert! I made my own decision," Thomas said.

Walsingham sighed. "I trow, Robert, 'tis most fatiguing, this hatred of yours. Why do you persist in thinking I wish Thomas harm?"

"Because Thomas knows more about you than most. He knows your contacts and methods. He knows how you think and what you are capable of. He knows enough, in a word, to get you hanged does he go to the queen."

"There, my fine Scottish friend, you err. Elizabeth is much more like to hang Lord Rotherwood does he bleat to the world the manner in which I have been protecting her vast interests."

Thomas laughed. "He has you there, Robert. Think on it. Elizabeth has the crown firmly in her grasp, and she is determined to keep it there. She would deal harshly were I or anyone else to publicly embarrass her most loved counselor."

Walsingham delicately peeled a long rope of skin from the apple. "So we come full circle, for the queen would be even more displeased were one of her favorites to meet with his untimely demise whilst in Scotland."

"Aye," said Robert, "especially if he were to bake in a pie of your making."

Thomas frowned at Robert, but Walsingham merely cut the apple into six even pieces. "Precisely, my astute friend. 'Tis for this reason I am especially indebted to you for saving my, ah, pie, as you so eloquently expressed it."

Robert looked anything but pleased, and Thomas hurried to head off any more discussion. "I had some difficulties in obtaining the letter."

The counselor's eyes were so light a gray as to appear almost colorless. "So I heard. It appears Maclean knew you were coming."

"What?"

Walsingham nodded. "The information had to have come from someone close to you."

Robert flushed. "Go ahead and say it. You think 'twas me."

"I do not. If I had thought such a thing, you would not now be in this room, Montley," said Walsingham sharply. He looked thoroughly affronted. "Don't underestimate my capabilities."

"Who do you think 'tis?" asked Thomas.

"I have my own theories as to who it might be. But of even more import, we must find out why the cunning Laird Maclean has been so eager to be of assistance to our cause. 'Twas most unexpected."

Thomas and Robert exchanged a look.

"I wouldn't have called Lord Duncan exactly 'eager,' " Thomas said cautiously.

"No?" The thin eyebrows arched. "What would you call it when he married you to his beloved cousin, gave you enough evidence to suggest that it would not be improper to behead his own queen, and then arranged for an, ah, even more valuable gift to await you here."

"How did you know of Fia's and Thomas's marriage?" asked Robert suspiciously.

"I have my ways," the minister answered with a wry smile.

The wonder that Walsingham knew as much as he did was lost as Thomas absorbed the last part of the sentence.

"He sent something here? To Rotherwood House?" he said slowly. He wished he hadn't sent Fia on ahead without him.

The minister skewered another apple slice and nodded. "Rotherwood House? Aye. Sent? Nay." His mouth turned down. "I offered to meet with him, but he waits for you. He wishes to deliver this gift in person."

"How did Maclean get here so quickly?" Robert asked.

"He must have left as soon as we did. Aye, and traveled night and day." Thomas gripped his sword. There was only one possible reason Duncan would make such a journey.

Walsingham took a bite of the fruit, his hooded eyes following every nuance of Thomas's expression. "He brought a generous gift, if I say so myself. Did he not tell you of it?"

"Of what?" Thomas heard his own voice, through a roaring in his ears like that of a cannon going off.

Walsingham patted his mouth with the small cloth.

Robert slammed an open hand on the table. "God's Wounds, stop this cat and mouse! Tell what you know."

"Patience, child," the minister said, a cool anger lighting his eyes. He turned to Thomas. "Duncan Maclean has gifted you with an entire army."

"An army?" Robert echoed hollowly.

Walsingham nodded.

"Have you spoken with Maclean?" Thomas asked.

"I tried. He has been infuriatingly reticent."

The roar filled Thomas's head. "How many are there?" he heard himself ask hoarsely.

"A hundred. Maybe more. Enough to occupy the entire street outside Rotherwood House."

As if through a mist, Thomas heard Robert ask, "Why would Maclean bring an army?"

Thomas didn't hear anything else. Duncan's last words to Fia rang through his ears. *"If you're not happy, I'll come for you."*

He was faintly aware of standing, of his chair crashing against the wall, of the startled expressions on both Walsingham's and Robert's faces, and of the thunderous roar Goliath made as Thomas yanked the door open and toppled the huge man from his seat.

Then Thomas was out in the street, blood pounding through him, hot and furious, as he ran. He was heedless of the damage he inflicted on those he pushed past and only dimly aware of Robert's steady footfall behind him.

All he knew was that Duncan had brought an army. An army to reclaim what rightfully belonged to Thomas.

Chapter Twenty-one

They were everywhere. Men in red, blue, and green kilts lingered by the house and massed at the gate, their swords strapped across their shoulders with insolent intent.

Thomas ground his teeth and started forward, hand fisted about his own sword. By the rood, but he would not let any half-dressed savage take his wife and—

Robert stood before him. "Hold, *mon ami!* Not only are we outnumbered, but we have no plan of attack. If we walk straight into their clutches, we'll never reach Fia."

Thomas looked around at the Scotsmen. Already he and Robert had been noticed, and the group about the gate had increased twofold. He cursed under his breath.

"What do you suggest?" he asked Robert.

"I haven't an idea. Deception and chicanery are your area of expertise, not mine."

Thomas stared at the house and rubbed his chin. There

was a side door that led directly to the major apartments. All he had to do was slip past the guard. But what would keep a Scottish army distracted for the time he needed to reach the door?

He cast a glance at Robert's profile. MacQuarrie was silently counting the guards, one hand absently resting on his rapier.

"Come with me," Thomas said.

Robert turned toward him, excitement lighting his face. "Aye? You have developed a plan of attack?"

Thomas grinned.

"What?" asked Robert suspiciously.

"I need a diversion."

Robert looked from the men to Thomas and shook his head. " 'Twill never do! There are far too many of them, and—"

"You've done it before," Thomas said, turning toward the house. "All you have to do is challenge one, preferably the strongest and the slowest."

"Halt!" A plaid-covered guard stepped from the crowd and stood menacingly in Thomas's path. "State yer purpose, English dog."

Robert was there in an instant, his lean form stepping between Thomas and the Scotsman. "Och, now, do my ears lead me astray, or are ye not a Douglas?"

Thomas hadn't heard Robert speak with so pronounced a Scottish burr since his first arrival in England years ago.

The man regarded Robert with a suspicious frown. "Aye, I am Kinnish Douglas. And who are ye?"

Robert swept an elegant bow that looked woefully out of place in the midst of the hostile Scotsmen. "Robert MacQuarrie, Viscount Montley, at your service."

An angry mumbling arose at the name, but Douglas looked almost pleased, his yellowed teeth showing in a wide grin. "Well, now. So I have the pleasure of meeting the Coward of Balmanach. 'Tis a rare honor, that," Douglas gibed, and then called out, "What do ye think, men? Do I let the Coward of Balmanach pass unmolested?"

The men broke into a jeering mass of shouts and yells. Robert seemed unconcerned, his eyes never wavering from Douglas. "Are you challenging me to a duel?"

"A duel?" Douglas sneered. "With a white-livered traitor as yerself? Nay, MacQuarrie. Ye deserve no such honor."

Robert clicked his tongue and regarded Douglas with polite disbelief. "If you're afraid, then so be it."

A dead silence fell. Kinnish's face flushed red. "Fool! Foul pretender! I am no more afeared of ye than of a wee ant!" He threw his cloak to the ground and drew his sword, the steel flashing menacingly.

Thomas regarded the huge two-handed claymore, careful to keep any expression from his face. Robert's long, thin rapier would make minced meat of this buffoon in no time.

Robert gave Thomas a quick wink and began to walk about, kicking loose stones out of the way, all the while ceaselessly taunting his foe. As he neared Thomas, he pushed Douglas's fine cloak toward him with a careless shove of his foot.

Thomas waited for the yelling to reach a fevered pitch, and then he slowly melted into the crowd, the cloak crumpled in his hands.

Duncan leaned back in the chair and stretched his feet toward the fire. " 'Tis a grand fireplace, though it still does not give off much heat. You'll freeze in this house, poppet. Duart Castle is warmer than this even in the midst of winter."

Fia crossed her arms and frowned. "Duart Castle is freezing cold on the hottest day of the year, and well you know it. Surely you've not traveled all the way from Mull just to compare your residence to a Sassenach's. Why have you come, Duncan?"

A sudden clamor arose from outside, and Duncan's brow creased. "Ferguson!" he bellowed.

The door opened, and a tousled head appeared. "Aye, yer lordship?"

"What in the blazes is going on out there?"

" 'Tis Robert MacQuarrie. He approached the front gate and challenged Kinnish Douglas," Ferguson said, giving a wide grin. "He'll rue this day's work if'n he lives long enough. There's none like Douglas with a sword."

Duncan snorted derisively. "Fools! Sapheads! Lackwits! There's none like MacQuarrie with a rapier. Douglas'll not last above ten minutes."

"Och, he's already lasted that long. They've been goin' at it fer the past quarter hour."

Duncan straightened in his chair. "What about the master of the house? Have you any sign of the Sassenach? Where you find MacQuarrie, you usually find that damned Englishman."

Ferguson shook his head. "Nay, yer lordship. There's no sign of him anywhere."

Fia sighed impatiently. "If there were, you'd be hard pressed to find him in yon madness."

Ferguson's color deepened. "We've been standing guard without, me and MacKenna. We'd never leave our post."

"Then how did you know MacQuarrie was fighting Douglas?" asked Duncan.

Ferguson bit his lip. "We just went to the window fer a—"

"If you leave your post again, I'll send you back to Mull skelping like a beaten dog."

Though Duncan hadn't raised his voice, Ferguson

gulped and scurried from the room as if the hounds of hell pursued him.

"Fool," said Fia. Thomas never would have been so quickly cowed. The thought made her chest ache.

"Aye. See what I have to contend with? 'Tis a good thing you are away from such lackwits." He gave the chamber an appreciative glance, his voice echoing hollowly against the high ceiling. "As much as I miss you, poppet, 'tis here you belong."

Fia followed his gaze about the room. 'Twas more than grand. Everything about Rotherwood House spoke of money and power. From the decorative plaster ceilings and heavy-timbered roofline to the marble floors, the house evinced the incredible fortune and command of the owner.

Her throat tightened. She had once thought to have Thomas find her someone of wealth and influence to sponsor her plays, and yet here he lived amid the splendor of a prince. To think that he had asked her to be his wife in truth had the unfortunate effect of making her eyes water.

"There now, lassie," said Duncan bracingly. "Don't look so stricken. I'm sure you'll get used to such grandeur." His gentle smile was accompanied by an even gentler pat on the back of her hand. "I couldn't have arranged a better match for you. You deserve to be mistress of such a residence."

Fia sank into the seat beside him and gave him a look of disbelief. "*Me?* Mistress of *this* house? You've been in the pixie dust to think such a thing. I can no more run a house of this size than I can make a cow give golden ale."

Duncan laughed. "Come, now! Where is the pert maid who chose to wander about the countryside with a sack of stolen silver and a poor, abused Sassenach in tow instead of marrying a nice, quiet Scotsman?"

"'Twas a sack of *borrowed* silver, and there is no such thing as a quiet Scotsman," Fia said, then smiled. "Thomas was a bit bruised from our meeting, wasn't he?"

"I don't think any man has ever been quite so happy to be captured." Duncan chuckled.

"Not with you threatening him every chance you got. Though I . . ." She halted and then frowned. "You are a scurvy hagseed to be turning the topic so. You still haven't answered my question. Why have you come?"

"I've come to pay a bride's visit to my own beloved cousin," he responded promptly, and with such an air of a schoolboy having memorized his lessons that she was hard pressed not to smile.

"'Tis suspicious you came to visit so soon. You must have left when we did."

"Nay. Not for several hours." Duncan eyed a large bowl of nuts adorning a delicate wooden table. He hooked one huge booted foot around the table leg and dragged it within reach.

Fia winced at the scraping sound that echoed throughout the room. "You've told me when you came, not why."

He took a handful of nuts, ignoring those that slipped from his grasp and rattled to the floor. "It occurred to me that I hadn't given you a proper bride gift."

"There is something unsavory about your tale, Duncan. Indeed, it reeks as strongly as two-week-old fish."

"Now, poppet—" Duncan began.

"If you won't answer with the truth, then don't answer me at all."

Duncan heaved a mighty sigh. "'Tis sufficient to say I came to see how you and the Sassenach were going on. 'Twas a misfortune I arrived ahead of you." He shook his head regretfully. "Your Sassenach must not be much of a sailor."

"He's a fine sailor! We ran into a storm," Fia returned hotly, only to catch a glimmer in Duncan's eye. She glared at him. "You're a devil today, aren't you?"

Duncan waved a hand, the gesture causing more nuts to drop onto the floor. "As mistress of this fine establishment, you can always have me thrown out."

"And how would I accomplish that? I've not seen a servant of the household since I arrived."

" 'Twas necessary to lock them belowstairs. They refused us entrance."

Fia dropped her face into her hands. "Sweet St. Catherine, Duncan! How could you? I'll never be able to face Thomas again! Once he—"

A muffled shout sounded outside the door. A voice she instantly recognized growled a command before something thudded against the wood panels. Fia was on her feet and halfway to the door before Thomas stormed into the room.

His expression was white-lipped and grim, his hands brandishing his sword as though he fully expected to meet a fire-breathing dragon. His eyes found her the second he crossed the threshold, and he stalked purposefully to her side, hauling her full against him even as he held the sword ready.

"T-Thomas!" Fia stammered. His clothing was torn, and a thin trickle of blood dripped from the corner of his fine mouth. His brown eyes glinted like burnished amber as he glowered at Duncan. Fia reached up with a cautious touch and wiped the blood from his lip. He looked at her, his gaze softening.

She should have reminded herself that she was angry with him. But she didn't. Instead, she smiled. She knew it was a silly, besotted smile, but she couldn't contain it.

"Are you hurt?" he asked softly, his eyes dark with concern. Fia leaned against him, powerless to stop herself from seeking his warmth. Every hurtful word he had spoken on the ship was forgotten in the intensity of his gaze, every ill thought she had ever harbored against him melted away in the heat of his warm brown eyes.

"Nay, I am fine." Her voice quavered, and his grip tightened in response, curling about her shoulders and holding her closer still.

She tried to school her wildly beating heart. Sweet St. Catherine, but why had she fallen in love with such a handsome man? Just looking at him from a respectable distance could make her stomach heat as though a fire were lit inside her. But pressed against him as she was, his perfect mouth mere inches from hers, she could no more speak than she could think.

Of their own volition, her fingers slid across his lower lip, her eyes fastened on that perfect morsel. Her own mouth felt swollen; it almost ached to be touched by his. As though reading her every thought, Thomas moaned and lowered his mouth toward hers.

" 'Tis a fine cloak ye have on, Sassenach." Duncan's voice rumbled over them like the cold waves of the sea. " 'Twould be a pity to have to run my sword through it just to pry you away from my cousin."

Fia flushed with embarrassment. Thomas stiffened, and his mouth thinned, but his arm remained firmly about her.

He glared at Duncan. "A pox on you, Maclean! Were you not my wife's only living relative, I'd slice you in two."

Duncan cracked a nut, his eyes gleaming with amusement.

Fia hastened to intervene before he could goad Thomas further. " 'Tis not so bad as it seems, Thomas. Duncan has only come to pay us a wee visit. He'll not be staying long though, will you, Duncan?" She cast a darkling glance at her cousin.

Maclean tossed another nut into his mouth and grinned. "Nay, poppet. I'll not intrude upon your newly wedded bliss for long." He made an expansive gesture to the chair opposite his. "Pray, come and join me, Sassenach. This puny fire cannot be expected to reach so far."

"What do you mean by invading my house with your accursed army?"

Duncan lifted his eyebrows. "Invade? I came in peace, as a relative."

"With over a hundred men?"

" 'Tis a bit much, eh?"

Thomas regarded him with a flat stare. "Where are my people?"

"In the larder." Duncan tossed shells onto the table and dusted off his hands. "They refused us shelter."

Fia shut her eyes and wished with all her heart that she would wake from this nightmare.

As though aware of her thoughts, Thomas slid his hand beneath her hair to rest on her neck. The touch was both warm and possessive as he pulled her head against his shoulder. To her further discomfort, his thumb began to trace featherlight circles on her sensitive skin. She risked a glance up at him, and for a moment his eyes locked with hers.

Duncan gave a muffled curse.

Reluctantly, Thomas directed his attention back to the laird. "Did you hurt any of my retainers?"

" 'Tis a piss-poor lot of servants you have, Sassenach. Not a half pint of backbone in the lot."

"God's Blood, you brought an army with you! Of course they were frightened!"

"I brought my men to protect me and mine. You never know what you are like to run into in this godforsaken land." Fia tried to warn Duncan with a frown, but he ignored her and continued. "In fact, we were viciously

241

attacked just after we crossed the English border."

"No doubt some honest landowner took offense at your carousing through his lands," Thomas replied through a false smile.

"Mayhap." Duncan yawned and stretched his arms over his head, the chair creaking loudly in protest. "I didn't have the time to ascertain the nature of his grievances. We trounced him right and well and continued on here."

Fia winced at the sound of Thomas's grinding teeth.

A loud knock fell upon the door.

"Enter!" bellowed Thomas and Duncan, their voices blending as beautifully as a chorus. For a moment they glared at one another, and then Duncan grinned and shrugged in apology.

The door opened, and a disheveled Robert was shoved into the room, followed by Ferguson. MacKenna ambled behind. Robert stumbled against a chair and stood unsteadily, one hand against his bloodied head. Fia tried to free herself, but Thomas's grip tightened.

"The laird is wantin' to speak to ye, ye cowardly traitor!" Ferguson rudely shoved Robert toward the fireplace. Robert stumbled into a stool and fell to the floor.

The guard lifted a foot to kick at his prostrate form, but Thomas was across the room in an instant, the flat of his sword slamming the Scotsman into the wall.

"You should never kick a man when he is down." Thomas's voice was as chilly as the wind that whistled across the Sound of Duart to rattle the windows of the castle.

"Why not? He's naught but a coward," said Ferguson, spitting blood onto the floor. "He deserves no more."

Thomas slammed the hilt of his sword into the grinning face.

Fia winced as the man went tumbling end over end, his arms and legs becoming inextricably tangled in the chairs and benches. Duncan's laughter rang through the room.

" 'Tis not funny," Fia snapped.

"Perhaps not," Duncan said in a stifled voice. "But 'twas well done. Indeed, 'twas very well done."

Thomas gave a tightly controlled smile. "You're too kind."

MacKenna went to the fallen man. "He's out cold, the fool. I'll put him to bed. He'll have a hell of a headache when he awakes." He lifted the inert body and dragged it out the door.

Fia helped Robert to his feet. He leaned against her with a thankful sigh. *"Sacre Dieu,"* he murmured. "My head has a thousand needles sticking in it."

Duncan smirked. "Douglas did you in, eh?"

Robert shook his head, then winced. " 'Twas not Kinnish but his brother. The filthy whoreson took me from behind."

Duncan's frown was sudden. "Took you from behind? One of *my* men? That cowardly lackwit'll be hideless when I finish with him!"

"It seems your army is peppered with cowardly lackwits," said Thomas.

"Och, I cannot believe this!" Fia declared, before Duncan could respond. "Here is Lord Robert, nigh unto death, and the two of you can do nothing but taunt each other like children! Come, Robert, let's leave the fools to bray and wrangle like the asses they are. We'll find the servants and see what chambers are to be had." Casting a sweeping glare at them all, she led Robert from the room.

Thomas watched until she was out of sight, relieved to see her leave. It was difficult to pay attention to Fia's grinning lout of a cousin while she was about, all flashing eyes and kissable lips.

Worse yet was her hair. He had almost lost his tenuous control then and there when he had slid his hand under the silken mass to caress the warmth of her neck. Sweet Jesu, but he wanted to run his hands through her curls even when they frothed about her shoulders and tangled beneath Robert's arm.

Thomas frowned. Damned if Robert hadn't been holding his wife a bit too tightly.

He peered into the hall, wondering if he should say something. He shook his head. Nay, every time he tried to speak with Fia, he ended up sounding like the veriest lackwit. Only when he held her did he receive the response he wanted.

He grinned. Maybe that was the key. Maybe he should do less talking and more touching. As soon as they were alone, he would—

"By the Holy Cross, Rotherwood, leave her be." Duncan's amused tone recalled him to his senses. "She's safe enough with MacQuarrie. He barely has the strength to stand, much less make love to her."

Thomas fumed silently to have been caught staring after Fia like a lad smitten by his first maiden. He managed a stiff smile. "You haven't yet explained why my household has been overrun by a loud, loutish army of Scotsmen."

Duncan grinned. "I suppose I owe you that much. MacKenna!" he bellowed.

The guard ambled into the room. "Aye?"

"Bring me the cask."

MacKenna nodded and left.

"Cask?" Thomas asked.

"Aye. I bring you something of great import." Duncan strolled to the fireplace and leaned a broad shoulder against the mantel. " 'Twas the reason I came."

"Couldn't you have just given it to me while I was on Mull?"

"I would have if it had been in my possession. It arrived two hours after you left."

Thomas raised his eyebrows but returned no answer. He disliked this sudden turn of events.

MacKenna returned with a small jeweled cask that he carried with the utmost care. He set the box on the table near Thomas and then left the room.

As the door closed behind him, Thomas asked, "Yet another wedding gift?"

"You might call it a wedding gift. Though not for you."

"For Fia, then."

"Nay." Duncan shook his head, his eyes intent on Thomas's face. "For Walsingham."

Thomas lifted his brows. "Walsingham?"

Duncan nodded. "Aye. As he dare not be seen with me, I am counting on you to deliver it for me."

"He said *you* wouldn't see *him.*"

Duncan's smile was black. "What Walsingham says and what Walsingham does are often as different as night and day. You should know that."

Thomas nodded. He was beginning to suspect Robert might have had some foundation for his dislike of the counselor. "Walsingham said you had brought an army as a gift."

Duncan shrugged. "If you need them, you've but to call. I must warn you, Sassenach, after today, Walsingham will stop at nothing to discredit me. He's a powerful man. I'm counting on you to protect Fia."

Thomas picked up the cask. Rectangular and made of rosewood, its surface was cut into an intricate pattern and set with sapphires and rubies. He looked up to find Duncan regarding him. "What's in it?"

The laird cast a grim look at the casket and spoke with telling softness. "Inside lies enough evidence of Queen Mary's trickery as could warrant her execution."

Thomas swallowed against the dryness of his throat. Walsingham's final evidence. He carefully set the cask back onto the table. Sweet Jesu, but he could use some ale.

"The Scottish queen has betrayed us all." Duncan's face was as frozen and hard as the Thames in the height of winter. "Walsingham has promised support for her babe, the prince, if she is deposed. She must be removed before she plunges Scotland into the bloodiest battle ever seen."

"War is imminent?"

"Already men draw lines in her name and dare each other to cross. 'Tis but a matter of time."

Thomas whistled silently. "Do you ask Walsingham to secure Elizabeth's support in overthrowing Mary?"

"Scotland doesn't need any more martyrs. We merely want Queen Mary sequestered somewhere safe."

"We?"

Duncan nodded. "There are twenty of us. Some of us have property and titles, some don't. But we all love Scotland too much to let Mary tear her apart."

Thomas saw the tightening around Duncan's eyes. "Has Walsingham promised you this help?"

"He has. Now 'tis only a question of whether he'll honor his agreements or not." There was a moment of silence as the laird absently stirred the fire. He looked up to meet Thomas's gaze. "You mustn't tell Fia any of this. I won't have her endangered."

Thomas nodded. After a moment, he asked, "Tell me, Duncan—the letter I took from the great hall—did Fia know of it?"

"Of course not. She knew you had come into the house to steal a missive of some sort, but I wouldn't let her see it."

Thomas experienced a surge of relief. She hadn't known. She had told the truth.

"I want your agreement, Sassenach, that you will keep Fia clear of this mess. Walsingham is no fool."

"You may leave Fia to me, Maclean. She's my wife, not yours."

"You don't have to remind me," Duncan said softly. His mouth twisted into a bitter, self-derisive smile. "I told my men we traveled here to bring that cask to Fia. They believe it holds the famed Maclean rubies.

"You needed a hundred men merely to protect a small cask of jewels?"

"The *Maclean* rubies, Sassenach."

"Do they even exist?"

"Aye, though if you can get Fia to wear them, you're a better man than I."

"Was there ever a question?"

Duncan's smile faded, and Thomas lifted the cask, the jewels winking red and blue. "What exactly will I receive for this service?"

"The sight of me and my men riding down yon street, headed in the direction from whence we came."

" 'Tis enough. I'll do it, though I don't understand why you must—"

"It doesn't matter." Duncan's voice cut through the air like a claymore. "Just take it to Walsingham, and tell the old fox I've paid my part of the bargain. We are now even."

"Even? For what?"

Duncan's shoulders shook, and his laughter boomed across the room. "For more than you know, Sassenach. For far more than you'll ever know."

Chapter Twenty-two

"Sweet Jesu! That hurts!"

At Robert's shouted protest, the rabbit scrambled madly off the bed and skittered across the room, his fat stomach never clearing the floor.

Fia smothered a giggle as she watched the rabbit paddle wildly to reach the safety of the red brocade window curtains.

"I lie dying, and you play with that rabbit," Robert complained.

"You've only a wee knot upon your head, and 'tis scarcely bleeding. If that's all it takes to kill you, 'tis a wonder you've lived this long."

Robert raised a hand to his right ear and gingerly touched the swelling. "You're a cold-hearted wench to call such a serious injury a wee knot. No doubt were I to lose an arm, you would call it a mere flesh wound."

Mary clucked her tongue. "Fie, Master Robert! Here's

248

her ladyship a-tendin' ye as if ye were her own bamkin, and what do ye do but cry foul!"

"Let her become busy elsewhere." Robert sulked, eyeing the herb-soaked bandage in Mary's hand with some distrust. "I would run and hide from you both were that hideous animal not standing guard over the doorway."

Zeus lay sleeping on his back across the threshold, his legs splayed in an ungainly sprawl, drool dripping from the corner of his slack mouth to pool onto the floor.

Fia regarded her dog with a fond smile. "Och, now, Robert, don't make sport of the poor beastie. He's worn out from chasing all the evil, villainous English cats from the courtyard. He was snarling and gnashing his teeth like a huge, terrible ogre. 'Twas a sight to see."

Robert snorted his disbelief. "He possesses naught but gums, and those he displays only when you are present to protect him, should any take up his false challenge."

"Och, no. He can be strong and brave when he needs to be," Fia protested. "You've just never seen him with reason. He must feel secure in your presence to sleep so soundly."

"Pathetic, mangy beast," muttered Robert, turning his face away from them all, as if the sight was too much to bear.

"Now, Master Robert, enough of that," admonished Mary. " 'Tis no wonder ye are a wee bit out of sorts, what with such a welt on yer noggin, but don't be takin' yer poor spirits out on the lassie. She's enough on her plate without ye addin' to it, hurtin' though ye be."

A slow smile curved his mouth as he turned back, grabbed Mary's rough hand, and held it reverently. "Ah, Mary! Only a skilled healer such as yourself would recognize the severity of my wounds. Even angels could learn tenderness and mercy from your gentle touch."

She disengaged her hand and patted his cheek.

"Enough of your foolery, Master Robert. Now let the mistress clean yer wound without any more of yer mischief." She glanced at the door and frowned. "Though we could do with some water. I wonder where that flitterin' missy is who promised to bring us some fresh water."

Fia wondered if Rotherwood House's stern, disapproving housekeeper would ever return. There had been instant animosity between the woman and Mary.

Robert gave a sad shake of his head. "Mistress Hadwell has never been a flittering anything. As a housekeeper, I believe she is superb. But she is a dour woman with a pinched mouth as would make a lemon green with envy."

"Ye have the right of that. She looks as if she sat upon a stick at some time and forgot to remove it."

Robert's eyes twinkled. "I've never been able to win so much as a smile from those grim lips, though I have jested and read poetry to her by the hour."

"Why does Thomas allow her to stay?" asked Fia.

"Mistress Hadwell has been with the Wentworth family for nigh on two score years. She's a superb housekeeper, too, for all her sour ways."

"I can't believe ye'd say she was a superb housekeeper," Mary scoffed. "There's more dust in here than out in the street. And as for Mistress Hadwell, 'tis obvious that 'Mistress Hadnone' would be a more fittin' name."

Robert choked on a laugh. "I fear you may be right, Mary. Only a well-stuffed codpiece would brighten that dismal face."

Mary ignored him and continued her tirade. "Aye, stiff and soured, she is. I could tell that the minute we released her and that parcel of withered goats his lordship calls servants."

"Now, Mary, you'd have been upset, too, if an army

of Englishmen came to Duart and locked you in the cellar," Fia protested.

"I think 'tis a wonder the poor Sassenach even has a house to come home to, with such whey-faced dribblers about. Well, I'm not waitin' fer the water any longer. I'll just go and get it myself." Huffing loudly at all the dust she imagined must be under the bed curtains, she stomped out of the room.

"How I wish I could witness that encounter." Robert sighed wistfully.

"Why? To goad them on?"

"Mistress Hadwell runs Thomas's establishment with an iron hand. She'll not welcome any interference from Mary."

Fia chuckled and perched on the edge of the bed. "I'd wager on Mary any day."

"Would you, indeed?" His voice had an unmistakable edge of eagerness.

She laughed. "Aye, though not with you! We still have one wager between us, and that one doesn't suit me well at all."

"An easy bet, that. I've naught to do but transform you from a winsome Scottish lady into a winsome English lady. Then you will secure the queen's sanction, and your plays will be the rage. Thomas can have no doubts then that you seek him for reasons other than the use of his fortune."

"That was never my intention."

"Then you sought to make him jealous," Robert suggested.

Fia smoothed the bed curtains. "I would never attempt anything so foolish."

"Of course," he said, plainly disbelieving. "Well, it makes no matter. I will win the bet. You've made excellent progress already."

"But not enough. Remember, Robert, that if you lose,

'twill take all your charm to find the amount of gold I will require to publish my plays."

He gave a negligent wave of his hand. "I would gladly publish your plays myself, wager or no. You've enough imagination to write a hundred plays. But, my sweet, should I win . . ." His smile widened into a blatant grin.

Her eyes narrowed. "I think 'tis time you told me the exact forfeit of our wager."

"Why? Do you think I mean to fail in my task?"

"Of course not. 'Tis just that the more I get to know you, the more aware I become of your tendency for mischief-making."

"Nay, 'tis nothing evil," he said and shook his head. Immediately, a flicker of pain crossed his face. "My poor head feels like an egg crushed beneath the heel of a boot. I'd like one good moment with that fiend Douglas."

"Aye, that would solve all. Then we'd have two broken heads instead of one."

His mouth curved sweetly. "Nay, you'd have but one, for I swear there would not be enough left of the wretch to bury, much less bandage."

Fia gave an inelegant snort. "Men. Fools and brawns, they are one and the same thing."

"A lovely sentiment," a deep voice drawled from the doorway. "Though hardly a welcome one to hear pouring forth from the lips of one's wife."

Fia jumped up guiltily from Robert's bed. Thomas leaned in the doorway against one powerful arm, his other hand cupped about a small bejeweled box that winked beckoningly in the light.

"I would enter, but this"—he gestured at Zeus—"thing halts me."

Fia called to the dog, but other than twitching slightly, he didn't respond.

Thomas lifted an eyebrow and looked steadfastly at the sleeping animal.

Fia called to Zeus once more. Again the dog twitched, but his snores did not cease. Refusing to meet Thomas's amused gaze, Fia stomped across the room and grabbed the dog by the loose skin about his shoulders. With much shoving and tugging, she hauled the slumbering animal from the door.

Finally roused, Zeus wagged his tail, thumping it loudly on the floor as the corner of his slack mouth lifted in a grin, though he made no move to help Fia. He was softly snoring before she had even walked two steps away.

Fia shot a resentful glance at Thomas and wryly sank into a curtsey. "Your path is now cleared, your lordship," she intoned.

With a sigh, Thomas deposited the small cask onto a table and hauled Fia unceremoniously to her feet. She tried to ignore the thrill that ran through her as his large, warm hands slid down the length of her arms to capture her hands.

"Enough, comfit. Though I enjoy your wit, I find it much more humorous when 'tis pointed elsewhere. If you must needle someone, why not sink your barbs into Robert? He is far more worthy of your scorn."

"A pox on you, Thomas," protested Robert. "I don't deserve such abuse!"

Thomas arched an eyebrow. "Really? Then can you explain why you thought it necessary to lay your bloodied head upon my bed and not your own?"

"Robert! You said this was a guest chamber!" She looked around the room, the rich red velvets and thick carpets suddenly making more sense.

" *'Tis* a guest room, as I am a guest and I am using this for my room," Robert said. "Besides, I am sore wounded and—"

"Sore wounded? By a mere bump on the head?" Thomas pulled Fia beneath one arm and lowered his voice

253

to whisper conspiratorially, "See how he plays upon your tender sensibilities? 'Tis shameless."

" 'Tis shameless," she echoed breathlessly, wondering how she was ever supposed to put moments like this into her plays.

He chuckled and pulled her hand to his lips. Her heart pounded so loudly in her chest, she was sure everyone in the entire house could hear it. Sweet St. Catherine, but this was too much. The back of her hand tingled and burned where his breath brushed against her skin.

Robert moaned loudly. "I'm too ill to move. Besides, this bed is softer than mine."

Thomas pressed a last, lingering kiss on the back of Fia's hand before sighing deeply and releasing her. "Duncan awaits you belowstairs, comfit. Best you go now before he comes looking for you."

"Duncan?" she repeated, clutching her released hand to her heart. As the sound of her own blank voice drifted through the fog surrounding her, Fia blushed. By the saints, but she sounded like the most besotted fool ever to walk the earth. Thomas must think her a total lackwit. Taking a shuddering breath, she nodded. "Of course. Duncan awaits."

Thomas smiled warmly. She looked like an angel, her hair a nimbus about her head, the curls caressing her neck, her cheeks lightly stained with color. Sweet Jesu, but he would give all he had to take her, to tell her . . . He glanced past her and met Robert's amused gaze.

Smothering the impulse to rail against the smirk on Robert's face, he returned his attention to Fia and said, "Aye. Duncan asked—"

"Asked?" Robert's voice was fraught with disbelief.

"Asked," repeated Thomas firmly, "for Fia to attend him before he leaves. Meanwhile, I will assist Robert in locating his own bedchamber."

Fia hesitated yet again, and he took her hand and led

her to the door, turning her about and gently pushing her in the direction of the stairs. "Speed your cousin on his way before his accursed men begin a brawl in the street. 'Twould take little for it to become an all-out war."

Fia nodded and walked down the hall, her skirts swaying with each hesitant step. Thomas watched her from the doorway.

"I lie dying, and all the world falls in love." Robert's voice drifted out into the hallway. " 'Tis a cruel, cruel world."

"What? Still in my bed? Get thee gone, lazy slug."

Robert gestured to the heavens. "Am I to receive no comfort? No care? No kind words?"

"None."

"Unappreciated. My genius is wasted. I don't know why I even try. First I am attended by a beautiful woman who showers her care only on a fattened rabbit and"— he gestured at Zeus's snoring figure—"*that,* whatever it is. Then comes a warm and generous maid, but she is too busy warring with the housekeeper to attend to me. And now you, so full of mirth that I scarce know you."

"You know me well enough." Thomas grinned and went to lean against the mantel. Zeus lay in the prime spot, his lethargic body stretched across the hearth. With a heavy boot, Thomas nudged the dog out of his way. Zeus's eye opened to a narrow slit, and he yawned, his gums bared for the world to see, before resuming his snoring.

"I knew the old Thomas," Robert said, sitting upright and sliding off the bed with surprising litheness. He tucked a pillow under each arm. "I knew the one who grumped and grumbled about life. The one who took the whole world as seriously as death and never laughed nor smiled."

"I was not so bad as that."

Robert raised his eyebrows. "The one who worried constantly whether or not he could meet the impossible dictates of a man long dead."

Thomas frowned into the fireplace. "My father was strict, not impossible. He was used to getting the best, and he had reason to expect it from his only son. Besides, I laughed and smiled, just not to the excesses you choose."

"Only when forced by politeness to do so. You take everything too much to heart, *mon ami*. You always have." He grinned. "Until now. She has brought you laughter."

Thomas rubbed the back of his neck. He *had* been feeling near giddy since Duncan had admitted Fia hadn't known of the queen's letter.

He shot a glance at Robert. "I asked Duncan if Fia knew the contents of the missive I stole from Duart Castle."

"What did he say?"

"He said she knew there was a missive, but he had kept it from her."

"Do you believe him?"

Thomas nodded.

"Wondrous! Now you can forget that crack-brained annulment plot."

Thomas wondered if it would be that easy. He had offered to marry her in earnest, but she had refused him almost coldly. Yet the heat of her reaction when he had won his way into Duncan's presence had been a reward in itself.

"So will you give up the annulment?" Robert asked impatiently.

Thomas shrugged. "Perhaps."

Robert's smile grew sly. "Simmons seems to think you and Fia became most, ah, intimate aboard ship."

"Simmons is a fool."

Robert tapped his chin. "Of course, there are many strange noises on a ship, all sorts of moans and creaks. He could be wrong, I suppose."

Thomas crossed his arms.

Robert grinned. "You lasted longer than I thought you would."

"Simmons possesses an unfortunate tendency to spread rumors."

" 'Tis no crime to bed your own wife. Admit it. 'Tis the one and only benefit of the married state."

"If you've developed a liking for wedded bliss, 'twould be easy enough to satisfy such a craving. I'll speak with the queen."

Robert scowled at Thomas's chuckle. "I think I liked you better without humor." He turned toward door, halting as he walked by the table. Sapphires and rubies winked at him. Robert's hand grazed the surface of the cask. "A pretty trinket. Is it a present for the beauteous Fia?"

Thomas shook his head. "Nay. 'Tis the rest of Walsingham's proof. I'm to deliver it along with Duncan's compliments."

Robert yanked his hand away as if the box were a live coal. "By the rood, but you're a cold fish to stand there and speak so calmly. Men would die for this!"

Thomas regarded the box thoughtfully. "Aye, I imagine they would."

Robert looked puzzled. "Why does Duncan provide so much for Walsingham?"

"He wishes for Elizabeth to secure the Scottish queen away to avoid war."

"Would Elizabeth do it?"

"Aye, if she perceived a threat to her own crown. I take it these letters may prove just that."

Robert limped to the door. "I've no head for intrigue today. 'Twill be difficult enough to sleep with *that* lying about," he said, gesturing at the cask. "I will most like have nightmares."

"I'll hide it, never fear."

Robert's eyes went past Thomas to the huge, carved rocks surrounding the fireplace. "The secret hiding place?" His voice filled with awe.

Thomas looked at the hearth with a frown. "If I can remember how to trigger the latch to release it, 'twould be the most secure place. It's been years since I have even tried."

Robert regarded him with a jaundiced eye. "I can't imagine it. A secret hiding place, and you've never used it. Had I one in my house, I would keep all my silks within."

Thomas rolled his eyes. " 'Tis not a closet, Robert. There's barely room for yon box."

Robert looked disappointed. He turned toward the door. "Oh. I thought 'twas of a decent size. Be sure to secure that box quickly. We don't know who can be trusted."

"True. And Robert, before you leave, replace my pillows. 'Twould make you even more sore if I have to yank them from beneath your slumbering head."

Robert frowned, and with a great show of injured dignity he lay the pillows on a chair by the door, carefully smoothing away imaginary wrinkles, and lightly fluffing them. Then, with a slight bow, he quit the room, slamming the door in his wake.

Chapter Twenty-three

"Och, now, and what might you be doing?"

Thomas jerked upright, slamming his head into the stone fireplace. A huge puff of soot billowed into the room, and he began to choke, one hand wiping his streaming eyes, the other uselessly fanning the ashy air.

As he staggered away from the hearth, one large boot came down squarely on Zeus's crooked tail. The dog howled in agony, and Thomas spun away, tripping over a chair and reeling backward, his arms flailing uselessly.

For the space of a second, he tottered on his heels, then crashed to the floor in a cloud of soot.

Fia blinked in amazement. "Are . . . are you all right?"

He moaned softly, and Fia tiptoed closer, peering through the haze at his blackened face.

Thomas's hair was no longer tawny gold but a dull, dusty gray. Soot splashed black trails across his head and shoulders, leaving only his neck and a small triangle under his nose the color of flesh. His eyes, which had filled with tears at the sudden fall of ash, were now so reddened that they could have frightened off the most stouthearted of heroes.

"Can you get up?" Fia asked, sinking to her knees on the floor beside him, heedless of the ash clinging to her gown.

"Aye," he choked, rubbing his eyes with the back of a grimy hand. "Only . . . give me a moment to . . . recover my breath."

In the silence that followed, Fia could almost hear Robert saying that Thomas was the luckiest man in England. *Sweet St. Catherine, but if this is the luckiest man in the country a-lying here in the soot, then God help England.*

She choked back a laugh, hiding her mirth by carefully wiping some of the soot from his face with the edge of her skirt. "What were you doing with your head stuck up the chimney?"

"God's Breath, comfit, but you scared me nigh to death. Do you never knock before entering a chamber?"

"I did knock," she answered indignantly, "but no one answered. Where's Robert?"

"In his own chambers, where he belongs."

"Oh. He must be feeling better." She tilted her head to one side. "Do you think you can stand?"

Before he could answer, Zeus shuffled over and sat beside Thomas. The dog's crooked tail thumped uncertainly.

"Och, look at that. Zeus has come to see how you are."

" 'Twas all his fault," Thomas grumbled, then glared at Fia's smothered giggle. "As for you, Mistress Mirth, 'tis not a laughing matter. I was nigh killed."

Zeus tilted his head curiously at the familiar voice. With a puzzled look, he leaned over and sniffed loudly

at the ash-blackened hair. His tail thumped as he recognized Thomas.

"What a sweet beastie he is," said Fia. "He wants to
make up."

Thomas looked anything but pleased, yet he still offered the dog a tentative pat.

Zeus leaned forward to take another sniff at the soot-
covered hair and promptly sneezed in Thomas's face.

"That . . . your . . . if
I . . . when I . . . I'll just . . ." Thomas reached for
Zeus, but the dog scrambled out of the way, his crooked
tail wagging as he scrambled under the high bed.

"That mangy, good-for-nothing, ill-mannered, foul-
smelling—"

"Half-eared," Fia added helpfully.

Thomas favored her with a flat stare. She bit her lip,
knowing instinctively that to burst out laughing would
be a grave error.

He regarded her silently. "We need to speak of our
marriage," he said, his voice abrupt in the silence.

All desire to laugh left her. "What is there to say?"

He brushed her cheek with the tips of his fingers. "I'm
not Robert, comfit. I don't woo with words." He gave a
half-grin that stole away power of speech. "I don't know
what soft phrases will thrill your heart."

She blinked. For a man who didn't know how to thrill,
he was doing a remarkably fine job.

"I never would have suggested we continue this marriage if I didn't think 'twould be successful," he said.

"There are reasons other than a babe?"

"Many more reasons."

It was more than she had hoped for. Fia knew her
happiness must have blazed in her smile, for his eyes
warmed to molten amber. Yet he made no move to touch
her.

"Is something wrong?"

261

"Aye," he replied. "Something's very wrong."

"What?" A tinge of alarm rose through her. He looked so serious.

His hands grasped her shoulders. "It has just occurred to me that I am so very, very dirty, whilst you are so very, very clean."

Before she could comprehend his intent, he pulled her against him and then rolled her under his length. She was trapped on the dusty floor, soot rising in a foggy cloud around them.

His ash-covered face loomed above her, his even white teeth gleaming as he grinned.

"You-you . . ." Words failed her.

His grin widened. "You must take your medicine." With deliberate slowness, he wiped his hand on the front of her dress, lingering an unnecessary length of time on the swell of her breasts.

A long smudge led down to where his hand cupped her intimately. She frowned severely. "I didn't think laughing was against either of our rules, so I owe no forfeit. All I did was enter the room. You were the one who acted as though you'd been caught stealing silver from the queen." Her eyes narrowed. "What were you doing with your head up the chimney like a—"

He kissed her. 'Twas merely an effort to silence her questioning, but as her lips parted and her tongue sought his, he forgot about the secret hiding place, Walsingham's proof, and everything other than the woman he held in his arms.

She strained against him, her arms about his neck, her tongue seeking his. Her hips lifted in an unconsciously wanton invitation. He had to steel his every nerve against the urge to immediately bury himself into her, so intense was the pleasure.

He looked into the smoky blackness of her eyes and gently bit her full bottom lip, laving his tongue against the mock injury. She moaned and closed her eyes, her thick lashes lying like black crescents on her cheeks.

He smiled gently at the gray streaks that marred her creamy skin and whispered against her mouth. "I hate to tell you this, comfit, but I fear I've shared a bit more of this soot than I intended." She blinked up at him, comprehension rising slowly in her arousal-clouded eyes.

To his surprise, she returned his smile and traced a finger down his cheek. "I've always wanted to make love in front of a fireplace." She chuckled, and the sound ran through him like a rushing brook through a parched plain.

"You look more like you've been inside a fireplace than in front of one." He took the opportunity to place a few small kisses alongside her delectable mouth and firm, rounded chin.

Her eyes melted into liquid pools of black. "With you, anywhere," she murmured, her voice carrying a huskiness that ignited him with the need to take her here, now.

His hands sank into the luxury of her hair, instantly welcomed by the silkiness of her curls. He ran his hands past her waist, to the curve of her hip, and on to the firmness of her thigh.

With an impatient tug, he pulled her skirts up until he could cup the roundness of her leg in his hand. Sweet Jesu, but this woman was made for his hands, he thought possessively, kissing her with renewed passion.

Fia gasped as his hands touched her leg and began their smooth ascent past her knee. Just as she tensed, his mouth, warm and demanding, was on hers, his tongue seeking, questing. She threw one arm around his neck and placed the other on his back, running it up and down the hardness of his rippling muscles. Sweet St. Catherine, but she forgot everything when he touched her.

Lost in the wonder of the feeling, she murmured, "I love you so."

The world froze. Neither spoke nor moved. Slowly, he pulled back and stared into her eyes. "What did you say?"

Even with his face and hair smudged with soot, he was still heart-wrenchingly beautiful. She swallowed hard, wishing the earth would open up and swallow her whole. "I . . . don't remember."

"Nay." Thomas put his hands to either side of her face and tilted her chin up, smiling softly. "Tell me, comfit," he whispered.

His eyes glinted like firelight playing across a goblet of mulled wine. Try as she might, she could not look away from those mesmerizing eyes. "I love you," Fia whispered, the words wrenched from her heart as surely as if he had placed her under a spell.

He didn't smile but slowly lowered his mouth to place a leisurely, almost reverent kiss on her lips. She groaned and kissed him back, her whole body writhing with urgent passion. His hands sank into her hair, and he plunged his tongue into her mouth in an insistent, seductive rhythm. Unconsciously she ground her hips against his, her hands tugging senselessly at his clothing.

He began to loosen her dress. As her skin was exposed to the chill air, her nipples hardened. He moaned, and his mouth, hot and insistent, covered one taut peak even as his hand cupped the other. She gasped, arching into him, her hands grasping at his hair.

"Don't stop," she breathed, and he increased his efforts. Somehow, without ceasing to ply his heated tongue to her breast, he managed to free her dress. He stripped it from her, his eyes burning as though fevered.

He lifted himself to look at her, his gaze moving slowly from her face down her neck and beyond, lingering with exquisite torture on her body until she thought she would burst into flames from embarrassment. "Sweet Jesu, but you are beautiful," he murmured.

She tugged at his shirt. "Undress," she whispered, pleading.

He stared at her, a beautiful smile playing across his chiseled lips. The soot was almost gone, only a trace remaining under his eyes to give him a rakish look. She ran her fingertips across his mouth, and he caught her hand, placing a heated kiss into the tender skin of her palm.

"Undress," she whispered again, tugging at his shirt laces.

"Nay, sweet lady, 'tis your turn to undress me," he whispered against her mouth, his hands never still.

She moaned and writhed as he nipped at her ear, his hand sliding up her thigh to brush ever so lightly against her moistness. She began to tug on his shirt, crying out when the stubborn lacing refused to loosen.

He chuckled deep within his chest and grabbed her frantic hands. "Softly, love! We have all the time in the world." His brown eyes glinted warmly into hers as he leaned forward to gently brush her lips with his. The kiss deepened, and she felt his hand slide between her legs to thread gently through the curls.

Hot, molten liquid rushed through her veins. She was afire with want. She threw an arm about his neck and ran her other hand over his shoulders, down his back and lower, her fingers kneading his firm muscles. She reached to cup his manhood, and he groaned into her mouth. She wanted to touch him, to hold him. Thomas moaned again as she stroked him through the cloth.

She tried to undo the lacing, cursing her trembling fingers with her every breath, yet still he did not help her. Frustration made her bold.

"Undress," she demanded less softly this time, thrusting her hips at him for emphasis. His eyes clenched shut as though he were in pain.

"Sweet Jesu, woman, do not move!" he hissed through gritted teeth, his face strained, a damp sheen moistening his upper lip.

For a second he lay still, his forehead dropping to rest against her cheek, his breathing rasping harshly through the room. Suddenly his fingers were tugging and yanking at his own laces with satisfying desperation. In an instant, he was naked, his skin warm against hers.

He pulled her legs apart and positioned himself above her, his eyes staring directly into hers as he lowered himself into her. There was an agonizing second of fullness as he ground his hips against her.

"Sweet Jesu," he whispered between clenched teeth. Before he could withdraw to sink into her again, she tensed and then threw back her head as wave after wave of pleasure rippled through her.

Heat rose and singed Thomas as she clutched her legs about him. Try as he might, he could not withstand the wet pressure of her reaction. Spiraling through heaven, she sent him over the edge without even moving.

For a moment they lay spent, legs intertwined as their breathing returned to a more normal pace. Thomas lifted himself to look down at Fia's flushed face. He couldn't resist placing a kiss on the corner of her mouth. It looked like a dewy cherry, ripe for tasting.

She peered at him from beneath heavy eyelids. "I have soot all over my clothing."

He chuckled. "Aye, and your face as well." He kissed her nose. "But you manage to look beautiful for all that."

She smiled as her eyes drifted closed.

"What's this? 'Tis but midday, madam, and yet you look to be asleep."

"I know," she murmured, not opening her eyes. " 'Tis just that you make me so very, very tired." She shivered, and a slight frown turned down the corners of her mouth. "I would sleep but for the cold."

He laughed softly, cupping her face between his hands. "I promise to have a roaring fire awaiting you next time."

She shifted on the floor and grimaced drowsily. "Only if you get thicker carpets. This is not much better than the planks of your ship."

"Witch!" he remonstrated as he spread her skirt across her and tucked it under her chin like a blanket. "I give you so much pleasure you nigh expire, and all you can do is complain of the hardness of the floor and the coldness of the room?"

" 'Nigh expire'?" she murmured. "Now you sound like Robert."

"I would rather be likened to your pig, King Arthur."

She chuckled, the sound settling around him with the warmth of a woolen cloak. He draped a leg across hers and pulled her to him.

She nestled against his chest, falling asleep almost instantly. He watched her a moment before a noise in the corridor reminded him of the activity within the house. It was very possible that some servant or other would come tromping into the room at any moment.

He gave a reluctant sigh and scooped her into his arms. He laid her on the huge bed as gently as he could. Other than snuggling farther into the mounds of pillows and blankets, she did not stir.

He smiled in contentment as he brushed her hair from her face. She loved him. She had admitted as much during their passion, unable to deny it. He tucked the cover under her chin and gently kissed her lips. She smiled in her sleep, a soft, sighing smile that whispered of magical dreams.

He laughed softly. Soon. He would tell her soon.

Chapter Twenty-four

Two weeks of heaven. Thomas sat on a bench beneath a tree and looked at the handful of blossoms he had gathered. He was somewhat astonished at the breadth and beauty of the gardens. In the eleven years since Rotherwood House had passed into his hands, he couldn't remember having spent more than a moment or two within the peaceful confines of the tended walkways or flower beds.

Until now.

He stared back at the house and wondered how he ever could have thought of Rotherwood House as dark, forbidding, and joyless.

The windows of the house stood open with nary a curtain drawn. Within the walls, the servants called merrily to one another, and doors opened and slammed with vigor. Somewhere a lute was being strummed as a callow youth practiced a colorful ditty. 'Twas as if the whole place had suddenly awakened after a long sleep.

Even the servants seemed more lively. All of them except Mistress Hadwell.

Thomas grimaced at the thought of the dour housekeeper. He had inherited her along with the house, and he had begun to think 'twas her presence that had long dampened his enthusiasm for the place. He would have to have a word with her about the way she spoke to Fia. It bordered on insolence.

"Hallo, there, Cap'n," Simmons's cheery voice rang out.

Thomas started and became absurdly aware that he was holding a fistful of flowers and staring at the house like some lovestruck poet. "Simmons," he said, dropping the blooms and dusting off his hands. "I was just, ah, checking the quality of the gardening."

"Aye, Cap'n, if'n ye say so." His first mate's bulbous eyes focused on the discarded flowers. "I've delivered yer message jes' like ye told me."

"And what did you find at—" Thomas began, only to halt as Fia's laughter, low and sultry, drifted down from an open window and caught his attention. The vibrant, husky laugh mingled with Robert's deep voice.

'Twas time Robert learned the value of home. His own home. Though the frivolous Scotsman's slight wounds had long since healed, he continued to haunt Rotherwood House. He exhibited an astonishing disregard to Thomas's broad hints that he must be eager to be on his way.

Robert's excuse for staying on was that he was bound by honor to train Fia for her presentation to the queen. Thomas wasn't sure he approved of such nonsense, though Fia seemed to derive considerable enjoyment from it. For that reason alone, he had made no complaints but silently ground his teeth at Robert's annoying presence.

"Cap'n?" Simmons interrupted his thoughts. "If'n ye

don't mind, me li'l Meggie is waitin' on me."

"Of course," Thomas answered absently, his attention still riveted on the window.

"I declare, Cap'n, but ye look to be moonstruck. 'Tis unnatural to see a growed man so addlepated." He directed a glare at the window and spat his disgust into a nearby bush.

"This from a man who sat in the street in front of Meggie's house and yelled the most horrendous love sonnets 'til she agreed to marry him. I'm still not sure whether she loves you or if she merely became crazed by all of that caterwauling."

"Cap'n, keep yer voice down." Simmons looked nervously around the garden. "Someone might hear ye."

Thomas chuckled and stretched out in the warm sun. By the rood, but the garden was a virtual paradise. He'd bring Fia here this eve and stroll about the walkways. He had discovered that his newfound joy tripled every time he shared it with her.

He wondered if the new carpet he had ordered had yet arrived. He had a prime spot in front of the fireplace already picked out. A little surprised at his own eagerness, he wondered at himself. Aye, something had definitely changed.

An idea struck him with the force of a blow—he had fallen in love. He looked at Simmons in bewilderment.

"What's the matter with ye, Cap'n?" Round eyes blinked anxiously. "Are ye ill?"

Thomas abruptly stood. By the saints, he loved Fia. He knew that since her own admission she'd wanted to hear him make the same. But some part of him held back, whispering to him of loss and betrayal.

"Trust no one," his father's voice whispered in his ear. A wave of uncertainty ran over him, and he clenched his fists against an ocean of doubts.

Simmons grunted, eyeing him with a severe frown. "Ye think ye've got the pox? I could go and fetch li'l Meggie if ye think 'twill help."

Thomas recovered himself. "Nay. I'm fine. Did you find the tavern?"

Simmons nodded. " 'Twas as easy as knottin' a rope."

"And the message?"

"That were a mite more difficult a task. I found that big man like ye said and asked to see Letty."

"Did you encounter any problems?"

"Well . . ." Simmons scratched his neck, casting a leery glance at Thomas. "Not 'xactly."

Thomas crossed his arms. "And what does that mean?"

"Cap'n, 'twas like this. I didn't have no problems 'til that poxy scriver took offense at somethin' me li'l Meggie said 'bout the lack of quality ale in the place. Ye know, 'tis a crime the way they try to cheat ye in a low tavern like that. If I owned a tap room—"

"Meggie?" Thomas asked, his voice rising. "You took Meggie with you when you went to deliver the message?"

"Well, now, Cap'n, it didn't seem like such a bad idea at the time, seein' as how she already knew all 'bout it."

Thomas felt the heat rise in his face, and Simmons hurriedly added, "It jes' slipped out, Cap'n, I swear it!"

"I should have you flayed. If I had thought you'd tell every person you knew, I'd have sent one of the servants here to attend to it!"

Simmons nodded wisely and rubbed his nose with a dirty sleeve. "Aye, house servants are a shifty lot."

Thomas closed his eyes. "Simmons," he said slowly, "what did Goliath say?"

"Goliath? Oh, that be the name of that lout! Well, Cap'n, after he and me li'l Meggie'd had their words, I

271

asked to see Letty, jes' like ye asked me to. He said she was not about."

Thomas frowned. "Not about?"

Simmons nodded. "Aye. He says she's gone to visit her mum up in the north country."

Thomas swore softly. For two weeks he had been trying to get a message to Walsingham to arrange for the delivery of Duncan's letters. The message from Goliath meant that Walsingham was out of the country.

Thomas frowned and rubbed his neck. He had tried to contact the minister through every route available, leaving word for him at his house, at court, and elsewhere. It was unusual that Walsingham hadn't even bothered to send an emissary in response.

In fact, thought Thomas warily, the whole business was odd.

"It seems to me, Cap'n, that the queen's man is playin' hard to git. That's a mite strange, seein' as how ye thought ye were both on the same side, so to speak."

"My thoughts exactly," Thomas said.

Simmons rubbed a sausagelike finger on the side of his nose. "Why doesn't he wish to see ye, Cap'n?"

"There's the puzzle, my friend." He sighed. "But 'tis a puzzle that will have to wait."

"Well, then, if'n ye don't need me fer anythin', Cap'n, I'll jes' be off. Me li'l Meggie is waitin' fer me."

Thomas nodded. "Give her my thanks for her assistance."

The first mate beamed. "Well, now, that will make her right happy."

Thomas wondered about the first mate and his colorful wife. "You and Meggie seem very content."

"We're like two fleas on a dog, Cap'n."

"How long have you been married now? Two, three years?"

"Well, now, I wouldn't 'xactly say we was married,

Cap'n," said Simmons with a nervous glance at the gate.

"Does she know that?"

Simmons pursed his lips. " 'Tis possible, I suppose. But I don't think she does."

"How did you pull that off?" Thomas demanded.

The first mate beamed. " 'Twas the neatest trick in the world. I had Pedro Alvida, the first mate from the *Queen's Parlay*, do the weddin'. I told Meggie he didn't speak no word of English. He done it all, right and tight, even give us a scrap a paper sayin' we was wed. He only charged me two pence fer the whole thing."

Thomas lifted his eyebrows. "What will happen if Meggie finds out?"

Simmons shrugged. "Now don't go borryin' trouble, Cap'n. I suppose if she found out, I'd have to marry her for real. Speakin' of trouble, I'd best go. Meggie don't like to wait, ye know."

Thomas nodded and watched the first mate leave through the gate. It seemed as if every relationship had an element of untruth in it. Yet both Simmons and Meggie appeared happy. He wished he could have seen the confrontation between Meggie and Goliath.

He ran an impatient hand through his hair. God's Blood, but what was Walsingham up to? It was highly unusual for the counselor to ignore his messages.

Fia's laughter again drifted on the scented spring air, and Thomas turned and headed for the house.

Walsingham be damned. He had no time to play devious games. He had more pressing things to attend to. Things like surprising his winsome wife with a particularly thick new carpet. Things like ensuring their privacy. He reached the stairs and bounded up them, already thinking of the pleasure he would take in sending Robert packing.

* * *

"Well, I never!" Outrage warred with revulsion on Mistress Hadwell's thin face as she came upon Lady Fia and Lord Montley cavorting most indecorously. Her colorless lips pressed into a straight line as disapproval stiffened her already taut back.

"Mistress Hadwell!" Robert opened his arms in a gesture of greeting. "You have come just in time!"

The housekeeper's eyes bulged, and Fia had to cover her mouth to smother her laughter.

Truly, Robert looked a sight. He stood poised on his toes, fantastically garbed in one of Fia's new dresses, the skirts barely reaching his shins, the full sleeves tied but halfway up his long arms, and the embroidered stomacher, gaping at either side, hanging across his chest like ill-fitting armor.

The most amusing aspect was the huge red wig sitting precariously upon Robert's black hair. The mass of curls slid to one side even as he simpered at the outraged housekeeper.

Her body as rigid as a marble pillar, aversion plain in her bloodless face, Mistress Hadwell looked from Robert to Fia. "Heathenish Scots! The late master would rue the day to see his own son cavorting with such."

Robert's smile disappeared. "Take care, mistress, that your tongue doesn't lead you to forget your station."

The housekeeper's nostrils quivered in anger. "I will go and see the master about this. We'll see who has forgotten his station." She looked past Robert to Fia and snapped, "And as for you, we all know why the master wed you. If he'd not been forced at knifepoint, he'd have no more married you than one of the kitchen maids." With a swirl of gray skirts, she stomped out the door, leaving Robert and Fia in silence.

Robert recovered first. He turned to Fia with a rueful smile. "Spiteful hag. I suppose I shouldn't have been acting the fool."

Fia ignored the cold ache caused by the housekeeper's jibes. "You were merely trying to amuse me. I'm afraid I was not a very attentive pupil today."

"Nay, your mind was elsewhere—mainly staring out yon window at Thomas." He grinned softly and pulled the wig from his head. "Don't look so crushed, sweet. Mistress Hadwell is as mud in a pigsty."

Fia's brow creased in confusion. "Mud in a pigsty?"

"Aye. It only smells if you roll in it. Ignore her! Come! Let's continue with our lessons. Your curtsey has grace, but you lack an imperial air. We must work on that. Style, my sweet, is everything."

He slapped the wig back onto his head and lifted an impossibly large fan. He tossed her a pouting smile and floated across the room in a surprisingly accurate imitation of a gentlewoman approaching royalty.

"You turn and bend and curtsey like so."

Fia found herself admiring Robert's grace and musical voice. "You belong on a stage," she said reverently.

He straightened and gave her a mock frown. "Aye, well, I just hope that I'm never again forced to such lengths as this to keep the attention of a woman." He shook his head, the red curls bobbing erratically. "You are ever hard on my pride. Now come and see how easily such a commanding air can be accomplished."

She rose from her seat and was immediately aware of the stiff skirts and petticoats that bound her. By the saints, but she hated her new clothing. " 'Tis too heavy, this skirt," she complained, kicking the stiff lengths out of her way as she went to stand by his side. "I am like to faint from the weight. And this stomacher is too tight. It presses my breasts up 'til they nigh overspill." It was worse than the makeshift dress she and Mary had prepared when they had been trying to scare off Malcolm the Maiden.

Robert assessed her rounded breasts where they

275

bulged over the edge of her neckline. "The ladies of the court wear far lower and far more revealing collars than yours, milady." He pursed his lips thoughtfully. "Though I must admit that there are few who show to such advantage."

"I shall probably catch an ague from such exposure." She tugged at her ruff. "This thing has been starched until it resembles a piece of wood."

Robert rolled his eyes heavenward, his breath hissing through his teeth in frustration. " 'Tis a pretty ruff, and it frames your face admirably. Cease your quibbling, woman!"

"Aye, I am to be silent though I am trapped by stiff skirts, a tight waist, and an overzealous ruff," she retorted, "whilst you cavort about in loose-fitting velvets and comfortable wool."

Robert ripped off his wig and threw it to the floor. Raising his hands, he addressed the heavens. "How can such a comely woman so hate the very trappings of beauty?"

"And how," Fia scoffed, "can such an ugly woman so love those very same trappings though they pinch and bind and scratch?"

"I am not an ugly woman! Were I to attempt the resemblance in earnest, save for my beard you would think me a beauteous maid." He began loosening the ties that held on his skirts and stomacher.

Fia knew he was probably right. He was an amazing actor when he chose to be.

He threw the garments onto a chair and took several swift strides about the room, hands clasped behind him. "How can I get you to understand the manner, the air you need?" He halted. "Fia, suppose you pretend that this is one of your plays."

She tilted her head. "A play?"

He frowned, stroking his beard as inspiration struck

him. "Aye. Pretend that you are the heroine from your play *The Beggar Prince*."

Fia bit her lip. "Mirabella?"

"Aye, the lovely Mirabella!" Robert rubbed his hands together eagerly and took another quick stride around the room. "Aye, you will be the beauteous Mirabella as she requests the aid of that shrewish queen—what was her name?"

"Elspeth."

"Aye! Evil Queen Elspeth! That demon of a woman, in league with the devil himself!" He frowned. "Though I must admit that your best villain was Theobald in *Clarence of Turnbridge*. But Elspeth will do. *I*," he said with a grand air, "will be the evil Queen Elspeth. *You* will be the lovely, innocent Mirabella, come to ask the evil queen to release your beloved from the dreadful death she has planned for him."

"But I don't—"

"Come!" He beamed. He grabbed up the wig and planted it on his head, going to stand by the fireplace. His chin rose to an unnatural height, his mouth pinched in vigorous disapproval. He stared down his nose. "Approach your queen!" His voice rose into the querulous whine of a displeased ruler.

Fia reached inside herself for her own emotions, then threw herself into her part, affecting an expression of feminine courage and determination. If Thomas's safety ever required her to approach a fire-breathing dragon, she would do so without hesitation. Lifting her chin, she swept across the room and sank into a deep and respectful curtsey before "Queen Elspeth."

"God's Blood, Fia, that was perfect!" Robert grabbed her about the waist and swung her around. "If only I had thought to enlist your plays sooner! I trow, but you are near ready to meet the queen."

Fia disengaged herself. "Do you really think this will

be enough, Robert? Or do we play at fools' games?"

He looked puzzled, his wig sliding to one side. "Fools' games? You fear we'll fail?"

She sank into the window seat and leaned against the cold pane. "I fear everything." She shoved and pushed her skirts so she could draw her knees up on the seat. Wrapping her arms around them, she stared into the garden.

There were times when she looked at Thomas that she thought she saw a tenderness in his expression that hadn't been there before. There had even been a moment when she thought him on the verge of declaring himself. But that moment, like all the others, had slid away without making her one whit more sure of her husband's affections.

"Don't look so saddened," said Robert bracingly. "You've made it to London, you have the benefit of a great position and the love of a notable man—what more could you ask?"

"Love? Do you truly think that?"

"The man is smitten beyond recognition. If love were the color green, our Thomas would look like a vine of ivy."

"So you say," she said, her voice dropping to a whisper, "but he does not."

"Fia, sweet, give him time. He's never before dealt with the fears and jealousies of passion. His father taught him that love was the ultimate folly. Believe me, he is wholly, completely besotted."

"Perhaps," she said, almost afraid to hope.

Robert frowned. "Come! Such a sad face will haunt my dreams, and I'll awake as hollow-eyed as a troll. Tell me what pretty trifle will lighten that brow. A silk fan? Jeweled slippers?"

Fia smiled and stood, determined to shake off the

frightful uncertainty that held her in its sway. "Nay. There's naught."

"Brave child. What you need is a diversion." He looked about the room. "What if I told you a tale of intrigue regarding this very hearth and a secret closet?" he whispered dramatically.

" 'Tis a true tale?"

He grinned and gestured grandly. "Aye. 'Twas a favorite hiding place for Wentworth treasures during less certain times," he said in a hushed tone.

Fia suddenly remembered Thomas's poking inside this chimney upon their arrival. She crossed to the fireplace and began to search the stones with anxious fingers. "Where is this hiding place?"

"God's Wounds," Robert protested, looking at the room's open door and frowning. "Don't alert the whole world. Besides, we can't possibly open it up. I was merely going to tell you about the hiding place and its bloody, macabre history." He sighed and pointed to an inconspicuous gray nook in one side of the hearth.

Fia's hands traveled around the edges of the stones in the area Robert had indicated. There had to be a release mechanism of some sort. "How do you open it?" She bent over to look into the hearth proper. "I saw Thomas looking within here."

Robert hesitated. "Fia, pray, don't look more. We can't—"

"Robert! I see a lever!"

He leaned into the opening. "By the rood! Pull on it and see if it opens."

Thomas walked quietly into the room and halted at seeing both Fia and Robert half inside the huge chimney. He felt an instant surge of irritation, but it dwindled when he saw Robert's soot-covered hand gripping the edge of the opening.

There was no way to open the panel from inside the

279

fireplace. One merely pressed on the left cornice of the mantel to open the hidden drawer. There was no way either could discover it. Silently grinning, he seated himself in a chair directly across from the fireplace and waited.

"Och, 'tis too dark. Can you get a bit of light in here so I can see?" Fia's voice echoed hollowly in the chimney.

"Of course," Robert agreed. He pulled back to grab a candle from the mantel. "This should do," he said. But when he turned to hand it to Fia, his eyes fell upon Thomas.

"Robert." Thomas nodded pleasantly.

"Did you find the light?" echoed Fia's voice. "Robert? Where are you?"

"Light?" Robert blinked at the candle as though he had never seen it before. With a false smile, he urgently tapped Fia on the back. "We don't really need light." He made a great show of setting the candle back on the mantel. "We were just, ah, just, ah . . ." He gulped at Thomas's arched eyebrows and pulled desperately on Fia's arm.

With a stifled curse, Fia backed out of the fireplace. "For the love of St. Mary, Robert, pray, stop jerking on my arm. 'Tis difficult enough to maintain my balance without you tugging on me. Did you find the—" Her eyes followed Robert's wild gaze to where Thomas sat. She swallowed and trained a wide, desperate gaze at Robert. "We are looking for . . ."

"Patterns. Aye, we were looking for patterns in the stone," asserted Robert, nodding vigorously. "Patterns to . . ." He stopped, his jaw working soundlessly as he tried to get his frozen mind to work.

Thomas rubbed his mouth in an effort to hide his grin. Robert's guilty monologue, issuing from his lips spotted with soot, was more amusing than any farce he had ever seen. And Fia's frantic expression was made all the more enjoyable by the smear of ash from her brow to her chin. A ragged red wig was impossibly tangled with her own hair and appeared to be growing out of the side of her head.

"To draw." Fia finished Robert's sentence breathlessly. "We were going to draw the patterns we found in the stone."

Thomas allowed his gaze to slip past them and back again, afraid to look at either one for too long for fear of bursting out laughing. "And what were you going to do with these patterns?"

Robert's eyes narrowed. "Pray, cease playing at cat and mouse!" His lips twitched. "You know what we were doing up the chimney. We were merely curious about your secret closet and were trying to find the latch."

Fia made a sound of muffled irritation. Robert cast her an apologetic glance. "He had already found us out, sweet. He was merely toying with us."

"Robert, I think 'tis time you returned home." Thomas had been looking for an excuse, and he decided this was as good as any.

"Home? But 'tis not yet supper!"

"Home." Thomas repeated.

Fia planted her hands on her hips. "But, Thomas, I need Robert to prepare me to meet the queen." She pushed back her hair, and Thomas became instantly aware of her magnificent breasts pushed into mounds above her stomacher.

The sight inflamed him. "You stand in danger of becoming unbound, milady. Perchance you will tell me why you are so dressed?"

Color stained her cheeks, but she gave a defiant toss of her head, almost dislodging the red wig. " 'Tis the fashion. There are those who bare even more."

281

Beside her, Robert nodded in agreement. "Aye, think of the Lady Belfort and her black brocade dress."

"I remember no such dress," Thomas said.

"Strange you should forget," mused Robert. "I remember it well. When you first beheld it, you said that all women should wear their breasts for display, as 'twould lessen the difficulty of choosing wh—"

"I remember," interrupted Thomas curtly, glancing uneasily at Fia. She was busily dusting ash from the edges of her skirt and didn't seem to hear. He glared at Robert. "Surely there are households other than ours where you are welcome."

"One or two," Robert said easily.

"Then go to one of them. Only, pray, set yourself to rights first. You look as if you had the plague."

Robert looked down at himself. "Alas! My poor lace!" he cried. He anxiously examined his doublet. " 'Tis ruined! Amber velvet, and 'tis stained beyond repair!" He sighed. "I shall leave, *mon ami*. I'm through with my work here, anyway. Your wife is now ready to be presented to the queen."

Fia's head flew up. "I am? Do you think so?"

Robert laughed and pulled his cape from the bed. "The only question that remains is whether Thomas is as ready for your presentation as you are. He will have to share you with more wags than just myself. And I am very, *very* nice compared to some of the hardened rakes that hang about the court."

Two pairs of eyes turned to him, and Thomas had to force himself to remain expressionless. By the saints, but he hadn't even considered that. He looked at Fia, who, even with her face stained with soot and a hideous red wig sticking out of her hair, was still the most beautiful woman he had ever beheld.

He wanted to lock her in his room and slit the throat of any who would take her from him. The feeling made him steel himself all the more against any thoughts of love. What if she found herself attracted to someone else? Once they reached court and she was besieged with the attentions of a dozen handsome lords, she might well realize that all she felt for him was a brief passion.

Thomas remembered how he had once thought his lust for Fia would cool when he saw her in comparison with the other ladies of court. He could have laughed at his own naïveté. Fia would stand out wherever she was, and he would love her no matter what.

He caught her gaze, and the excitement shining within her black eyes burned into his heart. With as much bravado as he could muster, he pasted a smile on his face and shrugged. "Ready? Of course I am ready."

Chapter Twenty-five

Her court dress weighed more than any other three outfits she owned. Fia felt like a trussed-up leg of mutton.

"Ye look wondrous, lassie," said Mary. "Master Robert was right about the green brocade. It looks wondrous on ye."

Fia looked down at the gown. The skirt and bodice were made of deep green brocade embroidered with small golden flowers. The modest neckline was accentuated with rows of pearls sewn into an intricate pattern. The long fall of her skirts draped into a perfect bell shape over the cone farthingale.

It felt strange wearing so many jewels. Her rubies glittered as if filled with light of their own. And just last night, Thomas had given her a strand of pearls. "For luck," he had said as he draped the necklace over her bare shoulders. Fia rubbed them absently. Even with such rich adornment, she still felt as if she were a duck wearing a swan's coat.

"Ye look like an angel, if I do say so meself," said Mary. "I'm proud to see ye're wearin' yer mother's rubies."

"Thomas thought they'd be perfect with this dress. This ruff is like to kill me before the evening is through."

Mary reached up to loosen the ties. "There. See if that doesn't suit ye better."

"It helps," said Fia. She rubbed her chest. "I vow I can't breathe."

"That'd be because of yer busks. Robert says all the women wear them, though I'm not so sure why. He says ye'll get used to it."

Fia didn't think anyone could get used to an iron and leather undergarment. " 'Tis easy for him to say," she protested. "And you. Neither he nor you have to wear one."

"Whist, lassie, the sad truth is, I don't think they make them in my size." Mary patted her ample hips. "Even if they did, I think 'twould be a waste of good leather. There's no holdin' in these curves."

Fia reached over and hugged Mary. "You're perfect as you are."

Mary gave her a tight squeeze in return. "There, now, lassie. Look what ye made me do. I've gone and dropped a tear on yer dress."

"If things go ill this evening, your tears won't be the only ones adorning this dress."

"Don't ye fret about this evenin'. All ye have to do is be yerself, and everythin' will go well. Och, that reminds me. Ye have a few gifts." Mary bustled to the bed and returned with a jeweled fan and a single rose.

Fia smiled. Robert had promised her just such a trinket. She tucked the flower into her neckline and hung the fan about her wrist. Finally, she was ready.

The door opened, and Mistress Hadwell stepped into the room. Zeus let out a low growl.

"Hush, now," said Fia. " 'Tis just Mistress Hadwell."

"I still think we should call her Hadnone," grumbled Mary under her breath.

The housekeeper's nose scrunched, as if detecting an unpleasant odor. "His lordship is waiting."

Mary snorted. "Let him wait. When he sees how well her ladyship looks, he'll forget all about the time. In fact, I wouldn't be surprised if he dragged her back up here fer a quick tumble," she added with a broad wink.

Mistress Hadwell's face reddened. Lips pressed into a furious line, she turned toward Fia. "His lordship requests that you wear your rubies."

"What do ye think is hangin' about her ladyship's neck even as ye speak?"

The housekeeper lifted haughty brows. "Oh. Those."

Mary planted her fists on her hips. "That's about enough of ye, ye pribblin' moldwarp! Ye'd better leave before I toss ye out."

"You wouldn't dare."

Mary rolled up her sleeves.

Mistress Hadwell's chin rose a notch. "That's quite enough. I was sent to deliver his lordship's message."

Mary spit into her hands and rubbed them together, a wide smile lighting her face. "Ye've done it. So be gone."

The housekeeper turned on her heel and scurried out the door.

Fia shook her head and gave a worried frown. "Be careful, Mary. She is a bitter woman."

"She's a dried-up old prune. Now here, let me see ye." Mary turned Fia toward the window, where the fading sun cast its last weak rays.

Fia tried to remember everything Robert had taught her about posture and comportment. "Well?" she asked finally when Mary didn't respond. "How do I look?"

Mary dabbed at her eyes. "Ye look fine, lassie. Like a fairy princess. Now get out of here before I begin bawlin' like a baby and ruin yer fine dress."

Fia gave her a swift hug. She didn't feel like a fairy princess. She felt more like Ursula, the maiden in her new play, *Pirate of Virtue,* as that fearless captive marched bravely to her death to prove her love for her handsome pirate prince.

Fia walked down the hall. Like Ursula, she wouldn't give up her pirate prince without a fight. "To the death," she mumbled as she marched, stabbing at the air with her fan, pretending it was a magical sword.

"I don't know who you're fighting, comfit, but I think you possess a more deadly weapon that that," drawled a familiar voice.

Fia dropped her fan. Thomas stood before her, resplendent in amber damask. His breeches were of a deep, rich brown that matched his boots and belt. Yet even as she thought how magnificently he was dressed, she was assailed with the desire to take all his fine clothes off, one stitch at a time.

He picked up her fan and opened it. "It matches your gown."

She swallowed the welter of desire that had closed her throat. "Robert sent it," she croaked.

"Nay, comfit. 'Twas I." He placed the fan in her nerveless hand and brushed his fingers over the rose at the opening of her bodice. " 'Tis lovely. Though not as lovely as you, milady."

Fia didn't know what to say. This wasn't the Thomas she knew. He seemed quieter, almost pensive. And ever so serious. "You flatter me," she finally replied.

"Nay, I tell the truth." He pulled her hand to his mouth and placed a warm kiss in her palm. Curling her fingers over it, he met her look of concern with a tight smile. "Whatever happens this eve, comfit, I want you to know—"

"Lord Montley has arrived, your lordship," said Mistress Hadwell, her face carved in disapproving lines.

Thomas dropped Fia's hand. "We'll be but a moment more."

"Lord Montley said 'twas late and—"

"We'll leave when we're ready and not before," Thomas snapped.

"Very well, your lordship," Mistress Hadwell said, though her eyes pinned Fia with an incriminating stare. The housekeeper spun on her heel and marched out of the room.

"She's a mite edgy," said Fia into the silence. Whatever magic had been between her and Thomas was gone.

"Aye." He rubbed his neck in frustration. "And damn inconvenient." He sighed. "I should replace her, but she's been at Rotherwood House for more years than I can remember. My father thought highly of her."

"Then she should stay," said Fia promptly.

His mouth thinned. "Nay. Robert told me she's been less than polite to you and Mary. I won't stand for such insolence."

Fia smiled. "You don't have to. Leave Mistress Hadwell to me. 'Twill take some time, but I can deal with her." She looped her fan back over her wrist. "Well, my lord, are we ready?"

He looked at her for a long, silent moment before proffering his arm. "Aye, milady wife, we are."

Power lay like a mantle about Queen Elizabeth's thin shoulders. Her dress was crusted with so many pearls and so much gold thread, it rippled and glowed like fire. Her slender, graceful hands and neck dripped with jewels, their vivid color startling against her white skin and red hair. She looked resplendent, vibrant, and furious.

Thomas stood before the dais, his head high, only the whiteness about his mouth indicating his struggle to contain his temper.

"I must go to him," Fia whispered to Robert.

"Nay. You can't approach the queen lest she deigns to recognize you. Let Thomas be. He knows what he is about."

Fia eyed the queen doubtfully. The interview had been cursed from the onset. Elizabeth had arrived incensed, her eyebrows low, a scowl on her face. Thomas's refusal to bend his knee to her anger seemed to infuriate her the more. Fia cast an uncertain glance at Robert.

Robert whispered, "Peace, Fia. Let Thomas deal with her. She is wont to be angered at any marriage made without her gainsay. Our only option is to ride through this storm and hope to find a safe mooring on the other side."

Fia began, "But shouldn't we—"

The queen's voice lashed out with all the crack and sting of a knotted whip. "I've already heard the details of this wedding. Walsingham has informed me. I came prepared to annul this farce and send the chit back to Mull with a clear message for that Scottish ingrate who dares force his wishes over mine. Yet you come and ask instead that I sanction the marriage. Even for you, Rotherwood, this exceeds all!" Silence filled the great hall as everyone strained to hear Thomas's response.

"Damn Walsingham," muttered Robert through gritted teeth. "I might have known he would be involved in this."

"Why?" Fia whispered.

"I'm damned if I know, but I begin to think there is more untoward than we realize."

Thomas crossed his arms. "What is done cannot be undone. We are married, the contracts honored, the vows given in a holy church, and the union consummated."

"Damnation, Rotherwood!" snapped Elizabeth. "You hang yourself with your own tongue."

"I don't know what lies you have heard, but I was not forced to wed. 'Twas of my own free will. I have no apologies to make. Only the offer to submit to pay whatever penalty you deem."

An almost feral gleam of anticipation raced through the court. So far, the ladies and lords who hovered about the queen reminded Fia of nothing more than finely feathered crows waiting to swoop in on whatever carrion the queen left in her wake.

" 'Tis not enough," Elizabeth said coldly.

Thomas shrugged dismissively, and a red tide swept up the queen's neck as her anger heightened. Her hand slammed onto the arm of her chair, her rings flashing a pattern of colors across the floor. "By God, Rotherwood, but you test me this day!"

Fia shut her eyes. Sweet St. Catherine, why didn't he make more of a move to protect himself? she wondered. Why didn't he tell the queen the truth, that he had been forced to wed? She took a steadying breath and opened her eyes.

Elizabeth was staring at her with open hostility. Fia ventured a smile. The queen snorted her disgust and twisted restlessly in her chair, averting her eyes as though sickened by the sight.

The silence grew. Fia wished Robert would loosen his hold on her arm. Her fingers were already tingling and would be numb did he persist in clutching her elbow with such brutish strength.

As though the words were wrested from her, the queen snapped, "Well, Rotherwood, have you anything more to say for your impetuous behavior?"

Fia could see Thomas struggling to control his own anger. "Nay, Your Majesty. I never sought to betray your wishes. I didn't seek a wife. Fate brought her to me." He smiled as he turned to Fia, a glimmer of humor in his eyes. "I've been told one should never fight fate."

Fia returned his smile with every bit of strength she could muster.

The queen kicked her footstool. It flipped off the dais and landed on the floor with a thud. Courtiers scattered to the edges of the room like chickens scattering before a fox.

"Damn your eyes, you pox-ridden churl," Elizabeth sneered. "Fate does not excuse your behavior! All my life I have heard of naught but the luck of your family. Well, let it be known this day that the luck of the Wentworths has left you." She motioned to the guards. "Take him to the Tower. I'll not have such impertinence from my own subjects!"

Fia's heart lodged firmly in her throat as Thomas ground out, "Then 'tis to the Tower. I cannot undo what is already done."

Fia reached for him, but Robert caught her arm. "Leave him be," he hissed urgently. "He knows what he's about. Likely she'll send him to the Tower only until her temper cools. Then she'll fine him some trifling amount, and all will be well."

Fia couldn't take her eyes from Thomas's straight back as he stood before the dais. He looked like a knight from ancient times facing down a dragon.

"Why doesn't he tell the truth?" she asked in a low voice.

"Because if he admits he was forced to wed, she would offer forthwith to annul the marriage. He doesn't wish for an annulment."

Fia turned to Robert. "He'd go to the Tower for me?"

Robert frowned. "Of course."

"Did you know this would come about?"

"Nay. We hadn't planned on informing Elizabeth that your cousin had anything to do with the matter. Alas, apparently Walsingham had already spread the tale." Robert rubbed his chin thoughtfully. "I wonder what evil that varlet plans."

"If he's the cause of this, I want to speak with him myself," Fia said darkly.

Robert nodded. "Come. There's not much we can do now. The course is set. We must figure out a way to get Thomas released quickly from the Tower."

Fia clenched her hands in the stiff folds of her skirt, watching as two burly men came and grabbed her husband.

Thomas turned and caught Fia's gaze. Within the frame of the ruff, her face was pale, and tears glimmered in her eyes. He smiled with a reassurance he didn't feel. But then she turned from Robert and marched toward the dais.

"Fia, no!" he said in a low, urgent voice. Beyond giving him a quick smile, she made no effort to halt. He looked to Robert, who stood with his mouth agape. Thomas struggled to pull his arms free, but it was too late. She was already at the dais, sinking into a deep, graceful curtsey. *Sweet Jesu, we are lost.*

"What's this?" said Elizabeth, her thin, arched eyebrows lifting. "How dare you approach Us!"

"Your Majesty, I am unversed in the ways of the court, though Robert MacQuarrie has been kind enough to give me a few lessons."

Elizabeth scowled at Robert. He flourished a bow of such exaggerated depth that the queen's thin lips twitched involuntarily. "Robert MacQuarrie is a fool and worse."

Fia nodded. "Aye, that he is," she responded sensibly. "But he is a dear lad for all his foolish ways, Your Majesty."

"A lad, is he?" Elizabeth quirked an eyebrow, surveying Fia. "Yet surely he has more years to him than you?"

"Years, perhaps. But I've had more adventures."

Fia smiled angelically, and Thomas saw the queen's swift frown. His own heart beat as though he were running, a cold sweat covering his brow. So much hung in the balance, and Fia knew so little of the capricious whims of a queen.

"Bah! What adventures could a chit like you have had?"

"Well, now, I've come all the way from the Isle of Mull to London, I have, to see the queen." Fia tilted her head to one side. "Surely that's an adventure."

"It takes more than that to make an adventurer, girl."

Fia bit her lip. "I suppose you are right. In truth, there are many things I've never done. I have never been a knight, nor a cook, nor a fish, nor a—"

"A fish? How could you be a fish?" Elizabeth demanded, her voice rising like the thin shriek of a gull.

Thomas winced at the shrillness.

" 'Tis interesting you should ask that very question, Your Majesty. I had a cousin once who fell and hit her head on a rock nigh on the very eve of her wedding day. From that moment on, she swore she was a fish." Fia sighed sadly. "And not an ordinary fish, either. Nay, Katherine thought she was a large speckled carp, the kind as mopes about the reeds, too lazy to move if the water's the least bit warm."

Thomas groaned and hung his head as he heard Fia's sultry, melodic voice describing Cousin Katherine's bizarre predicament. He was near to getting hanged, and she was telling a tale about one of her ill-fated cousins. His brow suddenly creased. Mary had told him that Duncan was Fia's only near relative. He lifted his head to regard his wife through narrowed eyes.

The queen waved a dismissive hand. "Carp or perch,

what can it matter?" She frowned for a moment, then asked, "What happened to this wench?"

"Ah. 'Twas a ticklish spot for my uncle, as Katherine was to marry a Campbell within the week. The Campbells, as you well know, are not known for their patience." Fia stared off into the distance, as though seeing the entire episode unfolding before her. "There was my unfortunate uncle, his house full of Campbells from the groom's party, and his daughter, the bride, who thought she was a carp. He was caught, as we Scots say, betwixt the devil and a rock."

"Ha!" uttered Elizabeth. "I've been there myself."

"Aye, I wager you have, your Majesty. Uncle Andrew was in a very sticky position. If he told the Campbells what had happened, there was a strong chance they would think it a trick to elude the wedding and thus dishonor them. Under those circumstances, they might murder him and his whole family right where they stood. Yet if he didn't tell them, how was he to get his poor daughter, now a carp swimming about the moat, through a wedding ceremony?"

"Was there a fountain within the castle?"

"Nay. A pity, for that might have served. They attempted to pull her from the moat and dress her in her wedding finery, but she would gasp and moan as though dying. So whilst my uncle tried to discover a way out of his difficulty, there Katherine stayed, flopping about in the weeds as naked as the day she was born."

Thomas exchanged a desperate glance with Robert. Dead. They would all end up dead. But to his astonishment, the queen leaned forward and asked, "Why, pray, was she naked?"

Fia leaned forward and whispered loudly, "Fish don't wear clothing, Your Majesty, and naught that poor Katherine's parents could say would convince her to let them dress her."

The queen nodded.

"A most desperate case, was my cousin," Fia continued. "The only way my uncle kept the wedding party from finding out about her sad state was to keep the wine and ale flowing so freely within the house that there was no reason for any to venture out. This is a powerful enough persuasion for most Scots."

Elizabeth's mouth twitched slightly, and Thomas felt his heart rise.

"I can well imagine," the queen said. "So what did your uncle do next?"

"Well, he ordered a big tub to be placed in the middle of the hall. Then he told the Campbell that his daughter would marry him only if she were immersed in the special fairy water of Loch Tuath. 'Tis a well-known fact that the waters of Loch Tuath are blessed by the small people. My uncle was hoping by this stratagem to win a delay of a few extra days. He was still praying Katherine would come about."

The queen looked skeptical but said nothing.

"Well, the Campbell, being a great believer in good luck, agreed to this strange stipulation. He immediately sent ten of his best men to bring back a goodly supply of Loch Tuath water for the wedding, enough to fill the large tub."

"Preposterous!" Elizabeth scoffed. "Surely the bridegroom knew something was wrong."

"Nay, Your Majesty. For you see, my uncle had laid by such a great store of whiskey that three entire clans could not have drunk him dry in anything less than a fortnight. Not only was the groom and his party satisfied to be feasting and drinking, but they were sorely saddened when the Campbell's men returned with the blessed water within two days, as it signified an end to their merriment."

"Hmph. I'll have to take your word about the quantity

of whiskey laid by in your uncle's cellars." Elizabeth
cast a disapproving glance at Robert MacQuarrie.
"Though I can personally attest to the love Scotsmen
have for the stuff."

Robert bowed and grinned. "Thank you, most gracious Queen, for noting one of my many talents."

"Hush, you preening coxcomb!" Elizabeth scolded,
though Thomas noted her gray eyes lightened with
amusement. She waved imperiously. "Well? I cannot
wait all day to hear the end of this story. Continue."

"Aye, Your Majesty. As soon as the blessed water
arrived, all the guests assembled in the great hall. There
sat the tub with the disrobed bride floating about and
blowing bubbles." Fia frowned. "I'm not sure why she
was blowing bubbles, for I've never seen a carp blow
bubbles. I would think you would have to be able to
purse your lips, and I don't think a fish could—"

"Fie, child, get on with it!" Elizabeth commanded.
"Were they married?"

"Och, aye, they were married." Fia nodded and smiled
sweetly at the queen.

The entire room was rapt, every eye on Fia, Thomas
noted. Even Elizabeth sat on the edge of her chair. Yet
Fia smiled on, as if unaware that all awaited her next
sentence with bated breath.

Elizabeth gave a sigh of impatience. "God's Teeth,
woman! Can you not finish a simple story? What about
the fact that the wench thought she was a fish? Surely
the bridegroom must have protested when he found himself so duped."

"Och, no, he didn't, your Majesty. You see, as the
wedding took place, my cousin was splashing and
thrashing about in the tub until the time came for her to
say her vows. My uncle kept proclaiming that 'twas the
blessing of the little people as were causing both the
water and my cousin to churn so.

"Things were progressing right nicely, until the time came to put the ring on her finger. Fish, of course, do not wear rings, so it took three men to hold Katherine down. During the ensuing struggle, my cousin hit her head soundly on the edge of the tub."

Elizabeth's eyebrows rose. "And then what happened?"

"Katherine was embarrassed to no end. One minute she was walking through the garden, and the next she wakes as naked as the day she was born in a tub of water with a hundred interested guests looking on. To this day, she'll not let even her maid attend her in her bath, and never a fish is served at her table, be it carp or salmon or else."

Elizabeth gave a slight smile as a ripple of laughter passed through the room. Her shrewd gray eyes rested on Thomas for several long moments before she turned back to Fia. "I trow, but the chit tells an amusing tale. Perhaps the Wentworth good fortune has been proven yet again."

Fia sighed woefully. "I fear you mistake the matter. I have brought Thomas naught but ill luck since we met."

Thin, arched eyebrows climbed toward queenly red hair. "How so?"

"Well, I knocked him from a second-story window, though that 'twas an accident."

Elizabeth peered at Thomas with amazed eyes.

"Aye, and I had need to steal his coins, leaving him penniless. Then my poor dog scared off his horse, and he was forced to take mine, and—"

"He *stole* your horse?" Elizabeth's lips twitched, and Thomas almost groaned aloud.

"Och, he had no choice. Then, of course, my horse bit his arm and laid on his leg and would not rise until he apologized."

"To the horse?" Elizabeth asked.

"Aye," Fia said. "Thunder dislikes Englishmen. She still tries to bite him every time he gets near, though Thomas was kind enough to carry both her and my dog—and the pet rabbit Thomas had found me in the dark Mull forest—on his ship to London."

"I trow, but I wish I had seen you after this journey, Rotherwood," said Elizabeth.

"He was a mite ragged," Fia admitted ruefully.

The queen's mouth quivered. "Of course. I'm surprised he put up with such monstrous ill-fortune."

"As to that, I fear he had has motives." Fia's brow furrowed. "He promised to sponsor me in coming to London. I thought he meant he would publish my plays, but I found out he meant something quite different."

"He did, did he? The knave!" Elizabeth tried to frown at Thomas, but a grin broke through her stern demeanor.

"Aye, but that was before my cousin Duncan hit him with his claymore and—"

"Cease! Pray, cease before I laugh myself insensible!" The queen pressed a hand to her quivering stomacher and waved to Thomas's grinning jailers. "Release him! God knows, the man has already been punished enough!"

Thomas straightened and stalked across the room, ignoring the laughter and jesting of the court, and pulled Fia to his side, squeezing the cold hand she placed in his. "Thank you, Your Majesty. Are we forgiven?"

Her gray eyes still shimmered with laughter. "I could send you to the Tower, did I wish it."

"Aye, Your Majesty. I am aware."

"And I could take away your lands, your title, everything you own."

Thomas's arm tightened about Fia. "But you won't."

Elizabeth's eyes narrowed on Fia. "Is the chit increasing?"

Fia stiffened, but Thomas merely laughed. "If the Wentworth luck still holds, she should be."

The queen snorted and stared at Fia. "She is an attractive chit, Rotherwood, but a hellion for all that. I will let the marriage stand."

"Thank you," said Fia, sinking into a deep curtsey, as Robert had taught her.

"Don't thank me. You will still be fined for this day's work."

Thomas felt a thrill of triumph. He bowed. "And I will gladly pay."

Elizabeth waved him away, saying acidly, "Then at least have the sense to look saddened, else I will think of some other, more painful punishment."

Thomas captured her waving hand and placed a graceful kiss upon it. "Your Majesty is ever gracious. Ever gracious and ever beautiful."

She scowled, though it didn't reach her eyes. "Get you gone, Rotherwood, before I clap you in the Tower." She turned to Fia and held out her hand, a smile curving her thin mouth. "And you, lady, I find interesting. Come see me again, and bring your plays with you. I desire to discover whether you can spin a tale on paper as well as you can into the thin air."

Fia curtsied. "Aye, Your Majesty, that would please me very much." She grinned up at Thomas, and he thought he had never seen eyes shine so brightly.

Chapter Twenty-six

Mistress Hadwell sniffed disdainfully, "The household has been using far too many candles of late."

Fia, sitting at her writing table, hunched her shoulders, straightened, then hunched them again.

"What are you doing?" the housekeeper asked with obvious distaste.

"Just working a mite of a crick out of my neck. 'Tis a common problem for people who sit up writing for hours at a stretch."

The housekeeper's mouth turned down severely at the corners. "I suppose, then, 'tis too much to ask you to deal with some of the problems of the household as a proper mistress should. Neither you nor that uncouth maid of yours have any idea how such a fine house should be run."

Fia bit back a sharp reply. She knew Mary had gained the respect of most of the other servants, and that fact grated harshly with the housekeeper, who had been the iron hand of rule before Mary's competent ways had challenged her standing.

A touch of sympathy for the woman welled in Fia. "I'm sorry if I seem distracted. You were saying something about candle usage."

"Aye, I was. Our candle usage has tripled since you and those . . . others arrived." Loathing pooled in her voice.

"That's because I do much of my writing at night."

" 'Tis a waste of wax." Mistress Hadwell glared down her nose.

"Then 'tis fortunate 'tis not your wax," answered Fia with a polite smile. A week ago, she had faced down a queen. Today she battled a household dragon. Life was stranger than any play.

Mistress Hadwell's nose flared in anger. Fia was fascinated. She wondered if the housekeeper could flare her nostrils at will.

Thin lips barely moving, the glowering housekeeper hissed, "Mistress, let me tell you—"

"There you are!" Thomas came through the door, Zeus lolling behind him. The dog's tongue hung out the side of his mouth, drool dripping with his every step.

'Twas becoming a common sight to see Zeus following Thomas about. Fia had even caught Thomas slipping food to the dog from his plate when he thought no one was looking. Zeus wandered to a corner and threw himself onto the floor, giving a sleepy yawn.

Fia's heart thudded as it always did when Thomas was nearby. He looked particularly handsome today, his blond hair mussed by the wind, his warm brown eyes crinkled with mirth.

"Mistress Hadwell and I were just discussing the need for more candles." Fia forced her attention back to the housekeeper, hoping Thomas would leave her to settle this for herself.

The aquiline nose quivered for a moment. "We were discussing, mistress, how so many candles are going to *waste.*"

Thomas looked from Mistress Hadwell's outraged face to his wife's determined smile. Fia caught the question in his gaze and gave an imperceptible shake of her head. He settled back to observe.

"Buy more candles," Fia said to the woman, nodding a dismissal.

"But—"

"That will be all."

The housekeeper turned to Thomas. "I beg your pardon, your lordship, but such waste is against—"

"You're right," Thomas announced.

The housekeeper shot Fia a look of venomous triumph.

"Och, now, and what are you about?" Fia demanded, her fists planted on her hips.

Thomas shook his head sadly. " 'Tis no use. I have been discovered. I fear 'tis I, Mistress Hadwell, who have been guilty of gluttony."

"You, my lord?"

He leaned toward the housekeeper and whispered, " 'Tis the glow of the candles. I love to see it play across my lady's soft skin, caressing her curves, lighting the silk of her hair, casting seductive shadows across her hidden, most secret places." He sighed, and his breath stirred Mistress Hadwell's iron-gray hair as he gazed past her to Fia. "I cannot seem to stop. Every time I see my beautiful lady lying naked in the soft light of the candles, I become a man crazed. I burn ten each night, sometimes more, just watching her sleep."

Though her cheeks were the red of a persimmon, the housekeeper's eyes remained glued to Thomas's face, her narrow brow covered with a light sheen of perspiration. Thomas took her limp hand. "You can see that I

am a sad case. Until my lady cures me of my addiction,
I must have candles." He patted her hand. "Many candles."

Mistress Hadwell nodded slowly, her angular body
quivering. "Candles. Of course. I will send someone to
fetch more today."

Thomas smiled sweetly and reached for Fia. He pulled
her into his arms and waved a hand at the housekeeper.
"That will be all, Mistress Hadwell." He ran a hand
down Fia's cheek, smiling into her eyes. "I've a need to
begin my cure."

Fia's legs went weak. She tried to control her racing
heart. Sweet Jesu, but the man could weave a spell when
he chose.

Mistress Hadwell's mouth opened and closed. Finally,
as though wresting herself from a deep sleep, she turned
and walked from the room with unsteady steps.

Fia tried to contain a laugh. "I don't think she'll ever
be the same, poor woman."

Thomas shrugged and tipped her chin up with the
back of his hand. "I have other things on my mind than
dour old housekeepers."

Fia smiled. "Like candles and a carpet, no doubt."

"Aye." He leered. "All that and a naughty, tempestuous Scottish wench."

She blushed, and he laughed, catching her up in his
arms and swinging her around. "Enough of your maidenly blushes. Where is the bold wench who straddled
me last eve? I was so sore and bruised that I could
scarcely fit myself into a codpiece this morn."

"She waited for you all day, Lord Lackard, as you
promised to take her for a walk about the gardens. Yet
you disappeared after breakfast once Simmons arrived.
Whence did you run?"

He laughed and set her gently on her feet. "From angel to shrew in the blink of an eye. You are a lady of many talents."

"Remember that well, my lord, for I shall be very shrewish indeed do you break any more promises."

He grinned and kissed the tip of her nose. "Then I must make amends! Come, let's walk about the gardens whilst there is yet light." He took her hand and led her to the door. "You are a brave lady indeed to face down Mistress Hadwell."

Fia sighed. "I feared the queen less than our housekeeper," she admitted.

"No wonder. With Elizabeth, all you need worry about is being tossed into the Tower. With Mistress Hadwell, you could be done in with damp sheets, ill-prepared food, and mounds of dust." He shuddered.

Fia laughed. "I know. I don't know what it is, but she makes me feel as if I were naught but ten years of age, with my fingers still sticky from stolen pastries."

"Rest assured, lady, you don't look to be ten years of age." He leered for emphasis.

Fia grinned. "You make me feel far from ten, my lord. Especially since your purchase of such a thick, soft carpet for our hearth."

Thomas opened the door and arched an eyebrow. "Only since the carpet?"

A soft blush colored her cheeks. For a moment, she looked adorably embarrassed, but she quickly recovered. "Well, perchance there might have been a time or two before the carpet. . . ." Her voice trailed off as she stepped onto the path.

The afternoon rain had lifted and left the garden fresh with dewy scents. Fia breathed deeply of the perfumed air.

Thomas felt a twinge of lust as he stared at her parted lips. Sweet Jesu, he would die for the taste of those rosebuds. But there was more to Fia than mere beauty. Since she had made her appearance at court, he had marveled anew at her strength and ability.

He caught her against him. "What other times have I made you feel womanly?" he asked her almost roughly, wishing he could take her then and there on the damp ground.

She twined her arms about his neck. "Are you fishing for compliments? I trow, 'tis most unseemly."

The silk of her voice seemed to creep into his codpiece and tighten it a notch. "Will I catch anything?" he asked, blowing softly into her hair where it sprung back from her face.

She shivered and pressed her lips to his cheek. "I refuse to add to your vanity. You hear enough compliments without my adding to the chorus."

He lifted her into his arms and strode to a bench. Placing her in his lap, he captured her hand and pressed a kiss upon the graceful fingers. "The only compliment of any worth falls from your lips alone."

Her black eyes widened as his warm mouth trailed to her wrist. Her breathing quickened, and she pulled her hand away. "You . . . you seem very different today."

"Different?" he asked, retrieving her hand and placing a heated kiss on the palm. "Nay, I am the same today as yesterday." He nipped softly at her fingers, the need to feel her beneath him growing as she shivered. Her breasts swelled behind the confines of her dress.

"Nay." Her voice had softened into cream. "You are not the same."

He pressed his mouth to the delicate hollow of her throat and murmured against her skin, "Perhaps there is a difference." He drew back to meet her gaze. "I love you even more this day. You, little thief, have stolen my heart."

Her eyes widened, tears filling their velvety depths.

"Och, now, look what you've done. You've made me cry."

He laughed and pulled her against him, sinking his chin into the softness of her hair. "If that makes you cry, comfit, then ours is to be a very, very wet marriage indeed. I vow to tell you daily how I adore your every breath."

She looked up at him and chuckled, the sound washing over him as soothing as warm water. "And I vow not to bring you any more ill luck." Her smile almost blinded him.

He had wrestled with the shadow of uncertainty that plagued him. It still whispered to him at unexpected times. But the longer he was with Fia, the less power the shadow had. No matter what his fears, no matter what the future had in store, he loved her dearly. He loved her humor and her energy, the way she approached every problem as if it were a dragon and she a silver-clad knight on a prancing charger.

He smiled. "I have all the luck I need right here, in my arms." He lowered his mouth to hers.

She tasted of cinnamon and cloves. He nipped at the fullness of her bottom lip, and she arched against him.

"By the rood." Robert's voice was sharp with impatience. "I travel nigh onto ten minutes through muddied streets and find you embracing a wench in the gardens." He halted on the path. "Sweet Jesu, but 'tis your own wife! Your reputation will be in shreds!"

"What do you want?" Thomas growled as Fia laughed.

Robert crossed his arms and rocked back on his heels. "Merely to tell you that I was thinking of visiting Letty this eve." His eyes met Thomas's for a moment. He added in a low voice, "Simmons and I have finally tracked the damned fox to its lair."

Fia frowned. "Fox? What fox?"

Thomas shot a warning look at Robert. "Nay, 'tis a manner of speech, sweet. There's naught for you to worry about."

Her eyes sharpened, and she loosed herself from his grip. "What mischief are you into that you think I might worry?"

Thomas sighed. "None. 'Tis but a promise I made to deliver something. I would tell you all if 'twere my secret to tell. But 'tis not."

She pushed from his lap and stood, regarding him narrowly. "Yet you have told Robert. Even Simmons seems privy to this secret."

He winced. Simmons's knowledge of the affair sounded damning even to him. Yet Duncan's stern warning echoed in his ears. He couldn't place Fia in danger.

This meeting signified something else, as well. It signified the end of his relationship with Walsingham. Thomas didn't need any more challenges. Life with Fia was going to be challenging enough.

He captured her hands and gave her a beguiling smile. "Come, comfit, I will be gone but an hour, and when I return I'll tell you all. By then 'twill no longer be a matter of honor." He held her hand to his heart. "I vow it."

Fia's mouth curved into a reluctant smile. "I suppose if you tell me this eve, 'twill be fair enough."

"Come, Robert," Thomas commanded, turning from Fia. "The quicker we leave, the swifter we return."

Robert lifted his eyebrows. "Was I keeping you?"

Fia chuckled. "Nay, 'twas more me keeping the both of you." She turned and walked toward the house, gathering a flower here and there as she went.

Thomas knew when he returned that she would be sitting at her desk, quill in hand, oblivious to the world. He turned and caught Robert grinning widely. "What?" he demanded.

"Naught," said Robert with a smirk. "I was merely thinking of the strangeness of love."

Thomas scowled and strode on to the stables. "Come! Night is already falling, and I'm long overdue for a talk with Walsingham."

"I trust you will ask him why he found it necessary to mention the circumstances of your marriage to the queen?"

"Aye."

"Ask him, too, where he's been hiding these past two weeks since the Maclean left that cask in your hands. I vow, but I smell a mystery."

Thomas nodded. "So do I, and I am determined to track it to the end."

Chapter Twenty-seven

Goliath held out a grubby hand.

Thomas sighed, tucking the bundle under his arm. "Is the incomparable Letty about?" he asked, digging into his pocket for the required payment.

"That she be," Goliath mumbled. He looked over Thomas's shoulder and grimaced.

"Hallo, my large, smelly friend!" Robert cried. He grabbed Goliath's outstretched hand and pumped it eagerly. "Verily, I have been dreaming of this meeting!"

A bemused look fell over Goliath. His shaggy brows lowered, and then, giving a wide and near toothless grin, he closed his massive hand about Robert's. His muscles bulged as he squeezed. Hard.

"Damn your sodding black soul," cursed Robert through clenched teeth. "How am I to reach for my gold if you crush my hand?"

The huge paw slackened its grip, and Robert twisted

free. Perspiration beaded his brow. "By the rood, but I would like to see you take on a bear!"

Goliath grunted. Robert wiggled his fingers. "You could have maimed the finest rapier hand in all of England. 'Twould have been a tragedy."

"Braggin' on yerself agin, eh, Master Robbie?" Annie asked, opening the door beside Goliath. Her green eyes twinkled mischievously.

A dull flush stained Robert's cheeks. Annie motioned them in, smacking Goliath on the shoulder when he tried to block their path, his hand outstretched. "Enough o' that, ye poxy dog! Letty pays ye enough that ye don't have to go beggin' like a ne'er-do-well."

Thomas entered the room and dropped into a chair. "How long will we have to wait?"

"Not too long," Annie answered, setting three mugs on the table.

"He's the devil to find." Robert frowned. "Where has he been?"

Annie turned a warning frown at Robert and glanced toward the open door. "Jes' keep your breeches on. Letty answers to none. She'll be 'round as soon as it suits her."

Thomas noted that while Annie's cheeks were artfully smeared with dirt, her neck and hair were remarkably clean. In the dim light of the tavern, such a detail would be lost amid the smoke and grime. But here, the willful Annie's masquerade was more obvious.

She looked at him and tipped her head. "Will ye have anythin' else wi' yer ale?"

"Nothing. We will wait," Thomas said. Annie nodded and slipped out the door, her skirts swishing as she turned the corner.

"Sweet Jesu, but I find that woman intriguing," murmured Robert. He went to the door and stared into the tavern. "Call me as soon as that pox-ridden swiver arrives. I want to see if there is any information to be had

310

from the redoubtable Annie." He paused. "I am but a call away, do you have need of me."

Thomas took a long draught of the ale. "Go. See what you can find. As soon as I deliver this parcel and gather some answers, we will leave. I've no wish to tarry."

"*You* may not wish to tarry, but I hope to be invited to do just that." With a wave of a hand, Robert disappeared into the taproom.

Thomas thought of Fia at home, awash in the glow of her many candles as she worked on her play. He loved to watch her write. Sometimes when she came to an especially difficult passage, she would silently act out the various parts, her face contorting in a variety of expressions. He grinned, and a feeling of peaceful contentment stole over him.

"You look most relaxed, Rotherwood." Walsingham's dry voice rustled like aged parchment. He carefully closed the door and tossed off his tattered cloak.

Thomas shrugged and opened his bundle. He laid the cask upon the table. "Maclean sent you this." He rocked back in his chair and planted a boot against the edge of the table. Sweet Jesu, but it felt good to be rid of the miserable letters.

Walsingham sat in a chair, his sharp gaze flickering over the jeweled surface of the box. "What is it?"

"Proof that the Scottish queen was indeed guilty in her husband's death." Thomas thought he saw a flash of disappointment in Walsingham's eyes. He frowned.

The minister reached for the cask and drew it to him. With a flick of his thumb, he broke the seal and opened the lid. There was silence as he stared into the box.

" 'Tis empty."

"What?" Thomas's chair slammed onto the floor.

Walsingham turned the cask toward him. " 'Tis empty." His eyebrows drew down until they almost touched. "Did you see these letters for yourself?"

311

Thomas shook his head. "Nay," he answered shortly. "The box was sealed. I saw the lead markings on it myself."

The minister gave a muttered curse and slammed the lid shut. "By all that's holy, we've been tricked." He slammed fisted hands onto the table. "Tricked by a Scottish bastard! After all I gave him! After all the chances I took! I should have known better than to have—" The minister halted and closed his mouth, seeming to think better of his words. He spread his hands on the table surface. "Forgive my outburst. I was distraught."

A faint roar rang in Thomas's ears as he stared at the counselor. "You knew of the letters before you opened the box."

Walsingham's thin lips folded into a frown. "The truth is, we have both been duped. Me for trusting in a Scottish infidel, and you for . . ." The reedy voice faded into silence.

The roar grew. Somewhere on the edge of Thomas's mind some shadowy fact lurked. Slowly he said, "You knew what was in the cask because Maclean had already told you. Because you had already paid him for it."

Walsingham licked his dry lips. "I have not—"

"You said 'After all I gave him,' " Thomas stated. He remembered Fia blithely explaining that Duncan had enough gold and silver tucked away to replace any trifling silver she might think to steal. He pinned Walsingham with a frigid glare. "Maclean did not seek money."

The bony hands closed into fists. "Nay." Walsingham's frown deepened. "He did not."

"The truth," said Thomas dangerously, a coldness seeping into his bones and chilling his heart. "I want the truth."

There was silence that was broken only when Robert opened the door. "The fair Annie has banished me from the tavern." He halted and looked from Walsingham to Thomas. "What is it?"

"The cask is empty. Apparently this is no wedding gift, as Maclean offered, but is the end of a bargain between our friend, Walsingham, and the Scottish laird. You are just in time to hear the truth."

Robert slammed the door, a grimness about his mouth. "The truth and this man have ever been strangers. I wouldn't believe him were he to swear upon his own blood."

Walsingham flicked a contemptuous glance at Robert. "There is nothing but the truth left."

Robert leaned across the table. "Then speak quickly, old man, else I will slit your gullet."

Walsingham shoved the cask to the center of the table. "Of course I will explain everything. I've nothing to lose now."

Robert pulled his rapier free and laid it on the table. "You have your life."

The counselor ignored him. He looked to Thomas. "My association with Maclean began the day after Queen Mary's husband was murdered. As you know, rumors began almost immediately, implicating her and her lover, Lord Bothwell, in the death. However, Elizabeth would not hear of Mary's involvement without conclusive proof. I had to find that proof."

"Did you approach Maclean?" Thomas heard his voice dispassionately asking questions, as though he had nothing at stake in this venture. He felt as though he were asleep, listening to this preposterous tale through the mist of a dream.

"Aye. Repeatedly. At first he resisted. But eventually he came to see how advantageous this arrangement would be."

"How did you buy him? Gold?" Robert sneered. "And Maclean would speak to me of honor."

"There are few things the Maclean holds of value. It would have made our negotiations much simpler had he wanted gold." Walsingham met Thomas's gaze for a moment, then regarded the cask.

The roar in his ears increased until Thomas felt the vibration in his bones. He leaned forward, not recognizing his own voice, so harsh and distant was it. "What was his price?"

Hooded gray eyes flickered for an instant. "I did what I thought was best. What needed to be done."

"What did you trade Maclean for the letters?"

The minister swallowed, and Robert's rapier lifted, the slender point brought to rest directly under the counselor's chin. Walsingham swallowed, the sound echoing throughout the room. A trickle of blood dripped down his thin neck.

"Speak!" Thomas commanded, his fists clenched on his knees.

"A bridegroom," answered Walsingham, gulping air. "I traded him a bridegroom."

"Mon Dieu!" Robert's sword arm dropped, his eyes wide as he turned to Thomas.

The roar rose and swelled. Thomas shut his eyes against the onslaught. The truth struck him with the solidness of steel against bone. *He had been sold like a bull at auction.* He felt as though his soul had been shredded. Anger, pure and hot, poured through him.

"Trust no one," his father had said. *No one.*

Thomas took a deep breath. "What of the letter I was sent to retrieve from Duart? What of it?"

Walsingham wiped the blood from his throat with a cloth. " 'Twas fabricated. Maclean was desirous of meeting you before he sealed the bargain. He swore to deliver the cask to me here, at the inn, the week after you married his cousin. It never arrived."

"I was a fool from the beginning."

"Nay, Thomas." The minister leaned forward and placed a hand on his shoulder. "Not a fool. Just loyal. The queen will—"

Thomas shoved the hand from his shoulder. "I was a fool. A blind fool."

Walsingham sighed. "Maclean knew all there was to know of you. Your holdings, position, everything. 'Tis a compliment of sorts. He could have asked far more, and I would have paid. Title, lands, anything. Instead, he asked for a noble bridegroom to wed his cousin and spirit her from his war-ravaged home." He shrugged. "I suppose all in all, 'twas easy enough to arrange."

The rapier flashed to the thin throat, the tip hovering but a hairsbreadth from the pale skin. "Sweet Jesu, Thomas," Robert cried, "let me slice this evil whoreson!"

"Nay," Thomas answered, and Robert reluctantly lowered his blade, his visage black with fury. A multitude of images swirled through Thomas's mind, foremost among them the picture of Fia calmly telling him that she intended to go to London whatever the price.

Whatever the price.

It had seemed coincidental that she had been fleeing the very castle he had stolen into it. It had seemed equally odd that she was on her way to London as well, he thought bitterly. As was the fact that his horse had been chased off by Zeus, leaving the two of them with naught but Thunder, whose slow pace had assured their easy capture. Then there was the fateful incident in the castle, when the chit had stolen his clothing and lured him into the hallway wearing nothing but his hose.

He stared down at his fists. It had all been planned. All of it. He could still hear Duncan thundering of Fia's honor and virtue and how 'twas now Thomas's duty to wed her. But it had been no coincidence that they had been caught in such a compromising position. The truth was, Duncan had planned the entire miserable episode.

315

Likely with Fia's full and artful complicity.

"You told the queen that Fia and I were forced to wed."

Walsingham's thin eyebrows lifted. "Of course. I knew she would grant you an annulment forthwith. It was the one weapon I had up my sleeve." He placed a hand on Thomas's sleeve. "I knew the queen would grant an annulment. I never intended for the wedding to stand. You would have been freed as soon as you set foot at court."

"Thomas, don't believe him."

" 'Tis true," said Walsingham, frowning at Robert. "Once I had the letters, there was nothing to hold me to the bargain. The queen would have annulled the marriage, and that little Scottish doxy could be sent home with no more ado."

Thomas pulled his sleeve from the counselor's grasp. "The queen will never annul the marriage, after our meeting last week. You know that."

"I hear your lady has a most persuasive way with words." Walsingham was silent for a moment, his hooded eyes fixed on Thomas. "I never planned on your falling under the chit's spell. None of the information I received mentioned that she was lovely."

"Did Fia know?" The words burned in Thomas's throat.

The minister hesitated, then nodded. "From what Maclean said, your lady was aware of all."

"He lies!" Robert ground out, his fist whitening about his rapier. "Don't believe him! Fia would never—"

"I have no reason to lie, you fool," Walsingham snapped. He turned to Thomas and leaned forward. "We were betrayed, you and I. They betrayed us both."

The words hovered in the air like rank perfume. Thomas could see his father's harsh face. *"Trust no one."*

"But Duncan had arranged a marriage for her," he said heavily. "Malcolm Davies—"

"Was a fool. Do you honestly think Duncan Maclean would welcome a marriage with a sniveling whelp like that? He wanted you to think Fia had a justifiable reason for fleeing so you would take her with you. He had set a trap to catch the two of you together in the outer bailey, in front of a host of witnesses. I hear you made it even easier than he had hoped."

It all made sense. Thomas stood up so suddenly the room spun about him. With a shuddering breath, he leaned on the table, his head low, struggling against the madness roaring in his mind.

"Thomas?" Robert's voice echoed as if through a long, deep tunnel. "What will you do, *mon ami?*"

Thomas looked into Robert's concerned eyes. What was he going to do? He met Walsingham's pale, considering face, hatred burning within him at the detached curiosity lighting the gray eyes.

"Damn your rotten, filthy soul, Walsingham," Thomas said with quiet intensity, fury burning through each word. His body yearned for release. He kicked his chair across the room, slamming both his fists onto the table, splitting the wood surface.

"Damn your soul and that little Scottish slut," he snarled.

Chapter Twenty-eight

If innocence had a face, it would have been hers. Curled on her side, her hand tucked beneath her cheek, she looked as untainted as a child. The rabbit snuggled against her side, curved against her warmth.

Thomas took a long drink from his mug and closed his eyes against the stinging burn of the whiskey as it slid down his throat. He welcomed the pain, savored it. If he did not feel pain at this moment, he would feel nothing.

Nothing but emptiness.

He leaned his forehead against the smooth wood of the bedpost and stared at his sleeping wife. Sweet Jesu, but he had declared himself to her just this afternoon. He winced at the memory. How she must have laughed.

Silently, he toasted her sleeping form and gulped the last of his whiskey. He frowned into the empty mug and turned to the fireplace, where the bottle rested on the mantel. Zeus raised his head and then lumbered to his feet, approaching Thomas with a wagging tail. Thomas growled at the dog, showing his teeth in a feral gesture. Zeus's ears flattened, and he slunk across the room, wiggling his way under Fia's bed until only a hind leg showed.

Thomas felt a little shamed at his display. The dog had done nothing. He stopped to coax the canine back to the hearth. "At least one of us should be warm and happy this eve, eh?" he asked the dog.

Zeus wagged his crooked tail hesitantly.

Thomas refilled his mug and returned to the bed. He was inordinately proud his steps wavered so little. By the rood, they could accuse him of having been duped by a Scottish wench, but he could handle his whiskey with the best of them.

He stared into the amber liquid and wondered why he had even bothered to drink. The agony of Fia's betrayal had disappeared late in the night, leaving a forlorn numbness, as if some part of him had been ripped asunder.

He gazed down at Fia once again. Her hair flowed across the pillow. How he had loved to sink his hands into those velvety strands. His loins tightened at the thought, and he smiled bitterly. Sweet Jesu, but he starved for her even as she poisoned him with her lies. His father had been right. Believe no one. Trust only yourself.

After storming out of the tavern, he had ridden to his house as though the very hounds of hell were nipping at his heels. Snarling at every servant who stood in his way, he had stormed through the house and thrown open the door to his chamber.

He had wanted to rant and shout and drive Fia into the street, but she had been asleep. And for some reason, he could no more wake her than he could leave. He felt a wave of disgust for his weakness.

He turned from the bed. It would be light within the hour. The time was swiftly approaching when he would have to speak with her. He walked to the fireplace. What could he say to a woman who had purchased him like a pair of shoes? God's Breath, but he wanted to kill her.

The thought almost made him laugh aloud. He wanted to kill her, and yet he could not even stand to rouse her from a peaceful slumber.

Fortifying himself with another swallow of the fiery whiskey, he threw himself into a chair. He willed the creaking of the wood to awaken her. She did not move, and he scowled. The time had come. He smacked the mug on the chair arm, heedless of the whiskey spilling over the sides. She stirred, and his chest tightened painfully.

"When did you return?" Her voice, heavy with sleep, had the consistency of honey. He stilled the urge to cover his ears to block out the sultry sound.

He took a gulp and wiped his mouth, staring at his hand with bleary concern when he saw how it shook. *Do not look at her. You will never be able to get through this do you look at her.* He forced himself to answer. "Not long ago."

Fia sat up and shoved her hair from her face, wondering at the curtness of his tone. His meeting must not have been as profitable as he had hoped. " 'Tis late. You said you'd be no more than an hour."

Thomas flicked a glance at her, his eyes almost black in the shadows. She wondered at his stillness. He slouched in a chair, legs sprawled in front of him, his shirt loosened to his waist. His unshaven face seemed to have aged overnight.

She felt the first flutter of fear. With a concerned glance at the mug he held so tightly, she asked, "Are . . . are you well?"

He laughed, a bitter, self-derisive sound that chilled

her. "Perchance *you* should tell me the answer to that, madam wife."

She scooted to the edge of the bed. He was different. Completely unlike the Thomas who had held her in the garden. "What has happened? You seem angered."

"Angered? I?" He exploded to his feet and crossed the room with the fury of a raging storm. He wrenched her from the bed, his fingers biting cruelly into her arms. "Am I not to be allowed even that?"

"Wh-what are you talking about?" She could only stare up at him, her mind racing furiously.

He sneered. "You and Duncan greatly mistook the matter if you thought I was a man of even temperament. Or wasn't that one of the qualities you sought in your bridegroom?" His breath, laden with whiskey and fire, fanned her face.

"Duncan never—"

"Lies!" He spat the word and shook her roughly. "All you speak are lies! I saw Walsingham tonight, you scheming harlot!" Through gritted teeth, he hissed, "Speak the truth ere I kill you."

Fia fought for breath and began desperately, "Sweet St. Catherine, but you're mad! I don't know—"

"Cease this pretense now." His eyes shot amber sparks, and Fia feared he would catch fire with such fury. Yet in a voice as cold as ice he bit out, "I am tired of your deceit. I met with Walsingham. I know every-thing."

"I-I don't know what Walsingham has to do with—"

He threw her from him. She fell against the bed, her shoulder catching the large wooden post. A cry was torn from her lips. Thomas winced as if he had received her wound.

"Sweet Jesu," he muttered, his voice twisted in an-guish. "You have but to cry out, and I suffer." He stum-bled to his chair and took a shuddering breath. "How am I to deal with you when I cannot even stand to see you bruised? How am I to send you away when I—." He closed his eyes, a spasm of pain washing over him.

Fia rubbed her shoulder, staring at him with concern. Whatever had happened last eve, Thomas was suffering the torments of hell. "Are you ill?" she asked, shivering at his haggard expression. Sweet St. Catherine, but she ached to hold him, to soothe away the agony she saw in his amber eyes.

He glared at her. "Aye, I am ill. I am sick unto death at the sight of my lying, manipulative wife."

She caught sight of the empty bottle on the mantel, and suspicion rose within her. "Thomas, tell me—"

"Tell you?" He turned red-rimmed eyes on her. "Tell you what? Tell you that you have brought your ill fortune into my house and I am now cursed with it?" He shook his head. "Nay. We have discussed enough. You will sit there until I have decided what to do with you."

She clamped her mouth in irritation. "You are breaking nigh every rule we ever had, my lord."

"Rules? You would speak to me of rules?" He stood with a lithe grace that made her throat contract, and he crossed to her desk. He pulled a parchment from a cubbyhole and held it out. "You see here our contract, Lady Rotherwood. Let me show you the worth I place on your word." He wadded the paper and tossed it into the fire.

Fia watched the flames lick hungrily at the parchment. Her heart withered into ash. But whatever ailed Thomas, she was not about to stand for his vile temper. "I know not what demons possess you this eve, my lord, but I will not bear your wretched manners."

She gained her feet shakily and crossed to the door. Grasping the handle, she threw it open. "Leave my chambers immediately. We will speak when you have slept through your ill humor."

He laughed. A low, taunting laugh. The sheer ugliness

of it made Fia shiver. "Aye, that would be most humorous, wouldn't it?" He grinned and stretched his long legs in front of him. "You would love to write Duncan of how you threw me out of my own bedchamber, wouldn't you? How amused he would be to see how well his plan has worked."

"Plan?"

His eyes narrowed, and his grin thinned into a bitter snarl. "You may think you have purchased a gullible, manageable bridegroom, but you are wrong, madam. And I intend to prove that very thing to you."

She frowned in confusion. "You make no sense."

"Determined to play an innocent to the last." He shrugged. "And why not? It has been amusing thus far. Let's continue this charade a moment longer. Allow me to recount my discovery. This very eve I found 'twas no coincidence we were thrown together at Duart Castle."

Fia thought he looked like an avenging angel, beautiful yet dangerous. She clutched her hands tightly together, trying to comprehend his meaning.

"In fact," he continued softly, "I found out that you and Maclean purchased me outright from Walsingham." The lines on his face deepened. "I was bought as a side of beef in a butcher's shop."

"How could that be? What—"

"Cease your playacting, madam," he snapped. "You know it all! I was traded for a packet of letters proving Queen Mary's guilt."

"You have been misinformed. Duncan would do no such thing."

"Duncan delivered those very letters into my hands and bade me carry them to Walsingham." Thomas chuckled harshly. "Or at least, he would have me believe that he delivered them as was promised. But the cask was empty."

Fia rubbed her head wearily. How to decipher all this?

"What happened, Fia? Did you and Duncan think Walsingham wouldn't tell me the truth? That you could make a deal with the devil and not pay?" His eyes raked her body with insulting intent. "Wasn't I worth even that? Perhaps I didn't meet your expectations? God's Wounds, but I made you cry with pleasure. Surely that was worth payment of some kind."

Heat washed through her face and then receded, leaving her cold and shaking. "I don't know anything of these letters, but if you mean to suggest that Duncan or I had any kind of dealings with Walsingham, then you err. I've heard Duncan mention Walsingham before, and he holds no faith in him."

He laughed harshly. "There is little trust on either side of that fence. But I am far from mistaken." He spoke with a quiet, merciless certainty that chilled her. "I will never forget the duplicity of your behavior. Never."

Fia took a deep breath, pain lacing through her at his words. "No more. I am tired and confused and . . ." She pressed a trembling hand to her head. Sweet St. Catherine, but this was a nightmare. She wished with all her heart she would awaken to find the Thomas she so loved nestled in bed beside her. Anything but this bitter, angry stranger who stared at her with such virulent hate. "No more. I-I cannot."

Thomas stared at her quivering lips. Pure desire, hot and immediate, raced through him. He cursed himself that she still had the power to stir his blood. "Don't bother to act so heroic, madam. There is no need."

"There has been some mistake. If I could but speak with Duncan, I could—"

"Duncan asked me to deliver those damn letters to Walsingham myself. I had the cask." His mouth curved into a self-derisive smile. "Sweet Jesu, he even told me to tell Walsingham that they were now 'even.' How he must have laughed to have me deliver the payment."

Fia wrung her hands and took a step toward him. "Duncan would not lie! Walsingham must be keeping the truth from you!"

"Do you think I have not considered that?" he snapped. "But what has he to gain from such a stratagem? What reason would he have to speak falsely? Duncan and you, meanwhile, gain all. Duncan found a fool to wed his cousin and spirit her away from war. And you, sweet, were ever loud in your demands to go to London."

"Nay!" She took another step toward him, her hand outstretched. "Thomas, you must listen to me."

He regarded her silently, his eyes hardening. "I know you for what you are, a liar and worse. There is nothing you could say that would make me believe else."

Her hand fell to her side. "Then there is naught left." Her voice rang hollow as disbelief and loss rippled across her face.

"Oho, a playwright *and* an actress!" He clapped loudly. "Excellent! Such unexpected talents!"

She stiffened. "Och, enough! You barge in here, calling me names and accusing me of vile crimes. Then you refuse to believe me no matter the truth. Well, I've had enough of your nonsense!"

"You have had enough? Well, so have I, madam. I have been made a fool a thousand times since we met." He threw himself into the chair, his face contorted in fury. "I even gave the queen one of your plays, hoping she would sponsor you."

Her lips parted in amazement. He had never said a word. Through her pain came a lightening, a thrill that he had thought her plays good enough to risk giving to the queen. "I . . . never knew you had read any of them."

He stared at her, his eyes lingering on her mouth. "I have read every word that has ever dripped from your pen." He met her surprised gaze and shrugged, a bitter smile curving his mouth. "I would have sponsored you myself, but I thought 'twould please you more if the queen took you to heart." His laugh was heavy with loathing. "I was a romantic lackwit, was I not?"

A smile trembled on her mouth. No matter what he said, he loved her.

"Well, madam, you will have no chance for fame and fortune now." He shook his head, staring into the fire with bleak eyes. " 'Twas all a lie."

Fia dropped her gaze, her throat tightening painfully. She wanted to tell him that she loved him now and forever, but he would just use the words to wound her more. Whatever lies Walsingham had fed Thomas, poisoning him against her, she must find the truth. Find the truth and cure him.

"You can't even look at me." His voice trembled with wrath. "Allow me to return the favor. Whatever maudlin feelings I possessed for you are gone, never to return. Never."

Clenching her hands into fists, Fia struggled for breath. "You are merely angered. In the morning we will talk, and this misunderstanding—and your abuse—will end."

He smiled, his mouth a grim curve. "Oh, but I have not yet begun. We have a lifetime together, sweet wife. Since we are legally wed, and I cannot undo what is done, then I will spend the rest of our time together reminding you of your trickery and deceit."

Fia closed her eyes. She gathered the last vestiges of pride she possessed and said tiredly, "Then there is no more to be said." She turned and went to the bed. Grabbing up the blanket and a pillow, she headed for the door.

Thomas reached it first. He kicked the heavy panel closed and leaned against it. "Nay, madam. You will not leave this room until I have decided your fate."

"Decided my fate?" Her brows drew together. "I vow, sirrah, but you test my temper. I want nothing more to do with you."

"What's this? You no longer desire my presence? Is your purchased husband too base, too loud for you?"

"And boorish and rude as well. I don't know what has occurred, but I am leaving before I listen to any more of your petty accusations. You come to me, drunk and angered and ranting, refusing the truth and crying foul at my every word. I will have no more of this foolishness." She lifted her chin, her hands clutching the blanket and pillow like a shield. "Move."

He pushed himself from the door, and for a heart-stopping moment Fia thought he meant to grab her. She backed warily away. He smiled, satisfaction curling his mouth. "Finally you begin to realize your danger. But 'tis too late, your fear. I know you well and true now."

"And I know you," she returned evenly, regarding him with dull eyes. "There is no more to be said to-night."

He returned her look for a long, silent moment. "You're right," he said wearily. "We will wait until to-morrow to continue this."

She nodded, a lone tear slowly coursing down her cheek. "Perhaps then you will be ready to listen to reason."

The lines about his mouth tightened. "Nay, sweet. By then I will know what to do with such a beautiful, willful little liar as you."

"Then there will be no tomorrow," Fia snapped in return. Sweet St. Catherine, how could she love this man?

"Oh, but there will." He reached into his pocket and pulled out a key. He opened the door and inserted the key into the outer lock.

327

"Don't!" she cried. If she couldn't find out the truth, how would she ever be able to disprove Walsingham's base lies?

"Oh, but I will. Do not think, Mistress Deceit, that Angus or Mary will come to help you. I will have them closely guarded. You had best be prepared to tell me all when I return on the morrow." He gave her a mocking bow, then slammed the door shut.

The sound of the key grating in the lock rang hollowly through the room.

Disbelief coursed through her. She sank to the floor, still clutching the pillow and blanket. "What will I do?" she whispered. "What will I do?"

Chapter Twenty-nine

A shaft of bright sunlight streamed directly into his face, the brilliant colors blinding him. Thomas groaned and closed his eyes against the glare, vaguely aware that he lay atop a sack of grain.

"Oho! It awakes!" Robert announced.

Agony pounded through Thomas's skull. The memory of the previous night wavered to the fore. Clamping his jaw against a wave of nausea, he struggled upright.

His squinting gaze noted the sun streaming though the window. 'Twas a beautiful day. He loudly cursed every gleaming beam, twittering bird, and dewy morning flower.

"You have come to a sad pass, *mon ami*. The earl of Rotherwood, most fortunate of men, asleep atop sacks of moldy grain."

Thomas tried to glare but decided it pained him too much.

"I feel as if I died sometime last week," he muttered,

grimacing at the foul taste in his mouth. He peered into the gloom enshrouding the corners of his makeshift bed-chamber until he found his mug resting on the floor behind him. Grabbing it up, he gulped the remaining whiskey, welcoming the acrid burn.

"Just what you need," Robert said, the slight sting of anger coloring his tone, "more drink."

Thomas stared blearily up at the Scotsman's unsmiling mien and decided not to waste strength making an answer. His head felt as if it were filled with wet sand.

"*Simila similibus curatur*," Robert murmured.

"Aye," Thomas grumbled. "Hair of the dog. A foul cure for a foul illness." He wished he could just wretch and be done with it.

"A foul illness for a foul temper is more like," Robert returned.

Thomas ignored him and dropped the empty mug, flinching as it clanged on the stone floor. Gathering himself with a deep breath, he stood. The world listed slowly to the right. He placed a steadying hand against the wall.

Light sparkled on the window. 'Twas a horrifyingly beauteous day. He wondered briefly if anyone had thought to bring Fia her breakfast. The idea of her locked in her room was painful; the thought of her going hungry was agony.

He immediately pushed the traitorous feelings aside. It would serve her right to miss a few meals. It would serve her even better if he locked her up for the rest of eternity.

He covered his eyes wearily. He should send her away and be done. Duncan would take her back, and Thomas would be free to return to his life as it was before he had ever met that saucy, conniving little thief. His existence would be orderly, with no unexpected twists and turns.

The very thought chilled him. He couldn't do it. He

could no more send Fia away than he could cut off his own arm. Rubbing a hand against the ache in his chest, he wondered if he should take her to his estates in Northumberland until he could decide how best to deal with her.

Time would lessen the hold she had on him. It must. He leaned his forehead against the coolness of the wall and tried to force his swollen brain to reason.

"God's Wounds, Thomas! You look ready to topple over. 'Twas but whiskey!"

" 'Twas an entire flagon of the stuff, and I would appreciate it if you would cease shouting."

Robert made a seat of a barrel of salted fish. "I spoke with Mary this morn. Of course 'twas difficult to hear through her locked door panel, but we managed well enough."

Thomas closed his eyes.

"She says she and Angus are confined by your orders. I hear Fia is also locked away." He waited for Thomas to respond and then asked loudly, "Do you want to tell me what possessed you?"

"Nay," said Thomas curtly, wishing Robert would have the decency to at least lower his voice.

"Hmph. Had I known what you were about, I wouldn't have spent near an entire evening tracking a certain fat, bumbling oaf to his filthy lodgings in an effort to discover the truth."

Thomas opened his eyes. "There is nothing more to be said. She lied to me. 'Tis enough," he whispered. " 'Tis more than enough."

Robert bared his teeth in a semblance of a smile. "You know, *mon ami,* I never before realized how greatly you resemble your father at times. It ill becomes you."

"My father was right. Trust no one. Look where trusting has put me."

"Trust? How can you speak of trust when you locked

331

away that wondrous maid who has done nothing but love and honor you? How can you speak of trust when you take the word of that spineless maggot, Walsingham, over the word of your own wife?"

Thomas rubbed his forehead. "I don't know."

Robert was silent for a moment. "She loves you, you know. You can see it in her eyes every time you enter a room."

"Love," Thomas scoffed, wondering how anyone could bear the pain. "I have never known it." He stared out the window, irritated by the beauty of such a vile day. "Whatever I felt for Fia is no more. It has to be."

Robert let out his breath in a hiss. "I can't believe you! You meet with the most incredible good fortune. You find a woman made for you, a woman who loves you, and you throw it away, you—"

"Silence!" Thomas roared, shuddering as the echo pounded through his head. "I will hear no more."

"Sod you and your festering anger. I have tried to help, be a friend when no one else would." Robert stood and stiffly turned toward the door. "I have wasted my time."

"Nay, you have not," Thomas said dully, rubbing his neck with a shaking hand. "I am the lost cause, Robert. Not you."

Robert leveled a steady gaze at him. "No one is a lost cause, *mon ami. You* showed me that."

"Then I was wrong. Before you leave, see to it Fia is fed decently. Take Mary to her." He drew a shuddering breath. Somehow he would find a way through this madness.

"I'll have Mistress Hadwell take her something to eat."

"Nay," said Thomas sharply. "Keep Mistress Hadwell away from her. I'm sure our argument last night was loud enough that the entire house heard it. Whatever

Fia's involvement with Walsingham's plot, she does not deserve the contempt of that harpy."

Robert planted his hands on his hips. "Sweet Jesu, Thomas, listen to yourself! You would protect Fia from mere scorn. You can't even bear for her to miss a meal. I trow, there is hope for you yet." He returned to his barrel and leaned forward, placing his hands on his knees. "Listen to me. You should know this. Walsingham—"

"Let it die, Robert. Walsingham told the truth."

"Some of it was true, I'll grant you. But as usual, he didn't tell you all."

Thomas stilled. A flare of hope lit the bleakness of his soul before he quenched it. "Nay, you've mistrusted Walsingham from the start. What would he have to gain by telling such a foul tale about himself? 'Twas the truth. It had to be."

"Lying is as mother's milk to that pox-ridden pig's bladder. He told you the truth, at least part of the truth." Robert's blue eyes were dark with sincerity.

The hope flared yet again. This time Thomas was unable to kill it. "What part?"

"There was a deal between Walsingham and Maclean. But the rest is fabrication."

Thomas took a deep breath. Anger rippled through him, leaving another jagged tear in its wake. Sweet Jesu, what if Fia . . . He refused to finish the thought. "Who told you this?" he asked harshly.

"Goliath, of course. Since he sits so near the door, I thought perhaps he heard more than one might imagine. I was right." Robert smiled sweetly. "Have you noticed that he has developed a certain fondness for my company? While I am oft followed about by gentle animals and small children, this is the first time I have had a giant so—"

"Robert," Thomas interrupted grimly, "just tell me what you found."

Robert grinned. "The only thing we know for sure is that Walsingham would sell his soul to protect the queen. That is, he would if he had one."

Thomas took a steadying breath. "Speak plainly, Robert. What did Goliath say?"

"Not much until his life hung right on the tip of my rapier. Then he sang as sweetly as a bird." Robert buffed his finger nails on his doublet, his mouth curved in an unpleasant smile. "One part of the bargain between Walsingham and Maclean was that Fia was never to know."

Thomas felt a moment of exultation. Joy, pure and sweet, coursed through his blood. She was innocent. Walsingham had used him, bartered him even, as though his life were worth no more than a pence, but Fia herself was blameless.

"She's innocent," he said aloud, as though testing the words. A huge burden lifted from his laden shoulders, and he wanted to shout with happiness. "She didn't know."

"Aye." Robert crossed his arms and looked at the ceiling. "A pity she's locked away in her room, else she could breakfast with us."

A stab of guilt hit Thomas. He sagged against the wall, seeing Fia's pale, desperate face before him. "God's Wounds," he whispered. "I accused her of so much."

Robert frowned. "Surely you said nothing that can't be unsaid. Once she realizes how Walsingham used you—"

"Nay, she tried to tell me, but I wouldn't listen." Guilt weighed him down until he could barely stand. He tried to close away the anguish he had seen in Fia's fathomless black eyes. He needed to go to her, tell her what had happened, explain everything.

And then he would deal with Walsingham. The idea of exacting vengeance gave his thoughts a more positive focus. He pushed away from the wall.

"Good!" Robert said. "Go on bended knee and ask her forgiveness. Surely she will listen if you woo her with flowers and sonnets."

Thomas looked around the room. He couldn't bear to think what he would do if he had killed Fia's love. "The key . . ."

Robert slid his hand into his pocket and withdrew a large iron key. " 'Twas on the floor." His eyes were somber. "Was it so necessary?"

"She threatened to leave," Thomas said in an emotionless tone. "I couldn't let her."

"You love her," Robert said quietly.

Thomas took a deep breath and held out a hand. "Give it to me."

Robert idly swung the key on one finger. "Perhaps I should release the sweet Fia and assist her in escaping such a rude tyrant."

"Do, and I will kill you," Thomas growled. "Sweet Jesu, Robert, but if Goliath speaks the truth, then we don't know what Walsingham is about. He is but a swift pace from madness."

"Forsooth, 'tis a miracle! By the saints, Thomas, but I have been saying the same to you these past five years, and you would have none of it! 'Tis time you saw the dark side of that conniver."

"Nay, I knew of it. But his motives were to strengthen England, as were mine." Thomas frowned at his empty hands and closed them into fists. "But there is a limit. I will not have him near Fia. We must find him." He stared at his fists, trying to grasp some elusive fact, some cloaked truth that lingered just out of sight. He raised his head and looked at Robert. "Why did Walsingham say Fia was involved in the trade if she wasn't?"

Robert's eyebrows lowered. "Does he need a reason? Such a loathsome pilcher makes mischief to amuse himself."

"Nay, everything Walsingham does is to a purpose, usually cloaked in some intrigue to benefit Elizabeth. He told me Fia was involved to gain something." He walked to the window and stared out. A cool breeze stirred the trees. What was the old fox trying to accomplish now? "Perhaps," Thomas said slowly, "he told such vile lies because he thought he knew how I would react."

"Like your father," Robert said, his eyes brightening.

"Aye. Never again speak to her or of her."

"He didn't know you cannot even bear to see her miss her breakfast." Robert absently tossed the key into the air and then caught it. He stared at it, frowning. "But why did he try to break her from you? What purpose does he have?"

"That's what we must discover." Thomas walked to Robert and held out his hand.

Robert grinned and handed him the key. "Release her quickly, *mon ami*. Though beauteous, Fia is hardly the type of damsel to languish long in a tower."

Thomas closed his hand around the cold metal. "Nay, she stays locked within her room until we find Walsingham. She will be safer inside than out."

Robert was aghast. "You would leave her locked up? She will be furious!"

"I know," Thomas replied with a grim nod. "But she will be safe. That's what matters most. Have a cold bath sent to my room. I will need my wits about me before I track this fox to his lair."

"Aye," replied Robert dubiously.

Thomas left the room, a surge of hope and excitement flowing through him. Once he had Walsingham's confession, he would go to Fia and explain it all, how Walsingham had tricked them both. Perhaps they could start anew. And if she couldn't forgive him . . . His hand tightened around the sharp edges of the key until it cut into his hand. He couldn't think of the possibility.

She had to forgive him. She had to.

A long wail, like that of a keening ghost, rose through the morning air and then dropped into painful silence. Thomas sat up in the tub and frowned as the moan rose again and melted into a low lamentation. The noise was fraying what few nerves he had left.

A brisk knock sounded on his door. "Enter," he called. The wail echoed through the house.

Mistress Hadwell marched into the room carrying a tray. She halted when she caught sight of Thomas sitting in the tub. She turned away, her face red. "I beg your pardon, your lordship, I didn't know—"

"Never mind that," Thomas said as he stood and grabbed a towel. The keening sounded again. "What in the devil is that noise?"

If it was possible, her back stiffened even more. " 'Tis nothing, milord. 'Twill cease in a moment."

Thomas dried quickly and pulled on his breeches. Another wail echoed.

Mistress Hadwell set the tray on a table. "Heathen Scottish hound," she muttered.

Zeus!

A stab of fear ripped through Thomas. He grabbed the key and his boots, brushing past Mistress Hadwell without a second glance. He raced down the passage, his unlaced shirt flapping about him as he slid to a halt in front of Fia's door.

The horrible moan rose again. Thomas dropped his boots and unlocked the door with hands that fumbled with haste.

The room seemed cold, empty. Trailing from the bed, knotted end-to-end, were the bed curtains. The makeshift rope trailed to the open window and disappeared over the sill. Zeus sat staring out the window, his face mournful. Nose quivering, a solitary brown rabbit regarded him from the bed.

Fia was gone.

Thomas's throat tightened in fear. He crossed to the window and leaned over the edge. No broken body lay in the garden. A heavy sigh of relief escaped him, and he sagged against the windowsill.

"What's happened?" Robert spoke at his shoulder.

"She's gone." He was amazed that he sounded so calm, as though his heart were not firmly lodged within his throat.

"What?" Robert leaned over the sill. He turned a stern face to Thomas. "Damn your temper! She has left you!"

Thomas stared blindly at the rose-fingered sky, his brow creased in concentration. "Nay. She left her animals. If she planned to leave for long, they would be with her."

Below them a servant crossed the walkways carrying a basket. Robert leaned out the window. "Hold!"

The man halted and looked up, shading his eyes with one hand.

"Have you seen the mistress this morning?"

The servant shook his head. "Nay, yer lordship. I jes' . . ." He trailed off, his mouth gaping in surprise, as he noted the makeshift rope hanging from the window.

Thomas pushed Robert out of the way. "Go on, man! What did you see?"

"I've been picking apples here in the garden all mornin', yer lordship, and I ne'er saw hide nor hair of the mistress."

"Did you leave the garden at any time?"

"Only when th' basket was filled. I was gone only a moment or two."

"When was that?"

"About a half an hour ago, yer lordship. It couldn't have been more'n that."

Thomas felt a stirring of hope. "Then she's can't be far."

"Aye," Robert murmured, "or perhaps she was long gone before this man even arrived in the garden. We've no way of knowing."

"Pardon me, yer lordship," the servant added eagerly, "but I did hear tell two horses are missin' from the stables jus' this mornin'."

"Which horses?"

The man scrubbed at his ear. "That be the strangest thing. One was an old bay, not worth more'n a few pence. But the other! 'Twas the ugliest mount ye ever saw, and as mean as a snake." He held up his hand. "The blasted thing bit me jus' yesterday."

Thunder. Thomas nodded his thanks. He shared a long look with Robert and then strode to the door, grabbing up his discarded boots. With more force than was necessary, he tugged them on.

Robert leaned against the bedpost. "She doesn't know anyone in London."

"Nay, she is alone," Thomas replied briefly, the ache in his chest swelling with each breath. Alone and lost, looking for God knew what.

A cold, wet nose briefly nudged his hand. Thomas smiled reassuringly into Zeus's concerned eyes, rubbing the dog's good ear. "We'll find her, Zeus, I promise. She couldn't have just . . ." His voice trailed off as he stared at the dog.

He remembered Fia facing the queen. She had been fearless. He rubbed his chin. By the saints, he would bet gold she was concocting a plan to confront Walsingham and overcome his scheme. *Sweet Jesu, surely she wouldn't.*

He looked at Robert. "Go and see if Mary and Angus are still locked in their quarters."

"You think she took them with her?"

"I'm hoping she did. If she's gone to do what I think she has, she'll need their help. I only pray it is enough."

Robert's eyes widened. "Walsingham," he breathed. "Good God, she's gone after Walsingham."

Chapter Thirty

"I've come to see the owner," Fia announced. Garbed in a coarse brown dress that reeked of stale onions, she tried her best to look like one of the dubious patrons of the tavern.

Beady eyes glared at her. "Letty'll not see th' likes o' ye." The giant stuffed a huge slab of meat into his mouth, red juice running down his chin and dripping onto his stained shirt.

Fia repressed a shudder. *A play. 'Tis just a play.* From across the room, she caught Mary's frown and shook her head. She could deal with this. "Tell Letty I've somethin' of hers she'll be wantin'."

The guard's eyes narrowed. He removed a cleaned bone from his mouth, wiping away the grease with a dirty sleeve. "Ye do, do ye? Suppose ye tell me what ye have t' sell?" His little eyes studied her, lingering appreciatively on her low neckline.

Fia crossed her arms. If she had thought her new

gowns cut low, she had neglected to compare them to those of the streetwalkers of London. The dirty dress lacked fastenings of any kind, the lacing having been discarded long since. The stained leather girdle did little more than push her breasts up into the ragged opening. Perhaps trading her new gown and cloak for this garment hadn't been such a masterly stroke after all.

But it was too late to think of that. It was too late to think of a lot of things.

Mary had wanted to charge up to Walsingham's fine house and demand the truth, even though she had known he was probably surrounded by guards and weapons. To Fia's surprise, Angus had come up with a better plan.

Mary's silent husband had known about the tavern. " 'Tis a fittin' location fer such vermin," he'd said.

'Twas a long statement for the usually taciturn man.

Mary had pledged her help. "We'll go with ye, lassie, and help ye find this miserable clotpole who dares to mess with ye and the master."

"Too dangerous," said Angus.

" 'Twill be less dangerous with the three of us," declared Mary.

Angus didn't move.

"The lassie needs to find out what happened to her Sassenach, love," Mary had said earnestly. "She'll be heartbroken if'n she doesn't."

Fia remembered how Angus's bland gaze had softened when he looked at Mary. After a moment, he'd nodded. Now Mary sat by the door, keeping her eye on their horses, while Angus hovered nearby.

Looking at Goliath, Fia was glad for their presence. She forced herself to smile. "Well, now, I might have a lot to sell. Ye ne'er can tell. Me name is Kate." She reached out and squeezed his arm. "Fine an' brawny, ye are, like a bull. And what be yer name?"

"Most calls me Goliath. I am very strong," he replied

with pride. Throwing the bone over his shoulder, he flexed a massive arm.

"My! What an arm ye have!" Fia wondered to see the giant grinning like a lad.

"I can lift three barrels at once." He beamed at her admiringly. "I bet I can lift a li'l wench like ye wi' but one finger." Goliath reached out with hands the size of platters.

Angus stirred uneasily as Fia skipped out of the way. "Not 'til I've seen Letty, ye don't." She lowered her eyelashes, hoping she could keep this lumbering romancer at a distance without resorting to her knife. "Perhaps afterward, if ye're still of a mind, I could be persuaded to serve ye."

"Ye can't git in. Ye might as well spend the time wi' me."

"I might, if ye've got the proper coin," Fia replied, noting with relief the dimming of his enthusiasm.

"I has t' pay, do I?" He regarded her up and down, as though she were a prime bit of beef. "How much?"

How much? Fia blinked at him. She wondered what Kate commanded for a brief pleasuring.

She was still involved in her calculations when Goliath leaned closer to rumble in her ear, "Ye know, Kate, I could get ye in to see Letty if ye were nice wit' me." His foul breath seeped through the gaps in his lecherous grin.

"Goliath, let the chit be," came a low voice. Fia turned and met the green gaze of a tavern maid. The woman held a mug of ale in one hand, the other resting on her hip as she surveyed Fia from head to foot, her critical eyes assessing every detail.

"What are ye doin' here?" the woman asked, her reddish hair curling from beneath a dirty scrap of lace.

"I came to see Letty. This lout was tryin' to charge me," Fia returned, frowning sternly at Goliath.

"Here, now, Annie!" Goliath defended himself, seeming to cower before the bright green gaze. "I wasn't doin' no—"

"Let her in," the woman interrupted.

"But I was tol' not t' let no one in but the coun—"

"Let her in."

With a great show of reluctance, the huge man opened the door. Fia scurried past, Angus close behind her. Annie lifted an eyebrow at the burly Scotsman. He positioned himself in a chair by the fire and crossed his arms, clearly intending to stay put.

"I'll go an' get ye a drink," the maid announced.

As the door closed, Fia gave a sigh of relief. She tested a rickety chair and sat on the edge. She waited, shivering at the dampness of the room.

The door swung open, and Annie returned. "Here," she said, plopping a mug on the table. Water sloshed onto the dirty surface.

"Thank you. I'm very thirsty." Fia offered a tentative smile.

"Aye, ye were so thirsty ye have forgotten how to talk," returned Annie, her own mouth curving in response. "Yer accent, Katie. Ye've lost it all."

Fia bit her lip. "I don't suppose you would believe *this* is a fake accent and the other my real one?" she asked hopefully.

Even Angus smiled at that. Annie's mouth twitched. "I'm no' such a fool as that."

Fia sighed. "Then I suppose I'll have to tell you the real story. You see, I'm hiding from the unwholesome regards of my evil uncle, the baron."

Annie's eyebrows lifted. "You're an heiress, no doubt?"

"Och, now you've lost your accent as well." Fia sniffed the air. "There must be an evil wind about as sneaks up and steals them."

Annie grinned reluctantly. " 'Tis difficult to remember, isn't it?"

"Aye, though you do it quite well," Fia said with an admiring look, wishing she had thought to smear dirt over her hands and face.

"I've had more than my fair share of practice, milady." Annie took a chair and regarded Fia with calm green eyes.

Fia sipped her water. "I have a message to deliver to Letty." She looked about the small room. "Do you work here? I mean, with Walsingham?"

Annie's frown was as quick and sharp as a strike of lightning. She glared from Fia to Angus and back. "Marry, but you are forthright! Hold your tongue, do you wish to keep it!"

"Is he so fearsome?"

"He can be."

Fia placed her hands on Annie's. "Then leave."

Annie's face reflected a moment of hope before she shook her head. "Nay, I'm of no account here. 'Tis you who should leave."

"I'm of no more worth than you," Fia returned.

"I know exactly who you are. He's been expecting you. For that reason alone, you should go quickly. There are other ways to discover things. I'll help you."

"He knew I was coming because I sent a message for him to meet me here. Walsingham and I have a thing or two to discuss."

"I don't know if you're very brave or very foolish."

"What do you know about Walsingham?"

Annie was silent for a moment. "He leaves nothing to chance. He knows *everything*."

"My dear Annie," came a raspy male voice, "you make me out to be a mystic. Lady Rotherwood will run in fear if you continue thusly." The man's dry tone sent a shiver up Fia's back. Walsingham stepped through the door and pulled a cloak from his shoulders.

Annie flushed and stood. "I-I was just—"

"Leaving," he finished and draped the cloak across a chair. "I will speak with you later." He dismissed her with a curt wave of his hand.

Annie exchanged a level look with Fia and then slipped silently from the room.

Walsingham sighed and crossed to close the door. "Servants. You can never train them properly." He looked at Angus. The Scotsman stared back with an impassive gaze, his hand resting suggestively on his sword. "But I err. Mayhap yours are better trained."

Walsingham found a chair and pulled it close to hers.

Fia wished he had sat farther away. Her knife was tucked inside her boot, but it suddenly seemed too far to reach. She shot a glance at Angus and was reassured when he winked.

She returned her attention to Walsingham. "There are several servants at Rotherwood who are difficult in the extreme. At least one I am sure you are familiar with."

"Why would I be familiar with any of the servants at Rotherwood House?" he asked.

"Because you needed someone who knew the house well enough to know about its secret hiding place."

He arched his eyebrows. "My, this sounds very dramatic, indeed. Why would I need to know the location of this, ah, secret hiding place?"

"To steal the letters."

He gave a dry laugh. "You've a wonderful imagination. But then, that is proven by your choice of clothing. Did you think this was one of your plays?"

Fia fingered her skirt. "I think this skirt was, at one time, a fine wool. But then, that may be my imagination speaking. At times, it lets me see things others do not," she said pleasantly. "In fact, 'twas that very thing that kept me from returning to my sleep this morn. You know how 'tis when you behold a puzzle. It lingers, annoying and teasing your mind until you are nigh sick of it."

He laid a hand on the table and splayed his fingers across the rough wood. "I'm afraid I don't see what any of this has to do with me."

"Don't you?"

"We are wasting time, my dear. Thomas knows everything." An unpleasant smile flitted across his face. "I hear he has all but cast you out. Perhaps you should return to Scotland. I could arrange passage for you on the next ship. You could leave today if you wished." His sympathetic smile encompassed Angus. "And your servants, as well."

Fia gritted her teeth against her anger. She would get the truth from this man if she had to draw it from him with the edge of her knife. "I've not come here to seek your help in leaving."

"Even though your husband so wishes it?"

"Thomas loves me," she returned hotly.

"And he shows it by locking you in your room? A strange love, if 'tis love at all."

Someone at Rotherwood House *was* helping this man. There was no way he could have known that unless someone had told him. Who could it be? If she wrote a play, who would she hide within the gates to tell all to the villain? "Perchance Mistress Hadwell has been assisting you?"

The sharp, steely eyes flickered briefly. "This is absurd. You are in no position to accuse me of anything. Thomas has already branded you a liar and worse, milady. You have no recourse but to return to Scotland."

Fia's smile faltered. "I'm not going anywhere. 'Twas his anger speaking, not his heart. Now, tell me of this bargain that was struck between you and Duncan, or I'll go to the queen."

Angus stirred, stretching his legs before the fire.

Walsingham regarded them both with the strange and incurious gaze of a serpent. "I don't know why I should oblige you. No one would countenance your word."

"Duncan would believe me."

Walsingham shrugged. "Aye, but who would listen to a Scotsman with a grudge speak against the country that rejected his cousin? No one. Go home, milady."

"Nay, Duncan wanted me here. 'Twas that very thought that kept occurring to me this morning. I remembered how happy he seemed when Thomas and I wed."

" 'Twas a wedding he'd planned himself. Of course he was pleased."

"Aye. He wished me out of the country in case there was a war. I know why he bargained with Queen Mary's letters, too. Duncan wants Elizabeth's help. He thought of a way to accomplish all his objectives at once." She smiled proudly. "There're few men who have Duncan's genius."

From the hearth, Angus nodded.

Walsingham frowned. "This is foolish—"

A crash sounded in the outer tavern. The minister came to his feet, a small short sword appearing in his hand. Angus stood as well, his own sword drawn and ready. Another crash followed, and then another, until Fia wondered if a single table remained standing upright in the outer room.

The door creaked open slowly. Goliath stood in the entry, a thin sluice of blood dripping down his cheek from where he had been knocked on the noggin.

"Speak, fool!" Walsingham snapped.

The giant swayed, his face pale. Fia noted his

strangely blank expression. With a gusty sigh, Goliath toppled facedown on the ground.

Walsingham stiffened. "By the rood, what is the meaning of this?"

Thomas stepped over Goliath's slumbering body. His eyes found Fia's. "I came as soon as I could."

Fia bit her lip. 'Twas too soon. She needed time to speak with Walsingham, discover his motives. The last thing she needed was to have to deal with Thomas's anger. Hurt pooled in her throat.

"Comfit," he said softly, "I was wrong."

The words were so simple, yet they released a torrent of emotion in Fia. She managed to meet his gaze. "Aye, you were."

His mouth curved slightly. "I'm sorry. I'll never doubt you again."

"Very touching," said Walsingham. "You have come just in time, Thomas. Your wife was telling me the most wondrous tale."

"If my wife says 'tis so, then 'tis so," Thomas answered quietly. "She never lies." He slid his sword into its scabbard and took Fia's hand. He looked like a tousled hero, his shirt undone and his doublet left behind. "Can you forgive me, comfit? I've a lamentable temper. I should have believed you."

Robert lounged in the doorway, his rapier at the ready. "Don't give him quarter, Fia! Make him sing for you!"

Thomas scowled over his shoulder. "Perchance you should secure the door. I wouldn't want any unpleasant surprises."

Robert chuckled. "Very well. Ah, Angus, there you are. Mary has hit some poor man over the head with a tankard, and I fear there's to be a war." Angus nodded and left.

With a brief salute of his sword, Robert disappeared back into the tavern.

Thomas sniffed the air, then looked down at Fia. "I see you've managed to be authentic in odor as well as dress."

She fingered the rough skirt, wrinkling her nose. "I thought I'd be less obvious if I came dressed as a tavern wench."

He pulled her closer. "You'd need more than a dress that reeks of onions to make you appear like a tavern maid."

Walsingham gestured impatiently. "Have you forgotten that she betrayed you? Think of the whispers, the laughter." He leaned across the table. "Think, Thomas, of your father and all he suffered. 'Twill be the same for you."

"If all I ever have to bear is the laughter of the court, then I am indeed the most fortunate of men." To Fia's astonishment, Thomas solemnly placed a hand over his heart. "There are many things worse than the laughter of fools. There is loneliness and lost love. There is a sadness so deep it wrenches your gut into a thousand pieces and you bleed with every breath. Worse yet, there is life without sun, without warmth. Life without Fia."

Fia stared at him. "Thomas! That was from my play *Duke's Paradise!*"

Laughter twinkled in his brown eyes. "I liked the heroine, but the hero was sadly lacking in certain virtues."

"Then I'll rewrite it." Her smile was blinding.

Thomas touched a strand of her hair. She was more precious to him than life. He lifted his gaze to the counselor, who stood staring at them with a slight frown. "Let's finish this. The truth, Walsingham."

"I suppose it doesn't matter now. The chit will get the whole story from Maclean, and you would believe every word." The minister sank into a chair.

"Aye," Thomas answered. "I would."

Walsingham sighed. " 'Tis simple, really. Maclean

wanted a noble bridegroom. 'Twas obvious he already had someone in mind. He knew everything there was to know about you—your title, lands, everything. All I had to do was deliver you. In exchange, he was to send the letters."

The minister shook his head. "Though you might not credit it, I tried to talk Maclean into choosing someone else—Essex, Hatton, anyone. But he was adamant. 'Twas you or none. I was at a loss."

"Not for long," said Thomas.

The counselor smiled. "True. I detected an error in his thinking. He didn't know Elizabeth. I knew the queen would never let the wedding stand once she discovered it had been forced. As soon as Maclean delivered the letters, I would make certain you were granted an annulment."

"You planned to trick Duncan from the beginning," said Fia.

"Aye, but your cousin was a step ahead of me the entire time. He had already thought of the possibility of an annulment."

Fia brightened. "That's why he arranged for Malcolm Davies to come to Duart."

Walsingham's thin smile appeared. "Aye. He arranged to allow Thomas to escape at the same time he held out Malcolm as a husband to you. He knew you would flee, and he hoped it would be together."

"And if we hadn't?"

The minister shrugged. "All he really needed was an opportunity to imply that Fia's honor had been lost."

"So why didn't he just do that when he found us in the forest?" Fia asked.

"I believe he wanted to give you the chance to choose Wentworth yourself. I hear you made it remarkably easy for him."

"Aye," replied Thomas. "Too easy."

Walsingham's mouth twisted in a smile. "He was very clever. He even arranged to have that twit, Malcolm Davies, present as witness to the wedding, should he ever need one."

"I thought Malcolm the Maiden a very strange sort of bridegroom for Duncan to have chosen," Fia said.

Thomas nodded. "That doesn't explain why Duncan gave the letters to me." He looked at Walsingham. "You were surprised by that move, weren't you?"

"Very. They were supposed to be delivered to me here, within a week of your wedding. I would have secreted them away and procured your annulment before you had even arrived. Maclean foiled that plan the minute he gave the cask to you and told you what it contained. You knew he and I had exchanged something for them, you just didn't know what."

The minister's smile slipped. "The only thing that saved me was the fact that the cask was sealed. I knew you would never open it."

"So you arranged to have the letters stolen," said Fia. Walsingham nodded.

"You miserable cur," Thomas said bitterly.

The minister spread his hands on the table. "If the queen had discovered the trade, I would have been severely discredited. She needs me now more than ever."

Thomas wondered if he had ever really known this man. "If Elizabeth knew where your scheming had led you, she would have ended your miserable life."

The minister's eyes glinted with reluctant appreciation. "You think it? I prefer to believe that she would let me languish in the Tower until she again had need of my services."

"Tell Thomas why you lied about my involvement," said Fia.

Thomas noted how her hands clenched about his sleeve.

Walsingham shrugged. "I thought if you sent Fia away in disgrace, 'twould make everything Maclean had to say look like the rantings of an injured guardian. 'Twould discredit him with the queen."

"I thought to send Fia away, but never back to Scotland," said Thomas.

"I erred. I thought honor was all that held you to the marriage, that you had merely been compromised by physical passion."

Thomas caught Fia's gaze. "I'm such a harsh jailer that I worried you would miss your breakfast this morn."

She laughed softly. "I ate on the way here. Mary insisted."

Thomas wanted to lift her in his arms and slowly kiss every last inch of her. He turned back to the minister. "Where are the letters now?"

"Safe." Walsingham stared at Thomas. "You know I didn't do it for myself. You know it."

They exchanged a long look. "Nay," Thomas said finally. "You did it for Elizabeth."

Walsingham nodded. "Everything for Elizabeth. Everything." He heaved a sigh. "Well, my friend, we are at checkmate. I can't tell the queen the truth for fear she would send me to the Tower or worse. You dare not tell her for fear she will cast aside this marriage you have come to value."

"She wouldn't do such a thing," said Fia hotly.

Thomas looked down at Fia's hand resting in his. It fit perfectly, the graceful fingers splayed across his rough palm. As much as he hated it, Walsingham was right. Elizabeth's pride was legendary. If she knew how a renegade Scottish lord had purchased a titled English bridegroom, she would demand an annulment forthwith.

Walsingham gathered his cloak. "I had best be on my way. The queen has yet to see the letters. I was waiting until I could tie up these few loose ends." He looked from Fia to Thomas. "Such passion. Had I known there was such a bond betwixt the two of you, I would have approached this in an entirely different manner."

Thomas kissed Fia's hand. "One moment, comfit." He crossed the short space that separated him from Walsingham and hauled the older man forward with a single hand bunched in his velvet doublet. "One last word. If you ever attempt to meddle in our lives again, have your sword drawn and ready. There will be no bargaining. Just you and me and my blade."

The minister staggered, then caught himself and smoothed his doublet with shaky hands. "Let's hope the need never arises."

"Yer horse is ready," said Angus, standing in the doorway.

Walsingham nodded and, with a final bow, disappeared into the taproom. Angus silently followed.

"Where is he going?" Robert demanded, storming impetuously into the room. "You can't allow him to just walk away."

"We have to," said Thomas. "If the truth ever came to the fore, Fia would most likely bear the brunt of Elizabeth's wrath."

Robert cursed. "It goes sore against the grain." He sighed longingly. "But I daresay you're right. I will at least make sure that scurvy hagseed doesn't lurk about to cause more problems." He caught Fia's eye and grinned. "I have won my bet, sweet. You were presented to the queen and were accepted. You owe me."

Fia raised her brows. "What exactly *do* I owe you?"

He threw back his head and laughed. "Just wait! As soon as I have chased Walsingham back to his lair, I will return, and we can discuss the conditions." With a quick salute with his rapier, he was gone.

"I warned you not to wager with Robert," Thomas said sternly.

She chuckled. "Whatever the cost, 'twas well worth it. You could never have taught me to curtsey with such grace."

"Before I give you the kiss you deserve, comfit, we need to talk about your propensity to disguise yourself and climb out windows. I almost died of fright when I saw your bed sheets hanging over the ledge."

Fia peeped at him through her lashes. "Did I ever tell you about my Uncle Donald? He used to dream about things before they would happen. One time he—"

"What does that have to do with bed sheets?"

"Because one time he dreamed—"

"Never mind," Thomas said hastily. "You don't even have an uncle."

"Perhaps 'twas one of my cousins. We Scots have such large families, 'tis difficult to remember who's connected to whom," she chattered breathlessly. "My third cousin married a MacDonald, only to discover he was her own son. Can you imagine what a shock that was? Of course, you could say 'twas what she deserved for marrying a MacDonald."

Thomas thought she was absolutely adorable. He wrapped his arms around her.

"I haven't told you about my cousin Margaret, either."

"Damn your Uncle Donald, your cousin Margaret, and every relative you ever invented," said Thomas as he kissed her soundly, silencing her the only way he knew how.

Epilogue

Sheets of rain obscured the muddy streets, yet the horse galloped furiously onward, urged by the steady hand of its rider.

Thomas cursed the rain, the mud, and his own lack of resistance. Why had he let Fia talk him into attending the play? It was her sixth in as many years, each one vying against the other for success, each one widely acclaimed as brilliant.

Though not published under her own name—her position at court made that an impossibility—'twas a well-known fact that Fia Wentworth, the charming Countess Rotherwood, was a successful playwright. Thomas had been unable to keep from bragging to one and all of her talents.

He slowed the horse when the lights of Rotherwood House glimmered in the night. He jumped down, tossed the reins to a waiting servant, and bounded up the steps, water streaming from his cloak.

"My lord," Mary greeted him, her face wreathed in smiles. " 'Tis a boy! Saints be praised, but ye've a bright cherub of a son with black eyes and the blondest of hair!"

"And Fia?"

"She's above and restin' as easy as ye could expect." Mary took the wet cloak from his nerveless fingers. "She's been askin' fer ye fer the past half hour. The vicar is with her now."

"The vicar?"

Mary's smiled faltered a bit. "Aye. I warned her ye would be none too pleased about that, but she insisted on naming the wee one as soon as he arrived, and—"

He ran up the steps without waiting to hear more. The vicar stood over the bed, a small infant in his hands. His angular face beamed with pride. Fia opened tired eyes, breaking into a smile as soon as she saw Thomas.

He went to her immediately. "You, madam, are impatient."

" 'Twas little Robin who would not wait."

"Robin?" He asked, a bit of a sigh in his voice.

She chuckled. "Aye." A giggle at the door announced the arrival of the other children. "There they are! Bring Roberta and Robbie here," she ordered the vicar.

Thomas turned a laconic gaze on the cleric, who shrugged helplessly. He held out the babe, and Thomas took the small newborn, wondering how it could sleep so soundly with as much noise as his brother and sister were making.

The vicar brought the two children to the bed and was rewarded with a beaming smile from Fia. Thomas watched as the old man's face suffused with color. The vicar was like bread dough in Fia's capable hands.

Thomas looked down at his other two children and noted that they each held an incredibly fat rabbit in much the same way he cradled the new babe. He grinned.

357

Heaven help them, they were all puppets to do Fia's bidding.

"Let us see the baby!" demanded Roberta, her blue eyes sparkling with excitement. "We brought Prometheus and Mercury to see him."

"I get to see him first," replied Robbie coolly. "I'm older."

"I'm four, and I can see him if I want to," retorted Roberta with a mutinous toss of her red-brown curls.

"You can both see him at the same time," Thomas said hastily as he lowered the babe to their level. "But keep those animals away from him."

"He's wrinkled," Roberta complained, scrunching her nose in disgust. "And all red."

"Aye, and too small to play with." There was no hiding Robbie's disappointment.

"He'll grow." Thomas said. "I promise."

The vicar grinned, still looking befuddled. "I know you parents would like to visit with your newest addition. Perhaps the children can show me the new baby rabbits? I hear they are a fine brood indeed."

Roberta grabbed the man's hand, her rabbit hanging over her arm like a pillow. "We always have new baby rabbits," she said seriously. "Mama says 'tis because we are blessed." She turned to Fia. "Isn't that right, Mama? Aren't we blessed?"

"Yes, dear. We are blessed," Fia answered, exchanging a warm look with Thomas.

"These rabbits are the biggest ever." Robbie took the vicar's other hand. "You've never seen any this big before."

"I would be honored to view them," answered the vicar as he allowed the children to lead him from the room.

Thomas ran a finger down the infant's soft cheek. "Robin, eh?"

"A wager is a wager, Thomas," Fia defended herself. "I vow I never thought we'd have so many children, else I'd have made Robert settle for naming but the first after him." She looked at the door. "Where is he, anyway? Robert never misses my plays."

"He was at all the rehearsals, but he missed this eve. He said to tell you 'twas important business." Thomas lifted his eyebrows. "He says you've inspired him to take his life in his own hands. You wouldn't know what he was babbling about, would you?"

Fia smiled. "Aye. 'Tis time he did."

The baby yawned widely, showing Thomas toothless gums that reminded him of Zeus. A twinge of sadness washed through him. He missed Zeus, though the dog's innumerable sons and daughters were probably now in the barn, escaping the rain and making life miserable for the old and decrepit horses Fia had collected. She had even managed to find an old nag that reminded him strongly of Thunder, gone these past three years.

He sat on the edge of the bed and laid the baby in Fia's arms. "I suppose Robin was the best name you could think of."

Fia's mouth twitched. "We can call him by his middle name. 'Tis from one of my plays."

Thomas sighed. "I'm almost afraid to ask."

Her face lit with laughter. "You should be. Jebediah. 'Twill be a trial for him to spell."

He laughed, unable to resist placing a gentle kiss on her forehead. "I suppose he'll get used to it."

She smiled shyly and threaded her fingers through the baby's wispy blond curls. "You know, Thomas, I just thought of another."

"Another what?" he asked with alarm.

"Another name. For our next baby." She peeped up at him, as mischievous and irrepressible as when he had first met her. "What do you think of Robertina?"

"I think, dear wife," he said as he kissed her nose, " 'tis perfect."

AUTHOR'S NOTE

(Please note: The historical portion of this note was compiled by Alasdair White who minds the Clan Maclean history forum.)

Though all of the main characters in this book are fictional, Clan Maclean and proud Castle Duart are not. I visited Castle Duart on the beautiful Isle of Mull and found myself standing on the battlements, staring across the blue waters of the Sound. A lively sea wind brushed across the waves and cooled the sun-warmed stone, and instantly, irrepressible Fia Maclean and her dark cousin Duncan were born. But the actual history of the Macleans is even more compelling than fiction.

The romanticized legend of the Macleans traces the family back to the time of the kings of Dalriada and the foundation of the kingdom of Alban, or Scotland, in 845 AD, though actual documentation starts much later. Historically, the progenitor of the clan was a man called Gillean, born some time around 1210. Clan legend has it that Gillean was a warrior of some repute whose favorite weapon was a battle axe and, consequently, he is more often called Gillean of the Battle Axe.

The eldest of Gillean's sons, Gillemoire, is found in the retinue of Robert the Bruce, earl of Carrick, who later becomes king of Scots. Gillemoire joined Robert in paying homage to Edward I of England in 1296.

There is strong legend, though little evidence, that the Macleans fought at Bannockburn.

It can be assumed that they were there because shortly afterwards, Maclean was in charge of the Castle at Tarbet—one of Robert's strongholds in Kintyre—and it is likely that this was a reward for services rendered. The Macleans were prominent in the court of Robert the Bruce where they appear in the Exchequer Rolls on a frequent basis in relation to the upkeep of Robert's castles in Kintyre and the inner isles. The Macleans, notable seamen, traders and inshore pirates, were also heavily involved in providing sea power to Robert.

By the time of Queen Mary and the setting for this book, the position of Chief of the Clan Maclean was held by Hector Mor of Duart who spent most of his life plundering and raiding the lands of his neighbors, eventually falling foul of the Privy Council and Queen Mary herself who had him arrested in 1567. He died in 1568.

I encourage you to learn more about the real Macleans and Castle Duart. The Castle can be found at www.holidaymull.org/members/duart.html. Clan Maclean runs a central website at www.maclean.org.

If you've ever had the urge to wander to far-off places and taste the richness and excitement of things-that-were, then visit this incredible castle where history walks amid some of the most beautiful countryside in Scotland.

TEMPTED
MONICA ROBERTS

Well, tarnation! Apparently the man who mail-ordered Hope Savage didn't expect her, for he seems a bit taken aback by her language and her duds. But whooey, is he a looker! The parson's saintly face makes the Appalachian firebrand weak in her knees—and the preacher's perfect body makes her want to wail a hymn of thanksgiving. Still, every time she gets a hand on the rascally fellow, he manages to skedaddle, shrieking about the Good Book. Heck, she's seen a few good books and she hopes to learn if what she read is true. There she is, waiting to be set upon by her new husband, and all he wants to do is make a lady out of her. Well, maybe she'll let him. Then perhaps she can show him that it's sometimes nice to be naughty, and that something heavenly can come from being tempted.

___52353-1 $5.50 US/$6.50 CAN

Dorchester Publishing Co., Inc.
P.O. Box 6640
Wayne, PA 19087-8640

Please add $1.75 for shipping and handling for the first book and $.50 for each book thereafter. NY, NYC, and PA residents, please add appropriate sales tax. No cash, stamps, or C.O.D.s. All orders shipped within 6 weeks via postal service book rate. Canadian orders require $2.00 extra postage and must be paid in U.S. dollars through a U.S. banking facility.

Name_____

Address_____

City_____State_____Zip_____

I have enclosed $_____ in payment for the checked book(s).

Payment <u>must</u> accompany all orders. ❑ Please send a free catalog.
            CHECK OUT OUR WEBSITE! www.dorchesterpub.com

Body & Soul

Jennifer Archer

Overworked, underappreciated housewife and mother Lisa O'Conner gazes at the young driver in the red car next to her. Tory Beecham's manicured nails keep time with the radio and her smile radiates youthful vitality. For a moment, Lisa imagines switching places with the carefree college student. But when Lisa looks in the rearview mirror and sees Tory's hazel eyes peering back at her, she discovers her daydream has become astonishing reality. Fortune has granted Lisa every woman's fantasy. But as the goggle-eyed, would-be young suitors line up at Lisa's door, only one man piques her interest. But he is married—to her, or rather, the woman she used to be. And he seems intent on being faithful. Unsure how to woo her husband, Lisa knows one thing: No matter what else comes of the madcap, mix-matched mayhem, she will be reunited body and soul with her only true love.

___52334-5 $5.50 US/$6.50 CAN

Dorchester Publishing Co., Inc.
P.O. Box 6640
Wayne, PA 19087-8640

An Original Sin

Nina Bangs

Fortune MacDonald listens to women's fantasies on a daily basis as she takes their orders for customized men. In a time when the male species is extinct, she is a valued man-maker. So when she awakes to find herself sharing a bed with the most lifelike, virile man she has ever laid eyes or hands on, she lets her gaze inventory his assets. From his long dark hair, to his knife-edged cheekbones, to his broad shoulders, to his jutting—well, all in the name of research, right?—it doesn't take an expert any time at all to realize that he is the genuine article, a bona fide man. And when Leith Campbell takes her in his arms, she knows real passion for the first time . . . but has she found true love?

___52324-8 $5.99 US/$6.99 CAN

BUSHWHACKED BRIDE
EUGENIA RILEY

"JUMPING JEHOSHAPHAT! YOU'VE SHANGHAIED THE NEW SCHOOLMARM!"

Ma Reklaw bellows at her sons and wields her broom with a fierceness that has all five outlaw brothers running for cover; it doesn't take a Ph.D. to realize that in the Reklaw household, Ma is the law. Professor Jessica Garret watches dumbstruck as the members of the feared Reklaw Gang turn tail—one up a tree, another under the hay wagon, and one in a barrel. Having been unceremoniously kidnapped by the rowdy brothers, the green-eyed beauty takes great pleasure in their discomfort until Ma Reklaw finds a new way to sweep clean her sons' disreputable behavior—by offering Jessica's hand in marriage to the best behaved. Jessie has heard of shotgun weddings, but a broomstick betrothal is ridiculous! As the dashing but dangerous desperadoes start the wooing there is no telling what will happen with one bride for five brothers.

___52320-5 $5.99 US/$6.99 CAN

Winks & A Kiss THE BEWITCHED VIKING
SANDRA HILL

'Tis enough to drive a sane Viking mad, the things Tykir Thorksson is forced to do—capturing a red-headed virago, putting up with the flock of sheep that follow her everywhere, chasing off her bumbling brothers. But what can a man expect from the sorceress who put a kink in the King of Norway's most precious body part? If that isn't bad enough, he is beginning to realize he isn't at all immune to the enchantment of brash red hair and freckles. But he is not called Tykir the Great for nothing. Perhaps he can reverse the spell and hold her captive, not with his mighty sword, but with a Viking man's greatest magic: a wink and a smile.

___52311-6 $5.99 US/$6.99 CAN